# A TRIAL IN LAFAYETTE COUNTY

A novel by Phillip D. Payne

𝔅ℭ𝔭

Beech Cottage Press
Lovingston, Virginia

First Edition: January 2014
Second Edition: October 2014

ISBN: 978-0-9908330-0-0

Beech Cottage Press
Post Office Box 299
Lovingston, Virginia 22949
publishing@beechcottagepress.com

Acknowledgements

Much of the advice, assistance, and review that prodded this novel along was provided by the same people with whom I worked professionally during my eighteen years as an elected prosecutor. Edward L. Watkins, at the time investigator for the Nelson County Sheriff's Department, was a constant source of technical guidance. Dr. Marcella Fierro, Chief Medical Examiner for the Commonwealth of Virginia, took some of her valuable time to advise me. Judge Michael Gamble offered his suggestions and observations whenever I asked. Mrs. June Harris faithfully typed my hand written manuscript.

Author Stefan Bechtel gave me encouragement and valuable editorial comments outside the legal realm. My eldest son Dandridge was the point man for navigating the electronic maze of a new method of publishing. Finally, and last for emphasis, my unlimited thanks to my wife Lisa Payne, who was as quick to encourage me when appropriate as she was to hold her tongue when I needed no further discouragement.

While readers familiar with an author's home will claim to find a character mirroring one of the author's acquaintances, such a comparison would be in error. Anyone having lived in a small town will find a player in this novel who is familiar, for human nature has a way of repeating itself from place to place. The events and characters in *A Trial in Lafayette County* are entirely fictitious and any resemblance of either to a real event or person is entirely coincidental.

# CHAPTER 1

Saturday, August 22nd

Deputy Horace Seay walked through the gate and made for the gurney sitting at the pool's edge. Two rescue squad members stood over a sheet covered lump from which protruded stiff, plaster-white arms and legs.

Bennie Thomas, the rescue squad chief, looked up at the sound of the advancing deputy. "Nothing more we can do for her Horace." The squadsmen had a bad habit of trying to resuscitate obvious cadavers, a policy which usually resulted in disturbed potential evidence. With the rescue squads and their families representing a thousand votes or more, Seay's boss, the sheriff, was not about to press for restraint.

"Damn Bennie. She's been dead. Who is she?"

"She's Senator Noble's daughter," answered Bennie. "We had to try, you know. The Nobles were expectin' it." He motioned toward Clyde Noble sitting in a corner with his head in his hands.

Seay lifted the sheet to look at the remains. She was clad only in the bottom of a two piece bathing suit. "Was she in the pool when you got here?"

"Yeah."

"Half naked?"

"Yeah."

"Was anyone here when she drowned, I mean like at the house?"

"No. The Nobles had just got home."

"Au-ight. Gene Roberts needs to be here on this."

Bennie nodded and began pulling the gurney away.

"No. Leave her for the time being." Seay pulled out a faded blue bandanna and wiped his brow against the stifling heat. Using his radio he informed the dispatcher of his findings and asked that the investigator be sent to assist him. "Notify the medical examiner, too." As he turned to approach the squadsmen gathered around Clyde Noble, he glimpsed Rita Noble, alone near the pool house, slowly folding a towel. "Poor woman," he mumbled to himself. He stepped back to the corner of the pool's enclosure and quickly photographed the gurney, the pool house, and finally, each quadrant of the pool area.

Seay was still trying to prod everyone away from the poolside when the investigator, Gene Roberts, arrived. Two other deputies were several steps behind him. Roberts was a big man, trim for his fifty-four years. He usually wore a coat and tie, but had not today because it was Saturday and he had been called away from a picnic at his home with his wife and grandchildren. Unlike most of the younger deputies who wore their hair close cropped like a Marine, Roberts's reddish blonde, and graying, hair was kept long enough to reveal a gentle wave. Roberts's terse instructions to the onlookers, coupled with his commanding physical presence which usually cowed miscreants as well as even the seasoned of the deputies, prompted immediate compliance.

One of the newly arrived deputies, Okra Alexander, began draping yellow tape on the pool fence while Seay and the investigator briefly surveyed the corpse. Mervin McIntosh, the other deputy, walked to where Clyde Noble sat and spoke quietly to him. Rita Noble, joining her husband at the wrought iron bench where he was sitting, stared coldly at the two men peering at the partially nude form. She arose from the bench and walked quickly to their side. "Can't she be taken away?"

Roberts looked into the face of the woman who, although obviously younger than her husband, wore her fewer years poorly. "Just as soon as the medical examiner gives us the word. I'm terribly sorry about your daughter. We'll move as fast as—''

"Miranda wasn't my daughter, she's my stepdaughter. What do you need to do?"

Roberts clenched his jaw at the error. He continued, "We have several things we should look at. Maybe it would be better if you and Senator Noble walked to the house with me while these other officers take care of those things."

Rita Noble looked at the tile beneath her feet and sobbed quietly. "This is so hard on Clyde. What...what do you need to find out about a drowning?"

"Let's walk to the house." He motioned to Seay to follow.

Rita Noble looked up. "You know who we are."

"Yes."

"Who are you?"

"Gene Roberts. Investigator for the Lafayette County Sheriff's Department. This is Sergeant Horace Seay."

"Miranda had a drinking problem. She was probably drunk," she volunteered. "Oh my God," she said as if to herself, "how will we handle this?"

Rita Noble followed Roberts to the bench where Clyde Noble, his face still in his hands, was sitting. "I'm sorry to impose on you, Senator, but Sergeant Seay and I would like to walk to the house with you to get a little more information."

A puzzled look clouded Rita Noble's face. "Now? Must we do that now?"

Clyde Noble arose slowly and wiped the palms of his hands on his pant legs. "Come on, Rita. They've got to do this. Even with a drowning." He then turned to Roberts. "Hello, Gene."

"Hello Senator," replied Roberts.

Noble, a member of the Virginia Senate, was of medium height and weight, with medium brown hair that was thinning rapidly; he was, in fact, medium in every respect, excepting his ambition and his ego. He straightened somewhat, as if in response to Roberts, and taking his wife by the hand, led her toward the gate.

Roberts waited for the couple to leave his earshot before leaning near the deputy who had been waiting at Noble's side. "McIntosh. Did he say anything to you?"

"Not a word."

"Do we know where the body was?"

"In the pool," answered Seay.

"They weren't here?" asked Roberts with a nod of his head in the direction of the Nobles.

Seay responded again. "No. They just got home is what Bennie told me."

Roberts peered sharply at Seay. "Okay Horace. You and I will talk to the Nobles. McIntosh, find out from the squadsmen where in the pool they found the body. Get a sample of the water. Ask them who was here when they arrived and what they were doing. Find out who touched what. Photograph the body and everything here. Tell the medical examiner that I want an autopsy."

Seay paused before responding. "You don't think it's a drowning."

"Hell no. Half nude young woman who's in rigor mortis, obviously dying some time ago with no one around. We can't assume anything. Dust everything with a surface. Pick up trash, if there is any. We won't get a second chance after today. If you think of anything else, do it. Do we know how she got here?"

Seay answered. "I think the Mazda out front was hers."

"Then impound that for us to go over. McIntosh. Comb the yard—" Roberts looked around the lush well-kept lawns of the Noble home. "Comb the grounds." He rolled his sleeves down and buttoned them, as an afterthought.

Roberts and Seay walked through the gate and up the brick steps to the terrace at the rear of the house. Once on the terrace, Roberts surveyed the rear lawn. From his vantage point the pool, no more than thirty feet away, was fully visible. After allowing the scene to sink into his memory, he walked through the French doors leading to the dining room.

* * *

The harsh brightness of the low sun pounded the fading summer landscape, casting hazy shadows which offered no relief from the relentless heat that is always August in Virginia. Thirty-six year old Evander Cross, whose slender frame was sprawled in a rocking chair in front of a large fan in his kitchen, rolled a cold can of beer across his face. "At least I won't have to do this again until this drought breaks."

"What?" answered his wife Polly. "Drink a beer?"

"Cut the grass."

"Tough luck. It looks like rain."

"Change of subject. Wanna do it?"

"Ev." Evander had long ago been shortened to Ev.

"It is Saturday. Saturday's an American tradition."

The telephone rang before Polly could say no. "It's Rita Noble, for you," she whispered to Ev.

"Rita Noble?"

Polly shrugged her shoulders as she handed him the receiver.

"Hello Rita."

"Ev. Something terrible has happened. Clyde's daughter Miranda has drowned."

Ev hesitated for a moment as he tried to recall a Miranda Noble. "That's terrible, I'm so sorry," he finally said, not knowing what else there was that he could say and beginning to fear the possibilities that would lead her to call him about such a thing.

"She...we don't know how it happened. But the child has had some problems and she drinks too much. I found.... Well your deputy says she has to be autopsied. This is too much for Clyde. We need you to intervene."

The request made Ev instantly uncomfortable. "When did this happen?"

"Yesterday, or last night. But we just found her today."

"The police have been there?" *Why did I ask that?*

"Certainly, several. One insisted that we be interviewed. And Clyde is sick with grief. I'm trying to...I don't want him hurt even more by his daughter going to Richmond to be cut up by those people."

"I know this is horrible for you, but an autopsy is usually done when the death isn't natural. I guess I should say it's done when there's a question about how the death occurred."

"Ev, she drowned. She was here by herself. She may have been drinking. She went swimming. But she drowned." Rita Noble's voice faltered. "There's no question...we're asking you to do something about this...this autopsy. It will be just too much for Clyde. Such a humiliation."

"I'll call the sheriff's department and find out what's going on, but I need to warn you that an autopsy isn't unusual."

"Well, it would be with us, with her."

"I'll check into it."

"Thank you," replied his caller.

Ev replaced the receiver slowly.

"What was that about?" asked Polly.

"Clyde Noble's daughter drowned."

"His little girl?"

"No. This child was Miranda. I guess she was by his first marriage."

"I didn't know he had any other children."

"A well-kept secret I guess."

"How old was she?"

"I couldn't tell you."

"What were you talking about an autopsy for?"

"Rita doesn't want one. Usually the family is demanding an autopsy. I'd better call the sheriff's department."

"Do you need an autopsy to tell if someone drowned?"

"There's more to it than that," said Ev as he dialed the department's number. There was much more than he wanted to contemplate. Clyde Noble was running full tilt after the Democratic nomination for United States senator, with the election still more than three years away, and the press would be interested in Miranda's death, even more so if there were foul play—or even just play. Moreover, Miranda Noble's existence, for all purposes, was not a matter of general knowledge. Rita Noble's clumsy attempts at maintaining the secrecy were doomed, thought Ev, since half the county's population owned a police scanner and no doubt already knew more about the drowning than did the Nobles.

Ev's call was routed to Gene Roberts. "Having a nice Saturday, Gene?" he asked.

"Funny you should call," quipped Roberts. "I figured you'd be one of the newspapers."

"Are they calling already?"

"Oh yes. I take it you know about the Noble girl."

"Mrs. Noble called me herself."

"Let me guess. She doesn't want an autopsy."

"Bingo. How old is the decedent?"

"Nineteen, but apparently with some mileage."

"I take it you don't think it's a drowning."

"I can't assume anything. Something's not adding up."

"I don't want to get too much of this right now. But I told Rita Noble that I would call the department about the autopsy. Now what should I give her as a reason?"

"The chief medical examiner wants an autopsy on every drowning, which is true. If that doesn't work, tell her what I already told them: that healthy young attractive women don't just drown in their father's swimming pool with the top of their bathing suits off. No one was there, so we don't know where to start. The Nobles said the girl wasn't even supposed to be there, didn't know she was there."

Ev fell silent for several moments as he pondered the news media scrutiny that was bound to follow. "How are you handling the press?"

"Willie Painter," answered Roberts by giving the dispatcher's name, "has already handled the press. The very first one that called got the lowdown, as much as he knew it. So I've had to give the same stuff to the others. Pretty basic. Nineteen year old daughter of Senator Noble found drowned in father's swimming pool. Alcohol involved. No witnesses. Being investigated."

"I thought the sheriff had a policy about those dispatch clowns giving the press statements."

"He does."

"Well, tell the sheriff to expect a call from the Nobles. Let him deal with them. An underage alcohol death won't look good for the campaign."

"Maybe drugs, too."

Ev unconsciously rubbed the bridge of his nose under his glasses. "What's your source?"

"The senator."

"Were you there first?"

"No. Horace Seay was. Merv McIntosh collected evidence."

"Okay. I guess I'll see you Monday. Can you have Merv and Horace in Monday morning? I'd like to talk to them."

"Sure. Enjoy your weekend."

Ev replaced the receiver and turned to face an expectant Polly.

"Well?" she asked.

"A drowning with no witnesses, and from Roberts's tone, no clues."

"Then it's not your problem, yet."

"Not yet." Evander Cross had been Commonwealth's Attorney—the county's elected prosecutor—for six years, and blessed with good fortune and the small population of rural Lafayette County, had yet to try a murder case.

Ev made the return call to Rita Noble and was surprised when she accepted his response without a quibble. *This is going to get weird,* he told himself as he rehung the telephone.

**CHAPTER 2**

Monday, August 24th, a.m.


On an August afternoon when it rains the fallen water turns to mist, almost steam, shrouding the countryside with more humidity and offering no relief from the heat. But sometimes the rain falls long enough to bring a brief respite from the summer oppression. On the morning following such a precious interlude the dawn breaks clear and cool, and the mountains are crisp, as in June, against the bright blue sky, neatly outlined as the sun slowly illuminates their towering undulations, freeing them for a few hours from the haze of late summer which blunts their peeks and mutes their dark green. Such was the rain on Sunday evening. It had miraculously restored green to the burnt pastures and fields, and revived a luster of freshness to the enveloping woodlands before they merged in the distance to form their blanket on the mountain slopes.

On these days Lafayette is a dazzling natural wonder. Stretching from the James River to the crest of the Blue Ridge, the county displays corn-filled river bottoms, then rolling acres of pastures before forested fingers of mountains and narrow valleys announce the steep rise of the Blue Ridge peaks. Neither a stoplight nor a drive-through burger factory litters the landscape.

Nestled in a cusp of the rain brightened Blue Ridge foothills lies Lafayette Court House, the eye-blink of a village which serves as Lafayette county's seat, so named long ago because it surrounds the quaint building where court has always been held. The original courthouse, almost two centuries old, had grown over the last few decades, and in the most recent addition, in the corner of the second floor, Ev Cross made his office as Commonwealth's Attorney. He paced the rooms as he wondered when Gene Roberts would finally make his appearance at the sheriff's department, for Roberts kept his own hours, and whether Roberts would have the beginning of an answer to Miranda Noble's death

Ev was hanging up from Minnie Patterson's weekly complaint that a neighbor's cat was defecating—not the word she used—in her garden when Roberts called. "It's too beautiful to be here today," he greeted Ev. "You ought to be fishing somewhere."

"I wish I were. Up here or in your office?"

There was no privacy, much less quiet, in the room that Roberts and deputy investigator Lewis Brown shared in the courthouse basement, a squalid collection of small rooms to which the sheriff's department had been relegated. "Yours. Mervin McIntosh there yet? He's supposed to come straight there."

"No. Why?"

"I want you to hear it from him. I'll be right up."

Ev poured a cup of coffee as he waited. Soon he heard Roberts and McIntosh enter the office lobby where they tarried for a moment while trading light banter with

Ev's secretary about the standings of various stock car drivers. Roberts led the way into the prosecutor's office. "News people call you yet?"

"Not yet. But they won't bother me till I have charges."

"They've damn near worried us to death."

Ev looked at McIntosh who was only a step behind Roberts. "I bet you're glad to be out today." Deputies who worked the weekend were supposed to have Monday off.

McIntosh smiled. "Oh well, didn't have much planned anyway."

"Who goes first?" asked Ev.

Roberts spoke, beginning with what he had found at the poolside. He reached the point where he and Horace Seay had walked to the house with the Nobles, and then asked McIntosh to pick up the story.

McIntosh scratched his head and cleared his throat before setting his styrofoam coffee cup on the floor beside his chair. "I started trying to dust for prints, which was nigh on impossible since there was nothing with a proper surface, except a vodka bottle, some cans and the refrigerator door. Bennie Thomas had got there first. He said the Nobles were at the pool, and that the senator was sitting where he was when I got there. When I asked about Mrs. Noble, he said she was picking up trash around the pool. So I asked what trash, and he said beer cans, he thought, and pointed to a large Rubbermaid like trash can. So I went over and looked in, and it was about half full, and all I could see was beer cans, a trash bag and such like. I noticed one of the cans had a hole in it, like a homemade crack pipe. I smelled it and it had the smell. So I marked the whole trash can as evidence and taped it. I found an ashtray with Marlboro Light butts in it, but it looked like someone had poured beer or something in it. I took it anyway. We searched the yard and found one can, a beer can, near the drive. I vacuumed the pool tile the best I could. One strange thing. I found her bathing suit top in a trash bag with a couple of beer cans, the bag I found in the trash can."

Roberts was watching Ev intently as McIntosh spoke. "What do you think, Ev?" he asked when the deputy was finished.

"I think half our damn evidence is mixed up in some trash can. But I'm jumping ahead. I take it you're still suspicious, Gene."

"Aren't you?"

Ev studied Roberts for a moment. A thinly veiled connotation of inquisition permeated the investigator's discussion of every case and suggested to the astute auditor that he was the subject of some ritual examination concerning his analytical ability. Ev concluded early in his career as a prosecutor that Roberts had been training young deputies for so long that he automatically structured every utterance in Socratic fashion, though not only to quiz the neophyte officers he was guiding, but also to test the reasonableness of the conclusions he himself was reaching.

"I take my cues from you," answered Ev.

Roberts smiled as if he knew his hand had been called. "The Nobles said Miranda was not supposed to be there, but they allowed that she came, at least recently, pretty often. The Nobles had been to Richmond; they left Friday morning to go to some political thing. Among others, Clyde Noble was in a conference for underage drinking. Rather ironic, wouldn't you say?"

"Did you sense that this child was not a part of the family that the senator wanted in the public's eye? I ask that because Miranda was never in any of the family photos in Noble's campaign literature."

"Could be. She lived with her mother in Charlottesville. She dropped out of college in the spring, and that's when she started showing up at the Nobles."

Ev shook his head. "I'm side-tracking myself."

"I asked them whether anyone might have been there when Miranda arrived. The maid usually leaves around two o'clock. They'd already called her, I guess before any of us got there, and found out Miranda wasn't there when she left. No one was supposed to be there."

"Where were the children? Rita's set."

"At Mrs. Noble's, the senator's mother. I went to see the maid, Clara Wood, a real nice old lady, lives in Red Springs. I asked her whether she knew anything about Miranda coming. She hesitated, and then said Jason Thomasson had called around noon on Friday, asking for Miranda."

"Who is Jason?"

"Mrs. Rita Noble's youngest brother."

"I see," said Cross softly.

"Mrs. Wood saw his number on the caller I D and called him back. He told her to tell Miranda to call if she showed up. I sent Lewis over to the Nobles to look at the caller I D. Luckily the caller I D, the telephone numbers that is, from Friday were intact. He wrote all of them down, but I haven't seen them since he wasn't on duty Sunday. Mrs. Wood also said Miranda was at the Nobles Tuesday and Wednesday."

"Have you talked to the Nobles about Jason?"

"That's where we are. I felt a little hesitant about bothering the Nobles again so soon."

"I take it you haven't heard from the medical examiner's office."

"I'm waiting for my call to be returned, that will probably tell the tale."

"How about prints?"

McIntosh weighed in at this point. "We got plenty off the bottle and the refrigerator. We've got to work on the eliminations. Thought we'd better give the Nobles a little time."

"I'll go to the Nobles today to get a list of people whose prints we can expect," said Roberts. "Then we'll work on getting their prints. And I've got to ask Mrs. Noble about her cleanup, again, now that we've found the pipe."

Ev took a sip of cold coffee. "First the autopsy business, then the cleanup at the pool, and now the slight omission about Jason."

"Uh-huh," agreed Roberts.

"When did she die?" asked Cross.

"The local M E's guess is between nine and midnight. The autopsy should narrow the window."

"And you're going to see the Nobles today?"

"Yes."

"What about Miranda's mother?"

"I drove to Charlottesville Saturday night. The woman was too distraught for me to ask her much, but I'll tell you one thing. The difference between her reaction and the other Nobles was like night and day."

"How so?" asked Cross.

"She was a wreck, like you'd expect. Mr. and Mrs. Senator were...were more like depressed, maybe it was shock. I don't know. Maybe I was just looking too hard. Anyway, the first Mrs. Noble didn't make any bones about her contempt for Clyde Noble, and that there might have been foul play was obvious to her because I was there. At the door she asked me to check back with her after she'd had time to collect herself, and I left it at that."

"I guess I'm up to date," said Ev.

Roberts nodded his head.

"Thanks," added Cross. "Thanks for coming in on your off day, Mervin."

McIntosh nodded as he arose from his chair. "No problem."

"Go on, Mervin. I need a few more minutes on something else," said Roberts. He waited for McIntosh to leave the room before continuing. "Something's really fishy. Maybe it is as simple as a drunk girl drowning. But you have to prove that, too. And you probably read that the sheriff called it an accident."

"Hank Burke. Nothing like an uneducated guess."

"As you might have heard, investigation is not Hank's strong point. Remember the Alphonso Thornton scandal, cost a sheriff and a commonwealth's attorney their jobs."

"Maybe Hank learned something."

"Maybe."

"Are you satisfied with the work at the crime scene?"

"Yeah, after we got there. But God only knows what Rita Noble and the rescue squad screwed up. We'll have to dust all those cans and cups, I guess. By the way, I asked for a full screen on the blood work. That means a delay."

"Well, it can't be helped."

"By the way. Do you know the name of their place?"

"No."

"Noble View. Pretty tacky. I'm going down to our cop cave and go over telephone numbers with Lewis." Rising to his feet and straightening his blazer, Roberts smiled wryly. "If the autopsy shows intercourse, this could be a capital case."

"Thanks for the reminder," grumbled Ev as Roberts passed through the door. He sat still for several minutes, staring at the empty threshold. The first question to spring to mind was the sordid history of Clyde Noble's two families, the public one and the formerly secret one. There was nothing that remained sacred in a criminal case, and people who intensely valued their privacy were rarely drawn into the courtroom, indeed they avoided it. Sexual liaisons, drinking habits, scars—everything was grist for the spectacle that was a trial. He had to know more about the relationship of Noble and his daughter. The trick was finding a source who would not betray his interest, a feat that was more difficult than obtaining the information itself. He toyed with his cup of cold coffee as he searched his thoughts for the proper informer.

* * *

Gene Roberts crushed his cigarette in Lewis Brown's ashtray as he looked at the list of names and telephone numbers Brown had handed him. Brown sat expectantly at his desk. "I take it you didn't ask the Nobles about these people?" Roberts asked his understudy.

"They weren't in the mood to talk."

"You want to go with me to the Nobles, today?"

"Not really," said Brown. "That woman was cold as ice when I was there. Act like I was gonna steal something."

Roberts shook his head and laughed quietly.

"There were two unavailables, too," added Brown.

Roberts jotted the additional information on Brown's list.

Brown pulled a cigarette from the pack in front of him. Joseph Lewis Brown had been a star athlete in high school, and had fared well in college as a cornerback, but not well enough for the pro scouts. Some of the other deputies believed that Brown had won his promotion to deputy investigator due to his past athletic prowess, as the sheriff had excelled at baseball in high school, a talent Burke had parlayed into a few years in the minors before they and he concluded he was going nowhere. Brown knew better. Hank Burke wanted to reward the black voters who had been his margin of victory in the election, and advancing deputy Brown to deputy investigator was an obvious vehicle, even if carried no pay increase.

Brown's title was also part of the political equation. Burke first thought he should be called an assistant investigator, then he started calling him a detective, and more recently he had switched to deputy investigator. Simply referring to Brown as an investigator was unacceptable because the Lafayette County sheriff's department had state money for but one investigator, who was paid considerably more than the road deputies, and Burke had no interest in lobbying for more money.

"Alright," Roberts informed Brown, "I'm going into the lion's den. Should be back in a couple of hours."

There were several cars in the Noble driveway, including the senator's gold Mercedes and Rita's green Suburban. *The color of money,* thought Roberts. Clara Wood greeted him at the door, and with downcast eyes, let him into the central hallway which was tiled in marble and oppressively filled with dark heavy furniture. In the adjoining room the Nobles and their guests sat talking in unctuously quiet voices. Clara Wood hesitated for a moment, as if thinking about whether to announce his presence or show him into the room. Opting for the latter she guided him into the room where the Nobles, without salutation or his introduction to the others, arose simultaneously and led him into the dining room, a room as forbidding and unfriendly as the hall, only bigger.

With Roberts seated on one side of the massive dining table and the two Nobles on the other, Roberts searched his mind for small talk and then jettisoned the idea in favor of getting to the point. Looking at Rita Noble he began. "I understand from one of the deputies that you were picking up around the pool area after you found Miranda."

"Yes. I picked up some cans and things and put them in the trash. I don't know why. Gave me something to do while we were waiting." She glanced at her husband. "I was too distraught to think about what I was doing. Why does this matter? I thought the sheriff ruled it an accident."

"I believe he mentioned that. Can you remember just what you picked up?"

"Some beer cans, I don't really remember."

"Do you know what kind?"

"Miller Lite, I guess. That's what we sometimes have in the pool house."

"Plastic cups?"

She looked away beyond Roberts. "I think so."

"Did you just put these things in the trash?"

"What else would I have done with it? Why does this matter?"

"We're checking the items in the trash for fingerprints." Roberts reached beneath his coat pocket flap and pulled out a plastic bag, taped shut, which contained a Miller Lite can. He laid the bag on the table and pointed to a hole cut in the can and the scorch marks. "This can has been used to smoke cocaine. Do you recall this particular can?"

Rita shook her head.

"Okay," he said, almost as if to himself. Next he pulled from his coat's breast pocket a copy of the list Lewis Brown had given him earlier. "One of the officers got the names and numbers from your caller I D. I need you to help me with the relationship of each to you or to Miranda."

Mrs. Noble took the sheet of paper from Roberts and without studying the contents she began reciting each name and the probable reason for the call. She hesitated at the seventh name. Roberts knew which one had given her pause. She looked at Roberts sullenly. "Jason Thomasson. He's my youngest brother."

Roberts said nothing.

Near the end of the list she paused again. "This Anita Smith. I don't know her." She turned to Clyde Noble. "Do you?"

Clyde Noble shook his head.

Mrs. Noble pushed the list across the table when she had finished. "I see a note here that the number for two calls were unavailable. Is there anything else?"

"Would it surprise you that your brother called for Miranda?" asked Roberts.

"No," answered the senator. "Mrs. Wood told us today about the call."

Roberts glanced quickly at Mrs. Noble who was watching her husband intently. "Were they seeing each other?" he asked.

"I don't understand why that matters," answered Mrs. Noble.

"Mrs. Noble. We've got to try to pin down everything that involved Miranda just before she died."

"For a drowning...an accident?" she answered. "What about the autopsy?"

"I don't have it yet Mrs. Noble."

"It sounded to me like everything was done."

Roberts drew a quiet breath and composed himself. "I can only move one step at a time. Please bear with me, I have to make sure of what happened. I don't like bothering you. There are just certain things we have to do."

"They were seeing each other, some," said Clyde Noble quietly. "I'm not surprised he'd call. He's talked to her here before."

Roberts decided to put Jason aside for the moment. "Can you tell me when she was last here?"

"That would have been Wednesday, she left Wednesday evening," answered Rita Noble. "Before dinner."

"And before that?"

"Tuesday. She came Tuesday. I believe I told you this on Saturday."

"Did she see anyone?"

"No," Rita Noble said wearily.

"I think that's all I have for you, Mrs. Noble."

"Rita. I'll be out in a minute, as soon as I finish with the deputy," Noble quietly suggested to her, but there was no room for debate in the tone of his voice.

Roberts's jaw twitched once at the obvious slight Noble had conveyed when he referred to the investigator as a deputy.

No one spoke as Rita marched hurriedly from the room. Only after the door had been pulled shut behind her did the Senator turn his attention once again to Roberts. "No one visited her," he said evenly.

There was silence for several moments as Roberts considered whether to delve into the reason for Rita Noble's hostile reaction to his efforts to accumulate the bare minimum of background information. His eyes followed Noble's gaze to the latter's folded hands resting on the table. He knew that Noble was aware of the suspicion his wife's behavior was arousing. "What was going on with Jason and Miranda?" ventured Roberts.

Noble pulled his hands from the table and straightened in his chair. "They both live in Charlottesville. He was seeing her…that's an outdated word, seeing. Using her is more like it, and Rita was against it. It wasn't very pleasant having Rita decide that Miranda wasn't good enough for her brother, that she'd get him in trouble. So now it looks like that happened. But if you think he might have killed her, you're wrong. The little son of a bitch didn't have a reason, let alone the guts to do that." Noble was looking unblinkingly at Roberts as he finished speaking.

"There were no other contacts when she was here, friends, maybe even people you didn't know?"

"You mean like drug dealers, don't you?"

"Anybody."

"We've been over that, and Clara can't remember either. Of course if the children answered the phone, they wouldn't know."

"How old are they?"

"Eight and eleven."

"Had she come before when no one was here?"

"Yes. At least once."

"At least once?"

"I had my suspicions about some other times."

"How long had this been going on?"

Noble looked away from his inquisitor before answering. "She started visiting a lot beginning in May. There were a few times this summer when...when we thought she'd been here when we were away, but we didn't press the matter."

"You wouldn't know if she'd met anyone, when you weren't here?"

"No."

"Did Jason ever see her here?"

"Once. Rita saw to it that that wouldn't happen again."

"To your knowledge."

"To my knowledge."

Roberts retrieved the list of telephone numbers and slowly folded the paper before returning it to his jacket pocket. There was something wrong with Noble's effort at cooperation, a sullen wariness, not unusual perhaps, but present nonetheless, which gave Roberts the sense that Noble was not hiding something as much as he was unwilling to face the things he knew. Roberts decided to leave the matter be. "We'll need a list of people whose prints would be expected in the pool area. I don't have to have them immediately, but it would be helpful if you started jotting down the names. We'll need to eliminate those people as we go along."

The request was met by a piercing glare that surprised Roberts, and for a moment it appeared as if Noble were about to speak, or more likely, lash out in response. Then Noble looked beyond Roberts briefly, as if to gain mastery of himself before answering. "Okay," he managed. "Is there anything else you need?"

"Not right now," Roberts replied as he arose from his chair. "I'm sorry I had to intrude, senator."

Noble stood, too. "Thank you," he said in a low voice.

The two men walked silently out of the room into the hallway leading to the front door. Roberts paused at the door and extended his hand. From the corner of his eye he could see Rita Noble seated in the adjoining room, her eyes fixed on the two figures at the threshold. "I'll be in touch."

Noble nodded in response and stood at the open door until the investigator was in his car. Roberts rounded the circular drive and fished for a cigarette as he slowly made for the state road. Horses grazed on one side of the road, kept in by a four board white fence, and in the distance he could see a tractor mowing another field. He made a mental note to ask the Nobles who worked on the farm, perhaps estate was the word, but for now he was anxious to return to his office to place a call to the chief medical examiner and learn the results of the autopsy.

The cramped offices of the sheriff's department were overflowing with deputies and police officers upon his arrival and for several minutes Roberts was unable to get to his desk while Miss Dora Temple, octogenarian treasurer of the Lafayette County Historical Society, took orders for walnuts and pecans, an annual fund raising ritual for the Society which was more social outing for Miss Dora than fund raiser. Miss Dora would make the same rounds a few months hence to deliver the orders and collect the proceeds. "Put the sheriff down for three pounds of each," said Lewis Brown after he had ordered a pound of pecans for himself. Miss Dora thanked him and jotted down the request before leaving the room.

"Does he ever say anything to you about doing that to him?" asked Roberts as he seated himself at his desk.

"No," answered Brown with a smile. "The stuff comes in and he pays for it, doesn't even question why. He can't argue with a voter."

Roberts tossed two styrofoam coffee cups in the trash basket as he looked at the pink message slips on his desk. "You'd think this bunch would have the decency to store their trash elsewhere."

"Ain't got no home trainin'," observed Brown.

Roberts grunted in response as he pulled the list of telephone numbers from his pocket. "This name Anita Smith rings a bell. Something to do with Jeff Smith maybe?"

"Drugs and Smith. Makes since."

"The Nobles don't know her. Can you look into it for me?"

"Sure. This afternoon alright? I've gotta handle a burglary."

Roberts waved his hand in acknowledgement as Brown left the room. Taking advantage of the quiet interlude, he dialed the number to the medical examiner in Richmond. Several transfers were required to connect him with Dr. Jeannette DeWease, the Chief Medical Examiner for the Commonwealth of Virginia.

"Hello Gene," she greeted him in her clipped delivery, the product of her Ohio childhood and her no nonsense professionalism. "I apologize for the delay. We had eight bodies this weekend. You're calling about Clyde Noble's daughter?"

"Unfortunately."

"She had petechial hemorrhages of the conjunctiva, and marked congestion in the lungs, with focal hemorrhaging. No water in the stomach and no temporal bone hemorrhages. Her lungs were red. She didn't drown, she was asphyxiated. Actual cause of death was, of course, heart failure."

Roberts leaned back in his chair and reached for a cigarette. "Can you rule out a drug overdose?"

"Yes, but we'll still need toxicology to determine the levels. That takes several weeks, if you push them."

"What else?"

"One would expect some evidence of a struggle, but there is none. It would appear as if she might have been unconscious when she was smothered. The toxicology will help with that. I did note a very slight perianal tear, and the presence of semen in the vagina."

"What is the time of death?"

"Between nine and ten-thirty p.m."

"What about this tear?"

"It wasn't a cut, probably a blunt object. But you needn't ask me, I have no idea how that little wound occurred, and the body being in the pool doesn't help matters. It could be sexual, it could be many things"

"Any chance of DNA in connection with the tear?"

"No semen. My preliminary thought is we'll find nothing because of the water."

"I'm afraid to ask whether there's anything else."

DeWease laughed before answering. "You're safe. That's about it. I guess your drowning has turned into a murder."

"You've got it."

"Call me if there's anything else. Otherwise we're going to release the body. Mrs. Noble has been, to say the least, persistent."

"How so?"

"Wanting to know why the autopsy was necessary. Asking how the victim died, when the body will be released, that sort of thing. Of course, we deferred all those matters to your office."

"When did she call you?"

"Yesterday morning and again this morning."

"Thanks Jeannette."

"My pleasure."

Roberts slowly replaced the receiver and squinted as he thought about what next he might expect from Rita Noble.

Roberts was adding to his growing report on the Noble death, and preparing what he would say when he called the Nobles with the autopsy results, when Lewis Brown returned from the burglary he had been to investigate. "You're right. Anita Smith is the grandmother of your little friend, Jeff Junior Smith the Third."

"I guess we know where her drugs were coming from."

"Want me to go see him?"

"Not yet. I've got to think about this."

Brown turned his attention to the pink notes on his desk. "What the sheriff want?" he asked after reading the first message.

"I don't know. Probably getting some heat from your burglar victim."

"Crap," muttered Brown as he walked toward the sheriff's warren.

Roberts fingered his Zippo lighter as he pondered the significance of Smith's appearance in the mushrooming scenario. Perhaps, he thought, Smith's drugs would provide a reason for Jason Thomasson to drive to the Nobles to see Miranda when he was only minutes away from her when she was in Charlottesville. He picked up the telephone and dialed Cross's intercom number. "Ev," he began when the other answered, "The CME says it wasn't drowning, but asphyxiation."

Cross was silent.

"Also semen in the vagina and a very slight rectal tear."

"Shit," mumbled Ev.

"I haven't told the Nobles. Think I might need to interview another family member first."

"Rita's brother?"

"Yeah. Clara Wood said he called on Friday, I guess I told you that. Clyde says he was seeing her, with dishonorable motives."

"That certainly doubles the trouble for Rita Noble. Where does he live?"

"Charlottesville."

"Why would he see her at the Nobles? They were both in Charlottesville. Besides, that sounds like the kind of sporting that both of them would be keeping quiet."

"That's my problem, too, except for the autopsy results on the sex angle. That's why I want to see him before telling the Nobles about the autopsy."

"They're going to raise hell."

"Why do you think I called you," laughed Roberts.

"Okay with me. But we should let them know today."

"I'm with you. There's one more thing. I think we've got her local drug contact. Jeff Smith."

"The Jeff Smith?"

"Yeah. Jeff Junior Smith the Third."

"I would put him down as suspect number one. He's already gotten by with one murder."

Roberts put a cigarette between his lips before answering. "I'm reading your thoughts, but I've got to deal with little brother first. I'm uncomfortable with the way Rita Noble reacted when I asked her about his call to Miranda. I may be too late already, but I don't want to give anybody any more time to coordinate their stories."

"Anything else?"

"No, but I'll keep you posted." Brown was walking out of the sheriff's office, which adjoined the room used by the investigators, as Roberts cradled the receiver. "Come on, let's go," he ordered Brown without looking at him.

"Don't you wanna hear what the boss wanted?"

"Sure," answered Roberts indifferently as he pulled on his blazer.

"He said he finally figured out what my title is. Lieutenant." He held out two silver bars of the sort used in the army. "But the sergeants are still in charge of the road deputies, so I guess I'm in charge of you."

"Silver. You made it straight to first lieutenant. Skipped second."

Brown grunted a short laugh. "Wait till my momma hears about this."

**CHAPTER 3**

Monday, August 24th, p.m.

Jason Thomasson's townhouse was north of Charlottesville proper, some forty miles from Lafayette Court House, situated in that part of Albemarle county that had been absorbing growth like a sponge, and positioned among the explosion of shopping centers, now referred to as malls and squares, and the dozen upon dozen of generic chain restaurants that were vulgar proof that Charlottesville was no longer a sleepy little hub for the University students and peripatetic rich who had made the town, when it was that small, a fashionably unique city speck in the heart of Virginia's fetching piedmont. Away from the corridor of malls, apartments, and fast food joints lay a circling and ever expanding belt of subdivisions, all new, and like everywhere else, saddled with monikers like Quail Run and Deer Ridge. Clyde Noble was responsible for a few of these cul-de-sac laced additions, contributing to a suburban sprawl that dwarfed, and nearly choked, its modest urban core.

Thomasson's residence, Cavalier Landing, apparently so named because it adjoined a three acre man-made lake which undoubtedly had not existed in the seventeenth century, had a worn edge to it. Two joggers, the male of the two running shirtless, gave Roberts's unmarked sedan a hard look, for a new Ford Crown Victoria, sprouting antennae and occupied by two very large men—one white, one black—in coats and ties, might as well have had 'vice squad' or 'FBI' posted in big letters on the doors.

The investigator and his newly denominated lieutenant walked to the door and waited for a response to Roberts's raps. In a few moments a rangy young man answered, his demeanor distinctly conveying his understanding of the purpose for the visit. He was unshaven and looked as if he had just awakened. Roberts introduced Brown and himself and Thomasson nervously confirmed who he was.

Roberts, first across the threshold, looked around the shabbily furnished room and made mental notes of the bare walls, the three beer cans on the table in front of the sofa, and the various socks and shirts strewn about the carpeted floor. "Are you a student?" Roberts asked.

Thomasson looked at the beer cans at the same time Roberts did. "Ah, yeah. Over at the community college. I took a course this summer. I'm trying to get my grades up so I can get into UVA."

*Good luck,* thought Roberts as he surveyed the dingy sofa and decided he would rather not sit there. Beyond the sofa was a dining nook that contained a cluttered card table and three folding chairs. Roberts motioned to the chairs. "Can we sit at the table and talk a few minutes?" He never interviewed someone, if he could help it, while standing.

19

Thomasson nodded lamely and walked to the table where he scooped newspapers and debris from fast food meals into an open cooler and shoved it into the corner. "You can tell I live by myself," he mumbled as the three took seats.

Roberts decided to get immediately to the business at hand. "We're investigating Miranda Noble's death. I know this is a bad time for you, but we've got to ask some questions. I'm told you were dating her."

"Some."

"Clara Wood says you called there, at the Nobles, on Friday."

"Yeah."

"Did she call you back?"

"Yeah."

"What was the reason for the call?"

"We were going to hook up that night."

"Did you go see her on Friday?"

Thomasson's face, already pallid, lost the rest of its color. "No. I mean I was. That's why I called. But I came home, here, to get cleaned up from work, and fell asleep."

Roberts and Brown, who were sitting opposite one another, exchanged brief glances. "Did you let her know you weren't coming?"

Thomasson looked from one man to the other. "No. I mean I tried, but I didn't."

"Are you saying you called again?" asked Roberts.

By now Thomasson looked physically ill. "I don't think I did." He glanced around nervously as if looking for something. "Do you mind if I smoke, if I can find them."

"Not if I can, too," answered Roberts. He smiled and offered Thomasson a cigarette, but he did not intend to allow the shaken younger man time to regain his equilibrium. "Now, do you remember whether you called her?"

"I didn't."

"What did you mean when you said you tried?"

Thomasson shook his head helplessly. "I don't know. I wish I had."

"Why were you going to see her?"

"Why?"

"Yes. Wasn't it easier to see her in Charlottesville?"

Motioning to the room behind him, Thomasson managed a wan smile. "Rita's place was a little nicer than this."

"I gathered Rita didn't like you seeing her?"

"They didn't."

"I got that impression, too."

"Look, I know you're gonna ask it, so I'll tell you. We were having sex. They knew I met her there once, when they were away. We had to be careful in

Charlottesville, because her mother would've shit if she knew Miranda was going out with me."

"How late did you work Friday?"

"Till five-thirty."

"Where"

"At Shiflett's Auto."

"Doing what?"

"I work in the parts department. Look. You probably already know it, but Miranda was screwed up, pretty, but screwed up. I mean she was into drugs and she drank like a fish, and, well, I wasn't lookin' to marry her. I was basically in it for the...sex."

"What kind of drugs?"

"Anything she could get her hands on." Thomasson jerked his eyes level with Roberts's. "I don't do drugs."

"Where'd she get it?"

"Not from me, but goddam, you can get the shit anywhere."

Roberts paused as he contemplated the confidence that was creeping back into Thomassson's voice.

Thomasson continued without being prompted. "That's probably why she drowned. Drunk or high. Is that what you're after? Her supplier?"

Brown, who was making notes, looked up and replied. "Yeah, we want that."

"I don't know. Well, Rita and Clyde had alcohol at their place."

"How old are you?" asked Roberts.

"Twenty-three."

"Did you ever buy her any alcohol?"

Thomasson hesitated before answering. "Yes," he finally conceded. "But I didn't on Friday. I mean, she drank mine when she was with me."

There was a brief silence as Roberts watched Thomasson who was peering at his cigarette.

"About her drug source," said Brown, "You know the name Jeff Smith?"

Thomasson looked up. "I've heard of him."

"Heard what?" persisted Brown.

"He deals. She mentioned his name once or twice. But I never met him. I'm just assuming she got stuff from him."

"Was she seeing anyone else?" asked Roberts.

"You mean like going out. I don't know. She was hot. I probably wasn't the only person she was...you know."

"One more thing about Friday," said Roberts, "did you go out after your nap."

"Did I go out?"

"Yes. Go anywhere?"

"No. I...it was late. I just stayed here."

"When did you find out she was dead."

"Rita called here Saturday, to tell me."

Roberts looked at Brown who was scribbling notes. "You have any other questions, Lewis?"

"No."

"I have just a few more," continued Roberts. "Have you ever been convicted of anything?"

"Just traffic."

"Any DUIs?"

"One."

"Oh yes. When did you last see Miranda?"

Thomasson sighed quietly. "Thursday night. She came over here. She'd been at Rita's a couple of days. That's one reason I was beat on Friday. I guess you can figure out what we did."

"I thought you said you didn't have her over here?"

"No. Sometimes she came here. We didn't have much choice after Rita told me not to see her at her house."

"But didn't you try to call Miranda at the Nobles?"

"She told me to call her there when she was here Thursday. She told me I could come after work, that nobody would be there. Look, you don't turn it down when it's offered."

"I suppose not," said Roberts. "Before Thursday, when did you see her last?"

Thomasson squinted for several minutes as he tried to recall the prior week. "Sunday or Monday night. Monday I think. She was at Rita's on Tuesday and Wednesday."

"How do you know?" asked Brown.

"She told me, on Thursday."

"Tuesday night and Wednesday night?" asked Roberts.

"Yeah."

Roberts arose from the table and pulled his pack of cigarettes from his coat. "Thank you for your help, Jason," he said, offering him the pack again. Gene automatically surveyed the small first floor of the apartment again as he waited for Brown to finish with his notes. There was much more he wanted to ask Thomasson, but he did not know enough to know where to begin, and he was not yet so desperate as to start bluffing.

"Yeah, thank you Jason," added Brown as he hurriedly poked his notebook into his pocket. "And I'm sorry about Miranda."

"Maybe this wouldna happened...if I had gone to see her Friday," said Thomasson softly.

Brown and Roberts again exchanged glances, but neither said anything in response. One lesson Brown had learned during his apprenticeship with Roberts was to keep quiet when his mentor was lost in thought, and Roberts was immersed for the first part of the return trip to Lafayette Court House. Ten miles out of Charlottesville Roberts broke the silence. "When we get back, run Thomasson's criminal history. When you find out where he was picked up on the DUI get a copy of his fingerprints and a mug shot, if they have one."

"Do you want me to radio that in to the office right now?"

"No. Half the world will pick it up on scanners." Roberts paused. "Which part of what he told us was truth, and which part a lie?"

The leading nature of the question irritated Brown because he knew that Roberts had already answered the question, or most of it, in his own mind. He hated these little quizzes and remained quiet for a few moments.

"What do you think?" pressed Roberts.

"I'm not sure," answered Brown. "He was mighty nervous talking about Friday."

Roberts reached into his coat pocket for his cigarettes. "That's bothering me, too. Not just his nervousness, but the whole bit. A young man like that doesn't just go home and fall asleep when he has a hot date waiting for him at Shangri-La. Then when he wakes up, he doesn't call. Hell, at his age, time doesn't matter. You'd think he would have just driven over there no matter what time it was."

Brown grinned. "You mean you were young once?"

"I've forgotten," said Roberts. "But if he were there, what would be his motive to hurt her?"

"Unless it was an accident of some kind, and he's afraid to say he was there."

"How do people get smothered by accident?"

"I don't know, I guess it's possible."

"The defense lawyer will say it's possible."

"Maybe she wouldn't put out and things got out of hand."

Roberts, who was driving, had not taken his eyes off the road during the exchange with Brown. "That's an explanation, but it doesn't jibe with what he's saying about her morality. It doesn't jibe with what Clyde Noble is saying about her morality. Still, you're right, it does provide an explanation we've got to consider." After a pause, "And something about Wednesday night doesn't jibe either. And then there's Jeff Smith. I wish Jason had been a little more convincing. Can you track down Smith today and find out if he will admit to knowing the girl. I've got to call the Nobles about the autopsy."

"I can try and find him. He doesn't work for the county anymore."

"Don't tip too much of your hand. Let's just get him pinned down. We'll work on the truth later."

The investigators' office was uncharacteristically quiet, with Brown dispatched on his mission to find Jeff Smith and the road deputies actually making their rounds in the county. Roberts sat pensively at his desk looking at Brown's notes of the Thomasson interview and debating whether to drive to the Nobles to tell them in person the autopsy results or to call the senator and relay the distasteful outcome by telephone. A lifetime of investigating crime had not made any easier the task of giving family members bad news, especially more bad news.

Willie Painter's gravelly voice, coming from the adjoining dispatch room, interrupted Roberts's musing. "Gene, pick up on line two. Clyde Noble."

Roberts pursed his lips in realization that the decision had been made for him. "Roberts," he said into the receiver.

"This is Clyde Noble. You've been to see Jason."

"Yes."

"We would have appreciated you telling us you were going to do that."

"I believe I told you this morning that I needed to talk to everyone who had contact with your daughter before her death."

There was a brief pause on Noble's end. "I can understand that you have to do certain things. But I don't like being kept in the dark. We don't know what the autopsy showed, which I'm told is complete. Is it?"

"Yes. Your daughter was smothered. Also, there is evidence of intercourse, and a slight anal injury." Roberts leaned his forehead into his free hand when he was finished.

"God," came the murmur from Noble's end.

Roberts instantly regretted having let Noble bluster him into the blunt synopsis of Miranda's death. He could hear the other man's breathing as he tried to think of some solace he could offer, but no words would form.

"Oh God," mumbled Noble again.

"I'm very sorry, Senator," Roberts finally managed. "The autopsy generated more questions, so I'll need to talk to you and Mrs. Noble again, but I can wait if you want."

"When did you find this out?" asked Noble, his voice regaining its firmness.

Roberts briefly considered avoiding a direct response, then thought better of it. "Just after talking to you all this morning." He decided to offer no explanation for his delay in reporting the results.

"I see. You wanted to talk to Jason first."

"That's correct."

"Well?"

"Senator, we have a long way to go in resolving this. I need a lot more information."

"Like what?"

"I mentioned the fingerprints, the list of people we should expect to have been in the pool area."

"Have you involved the state police?"

"They'll assist if needed." Roberts was always irritated by this question, not just because it always was asked, but because the public mistakenly perceived that anything remotely complicated, or serious, was the domain of the Virginia State Police. In the twenty-eight years he had been in law enforcement, he could count on one hand the times the state police had been of any real assistance in one of his criminal investigations.

"I take it that means no."

"We aren't at the stage where they can help. Should—"

"You suspect Jason?"

"It's too early, Senator. Should I make an appointment for tomorrow?"

"No. Ask me now."

"I saw a man bushhogging near your place. Do you have farm employees?"

"Just Hector Lopez. He lives in the little frame house on the state road about a mile from my home. His wife cleans house, but only when Clara is here."

"Anyone else live there?"

"Their three children. The oldest one is probably fourteen."

"Would there have been any other maintenance people, delivery men, people of that sort at your house last week?"

"Roberts, there is always somebody coming here. The only one who comes to mind is Roger Snidlett. He's a logger, about sixty. He took a dead tree out of the yard last week, Tuesday or Wednesday. He's worked for me off and on for twenty years. Look, I'll ask Rita and Clara, but I can tell you, nobody unusual was here, not while we were."

"Okay, that will help."

"I think you're on the wrong track with Jason. I've told you he wouldn't do it. I don't have any use for him, as you can probably tell, but I see no reason to waste time with him."

Roberts's jaws twitched as he listened to Noble tell him how to do his job. "I hope you're right," he said patiently.

"Just so you'll know, Rita has instructed him to see our lawyers."

Roberts was speechless. He had not expected to work easily with Clyde and Rita Noble; people with means and power were frequently more demanding and less trustful than the routine victim of crime, for most victims were poor and beaten down—crime for them was just another lousy hand dealt by fate. But even with his reservations about the Nobles Roberts had not expected outright defiance from them, even if a relative had to be considered, in order to be eliminated, as the killer.

"Thank you, Senator," he answered coolly. "Please call when that list is ready." He put the receiver down slowly after he heard a click from Noble's end.

* * *

Paula Noble taught third grade in the Charlottesville public schools, the profession she was pursuing when she married Clyde Noble. They delayed starting a family so that she could work while Noble bounced from one job to the next. Between jobs, and to placate his mother, Noble agreed to manage temporarily his father's small construction business after the older Noble suffered a crippling stroke which left no one to finish the two houses under construction, and no one to provide for a wife and for two children still in high school. Growing up in a cash-strapped family honed an ambitious edge to Noble, hence he never viewed himself as a contractor struggling with alcoholic painters and temperamental bricklayers, but as a corporate CEO or perhaps, a financier.

From the less than modest start, Noble expanded his father's simple operation until Paula no longer needed to work, and then to the point where he needed not just artisans, but sales staff and secretaries. An equally ambitious Rita Thomasson was a part of the expansion, and with a single-mindedness of purpose that was no secret for one minute to either Noble or herself, she aimed directly for the source, captivating her employer in a time-tested manner that Paula came to realize only when Noble packed his clothes and left their home. Noble's succubus had no need for a ready-made family, however, and while there was no rancor over Miranda's custody, the issue of money was not so easily resolved. Finally realizing the value of a clean bill of sale, as well as the avoidance of repeated spectacles in court, Noble ignored his new love's adamancy about her future wealth, paid Paula what her attorney was demanding, and returned to Lafayette County to build the mansion his new wife wanted.

After ending his difficult conversation with her former husband Roberts called Paula Noble to tell her what the autopsy suggested and to schedule a time when he could come talk to her. Listening to her quiet questions he felt somewhat embarrassed that his attention had been absorbed by Clyde and Rita, and he could not refuse her invitation to come talk to her that evening. He knew that part of Paula's motivation was human nature: the insatiable and inexplicable desire to hear and rehear every fragment of the last moments, no matter how painful, of a loved one suddenly ripped away, and the notion that, somehow, there was an explanation which would pin the blame on some outside source, thereby removing the onus of fault from the lost one.

Roberts negotiated the tree lined street leading to Paula Noble's home and pulled into her drive. She greeted him at the door before he could knock. The original Mrs. Noble was tall, blonde and lithe, a striking woman even in her grief and Roberts found himself comparing her to the second Mrs. Noble, who, despite her youth, had a natural

26

hardness about her eyes and mouth which, unless she forced a pleasant demeanor, made her appear older and unapproachable. Rita Noble was smaller, too, yet her slenderness was too pronounced, almost abnormal, and had the effect of accentuating the many little facial lines that tainted her once attractive features making her look a little worn, like a small town cocktail waitress who should have found other work many years ago.

Roberts smiled in response to Paula's invitation to enter, unusual of itself for Roberts, whose professional scowl had become his natural persona. He took the seat she offered without his customary survey of the room.

She sat down across from him. "I really appreciate your coming this late. I don't know what I can offer that would help, maybe you should tell me what you need."

Roberts had expected family members to be with her, although he was not disappointed, for the extra people with their unrelated questions and irrelevant observations tended to keep an interview out of focus. "I'd like to know a little about your daughter. A brief sketch, if you will, of the past few years."

"There's so much to tell, I'd never really thought about it, about telling about her life like this." Her concentration drifted away from Roberts, toward the wall behind him, as she spoke.

"Let's start with school."

There was a long pause.

"She was a good student. She went to middle and high school at St. Anne's Belfield, where she graduated last year." Paula shook her head gently. "I teach in the public schools, and I was afraid there were too many bad influences, do you know what I mean?"

"Yes."

"She wanted to go to UVA, but didn't get in, so she took her second choice, James Madison. She wouldn't consider my school because it was all girls. But she didn't stay. She dropped out this spring, wouldn't complete the semester."

"Do you know why?"

Paula shook her head. "Well, maybe I do," she corrected herself. Glancing around the room, she again hesitated. "You know, we never know what's in their minds. I guess I didn't, or couldn't understand what it was like to have your father forget you existed. He quit visitation with her not long after the divorce. She didn't like going to see him, I think Rita made it difficult." Paula interrupted herself with a quiet sigh. "She started pushing the limits when she was a junior in high school. I thought it was the fast crowd, you know, the rich kids whose parents go to Europe for a month and leave their child with the keys to the Volvo and a couple of credit cards. And to some extent it was. Some of those kids have about as much relationship with the parents they live with as Miranda had with the father she never saw.

"I knew the kids were drinking. But I thought we'd made it when she went to college. Then she called here one night and asked if it would be alright to call her dad.

What could I say? I don't know what came of that. But it just seemed odd. Anyway, I think she had gotten lost. All of a sudden, after thirteen years, she wanted her father in her life. I mean...I don't know what I mean. You think you've done your best, and then you find out that wasn't good enough."

"What about drugs?"

Paula took a deep breath. "Clyde told me there were drugs. I thought I would see it, but I didn't, until he told me."

"Clyde told you?"

"She got stopped at school for drunk driving, with marijuana. It wasn't her car. She didn't call me, she called Clyde, and he hired her a lawyer. He told me. Then when she started going to Lafayette, he called again, telling me she was drinking and he thought there might be drugs. He called me," she emphasized, "like I was the only one who could do something about it." She dabbed at a corner of her eye with a tissue and fell silent for a moment. "I know you told me on the phone that you were...that you didn't have much to go on, but are you saying the drugs and the alcohol played some part in this? I don't understand...what this has to do with it, with someone killing her."

"I'm not sure it does. I hope not. But I need to re-create what was going on, before it happened. Some part of what you tell me is going to be related, I just don't know what part that is."

"Had she used drugs that night?"

"We don't know yet. It's possible."

"She was so different these last few months. Up and down. Unpredictable." Paula clenched her fists and stared at them. "Why didn't I see it and do something." She opened her hands and laid them gently in her lap. "What else can help you?"

"I think you knew she was seeing Jason Thomasson."

"Oh yes. I knew. Sort of the ultimate Thomasson revenge. I didn't like it, but what could I do."

"You didn't interfere?"

"Every mother interferes." Paula's eyes firmly met Roberts's. "What are you saying? Did he have something to do with this?"

"He talked to Miranda by phone last Friday. He said they were to meet, but it didn't happen."

"Oh God...oh God," murmured Paula, staring into her lap.

Roberts said nothing, knowing that anything he volunteered would excite more of the same suspicion in Paula that Thomasson's story had created for Brown and him.

"Are you holding something back? You think he did it?"

Roberts was relieved that her question was straightforward. "I need to remind you that I'm still trying to establish everything that preceded your daughter's death. At this point, everybody's a suspect and, in a way, nobody is. You need to keep in mind that somebody had to be the last person to see her or talk to her."

"He was the last?" she asked in an almost inaudible voice.

"He's the last to talk to her that we know about at this point."

Paula arose from her chair and walked to a candle stand in the corner of the room. She picked up a small frame containing a picture of Miranda holding a hockey stick and wearing the scarlet of St Anne's, and studied it aimlessly. "I can't think right now. I don't want to think right now. Those Thomassons. Jason moved here a couple of years ago. They're from Pennsylvania. Pittsburg I think. Don't ask me how they got here. Anyway, they met at Clyde's, Miranda met Jason there, I should say." Paula put the frame down and turned back toward Roberts. "Did Rita tell you that she didn't want Jason seeing her? That little bitch." She pursed her lips together for a moment as if contemplating her profanity. "Miranda was really hurt, because her father seemed to go along with Rita. That's when I intervened, told Miranda to take a hint. All of this because she wanted to see her father." She sobbed softly, and quickly turned to face the corner.

"Did Miranda tell you her plans for Friday?"

"As much as a nineteen year old will tell you. She said she was going to Clyde's. I didn't know that...that they wouldn't be there. As you can understand, I don't call Clyde to verify these things. At her age, well, I just had to accept it, at least that's what I was telling myself. She'd been there earlier in the week. She was there Tuesday and Wednesday night."

"Both nights? Spent the night?"

The interruption did not distract Paula. "Yes, she came home early Thursday, slept all day." As if thinking aloud, she continued. "She was going there Friday to meet Jason, so I wouldn't know, wasn't she? Did you talk to Jason? Did he say that?"

"I think they were trying to dodge you and his sister. Let me ask you this, did she get any calls here, or visitors, by people you didn't know? Just anything that looks unusual, in retrospect."

"I thought about that after you called me, racking my brain. Nothing. Just her slipping around to see Jason."

"What about Thursday night?"

"She said she was going out with some school friends." Paula turned from the corner and walked back to her chair. "What do you know about Thursday night?"

"She was with Jason."

"I thought so. You weren't going to tell me were you?"

"I'm not trying to keep things from you. But at this point there is so much I need to know. When it fits together, I can explain it to you."

"You're saying there're things you're not telling me." There was an edge to her voice.

"You have to trust me a little. There's no use in me speculating. That will serve no purpose. I promise you, when something begins to make sense, I'll explain it to you, and ask more questions."

Paula grasped the top of the chair. "I can't. I can't handle this not knowing. Somebody killed my child and you can't tell me?"

"No. I'm sorry. I can't tell you. That's why I'm here."

Paula put her other hand to her face and rubbed her temple. "I'm sorry. Of course you're trying. But please don't keep things from me. And don't worry. I won't say anything to Clyde. If I ever have to speak to him again, it will be too soon. Trite, huh? Oh, damn that man."

"You were reading my mind. It's best that you keep our talks to yourself."

"You don't trust them either, do you?"

Roberts felt vaguely trapped by the question. "It's not that," he managed.

"Well, I don't. You know as well as I do that this sort of thing would not look good in an election, leaving aside that dear little Jason is involved. That witch. Her brother too good for Miranda. The rumor in town is that he left Pennsylvania to get away from whatever he'd done there, or not done. You know he hadn't gone to college?"

"He said he was working on it. What do you know about the Thomasson family?"

"Mostly what I learned when Rita was still just an employee. They certainly weren't from a Main Line family. Her father was a real estate salesman, or maybe insurance. There was something about Rita, she was running from something too. But who knows what. If Clyde knew, he kept it to himself. The Thomassons aren't the kind of people to talk about where they're from, which is never a good sign. Anyway, since she married Clyde, she's become a part of the in-crowd. Where money and power are concerned, people don't ask questions, or don't care."

Roberts sat quietly for a moment. "Do you have a recent photo of Miranda we can have?"

"I'm sure I do. For what?"

"When we interview people, we like to be able to have them identify the person we're asking about."

"Just a minute." Paula left the room. She returned in a few moments and handed Roberts a picture of a smiling Miranda, her blonde hair tumbling to her shoulders.

"Thank you. Do you need it back?"

"No. It's a duplicate. From last fall, at school." Paula sighed and seated herself slowly in the chair across from Roberts. "This isn't real," she uttered quietly.

"I think this has been enough for tonight. Do you have anyone here with you?"

"My mother and sister came this morning. I sent them out to dinner when you called. I needed some time to myself, and to talk to you."

"Good, I'm glad someone's here with you." He paused a moment. "I think I'd better go now."

"Thank you." Paula did not move as she once again stared into her lap. "The funeral's tomorrow. The funeral. Oh dear God."

Roberts looked at Paula briefly before deciding to let himself out. "Good night Mrs. Noble."

She nodded in response.

On the return trip Roberts turned the bits and pieces of information over in his mind, uncomfortable that he did not believe Jason and at the same time trying to divine what possible reason he would have had to kill Miranda Noble. Either something was missing, or he was missing something. Intuitively he accepted that the former was the case. And then there was Wednesday night: he could not account for Miranda's whereabouts, which suggested there was someone else he needed to talk to.

Roberts went by the office to check for messages before returning home. The place was almost quiet, just an occasional radio transmission disturbed the silence with an indecipherable noise sounding like the blur of static that passes for a voice over the speaker at a fast food drive-through, and he could hear the night dispatcher, Reginald Williams, grumbling a response. He walked into the dispatcher's room and asked whether there was anything for him. There was no use checking his desk as Williams had never, in twelve years, delivered one of his cryptic notes to the recipient.

Williams leaned back in his chair and peered over his glasses at the tablet he kept in front of him. "Nope."

"Did anyone call me?"

"The sheriff was lookin' for you, but he said it could wait. I think it was about the funeral tomorrow."

It occurred to Roberts that he did not know where the funeral would be conducted. If in Lafayette, and given that Senator Noble was a survivor, he could safely assume that the sheriff would want all deputies on duty, including the investigator and his lieutenant, to be available to direct traffic. The sheriff followed his predecessor's routine of attending every funeral in the county, and that usually entailed at least one uniformed officer tending to traffic. "Where is the funeral, Reggie?"

"He said Charlottesville. Sure been hot," continued Williams. "Must be that damn El Caminyo."

"Sure has," said Roberts, deciding that he wouldn't spoil Williams's misconception that the Chevrolet Motor Division was conspiring with El Niño. He left the tiny dispatch room and walked to his desk where he found a pink message slip from earlier, before Williams came on duty. It listed a newspaper reporter's name. "This can wait," he mouthed to himself.

**CHAPTER 4**

Wednesday, August 26th

Ev Cross sat at his desk, his eyes trained unseeingly on the window, as he contemplated his conversation with Gene Roberts. A death that was not a simple drowning, an injury that suggested forced sex, and the surfacing of Jeff Smith were harbingers of a thousand new complications. His thoughts teased him with the possibility that he had a morbidly fascinating murder to try before the world, and the same thought reminded him that he could flounder along the way with all the eyes of the press carefully documenting his demise. He had never rid himself of a lawyer's curious propensity to question his own abilities, a feeling that he was somehow inadequate and that, eventually, he would be discovered.

No case was too insignificant to conjure the image of his professional self suffering public humiliation for an error that only an incompetent could manage. There were days when he thought he had finally met his fate, days when he had lost cases that he thought he should win. The emotion of inadequacy following a loss in a jury trial is without equal in its evisceration of the ego, and in the ensuing certitude that whatever else may be true, one's calling in life most surely is not the practice of law. In the damning hindsight which bedevils every lawyer who has dueled in the courtroom, there are a thousand what ifs, as sound and indisputable as a Southerner's analysis of how Gettysburg could have been won. Soon, though, the self-doubt recedes as other challenges rise to the fore, and after calmer retrospection the mistakes that loomed so large fade. They fade in part because every trial is a strictly human endeavor fraught with all the vicissitudes that human frailties can muster, and even the perfectionists of the bar must acknowledge that they can neither foresee nor control every whim of man's unpredictability.

The ring of the telephone interrupted his thoughts as he listened for his secretary to answer the call. She did, and in a moment she paged him on the intercom. "Are you here to talk to Mrs. Noble?"

"No. Tell her I'm going to court," Ev answered without hesitation. He always felt uncomfortable asking Linda to cover for him—he had not brought himself to call it lying—but he knew that Rita Noble must be calling about the autopsy, and he was not going to second guess Roberts's wanting to hold the results until after he had spoken to Thomasson, nor was he going to offer her an outright canard by saying that he was not yet aware of the report's contents. He picked up his files and walked from his office into the room which his secretary shared with the public's waiting area. "Well, I am on my way to court."

Linda cast him a knowing smile. "I wondered whether you wanted to talk to her. It's more than a drowning isn't it."

"Yep."

Linda Wood was the only secretary Ev had ever hired; hence she had worked for him for twelve years, beginning in the days when Ev, freshly graduated from law school, had returned to Lafayette County to hang out a shingle, and during the first lean years of which he was frequently late with her paycheck. She knew his moods as well as Polly, whose marriage to Ev predated Linda's employment by only a few months, and one would often forewarn the other when events cast him in a foul humor. The Commonwealth's Attorney suspected that Linda and Polly had already dissected the death over the telephone.

"The rumors are already flying," she continued. "Someone told me at church that she'd been raped. I didn't ask their source."

Ev paused at the door. "That might not be far off, for all we know." He then related what Roberts had told him.

Linda shook her head in the fashion she reserved for all bad news. "This ought not happen to a parent," as she reached for the ringing telephone. "It's Wil Bledsoe. Do you want to take it?"

Wilmer Dale Bledsoe, the most successful lawyer in Lafayette County, was humorous, hardworking, and skillful, and equally vain, profane, and opinionated. He was quick to invoke any racial, sexual, or ethnic epithet that seemed to fit the moment, and yet managed to represent almost every person mangled in a car wreck or on the operating table, especially those who were black, or poor, or illiterate, as well as the more well-heeled who not-so-secretly harbored the incorrect notion that his effectiveness sprang from craftiness instead of wits. In a profession where even two button single-breasted suits are sometimes considered casual, he preferred the double breast and cowboy boots.

"Hello Mr. Commonwealth," said Bledsoe brightly.

"What do you want?" replied Ev in feigned disinterest.

"Capital day idn't it. I'm surprised a government type like you would be in."

"Election's next year."

"That's right. Don't make a damn how much you're there, so long as it's Mondays and Fridays."

Ev laughed at the piece of advice regularly offered by Bledsoe. "I'm heeding your suggestion."

"Look. I represent this pinhead named Pup Tower, he ain't much, but he didn't have much going for him anyway. Have you seen a warrant on him?"

Ev answered that the name did not ring a bell.

"Well, Pup got charged with smacking his girlfriend a couple of weeks ago. Mind you, it was an open hand slap, not a fist. She got a warrant and a protective order and now he can't get his clothes, can't get his guns, hell, he can't fart."

Ev started rifling through the misdemeanor warrants stacked on a shelf behind his desk. "What's her name?"

"Let's see. It's Crystal Ricketts. You know those damn Ricketts. An open hand slap ain't nothin' but sign language to them."

Bledsoe continued talking as Ev looked for the papers on Pup Tower. "I guess you boys are busy with Clyde Noble's daughter. One newspaper quoted the sheriff as saying that everything pointed to accidental death."

"No one can accuse Hank of hedging his bets."

"That poor girl. I guess she was sorta cursed."

Ev found the papers he wanted and laid them aside. "How's that, Wil?"

"When Clyde divorced his first wife, Paula, he dumped his daughter as well. I handled the divorce. Back then I did a lot of his work, when he was moving from construction into development. That's when he was married to Paula. They had the one girl Miranda. He got a good deal on some land in Albemarle, and away he went. He set up his own sales staff, and hired Rita Thomasson. She used to bring papers to the office, and I'm tellin' you, she was easy on the eyes. She musta been easy, period. It wasn't too long before Clyde came to me about separation papers. Long story short, Rita got a sugar daddy; he's ten years older than she is. Paula got the kid. He didn't put up a fight about custody.

"He quit using me as much after the divorce, and then quit altogether. Farnsworth and Conte in Charlottesville got all his work. I think Rita wanted a nice, clean break with the past. When he ran for the state senate, what, about six years ago, I supported him. But I hadn't seen much of him until last year when he called to ask me to represent Miranda on a drunk driving and marijuana charge. First time he'd retained me in years. I guess he was embarrassed for Oliver Farnsworth to know he had a screwed-up daughter from another marriage. He told me she was having problems with drugs and booze and her mother had thrown up her hands. It was a first offense, so we got probation. She was a pretty girl. I don't know what happened to her, had a sorta lonely look about her. What do y'all think happened?"

"We don't know enough to know what to think."

"What is Hank doing offering opinions on it?"

"My guess is the Nobles want everything kept quiet. Politics. Hank isn't going to rock the boat."

"Yeah. That bitch Rita has her eye on a Georgetown address. You'd think Hank would have enough sense to keep his mouth shut."

Ev laughed at the characterization of Rita Noble. He knew that Bledsoe had counted on Clyde Noble's support five years earlier when Bledsoe sought the General Assembly's appointment as a circuit judge, an effort that failed in no small part because Noble had remained neutral. Instead, a Republican lawyer in the county, Jim Crawford, had secured the position. "You don't like Rita, I take it?"

"I don't give a rat's ass. I just know what she is. Reminds me of my first wife."

Ev decided to leave the matter of the judgeship alone. "Miranda was messed up?"

"Yeah. Hank may be right. That's the kind of person who ends up dead. What about Pup? Do you have any idea what you want to do with that? He says they're going back together."

"She hasn't talked to us. I'll just put the case on, let them tell their stories to the judge. Why do you fool with these court appointments anyway?" Bledsoe had once told Ev that he averaged a quarter million a year from his practice. The hundred dollar fee the state paid him for handling a case like Pup Tower's was not merely ludicrous, it was costing him money.

"The judges have to appoint somebody. If we don't spread it around, then just a few guys will have to do it all. I figure it's only fair to the judges and the bar." Bledsoe was not being entirely forthright, for while he regarded his motivation as altruistic, the fact remained that the indigent defendants he represented by court appointment often returned with paying work, like divorces and custody disputes, culminating with a nice personal injury suit when a hand got lopped off at the workplace. "I mean, hell, have you ever thought about what the district courts are?" asked Bledsoe, referring to the two lower courts, General District, where traffic cases and petty criminal matters are heard, and Juvenile and Domestic Relations, where custody, child support, and crimes among family members and by minors are handled.

Ev, knowing that he was in for one of Bledsoe's digressions, leaned back in his chair and took off his glasses. "Probably not along the lines you have."

"Society has to have some way to manage the mob. In the past they used feudalism, slavery, serfdom, castes, one owner factory towns, all manner of ways to deal with people who couldn't manage themselves. I mean they had to have a labor force, and they couldn't let this bunch breed and fight and undermine organized society. So when we got enlightened, we got rid of the old systems on the theory that people would look after themselves. Of course that couldn't work, especially after the free love and sex and welfare revolution of the sixties, so we started channeling them into the courts.

"Think about the great common law, that dealt with land and contracts, and the push and shove of government. Hell, the criminal law dealt only with rape and murder, and stealing of course, big stuff. Now we drag 'em in for slapping one another, for cussin', and to fix support for their bastard children, and in general to give 'em a place to scrap with each other because nobody else has the authority to referee. Instead of a grand duke or a foreman, we have lawyers and district judges and probation officers. The only time you see responsible, self-respecting people in district court is when they're victims or when they get a speeding ticket."

"Well, I've never thought of it like that," laughed Ev.

"Am I right? The Towers, the Ricketts, half the spades and wetbacks, they're all you see. You're the new overseer, and the judge is the king or master or whatever. We defense lawyers sorta round out the enlightenment factor, to give these Neanderthals someone who can translate for them, both the rules and their stories. I read the other day that the first juvenile court was created in Chicago at the turn of the century to manage the immigrant children who were running amok, to try to instill the American way. Even personal injury work is part of it. In the old days, laws and tradition made the upper classes look after the maimed and the old on the bottom rung, at least a little. Now we lawyers get' em SSI or sue for damages, that way the rest of society doesn't have to fool with 'em."

"You're being mighty hard on the people who made you rich."

"I didn't say I didn't like 'em. I wouldn't trade this job for anything. I'm just pointing out a fact of modern society. The law thinks for those folks who can't think for themselves."

Ev straightened in his chair. "There's more truth to what you say than I want to think about right now."

"That's why all this court ordered counseling for alcohol and domestic violence won't work," continued Bledsoe.

"Why?"

Bledsoe chuckled. "Because all these people can handle is the boundaries, the limits that keep them from landing in jail."

* * *

Ev had finished his morning in General District Court, and the small courtroom that was the forum for petty crimes, traffic violations, and preliminary hearings for felonies was almost empty; only Judge Abner Lincoln and Ev remained. Lincoln was signing the last of the warrants and summonses he had tried that morning and Ev was gathering his files. The bailiff, Okra Alexander, stuck his head through the door that led to the clerk's office, where some of the defendants were surrendering their drivers' licenses and setting up payment schedules for their fines. "That all till one-thirty?" he asked.

"That's it," answered Lincoln. "No more guilty bastards out there to try are there?"

Alexander laughed. "I'll check." He walked through the courtroom to the door which led to the hallway that also served as a lobby. Alexander, fresh out of the navy, and a city kid, had discovered an opening in Lafayette's sheriff's department when visiting his wife's uncle in the county. One month into his new job he had mistaken an old man's okra plants for marijuana and after pulling all the plants and presenting them to the sheriff, he landed a new first name.

Okra returned quickly. "Nope. You're done. See you at one-thirty judge."

Once the door was closed, Lincoln arose and walked around to the front of the bench. "I take it the Noble case will be a bad one."

"I'm afraid you're right."

"Why did Hank call it an accident so quickly?"

"You know Hank Burke," Ev prevaricated. Lincoln and Clyde Noble had been confidants, politically, before Lincoln was appointed as General District judge, an appointment in which Noble's help had been critical. Ev decided that the two might still be close and that he had best keep his opinions to himself.

"Yeah, I suppose I do. See you next Wednesday," replied Lincoln.

Ev once again gathered his files and walked the labyrinthine route to his office in the rear of the building. Hampton Coleman was waiting for him when he arrived.

Coleman was in his seventies, a heavy man who considered himself portly, and if accoutered with a cigar, which he frequently was, he looked the political boss he had always fancied himself. He took himself very seriously, and expected others to do the same. For decades he had been chairman of the Democratic Party in Lafayette, until toppled eight years before by an ungrateful coalition of newcomers, mostly old hippies, led by Bill Posner, a flower child who had outgrown his pony tail and gained election to the county's Board of Supervisors, and by a handful of blacks who had been promised positions of power by their new allies.

In the fallout of the scandal over the murder of Alphonso Thornton, the murder that had Jeff Junior Smith associated with it, another victim had been Bill Posner who lost his Supervisor seat because he was the rumored reason for the inept investigation of his son's involvement in the killing. Posner had been the point man in toppling Coleman from his chairmanship, so when the chairman's election was next held, the coalition's thin majority unraveled with the desertion of its disenchanted black adherents and Hampton Coleman recaptured the prize.

Ev had known Coleman all his life, not because of politics, but because Coleman was a friend and contemporary of his parents and Ev's uncle, and was a cousin of the uncle's wife, Virginia. Despite these connections Ev had never been comfortable in Coleman's presence, as there was always a condescending air about the older man which failed to mask a determined arrogance. Coleman had greeted Ev's Democratic candidacy with the vocal enthusiasm of a chicken that has just laid an egg and immediately had taken to treating Ev like a fellow warrior in the political wars, none of which, with the exception of his own, Ev cared about.

Coleman greeted Ev with a broad smile and a moist handshake that once again reminded Ev of his reservations. They walked into the prosecutor's office and Coleman closed the door, another harbinger that made Ev uneasy. Both men sat down and exchanged a few pleasantries about Ev's uncle until it was clear that Coleman was ready to get to the point of his visit. "Ev," Coleman began, "what is going on with this terrible thing about Clyde Noble's daughter?"

"You probably know as much as I do," answered Ev vaguely. He detested being quizzed about an ongoing investigation.

"I saw Clyde after the funeral. He seemed to think that his brother-in-law was being investigated. That can't be, can it?"

Ev forced a nervous smile. He knew that the visit would have an angle, but not this one. Noble had remained aloof while Bill Posner and his allies carried off their *coup d'état*; a perfidy, in Coleman's eyes, that was particularly unconscionable given the years of work he had dedicated to getting Noble into the state senate. But in the chameleon tradition that shades most political relationships, Noble had again embraced Coleman after his return to the chairmanship, calling him the 'old warhorse,' and Coleman was more than happy to forget that the man who might be the next junior United States senator had once abandoned him.

Ev's smile was still stuck to his face, but he knew where this exchange was going and he did not know how he could placate the old man without further riling his suspicious nature. The last thing he wanted with the election coming the following year was for Coleman to start looking for another candidate, which he had no doubt the other man would do despite the connection with the Cross family. "I don't think I'd put it that way," he began diffidently. "Right now, I don't believe the sheriff's department has a suspect."

"That's not the impression I got. He said they've been to question the boy, and apparently, it wasn't pleasant."

"I hope they're questioning everybody." The response did not sound like he had intended it.

Coleman screwed his lips together before responding. "That makes sense, but don't you think you had better be careful with how this boy is handled?"

"I'm not aware he's being given any, ah, bad treatment."

"Well, it just seems to everyone that he's being...treated like he did it." Coleman's face darkened. "It could be very embarrassing."

"He's not charged with anything, Mr. Coleman." Having known the older man since childhood, Ev had never reached the point where he considered it appropriate to become more familiar, if addressing the other man as Hampton could be considered less formal.

"What about the sheriff saying it was an accidental drowning?"

Ev sighed unintentionally, and hated that he could not retract it. "He was wrong," he said quietly.

"That's my point. First the sheriff making that remark, then this boy coming up as a suspect. It makes you all look like you don't know what you're doing. That kind of flip-flopping reminds me of Conway Lawson and the Thornton boy's death."

The analogy surprised Ev. "I think the only thing the Thornton case and this one have in common is a politico is involved, and this time nobody's playing favorites." The words had leapt out, and he had a sinking feeling as he watched Coleman's eyes widen.

"I didn't say that," the older man responded, a menacing, unpleasant tone in his voice.

"Mr. Coleman. No one will know about Jason Thomasson unless the Nobles or Jason let it out. You know, they know, we have to question everybody."

"I want to tell you again, this is not about questioning, it's the accusatory way it's being handled." He paused for a moment. "Ev, Clyde is going to run for senator, you know that. Anything that involves him is going to make it into the news. Having his brother-in-law investigated for murdering his daughter is...could create real problems."

Ev could feel his face flushing. "I don't believe I'm following you."

"Clyde said there's no way Jason could have killed that girl. Now I'd think a father would be the most aggressive of all if he thought you were onto the one who did it."

Ev wanted to tell Coleman what he thought of Noble's objectivity, but he knew this was no time to challenge Coleman, and anyway, at this point, he simply wanted the conversation to end. "Gene Roberts's handling the case, and I have great faith in his abilities. I can't start telling the sheriff and Roberts how to run the sheriff's department." The latter excuse, he thought, was on firm ground, since Hank Burke was a fellow Democrat and because anyone who was familiar with local government knew that the sheriff's department was a one man show: the sheriff's.

Ev's reference to the independence of the sheriff's department slowed Coleman briefly, and he peered at Ev for a moment, as if digesting how to best handle the problem. "You've got a lot more power than you realize."

"Not that much."

Coleman leaned forward slightly, which was not much given his girth. "Do you, and Roberts, really think this Thomasson boy could be involved?"

"That's what I'm trying to tell you. We don't know much yet." He paused and took a breath. "You know, I...there's really so much I can say. It is an ongoing investigation." He knew Coleman needed to be told that none of this was his business, yet he could not bring himself to use the forthright language that was running through his mind.

Coleman shook his head. "Let's look at this another way. If you all foul this up, it's going to be covered by the press start to finish. How is that going to make you look? The word is that Robbie Fleming might run for your position next year, as a Republican. How will this look for you and the sheriff, another messed up case with all these fits and starts?"

"I know what can happen when a big case goes south. But I...but we have to work this one like any other."

"I know that. But you've got to be careful how you work it. There's more at stake than just solving the murder. Look Ev, you've got two jobs. One is commonwealth's attorney. The other is politician. And they're Siamese twins, except they can't be separated and survive."

Ev leaned back in his chair, as if to restore the space that Coleman had taken when he hunched forward. "I know that. I'm aware of what can happen to reputations. But you know anything that gets out, like the accident bit, will be coming from the sheriff or one of his dispatchers. If people keep their mouths shut, there won't be any more fits and starts."

Coleman squeezed the arms of his chair and then stood up. "You've got a lot to learn, Ev. I've been through all this before, and so has your uncle. Ask him about it sometime."

Ev arose, too. "Thank you Mr. Coleman," he replied stiffly. Coleman turned abruptly and left the room at a brisk pace. Cross abandoned his intention of escorting the other man as it was obvious that Coleman was in no mood for further civility. For several minutes Ev stood behind his desk, staring blankly at the empty chairs before him, while an uncomfortable nervousness stirred in his stomach and Coleman's remarks swirled in his head, and he began to wonder just what it was that Coleman had expected him to say, or do. Already he was regretting that he had not told Coleman that politics made no difference and that he did not give a good goddam about the senate race, and now he felt that he had been spineless. He didn't want to acknowledge Coleman's observation about his own dual existence either, but there was too much truth in his statement for him to shrug it off.

Coleman's remark about power also nettled him. It was true that he, the prosecutor, the elected commonwealth's attorney for Lafayette County, had the final say in who was charged and with what, and whether the scofflaw was going to be convicted of a felony or a misdemeanor; and by either plea agreement or recommendation he could also frequently decide whether a defendant would serve time and for how long. This power was not lost on the public, who referred to him as 'the Commonwealth,' or the 'county man,' and who in addressing him almost always called him Mr. Cross, regardless of the age of the person speaking to him. Yet aware of all this, he did not accept that he was so omnipotent, especially when it came to a serious case, and wondered why Coleman had mentioned it. Enveloped in his inquietude, he walked into the lobby and looked at Linda Masencup.

"He left in a snit," she observed.

"Yeah," said Ev. "That was a weird conversation. It probably won't be the last one, with this case."

"How is he involved, or is everybody?"

Cross smiled at her characterization. "You're right. He's not involved, and yet everybody is. Politics. He's worried about Clyde Nobles' political future, and mine, too, but only because a Republican might beat me."

"Well, you knew that was bound to come up."

"Unfortunately, I did." Cross paused for a moment. "I'm going to the sheriff's office, and then to lunch." Preoccupied as he was, he left his office without the mail.

He found Roberts at his desk fielding a telephone call from Minnie Patterson, who still had not resolved her problem with the infringing cats. Roberts managed to conclude the conversation by promising to have someone speak to the felines' indifferent owner. "Damn," said Roberts after he replaced the receiver, "we need an early frost to kill her tomatoes so this crisis will pass."

Ev took off his glasses and laughed as he rubbed his eyes. "That's what I told Linda. Cats seem almost appealing at this point. Have you talked to the sheriff?"

"About the Noble case?"

"Yes."

"Yeah. I briefed him yesterday. He's uptight about his calling it an accident. The ghost of Alphonso Thornton is haunting him."

"Did you tell him to keep his mouth shut?"

"I dropped the biggest hint I could. He didn't need much coaching. He knows he made a mistake and he's worried about it."

"Where are we?"

"Did I tell you about the interviews on Monday?"

"Brown told me about Jason when I saw him in court this morning. Who else did you talk to?"

"Paula Noble."

"Any help?"

"The biggie is that Miranda came home Thursday morning. The Nobles said she left their place Wednesday night."

"Jason?"

"No. He saw her Monday, he thinks, and then Thursday night. So I've got about twelve hours to account for, which probably means there's someone else to talk to, that is if Jason's telling the truth. I doubt she up and decided to camp somewhere in her car by herself."

"Damn."

"I can't get over how different Paula's reaction is from Clyde Noble's. But she's not a basket case, that woman has a lot of class."

Cross put his glasses back into place. "You'll be interested to know that Hampton Coleman paid me a visit to complain about your talking to Jason. Noble had bitched to him."

"That supercilious sack of shit. What does he want us to do?"

"Politics. He wanted us to be careful with Jason, might affect who the next senator is. But whatever his intentions, I guess I agree that we need to be careful about what goes public."

"The hell with him. Don't they ever learn? Anyway, I haven't told the press anything but that the death now appears to be intentional, read that murder. I read Willie Painter the riot act, so I hope he won't be givin' any of his personal views to the press. I just hope the sheriff doesn't step on it again."

"There's not much to work with."

"We've got to get all the forensics back. Toxicology, isolate DNA, everything."

"What about drugs?"

"That too. Lewis still hasn't been able to track down Jeff Smith. I guess he's dodging him, but that's natural. The little punk is a drug dealer."

"Do I detect a hint of frustration?"

"Hell yes."

"Lewis said Jason was not too convincing."

"That's why the Nobles are crying, I guess. His story about Friday night is pretty weak, but why would he hurt her? And I have to agree with Noble, he doesn't look like the type to kill someone."

"Could he be lying about Wednesday night?"

"He could. But he volunteered that he saw her Thursday night, and there were no witnesses, as far as he was concerned, so he didn't have to admit that. He volunteered that she was his sex kitten." After a pause, "I don't know."

Ev thrust his hands into his pockets. "Okay. Let me know." He walked toward the door and stopped in the threshold. "Did Miranda's mother give you any names?"

"Nope."

Ev nodded his head, then left.

Roberts watched the other man's back as he disappeared into the hallway. He pulled out the legal pad on which he had made a list of things he needed to do in the investigation and looked it over without giving serious thought to what he was doing. He was doodling on the corner of the sheet, rethinking Thomasson's story, when Lewis Brown walked in.

"I tracked down Jeff Smith today, at his grandmother's," said Brown.

"And?"

"He beat around the bush for awhile, said he didn't know Miranda. Then he changed his story and said he'd seen her at the Quik Mart, with some white dude, but couldn't remember who she was with. He said he thought she'd gone to a few parties, which for him, means a drug party. He said he didn't know when he'd last seen her and didn't know her number. So I told him that we traced the call to his grandmother's phone. That's when he said his cousin had taken a number for him Friday, and when he called, he got an answering machine, so he hung up. Figured it was a wrong number."

"The Nobles don't have an answering machine."

"I know."

"Smith has a pager, doesn't he?"

"I'm sure he does."

"Did you ask him if she used crack?"

"I asked him if he sold any to her, and he flapped around about how he was tired of the cops harassin' him. All we did was harass the brothers. So I told him we'd be in touch."

"He's lying."

"I figured he'd do that."

"But you didn't ask whether he knew her to use crack?"

"No, I didn't ask it that way," Brown answered quietly.

"Jason might've hedged a little bit on how well he knew Smith. You ask him about Jason?"

"He said he'd never heard of him."

"But he'd seen Miranda with someone he didn't know?"

"Yep."

"That could be our boy."

"That's what I was wonderin'."

"Make a good report."

"I did better than that. I taped it."

"Did he know?"

"Yes."

Roberts broke into a rare smile. "Good work."

"Do I get a raise now?"

"I guess the sheriff didn't tell you that rank means nothing on the pay scale. He could have made you an admiral. Talk to your legislator."

Brown sat down at his desk and chuckled quietly. "I knew that." He sat silently for a moment, hesitating. "Hey. I gotta problem. You remember that break-in I worked Monday. Well there's been another one, just up the road."

"Do you think they're related?"

"Both happened in mid-morning, best I can tell. Guns were taken at each house, and a little spare change. And get this, some women's underwear."

Roberts shook his head and looked toward the ceiling. "Oh no. How'd they get in?"

"In the first one, they just walked in the back door, wasn't locked. Today, they broke a window beside the back door."

"Good old Lafayette County. People still don't lock their doors. Where is this?"

"Lebanon Cove Road. I gotta go back to talk with the neighbors. I thought maybe you could come along."

"Why of course, Lieutenant. We don't have much else to do."

Brown did not appreciate the sarcasm, but he decided to keep his thoughts to himself.

* * *

The Crosses' two boys were prancing in the sprinkler that Polly had put on her flower garden. Will was five, Sam eight. The few flowers which had survived the heat stood no chance against two little boys, but at least they were not fighting, which was their usual pastime. Inside Ev found Polly at the kitchen sink. "This is where I left you this morning," he said.

"That's because all I do is feed a bunch of men and then clean up after them. And answer your damn mother's calls. Teaching was a whole lot easier."

"Okay. What happened today?"

Polly pushed a damp blonde lock out of her face before placing her hands on her narrow hips. "I made the mistake of answering the phone. Your mother was already blitzed, so she told me for the third time that she was going to your sister's. Amanda has the two most beautiful children and are so well behaved and Richard is making so much money that they are going to Martha's Vineyard and she's going with them to watch the two little angels so Amanda and Richard can visit with all their new rich friends who always go to Martha's Vineyard, all of which she told me twice yesterday when she called here drunk."

"Why didn't you claim an emergency and just hang up."

"She'd just call back. I guess she's cramming in one last booze fest before she gets to Amanda's, since she has Amanda fooled into thinking that she only has a glass or two of wine."

"Can't Amanda tell she's been drinking when she calls there?"

"Ev. Your mother has a caller I D. She won't answer if she's polluted."

"Maybe we ought to get caller I D. Then you could avoid her calls. I could avoid some of mine, too."

"I should have known what I was in for when I married a mother's only son."

"You should have married a favorite child."

"That would have left me with Amanda."

"And that's not legal in Virginia. Maybe you should go jot this down so you can write about it."

Polly, imprisoned with two young children, had found time to write. What to write was the problem. She had submitted a few articles to magazines but was yet to be published. A novel about her mother-in-law was forming in her imagination and she kept notes of the Margaret stories that were her lot from day to day.

"Maybe. What about the murder?"

"Spinning our wheels. Jason Thomasson is sleazy and suspicious, but I don't know. And get this. That windbag Hampton Coleman came in and jumped me for the way Jason was interviewed"

"Why?"

"Politics."

"I've never liked him."

"Speaking of politics, next year's an election," he replied. "If I lose, you could be teaching again."

Polly rolled her eyes. "I didn't say I wanted to be teaching, not yet. But give me time and I might change my mind. Besides, who's going to run against you?"

Ev shrugged. "Yeah, why would any of them want to take a pay cut? Anyway, that Jeff Smith is still in the picture."

"Jeff Smith?"

"The little drug dealer who was suspected in the Alphonso Thornton murder, the one who was pals with the supervisor's son."

"What did he do?"

"We don't know. The number to his home was on the caller I D. Roberts suspects that he was her drug source."

"Why didn't they charge someone in the Thornton murder?"

"Besides the kind of police work Hank Burke is capable of? Anyway, I don't know all the details."

Polly opened the refrigerator door and leaned in. "We've got to get this light fixed."

"I know," agreed Ev.

"Is the sheriff really as stupid as he sounds?"

Ev chuckled at the question. Hank Burke had been the investigator, in the loose application of the term, in the Thornton murder. The reek of political cronyism permeated the affair, and Ev's predecessor and the former sheriff Conway Lawson both resigned. With Lawson back in his prior calling as a logger, Burke and seven other hopefuls battled for the voters' blessing. There is nothing like an open sheriff's race in a rural county to excite the dreams of little men who have never had power over their own lives, much less that of others, and to cause voters to actually discuss, in checkout lines and after church, those men as candidates. Burke managed to convey an air of experience that belied his utterly insufficient grounding.

Ev thought about Polly's remark for a moment before responding. "He's not bright, but he's got some savvy hidden in there somewhere."

"Well, just think. You could be shuffling paper in some big firm without all this excitement."

"Yeah," retorted Ev, "and making about two hundred grand. I guess I saw myself raking it in like Wil Bledsoe." He paused. "It's a little late for me to worry about it now."

Ev could not bring himself to wear the double-breasted suits and cowboy boots that served Bledsoe so well, and he was not born with Bledsoe's talent for silly banter, which the latter laced with double entendre and adroitly veiled condescending humor. Construction workers, waitresses, and assembly line cogs saw something of themselves in Bledsoe because he could tell a joke like the ones they exchanged on the job and because he could read their minds and let them know he was doing it without saying so; in short, they sensed that he was one of them even if he had accumulated a small fortune.

"Where did Wil go to law school?"

"I don't even know, some no-name place. He might have even gone at night. But the school doesn't matter, though no one tells you that at the time. There was a maxim in law school that A students make professor, B students make judge, and C students make money. Boy is that true."

"I don't guess you're going to teach. But what about a judgeship?"

"I'm not political enough. Besides, all the judges who sit in Lafayette are pretty young, who knows when a seat will come up. In the meantime, I'm thirty-six, no clients, and dependent on the voters for a job."

Polly watched him closely for a moment. "Don't worry about it until you need to." From the corner of her eye she saw Ev looking at her.

"Wanna do it?" he asked.

"I saw The Look. And no. The children are right outside." She faced him and feigned a look of disapproval. "Is that all you think about?"

"You know the old saying. Women need to be in the mood, men need to be in the room."

"Then leave the room."

"Later?"

"Maybe later. Maybe if your mother stops calling."

"Blackmail."

Polly smiled wickedly.

# CHAPTER 5

Thursday, September 3rd

The Lafayette County Juvenile and Domestic Relations District Court, commonly referred to as J&D court, and by Wilmer Bledsoe as the kiddie court, is in session every Thursday in the same room that houses the General District Court on Wednesday. The docket almost always falls behind schedule in the parade of custody and child support cases, randomly interspersed with the trials of domestic assaults and the hearings on charges against miscreant juveniles. In the crowded hallway grandmothers and mothers sit patiently on hard benches, grabbing at little children and thrusting bottles into wailing mouths as they wait for their cases to be called. Others, mostly men, wait downstairs just outside the entrance to the courthouse smoking cigarettes and dreaming up the excuses they intend to give the judge for why they are two years behind in child support payments, or for why they had to black a lover's eye.

Unlike General District Court, when litigants and witnesses pack the small chamber to await the calling of their cases, J&D customers come in only when their cases are announced. As the day progresses and the docket falls further behind, lawyers and deputies accumulate on the benches of the courtroom, a room designed for office space sixty years before, and whisper among themselves as they too wait. The delay often speeds the docket, for exasperated attorneys with other hearings in other counties often forge a resolution of their clients' disputes, or cut deals with the commonwealth's attorney on minor criminal charges, leaving for the judge the ministerial task of blessing the result.

Judge Mary Jane Chandler had paid her dues on the other side of the bench and to the great relief of the bar who practiced in her court she had not forgotten what is was like to try to wrench a living from the unfortunate rung of humanity who were forced to play out in her court the sordid parts of their lives. She knew the tight schedules that plagued attorneys and she always made an effort to adjust the docket when someone found that he was supposed to be in two places at once. But she had been a judge only five years, and most J&D judges did not start to unravel until they had served for a decade, when they began to experience social atrophy, delusions of grandeur, and irritable weariness.

On this Thursday, Ev and a fellow lawyer, Alec Dickson, were sitting near the rear of the courtroom cursorily scanning the files in their laps as they waited for Chandler to finish a custody hearing when Wilmer Bledsoe sauntered through the door, a devilish gleam in his eye, looking every bit like a man who has just told a woman an off-color joke, which he had. "Hello fuckheads," he greeted them in a voice audible beyond the two lawyers.

Ev smiled into his files while Dickson shook his head. Chandler looked over the man and woman who had been telling her their stories in hushed tones. "My Mr. Bledsoe, your voice certainly does carry in this room," she said evenly.

Bledsoe smiled at Ev and plopped down beside him. Leaning toward Ev he spoke almost quietly. "Have you heard the one about the bride?"

"Why the bride is smiling when she walks down the aisle? Yeah, I've heard it." answered Ev.

"Have you Alec?"

"Yeah."

"I just told that to the clerk, she turned red as hell. Too close to home I guess." Bledsoe stood up abruptly. "Ev. Can we go talk about that Tower case?"

Ev nodded and followed Bledsoe into the hallway and through another door to the tiny room that housed the coffee pot and facsimile machine, and doubled as a conference room on court days. The two men leaned against opposite counters, facing one another.

"You have any more thoughts on Pup Tower?" asked Bledsoe.

"I wrote the victim after you called, but got no response."

"They both came to the office yesterday, they're back together. She doesn't want to prosecute him, said he got drunk and backhanded her, by accident. Why don't we just take it under advisement?"

"No. She thought enough of what he did at the time to go get a warrant. Let the judge hear it."

"You're not after any jail time are you?"

"No. This probably calls for counseling. That's more punishment than a few days in jail."

"For a guy like Pup Tower, you're exactly right. And he doesn't even know it. I told him he'd probably get some counseling, and no jail, and they both were happy as larks. Can we just agree to that disposition?"

"I guess so, Wil. Save his girlfriend from having to lie."

Bledsoe shrugged his shoulders and turned to the coffee pot. After filling two styrofoam cups, he continued. "You know, there're three legal things that'll get a man in trouble: his mouth, his booze and his pecker." He ignored the hand-lettered sign requesting two bits per cup.

Ev smiled and picked up one of the cups. "Is that the gem of the day?"

"Take Alec Dickson. Booze has almost got him."

"How's Alec doing? I don't see him much now that he doesn't take court appointments."

"Alright I guess. His son moved back with him for awhile after Alec and Connie got divorced. He told me the other day the boy will be in his last year of college this fall. But I'll tell you, that Connie reminds me of my own first wife."

"I didn't know her very well."

"You didn't miss much. Which one?"

Ev smiled before answering. "Connie Dickson. I never met your first wife."

"Then you were lucky. Of course, I'll admit when you have a wife like Connie, one of the big three is bound to get you."

Several taps on the door interrupted the exchange. Gene Roberts pushed the door open and looked in. "Ev, are y'all busy or just killin' time?"

"Come in," said Bledsoe. "We're only talking about mankind in general." He put his unfinished cup of coffee on the facsimile machine and left the room.

"I'm sorry I haven't gotten back with you," said Roberts, "I've been chasing rabbits."

"Any luck?" asked Ev.

"I got a call from the lab this morning, I've been raising hell with them since last week. Jason's prints matched two on the vodka bottle. And the blood screen on Miranda showed cocaine and alcohol, not enough to kill her, but the blood-alcohol was point two-nine.

"She was blitzed. Could the combination have been enough?"

"The CME says no. She very likely could have passed out."

"That doesn't mean Jason was there that night."

"No. I've got to work on that, since he's been there before. I'm going to see him again. I finally got all the elimination prints of the people the Nobles provided me. That was like pulling teeth. They gave me seven in all. I'm carrying them to Richmond tomorrow, I hope."

"Who were the seven?"

"The Nobles, their two children, Clara Wood, and Mr. and Mrs. Hampton Coleman. I also got Hector Lopez, the farm hand, or whatever he is, to come in too. "

"That old bastard. I didn't tell you that Coleman came to my office griping about the investigation, did I?"

"You did."

"That's probably why he was so wrung up last week."

"He wasn't too pleased when he and his wife had to come to the office to be printed. Coleman has been trying to get up with Hank for a week. Hank's been dodging him."

"That's smart, real smart for Hank."

"I told Hank to be damn careful, the political bit. He knows enough about that anyway. But you never know what he might say if Coleman were to put the screws to him."

Ev was looking at Roberts without listening. "Can you imagine Coleman floating in the pool?"

"I decided not to ask why Coleman was at the pool."

"Have you got some prints to work with?"

"A few. Besides the vodka bottle, we got some off a few cans in the trash and from the one we found by the driveway. I'm asking them to run them through AFIS." AFIS was the acronym for the state forensics laboratory's computerized inventory of fingerprints.

"I talked to Hector Lopez," continued Roberts, "who saw nobody at the Nobles on Friday, but he didn't go to the house, said he was working on a fence in the woods all day. He seemed believable. His boy, fourteen, cut grass there Wednesday. His wife doesn't speak English, or won't admit she can, you know the game. I need to get Brown to talk to her. I didn't see much use in having her husband translate for her."

"A lot of questions."

"I know. I also got up with the logger, Roger Snidlett. He and his boy were there on Wednesday, to cut down a dead maple. He said he'd been shown the tree a couple of weeks before, and didn't talk to anyone that day. He and his son came, did the work, and left."

"Who's the son?"

"Lester Snidlett. He's the one everyone calls Lester Hester. I haven't talked to him. Oh yeah. The beer can cut to smoke crack, in the trash, had some latents, which were pretty poor. I doubt they can be matched."

"What's next?" asked Ev.

"I've got to go with Lewis to interview another burglary victim, on Lebanon Cove Road. If I can get that out of the way, I'm going to see young Jason Thomasson. Noble told me that they'd referred Jason to their attorney. Do you think that presents a problem?"

"No lawyer called me. How about you?"

"Nope."

"Then don't worry about it."

"That was my thought."

"Anything else?"

"Did I tell you that Lewis had tracked down Jeff Smith?"

"You did. On Friday."

Roberts laughed and shook his head. "Hell, I can't remember what I've told you and what I haven't."

There were several raps at the door before Okra Alexander pushed it open. "Are you ready for the Tower case, Ev?"

"Okay," answered Ev. Okra left the door ajar and could be heard announcing the case in the hallway. Ev turned back to Roberts. "Is there anything I can do, to help you, so that you have more time for this case?"

"Not really. I can't push it much harder at this point, except to badger the lab."

Ev glanced at Roberts and then looked at the floor. There was no use in trying to hurry Roberts; he was going to proceed at his own pace, but the inching progress on the case was making Ev uncomfortable. "I'll check with you later, then." Ev walked out of the coffee room, across the hall, and into the courtroom.

Pup Tower and Bledsoe were already seated at counsel's table on the left. To the right, at the table used by the Commonwealth, sat an emaciated young woman, obviously anxious as she waited for the proceedings to start. Crystal Ricketts's thin brown hair hung limply, coming just below her shoulders, and her long nose was made more prominent by her sallow sunken cheeks and hollow eyes. Cross walked to the bench and waited for the judge to arraign the defendant. As he waited, he watched the expressionless Pup Tower who was busy picking at his rough work-darkened hands. Tower, though equally sparse, displayed hard long muscles on the arms that were bared by the blue tee-shirt he was wearing, across the front of which was printed 'Lickity Split Trucking.' Beneath the lettering was the silhouette of a woman's spike heeled shoe sitting atop a truck tire. Facially, he sported a small beard—close cropped whiskers and mustache that circled his mouth and extended to just below his chin— that Bledsoe, in keeping with his prurient thought process, called a mangina.

All four faces turned to Chandler when she broke the quiet. "Is this Mr. Tower?" she asked, looking at Bledsoe.

"Yes ma'am," answered Bledsoe.

"Is the defendant ready to proceed?"

"Yes ma'am," he again responded. "We have a disposition worked out on this one."

Bledsoe explained the agreement; the judge asked whether everyone was satisfied, and with a few words on the back of the warrant, the case was over.

Pup Tower dropped his hands into his lap and looked up at Bledsoe. "Well?" he whispered gruffly.

Bledsoe turned to Tower and told him to go back into the hallway. Tower pushed away from the table and followed his attorney's instructions. Crystal Ricketts hurriedly arose and walked out of the room at Tower's side, tentatively leaning toward him and whispering in his ear as they went. Bledsoe remained where he stood as he watched the two until the door was closed behind them.

Alec Dickson walked to counsel table as Bledsoe prepared to leave.

"Having to meet a guy like that is the main reason I dread clients coming in," said Dickson. "I never dreaded seeing the clients when I was in a big firm. Then again, I didn't see too many."

"Come on Alec. That's the best reason to practice law here. There's nothing like the entertainment these people provide, and we're getting paid for it. I wouldn't trade it for anything." Bledsoe waved the file clutched in his hand as a gesture of farewell, opened the door into the hall, and began humming as he pulled the door closed behind him.

"I wish I could find all the pleasure in this that he does," groused Dickson.

Cross nodded in agreement. "I'd probably like it too if I made what he does out of it."

* * *

After talking with Cross Gene Roberts left the courtroom and descended the two flights of stairs which wound their way to the sheriff's office in the basement. There was no mistaking Cross's concern about the slow progress he was making in the resolution of Miranda Noble's death and there was little he could do about it. Lewis Brown was to meet with him at ten o'clock to go over the burglaries in Lebanon Cove—there were now five—which they were to visit another Cove victim. The burglaries were the very sort of distraction he should abandon, but Brown did not ask for help unless he believed he was in over his head, and anyway, next year was an election year and the sheriff would not countenance establishing priorities, at least not where five households, containing ten votes, were concerned.

Roberts picked through the pink messages on his desk, all of which had some voter's name written across the top. At the bottom was a note that Minnie Patterson had called yet again; there was no message, but none was needed. He looked at his watch; Brown was five minutes late. Roberts slid into his chair and picked up the stack of incident reports that the deputies had left for his review. Beneath them was a pile of printouts with a brief description of each call received by the dispatchers.

Lewis Brown walked in. "Sorry I'm late."

"That's okay. Let's go. Who're we going to see?"

"My latest victim said he couldn't miss work, so we'd have to come see him at night."

"We've all got our priorities," groused Roberts. "Give me a run down."

"Sure. But where we goin'?"

"To my car and then to Charlottesville, if you've got time. Jason isn't working today, according to his supervisor at Shiflett's Auto." Roberts pulled a cigarette and lighter from his pocket as he spoke.

"Well, this may be the only time I'll get to tell you about the burglaries. What I got is five break-ins, all happening when people are at work. The houses are all on Lebanon Cove Road, but every one of them is off the road and they're within a half mile of each other. The entry's always in the back, either through a door or window. It looks like he tries to get in without force unless he has to, then he breaks a window. Only thing taken is guns and cash, and one camera."

"And underwear."

52

"Oh yeah. That too."

"Any idea whether there's more than one person doing this?"

"You mean like an accomplice?"

"Yes." Roberts drew the word out.

Brown looked at Roberts out of the corner of his eye but decided to leave the commentary be. "The first one, the one on August twenty-fourth, it had rained the day before. I found two sets of footprints in the back. One was running shoes, the other looked like boots."

"Could you make a cast?"

"No. The owners went back there while I was inside and tramped all over them."

"Damn Lewis."

"Don't say it. I shoulda secured the scene."

"Any clues from neighbors?"

"One man says he's seen a blue Ford pickup on the road, one that doesn't belong to anybody who lives in the cove. But that's all I have on that."

"Who'd you want me to interview with you today?"

"Dillon Klobb and Naomi Prendergast."

Roberts turned the names over in his head, without success. "Who are they? Two different victims?"

"No. They live together. Naomi called Klobb her partner."

The more sophisticated of those who lived together without the benefit of clergy were now calling their co-habitants partners while the less well-heeled liked the ring of fiancé. The old standbys, boyfriend and girlfriend, were obsolete across the board and the government's laughable attempt at definition, significant other, had never developed a following. "Why did you need me with them?" Roberts asked.

"They wanted the investigator. A lieutenant wouldn't do."

"No suspects, I take it."

"There's a few teenage toads who hang out at a house near the end of the cove road." Brown continued to list odds and ends that he thought pertinent until he realized that Roberts was not listening. For a long while both men were silent as Roberts's mind churned Miranda Noble and Jason Thomasson, and all the things which were not making sense. He did not speak again until they were parked around the corner from Thomasson's townhouse in Cavalier Landing.

Brown grinned slyly. "You don't want him to see us coming?"

Roberts took off his sunglasses and slid them inside his coat. "Habit I guess." The two walked to the door where Roberts knocked several times. When he got no response he knocked again, this time more firmly.

They heard Thomasson's muffled voice from within. "Hold on. Shit." Then loudly, "They're here." Clad only in a pair of briefs and a sweat shirt minus its arms, he pulled the door open abruptly while looking over his shoulder. When he turned red embarrassment washed over his startled face. He looked over his shoulder again before speaking. "Damn," he muttered, "I thought you were someone else. Okay. Look. I got a friend upstairs. Do you mind?"

Brown, smirking to contain his smile, looked at Roberts.

"Where should we wait?" asked Roberts.

A tinkling voice wafted down the steps. "Is it them Jason?"

Thomasson turned his head slightly. "No!" he called back sharply. Facing his two unwanted visitors again, he answered Roberts. "Just come in and sit at the card table. Let me get her out of here." He turned on his heel and disappeared up the steps.

Brown shed his smirk and grinned broadly. "Damn you're a hard man Gene."

Roberts ignored the badinage. "Let's take our usual places." They walked to the card table and cleared the bachelor detritus which covered it. A few minutes after they seated themselves they heard two sets of footsteps descend the carpeted stairway. Thomasson appeared first, having added a pair of blue jeans to his attire, followed by a diminutive and very uncomfortable looking girl who made straight for the door without turning toward the two men sitting in folding chairs at the table. Thomasson hurriedly closed the door behind her and then walked to the table.

"Sorry for the intrusion," began Roberts, "we needed to talk to you again."

"I mean damn, couldn't you have called first?" Thomasson ran a hand through his disheveled hair to get it out of his face as he pulled out one of the chairs. "What is it now?"

"I'll call first next time. What I need to tell you is that we identified your prints on the vodka bottle in the pool house."

Thomasson, blanching, said nothing.

"Do you want to tell us about it?" pressed Roberts.

Thomasson looked at the center of the card table. "I've been there before. I was there a week before she died. I had a drink out of the bottle."

"What day?"

"On Friday, I think."

"I guess your sister can verify that."

There was a long silence. "No she can't," Thomasson finally answered. "Miranda and I were riding around, and we stopped there and went for a swim. Nobody was there. Rita doesn't know it."

Roberts knitted his brows as he glanced at Brown. Leaning forward and placing his arms on the table, Roberts continued. "Riding around?"

"Yeah. We hooked up here and just went riding around."

"Your sister's home is almost thirty miles from here, right?"

"Yeah. So what. I told you we didn't hang here much."

"And that's the only reason you went there? To swim?"

"Use your imagination."

"Did you do anything else, like go see Jeff Smith?"

"I told you I didn't know him."

"Where else did you go?"

"Lots of places. We might've stopped for some beer at that little place near Rita's. What's that little area called?"

"Onan."

"Yeah. I think I got beer at the country store there. Then we came back to C-ville and hit a few places. That's all I remember."

Roberts pursed his lips for a moment as he contemplated Thomasson's story. The lack of evidence left him with little room in which to maneuver; all that he could do was accept Thomasson's answers. He wondered whether Thomasson had taken his sister's advice to see a lawyer, but he dared not raise the issue since Thomasson had not. Under the circumstances the best he could do was nail down Thomasson's story and then test it later against other information, if there ever were any other information.

"When we were here last you said you saw Miranda Thursday night, the Thursday night of the week she died."

"Uh-huh."

"What about Wednesday?"

"She was at Rita's."

"Okay."

Thomasson took his eyes off the center of the table and looked steadily at Roberts. "She told me she was at Rita's. I didn't see her Wednesday."

"How did you make plans for Thursday?"

"She called me at work Thursday afternoon. What's this about?"

"Just pinning down where she was."

"Well ask Rita then, if you don't believe me."

Thomasson's firmness piqued Roberts's curiosity. He was onto something, but he didn't know what it was. He pulled out his cigarettes as a distraction and offered one to Thomasson before continuing. "Is Rita mad at you?"

The younger man looked away. "Hell yes, she's pissed. She didn't want me messin' with Miranda, then I was sneaking around her place meeting her. Now I'm being questioned by you guys. And I know you're thinking I might have done it. Shit. What can I do? All I can tell you is what happened, and that I didn't do it." He picked up Roberts's lighter and lit the cigarette.

"Did you ever go to any parties, anything like that when you and Miranda were in Lafayette County?"

"No."

"Did you go hang out anywhere?"

"Where the hell you gonna hang out in Lafayette, except the Quik Mart?"

"Did you go there?"

"Yes."

"Often?"

"Maybe twice. She knew some of the guys. I figured she was banging them, so I wouldn't go there anymore."

"Why did you go there?"

Thomasson twisted in his seat and did not answer immediately. "I think she went there to find out where to get crack," he finally replied.

"Did you go with her to buy crack?"

"Once. We left the Quik Mart and drove to some back road. She was driving. I don't know where it was, except it was out in the sticks. The place was like a burger drive through. It was that crowded. She got out and went up to some black dude and bought some. I stayed in the car. She said they wouldn't sell to her with some strange white dude with her."

Brown tapped his pen on his pad. "Did she say who he was?"

"Later, I think later she said she got the shit from Jeff Smith. I guess that was Jeff Smith."

"She got it from him more than once?" asked Brown.

"I'm sure she did, but I wasn't with her. She'd say something like, 'I saw Jeff last night, you want to smoke some?' But I told you, I didn't touch it. She was getting scary. She was on it too much."

"How do you know how much she was using?"

Thomasson looked at Brown before answering in a subdued voice. "She'd ask me to loan her some money to buy it. I think that started in July. I did once, but shit, fifty or sixty dollars adds up in a hurry, so I told her to forget it. She got pissed. Anyway, I thought that was a bad sign, cause she always had money when we first started going out." A queer smile bent Thomasson's lips. "One time she said she wouldn't, you know, do me, unless I loaned her the money. Man. I knew it was about time to cut that bitch loose."

"When did she say that to you?"

"That Friday night I was telling you about. I mean she didn't cut me off, but it was...she was gonna try that threat again."

"But you saw her again," interjected Roberts.

"Yeah."

"When was the last time she asked for money?" continued Brown.

"Thursday night. She asked Thursday, but she didn't get mad or anything. She was kinda weird, but not mad."

"Kinda weird?" repeated Brown.

"Yeah. Like she had something on her mind."

"Did she have any drugs on Thursday?"

"No. Just beer, and some vodka."

"What kind of beer?" asked Roberts.

"Coors Light, that's what I drink." A weary resignation marked Thomasson's face. "And you probably found some at the pool."

"We did," answered Roberts.

"That's what we drank at the pool," Thomasson said in a low voice as he leaned sideways and picked up an empty Pepsi can to use as an ashtray.

Roberts put his cigarettes and lighter in his coat pocket. "Anything else Jason?"

Thomasson shook his head as he toyed with guiding the spent ashes into the can's mouth.

Roberts looked at Brown. "You ready?"

"I'm ready."

# CHAPTER 6

Friday, September 4th

Polly guided Sam from one room to the other as she hurried him in his preparation for school. Ev was sitting at the kitchen table and wondering how long it would take his oldest son to finish preparations for what seemed like a military airlift to a foreign country. Ev had a trial that morning, and even though the judge and not a jury would be hearing the case, he was nervous and impatient, as he always was the morning of a serious case. He arose from the chair and aimlessly circled the small kitchen several times as he fought the desire to call to Polly and Sam to hurry their efforts. Will walked softly in, rubbing his eyes, as Ev paced.

"Does he need a jacket?" called Polly from the bathroom.

"Suppose to be in the nineties today Polly. Can you hurry?"

Polly walked into the kitchen as the last edged words fell from Ev's mouth. "He's brushing his teeth. Look. This is my last week of peace, don't spoil it."

"Last week?" said Ev.

"Yes. Your mother returns tomorrow or Sunday or Monday. I wish Amanda would take her on more vacations."

That Amanda was Margaret Cross's favorite didn't seem to bother Ev, but it was a constant source of irritation for Polly, that and her drinking.

Margaret McCloud Cross, the youngest of six children, was reared in a South Carolina farm town which pursued its decline throughout her childhood. Her father lost his five hundred acre farm two years before Margaret's birth, and with the proceeds from his last cotton crop, bought a struggling hardware store in the center of the three street town that served as the county seat. Ivanhoe McCloud had not been much of a farmer and proved almost as inept selling nails and seeds.

Margaret grew up in the nether world of gentry gone broke, whose status existed only because of the past, and because there were land-poor farmers and black sharecroppers who had even less. Her exposure to her cousins in Charleston made her enviously aware of what she didn't have—her grandmother had been born on the Battery—and the rest of her life was spent making certain that she did not repeat the pinched years of her depression-era youth. She was consumed with herself.

Lucius Cross met Margaret while he was still in the army, on his way back to becoming a civilian following the Korean War, the second war in which he had fought. Lucius's father was a founder of the First National Bank of Lafayette, and besides that Margaret needed to know nothing else. She abandoned her Presbyterianism for the Crosses' Episcopal Church, secretly agreeing that Presbyterians were Baptists without enough money to be Episcopalians. New position and money required a child; she bore Amanda as proof of her commitment. But children were work and an accidental second child, Ev, was not part of her myopic plan. One child was an insurance policy: duty done and duty imposed; a second was not going to increase the return. Contrary to every tradition which formed her world, the appearance of a son, particularly an only son, was not a proud accomplishment but rather a needless additional burden.

"Damn. I forgot she was away. Have you checked the house?"

"Yes Ev. I have been over there every two or three days. Who did you think was going to feed her cats?"

Ev shrugged and looked toward the narrow hallway leading to the bathroom. "I don't know. My mother and her cats haven't been my top priorities lately."

"You mean you haven't noticed the quiet? Come on Samuel Cross."

Sam appeared in the kitchen with his book pack strapped to his back.

"Who brung you to school, Daddy?" he asked Ev on the way to school.

"Brought me to school," snapped Ev. He was in no frame of mind to ponder the educational atmosphere that had degraded his son's grammar in less than a week.

"Who brought you to school?" tried Sam again.

"I rode the bus."

"Neat. Why can't I ride the bus?"

"Just can't."

"You did."

"Maybe when you're older."

"I am older. Second grade."

"Older than that. We'll see."

"Third grade?"

"We'll see."

Sam crossed his arms and pouted.

* * *

Ev usually arrived at his office before Linda Masencup, so his first task was to brew a pot of coffee. As he waited for the coffee he sat on the edge of the table in the room that served as his library and conference room. The heavy September sun streamed in through Venetian blinds as he thumbed through the file folder for the ten o'clock trial, and amid the quiet of the early morning he read again his notes from his interviews with seven year old Quanisha, the little girl who had been molested by her mother's live-in boyfriend, or fiancé, or partner, or whatever he was.

As he read what Quanisha had told him, Ev thought about the ride to school and how he had been abrupt with Sam. A tug of guilt pricked him and he chastised himself for not having taken better advantage of the morning's brief opportunity with his son.

The telephone rang and he contemplated letting it ring; whoever it was would call back when Linda was there to answer it and maybe shield him from a problem about which he could do nothing. People did not like hearing that their problems were beyond the reach of the criminal law, especially when that meant they needed to hire a lawyer. Ev laid the file aside and answered the call.

"Ev, this is Rita Noble," was the reply. "I wonder if you know that your sheriff's department is still treating my brother like a criminal."

The piercing statement made Ev immediately regret having lifted the receiver. "Mrs. Noble," answered Ev in measured tones that belied his rising anger, "I think all they've done is talk to him."

"Well you better talk to them." Her tone was imperious. "They burst in yesterday and practically accused him of killing her. This is too serious for that Barney Fife who calls himself the investigator."

Ev held his tongue and let her continue.

"Now it's been two weeks since Miranda died and you have gotten nowhere. All I can see is that they keep going to Jason and try to trick him into saying something that will make it look like he did it. I can't believe we're being treated like this."

Ev could not focus on her words, rather he was hearing her grating voice, an almost nasal voice, which was devoid of accent and sounded like that of many another irate newcomer who assumed that every native was functionally illiterate or involved in a conspiracy loosely attributed to the good ol' boy network, or both. He opened his mouth to respond, but Rita Noble spared him the effort.

"Now I'll tell you. Clyde is too nice to say anything, but it has to be said. Your people working on this case don't have any idea of what to do. If she didn't drown, as your deputy insists, then somebody had better get to the bottom of this. I just can't believe that they keep going to Jason, and pushing into his apartment like storm troopers when he's told them he was not here that Friday. I think you'd better investigate these drug dealers in Lafayette who were selling her this stuff. They would have a lot of reasons to kill her. They got every penny of her money. She probably owed them a fortune. She was always asking Clyde for more money, but we knew why she wanted it and he wouldn't give it to her."

Something in the last comment piqued Ev's interest, and not just the fact that a second wife would manage to mention money in the same breath as her stepdaughter's death. "Have you told Gene Roberts about this?"

There was silence on the other end of the line for a moment. "I'm sure Clyde told him about the drugs, but I haven't been present for all their conversations." Her tone was still huffy, but the derisive edge had evaporated.

"About the money I mean."

"Well I'm sure Clyde said something."

"Did she ask you for money?"

"Certainly not." The question had restored her acerbic tone. "Now I'd like to know what you're going to do about this harassment of Jason."

It was a presumptuous, accusatory question, like being asked when you stopped beating your wife, but framed like a statement, and one Ev loathed hearing. He had no idea what had gone on other than what she was telling him and though he knew that what she was describing was not Gene Roberts's style, any comment he offered in response was sure to be off the mark, or at least, misinterpreted. Ev decided to sidestep her demand by answering a question with a question. "Were you there, did you see all this?"

"Of course not."

"How do you know all this you're telling me?"

"Jason is my brother."

"I'm sure Gene Roberts is doing his job properly. But he hasn't discussed it with me, so—

"They don't keep you informed on these things?" Her intonation dripped incredulity.

This was another question Ev did not want to hear. For some reason the populace thought he had omniscient knowledge of every fact at every stage of every investigation; yet reality was to the contrary, for in the normal course he knew almost nothing until an officer had a question or when the investigation was beginning to fall into place. "I'm kept informed as the situation may require, but this morning I have court and I can't do two things at once."

"Well I hope they'll inform you of this. I can't believe this county operates this way."

Ev recognized this as the first salvo in the functionally illiterate and good ol' boy conspiracy critique, and he was in no mood to sit through it. "Mrs. Noble, I've got court, I've got to go."

"You understand that I'm expecting you to take care of this?"

"You've made yourself perfectly clear. Thank you."

"Good then. I'll be expecting to hear from you. Goodbye."

Ev rang off gloating over his last response, then caught himself in mid-gloat. He knew her unspoken threat was a political one, and with that thought, he wondered why, when he had been a guest in her home on a first name basis several years ago, even if only for the purpose of separating him from some of his money, he had now elevated her to duchess by referring to her as Mrs. Noble, especially when she was near the same age as he. Returning his attention to Quanisha's file he forced Rita Noble out of his mind. At nine-thirty Ev downed the last of his coffee and left his office on his way to the circuit judge's chambers. He knocked at the judge's door and heard Jim Crawford respond.

Crawford was a big man in his late forties who had played football in college until a knee permanently buckled, and as a native of New York and a Republican, he was somewhat of an enigma for Lafayette County, as most of his fellow northern transplants, except those who were retirees, were former flower children, and definitely were not Republicans. Like Ev, however, he was not partisan in his politics, and like many lawyers he had affiliated with a political party principally to advance his career. Ev got on well with Crawford and could talk to him without fear that he would be repeated, a courtesy Ev appreciated as he often felt isolated manning his one-lawyer office.

"What's news?" boomed Crawford when he saw who had knocked. Like the judges of the other two courts for the county, Crawford was in Lafayette only once or twice a week; the rest of the time he was sitting in the other jurisdictions which together with Lafayette made up the judicial circuit.

"Not much."

"How about the murder. Is that getting anywhere?"

Ev seated himself in one of the chairs in front of the judge's desk. "Funny you should ask. Rita Noble called me just this morning to ream me for her brother being questioned about the thing."

Crawford laughed. "She's a piece of work, isn't she?"

"I guess that's one way to put it."

"He's not really a suspect is he?"

"I don't know who to suspect."

Crawford picked up his pipe and began packing it. "How's Clyde reacting?"

"I haven't talked to him, that's been Gene's mission. Rita let me know, though, that Clyde was too polite to chew me over Jason being questioned."

"Don't believe that. When he unloads, you'll know it." Crawford lit his pipe. "Maybe Clyde doesn't share her concern."

"Roberts hasn't been able to read him. Rita is printed in big bold letters."

"Let me give you the observations of a yankee. A lot of northerners mistake politeness in you southerners for weakness. Then when you finally get to the place where you need to stake out your position, they think you're two-faced. With a Rita Noble, you had better just lay it on the line. She'll back off."

Ev studied Crawford for a moment as he pondered the remark. "That's an interesting theory."

"That's the sort of stuff I think up in my spare time when I'm sitting in here waiting for lawyers to try to settle their cases." Crawford looked at his watch. "It's about time for your case. You better go out ahead of me. We don't want the defendant to think we're in cahoots."

The trial did not take long, despite a slow start by Quanisha and a lengthy, lie-riddled effort by her mother to exonerate her unemployed partner, and at its conclusion Crawford found him guilty. It was after one o'clock when Ev returned to his office. In the quiet—Linda Masencup had already left for lunch—he first hastily read the pink telephone messages neatly spread in a line across the center of his desk. One of them informed him that Polly had taken the boys to the doctor in Charlottesville. When Varney Mitchell walked in, Ev was looking through his mail in a languid effort to shake the dark mood that always enveloped him after trying a child molester.

Mitchell was a reporter, the only reporter, for the weekly newspaper, the *Lafayette County Times*. He was young and short with thick dark hair that he had trouble keeping out of his eyes and his attire was always rumpled, looking as if it went to his back straight from the clothes dryer. His tortoise shell rimmed glasses were perpetually sliding down his nose, especially when he was jotting notes on a dog-eared little pad that he would produce from a coat pocket. He was right out of central casting.

"Have you got a minute?" asked Mitchell.

"Sure Varney. What's up?" He glanced up at Mitchell and saw that his necktie was askew, as if someone had given it a firm yank in an effort to choke its owner.

"What's going on with the Miranda Noble case?"

Ev leaned back in his chair and peered blankly at the window behind Mitchell. "We don't have much. We haven't been able to put anyone at the Nobles the night this happened."

"Is this Jason Thomasson a possibility?"

The question returned Ev's attention to Mitchell's face. He wondered how Mitchell knew about Jason. "He was the last person to talk to her, that we know of. But he hasn't impressed Gene Roberts as the likely sort. How'd you find out about him?"

Mitchell smiled. "The sheriff said he'd been interviewed, and cleared."

"And cleared," Ev repeated flatly. Mitchell's remark gave him every reason to believe that Rita Noble had made a call to the sheriff with the same message which it had been his misfortune to hear earlier that day.

"Yeah."

"I don't think anyone's been cleared."

"I can't report that can I?"

"I wish you wouldn't."

"How does this delay affect you? Two weeks and you still don't have much."

"It's nerve wracking, but it's certainly not unusual."

"Have you got anything else, like fingerprints or DNA?"

"We've got prints, and there was semen, so we'll have DNA, but they might not help."

"Semen. Could she have been raped?"

"That's one possibility." Ev decided to keep the fact of the perianal tear to himself. "There are drugs and alcohol, too. But it's not clear how they fit in or whether they fit in at all."

"Is there anything I can say other than that the investigation is ongoing?"

"I'm not comfortable with anything else at this point."

"Okay," responded Mitchell. "It's pretty interesting. These criminal cases always fascinate me. I've gotta run. Will you let me know if anything develops?"

"I'll do my best, Varney." For several minutes after Mitchell left Ev sat at his desk thinking about Jason Thomasson, alternating his gaze between the telephone messages that he did not want to return and the window opposite his desk. When he did pick up the telephone receiver it was to call Gene Roberts.

"Roberts," answered Gene gruffly.

"Damn. I can't believe it. I caught you at your desk."

"Yeah, lucky you."

"Mrs. Noble called me this morning." Again he had referred to her formally, and regretted it.

"I bet she did."

"Who goes first?"

"I will. We popped in on Jason yesterday, interrupting a little whoopee, and interviewed him again. Two things are pretty clear. First, he did not see her or talk to her Wednesday night, and Wednesday night is really beginning to bother me. Second, she was into the crack pretty heavily. He had been with her to some back road where he said she bought it. Just before her death, she was tryin' to get him to give her money for the stuff. That didn't work, so she threatened to withhold the favor of her multitude of talents to try to wring money from him."

"That sounds like something I just heard from Mrs., ah, Rita."

"Funny you should say that."

"Why?"

"Rita called the sheriff this morning and told him that Miranda was after her father for money, which she figured was for drugs."

"That's a real coincidence. When she told me about the money business, I asked if she'd told you. She had to collect herself, and then she said she was sure Clyde told you all about it. Obviously she thought otherwise, so she called Hank."

"Sounds like she's decided on a theory of our case for us."

"What else did the sheriff say?"

"To hurry up."

"Did he say that Jason had been cleared?"

"Say what?"

"Varney Mitchell told me that the sheriff said Jason was cleared."

"Bullshit."

"I wonder if he told Rita that."

"God only knows what he told that woman. He sure didn't tell me that."

"Are we going to have to have a little talk with your boss?"

"Sounds like it." Gene paused for a moment. "I can't believe that."

"What else is there worth reporting?"

"I called the lab and requested a DNA analysis on the semen. That'll take awhile, that's when they get to it. I'm trying to figure out a diplomatic way to get Jason to give up a blood sample. Of course we can expect to find his DNA in her, or should anyway, but we also need to be able to eliminate him if there's anybody else's in there. I also want to grill Jeff Smith. My bets are that she was about ready to start bartering with Smith for the crack, if she hadn't already started. But who knows."

"This is just getting worse," said Ev.

"Has Mervin spoken to you?"

"Not about anything in particular."

"He's been running surveillance on Smith's operation and trying to put an informant in for a few buys. He started about four weeks ago, and I told him to keep it between him and me. I haven't even mentioned it to Brown. What Jason told me sounds a whole lot like Smith's retail outlet, which is a place off a back road near Oak Grove that they call the Sand Lot."

"A place?"

"A little clearing in the woods. I don't know where the hell the name Sand Lot came from."

"What can you learn from Smith other than that Miranda was a good customer?"

"That's why I'm not ready."

Ev smiled at Gene's evasiveness. "Okay. Anything else?"

"What else do you want? We've got another burglary in Lebanon Cove. Seay is working a shooting, but don't worry, the victim ain't dead. The sheriff is all over me about the burglaries. Shit. I should have a helluva Labor Day."

"I'll think about you, Gene."

"Yeah, thanks."

Ev put the receiver back into place and looked at the clock on his desk. It was almost two and he had not been to lunch. He debated whether to go and then decided against it, taking up instead one of the telephone messages.

* * *

With his tumbler filled, Ev went to the front of the house to the room Polly facetiously called the living den, which served as their den, parlor, and entrance hall—as the front door emptied into it—and settled into a wing chair. Sitting alone with a drink in hand brought to mind his first trip to a Commonwealth's Attorneys' conference, the spring meeting. He wondered why this forgettable experience should drift to the surface of his thoughts; maybe it was the highball in his hand, but he was ruminating and he succumbed to the recollection.

The meeting was held in Williamsburg in late March, where, in welcome contrast to the winter that still prevailed in Lafayette, the soft breath of spring was

65

freshening the land. The faddish Bradford pears, whose unnatural conical symmetry was becoming more ubiquitous in Virginia than even her own delicate dogwood, were in full bloom, looking like a giant white version of a child's spinning top inverted, and beneath them daffodils and flowering quince provided swatches of yellow and red.

The conference itself did not meet in restored colonial Williamsburg where the dogwoods still reigned, but in one of the modern hostelries that lined the roads leading to the new version of the old town, this one a Conference Center and Inn named after a minor Confederate general and built around a few lumps in the soil that had once been secessionist earthworks. The inn's first set of glass doors led into a wide, shallow vestibule, the right side of which was occupied by a framed thirty-six star version of the Union's colors, and the left, by an identical frame whose contents were obscured by brown wrapping paper patched together with masking tape. These heroic efforts notwithstanding, a tear in the paper revealed enough fabric to identify the occupant as the battle flag of the former Confederacy.

Ev, late for the first session of the conference, eased himself into the rear of a chamber only slightly larger than a football field. The massive collection of bored faces surprised him at first, for he had never given any thought to the number of assistant prosecutors required to handle the transgressions of the major urban areas. But here they were, a great number of them very young, younger than he, who staffed one hundred and twenty-one offices across the state. He spent the next two hours trying to spot a familiar face.

After the first session a meeting of the elected prosecutors, one for each jurisdiction, convened in a much smaller room to discuss the business of their organization. As he scanned the room, sitting beside no one as he was, he decided that the association was a neatly arranged caste system modeled on the Hindu version.

Near the bottom, hence not present at the second gathering, were the assistants, the scores of drones who did the work in the urban areas; Ev decided that these were the Sudras. Their bosses, at least most of them, from the big population centers, who obviously considered themselves the Brahmans, rarely if ever set foot in a courtroom, but spent most of their time chairing committees and commissions, or attending national conferences, or in Richmond rubbing shoulders with the legislators, and at this meeting they were congregated near the front of the room waiting their turns to offer their opinions on everything. The Brahmans listened attentively with the contented air of royalty, smug in their self-anointed superiority. With time Ev determined that the Brahmans were comprised of two classes. Some were trial lawyers without equal who could have made fortunes in a big firm, but liked the gritty entertainment and power of prosecution. The others, schooled in the love of advancement for its own sake, were stuffed shirt *prima donna* asses.

The Kshatriyas—the warriors—were comprised of the prosecutors from smaller jurisdictions, with few or no assistants, who had served in their positions since shortly after Moses received the Ten Commandments, and who had tried everything from capital murder cases to fistfights between six year olds. The Kshatriyas sat together in little clumps, talking among themselves and generally disagreeing with much of what the Brahmans had to say. Many had the hunted look of a combat veteran who had seen too much to take anything for granted, exuding a combination of cynicism and humor that could melt into a sincere warmth which charmed jurors and garnered votes.

Then there were Untouchables, the neophytes from tiny counties who had for a staff one secretary, and perhaps, a part-time assistant, or were part-timers themselves. The Untouchables did not even know their fellow outcasts because they were scattered around the state, separated geographically by Brahmans and Kshatriyas, and at this meeting they again were scattered around the room, listening quietly to the proceedings. Like the new kid in school they did not know what to say, and most had the good sense to realize that no one wanted to hear from them anyway.

Except for acknowledgements from the handful of prosecutors Ev knew from the old days, he might as well have been a manikin at the meeting.

This second meeting concluded the day's formal business and one of his old acquaintances, a Kshatriya, guided him to the hospitality suite. Ev got a bourbon and water from the bar and lost this one familiar face in the process; now he found himself standing in the middle of the crowded room, where Brahmans talked to Brahmans and Sudras talked to Sudras, and so on, and he doing nothing but wondering how many sips he had taken from his drink in the last sixty seconds. The highball vanquished for the lack of anything else to do, he went to the bar again as an excuse to move from his isolation in the midst of the confabulation.

Ev lingered at the bar wondering what to do next. Should he walk up to someone who looked like another Untouchable and try some threadbare, transparent cocktail party ice-breaker, like the favorite yuppie line, "Well what do you do?" But that was obvious. "Where do you practice?" was out, too, since everyone wore a name tag with his jurisdiction prominently displayed. "Have you tried any good rape cases lately?" was more absurd than it sounded because Ev had been prosecuting for three weeks and had been confronted with nothing more serious than brawls and speeding tickets. He unconsciously shrugged his shoulders and killed the second drink faster than the first.

He overheard some of the crowd making dinner plans; for dinner he realized that his options were to search out someone he knew and invite himself to go wherever that fellow was going, and with whomever he was going, or to eat alone. In frustration he got a double and left for the quiet of his room where he could commiserate with himself.

The dead silence of his room was as discouraging as the noisy hospitality suite, but it hastened him to a decision. Pulling on an overcoat that had belonged to his father, he struck out on foot for the restored area, for he dared not drive now after having had something to drink. What would it look like for the commonwealth's attorney to land a drunk driving arrest while at a prosecutors' conference? The first eatery he attempted was closed and after walking most of colonial Williamsburg he finally found Raleigh's Tavern open. Having failed to make reservations, he spent another thirty minutes sitting by the door, his mouth going dry, waiting for an opening as knots of tourists finished their meals. Finally, shown to a dim candlelit corner, he shared a bottle of wine with himself over chicken stuffed with Virginia country ham and wondered what in hell could be worse than what he was doing.

That first winter meeting had been a fitting precursor to his subsequent existence as commonwealth's attorney—always around people, but insular, answering to no one, yet serving at the whim of thirteen thousand citizens, empowered to make decisions that could spell, literally, life or death, with only his conscience and wits as his mentors.

**CHAPTER 7**

Monday, September 7th, a.m.

Joe Lewis Brown parked his Crown Victoria at the side of the Onan Trading Post, leaving the engine and the air conditioning running, as he looked through the pile of files and papers on the passenger seat for the two manila folders Gene Roberts had given him. The Trading Post, its clapboards dusty white in the determined September sun, was an old rambling building that housed a store on the first floor and the proprietors' living quarters on the second. Like vapors from a fissure, the Labor Day heat drifted off the pavement around the gasoline pumps in front of the store's covered front porch, imparting the appearance of a gentle undulation to the drink machines and newspaper boxes which lined half the store front. In a long flower box under one of the many windows petunias drooped their wilted heads like old men at a funeral.

Brown found the two folders and opened them. In one was stapled the photograph of Miranda and in the other six photographs of young white men—a photo line-up—one of which was Jason Thomasson. Brown glanced up from the folders and looked around the store lot. An old pickup truck was parked at the other end of the building. He had ignored Roberts's admonition to make an appointment, and now, as an afterthought, he wanted to assure himself that the business was not filled with customers. Satisfied that the store was not crowded, he closed the folders and opened the car door. The heat smacked him with a vengeance as he stepped out, and patting his pocket for a spare set of keys, he closed the locked door with the car's engine still purring.

Inside the Trading Post air conditioners mounted in the walls groaned loudly, almost as loud as the roaring motors issuing from the speedway on the screen of the television set which sat beside the cash register on the checkout counter. A man in his thirties with curly red hair sat perched on a stool behind the counter, his eyes fixed on the television and his left hand toying with a pack of Marlboro cigarettes at his side. Brown spotted the owner of the pickup, a muscular young man wearing a tee shirt and tight faded blue jeans, approaching the counter with a carton of beer. "Hello Manfred," Brown greeted the red haired man.

"What's doing Lewis," he answered with only a brief glance from the television.

Brown moved toward the large coolers near the rear of the store and walked slowly in front of them until he found a row of Mountain Dews. "Nothin' much," he replied. He lingered at the coolers with a Mountain Dew in hand while the pickup owner paid for his beer.

"Y'all must be pretty quiet today," Manfred called to Brown as the storekeeper handed change to his customer.

69

The man buying the beer looked over his shoulder. "Don't worry. I'm drinkin' these at home." He laughed aloud as he swaggered to the door. "Don't let your meat loaf Red Man," he said to the clerk in parting.

Brown walked to the counter and laid the folders down. "Red Man?"

"Yeah. That's a nickname I got and can't get rid of."

"Was that Lester Snidlett?"

"I thought you'd know of him. I mean, I guess most of the cops do."

"Oh," said Brown, wondering what Manfred meant by the remark. "We played ball in school together. You know Miranda Noble?"

Manfred turned from the television to face Brown. "Uh-huh."

"Did she come here?"

"Oh yeah."

"How about Jason Thomasson?"

"Never heard of him. Y'all still workin' on that?"

"Yeah." Brown opened the file with Miranda's photograph. "This her?"

Manfred peered quickly at the picture of Miranda. "That's her. Damn she was pretty."

"Did she ever have anyone with her when she came in?"

"Yeah, a skinny guy was with her a lot."

Brown opened the folder containing the photo line-up. "Any one of these the guys?"

Leaning forward and squinting slightly, Manfred Fitzgerald studied the photographs for a moment. "Yeah. Is this Jason Thomas, or whatever?" he asked, pointing to the picture of Jason.

"Thomasson. When did you see him?"

"Oh he come in here with Miranda pretty reg'lar. By hisself too. Usually bought beer or gas."

"When did you last see him?"

"Oh I don't know. Couple of weeks. He hadn't been back since the girl died."

"Can you remember the last time he was here?"

Manfred scratched his red thatch and grunted a quick laugh. "I can't remember yesterday Lewis."

"Was it before August twenty-second?"

"August twenty-second. What was that? A Sunday?"

"Saturday."

"The day she died?"

"Saturday was the day we found her."

Manfred quit scratching his head and picked up the pack of cigarettes. "You know. I remember him comin' in the night before she died, well Friday night. It was the night before it got on the news. Miranda had come in earlier to buy something with a check, cigarettes or something like that, and wanted to write it for a lot, like fifty over. But I wouldn't take her check 'cause the last one bounced, so I told him she'd been in to get some cigarettes earlier, and he ought to take her some. I figured he was going to see her."

Brown put the Mountain Dew on the counter. "Did he buy her the cigarettes?"

"Sure did."

"What kind?"

"Virginia Slims. Maybe Marlboro Lights."

"You're sure it was Friday?"

"Yeah. Because the next day, when we heard it on the news, well I probably heard it on the scanner first, I said to Phyllis," Phyllis was his wife, "Damn, she was just in here yesterday afternoon."

"When did she bounce the check?"

"A couple of weeks earlier. Miz Noble came in and paid it and said they weren't coverin' any more of her checks. That if I took any more it was my problem. Poor girl."

"Do you remember what time he came in?"

"This Jason? I don't know. In the evening, but it wasn't late."

"Was it still light?"

"I think so, yeah." The door opened and several young people walked noisily into the store. Manfred looked at them and threw his head back in greeting. "I bet you think this Jason had something to do with it. I hadn't thought about it until now. Didn't make the connection."

"Just tryin' to cover all the bases," answered Brown. "Hey, thanks for the help man." He pulled four quarters from his pocket and handed them to Manfred.

Manfred rang up the sale and returned some change to the lieutenant. "No problem."

Brown turned and walked toward the door.

"Don't you want this drink?" called Manfred.

"Oh yeah, thank you," answered Brown sheepishly. He walked back to the counter and retrieved the Mountain Dew. Outside, Brown exhaled heavily, excited with his discovery and embarrassed that he had not been to interview Manfred earlier when Roberts had first told him to do so. He pulled at his tie as he walked to the car, and pausing as he dug into his pocket for the keys, he smacked the top of the sedan with his other hand. "Now we're cookin'," he congratulated himself.

Gene Roberts was walking away from his car when Brown turned into the parking lot beside the courthouse. Brown rolled his window down before his car came to a halt. "Hey Gene," he called.

Roberts stopped in his tracks and stared at Brown. "What?"

"You gotta minute?"

"I sure do. I thought we were going to the cove to talk to some of your victims."

"Come on. Get in."

Roberts shook his head as he reversed his course. Once inside the coolness of the lieutenant's car, he looked at Brown expectantly.

"You ain't gonna believe this. I've been over to Onan Trading Post—"

"About time," grumbled Roberts.

"—and interviewed Manfred Fitzgerald." Brown spilled out what he had learned in quick sentences.

Roberts listened without further interruption. When Brown was finished, he looked away and pulled a pack of cigarettes from his shirt pocket. "The little son of a bitch has been lying," he observed quietly. Turning back to Brown, he continued. "She wanted fifty in cash? Sounds like she needed some drug money."

"That's what I thought."

"Rita Noble wasn't kidding when she said they weren't going to give her money. But she got the stuff somewhere that night. Damn." He paused for a moment. "Come on. Let's go to the cove and get that out of the way. I want to go to Charlottesville."

The Klobb-Prendergast house was a rustic red wood-sided structure of one story set in the woods well off the road. A boxy Toyota van and an old Volvo were parked in the shapeless gravel driveway that blended into the sparse grass at the dwelling's door. On the rear of each were a multitude of bumper stickers, some over top of the others, carrying messages like Meat Is Murder, Clinton-Gore, Noble for State Senate, and Practice Random Kindness and Senseless Acts of Beauty. At the edge of the thin, overgrown grass which surrounded the house was an old Volkswagen bus, much of its body covered in honeysuckle and poison oak vines and the remnants of illegible stickers. The orange and black of a New York license plate peeked through the weeds growing in front of the bumper.

"What is this?" asked Roberts, "the Woodstock museum?"

The two men left the car and approached the house. Naomi Prendergast, clad in a tee shirt and blue jean shorts, her iron gray hair falling carelessly below her shoulders, appeared at the screen door before they could knock. Dillon Klobb, his curly blonde hair in a long platted ponytail, joined his partner at the door. Haydn's Farewell Symphony drifted softly from another room as first one and then the other spoke. Roberts listened patiently to the same information that Brown had related and dodged a request to post a deputy at the cove entrance.

Brown smiled as he turned the car around. "Now what did you think of that pair?"

Gene cast a stony glance at Brown as he reached for the cellular telephone. "All I want to know is why you brought me up here."

"I told you. They wanted *the* investigator."

"These women are going to be scared to death with some little snot stealing their panties. The case of the panty pincher." Gene finished dialing and waited for several moments with the telephone to his ear. "Hello. Jason. This is Investigator Roberts. I'd like to talk to you today." There was a pause. "You asked me to call beforehand the next time." There was another longer pause. "I'd really like to come today. In fact, I'm on my way now." There was a longer pause still. "Well, that won't suit. We won't need much of your time. I'll be there in about fifteen minutes." Roberts listened for another several minutes and then ended the call. "He didn't want to be bothered, Lewis."

"Then when are we going?"

"Oh we're going, but he didn't like the idea."

"He probably won't be there when we get there. Fifteen minutes. Are we flying?"

Roberts pulled his sunglasses from his coat pocket. "He'll be there. Now tell me what you have with the burglaries."

"Not much. I still have a feeling those toads at the Botas are involved, but that's just a guess."

"Didn't you tell me about a vehicle in the cove that someone said didn't belong there?"

"Yeah. But I don't have a license number."

"Maybe we ought to follow Klobb's suggestion. Put someone on the road to monitor who goes in and out."

"Someone?"

"Yeah."

"You mean concealed, to take down plates."

"Yeah."

"Someone like me." Brown looked at his mentor who made no response. "Okay."

# CHAPTER 8

Monday, September 7th, p.m.

Jason Thomasson opened the door before Gene knocked. "Is this going to take long?" he asked impatiently.

"I hope not," replied Gene as he and Brown walked in. All three went automatically to the card table which was free of its usual debris.

"What is it now?" asked Jason. "I gotta be somewhere."

There was no response as Roberts and Brown seated themselves across from one another at the table. Jason looked from one to the other before plopping down in the remaining chair.

Roberts pulled a small tape recorder from his pocket and positioned it on the table. "Do you mind if I record this?"

Jason's eyes widened noticeably. "Why? I mean I guess not."

"Thanks." Gene mechanically stated the time, date, and place, and the names of the three sitting at the table. "Okay. I want to ask you some questions about Miranda Noble. You've already told us at an earlier interview that you last saw Miranda on Thursday, right?"

"Yes."

"You told us that you had plans to meet her Friday night at the Nobles but that you didn't go?"

"That's what I told you, yeah."

"That you fell asleep and ended up staying here, at your apartment."

Jason looked at Gene a moment before answering. "Yes."

Gene folded his hands on the table. "You've been to the Onan Trading Post, right?"

"Yeah." Jason was now staring into his lap.

"The Trading Post is about two miles from the Nobles, wouldn't you say."

"I guess. That's about right."

"There's a red haired fellow who works there, owns it in fact. Manfred Fitzgerald. Do you know who I'm talking about?"

"I know who you're talking about. I didn't know his name."

"Manfred says you were in his store on Friday evening, the night Miranda was murdered, and that you bought her a pack of cigarettes."

The blood drained from Jason's face in the quiet that followed Gene's statement. His lower lip quivering slightly, he seemed oblivious to the two sets of eyes boring into him. For several minutes the three sat in silence. "Am I under arrest?" he finally asked in a shaking voice.

Gene and Brown exchanged glances. "No," answered Gene.

"Well I was there. Like I saw her Friday night. But I swear to God I didn't kill her." Softly, as if to himself, "I couldn't kill her."

Gene pulled his cigarettes from his coat and removed two from the pack. He pushed one across the table until it was at the edge where Jason sat.

Jason took the cigarette with an unsteady hand and lit it with the lighter Gene offered him.

"Tell us about Friday night," said Roberts evenly.

"I went there. She was at the pool. She was high and I thought she'd been smoking crack. But she was laughing and took off her bathing suit and jumped in the pool. I did too. And I...you know...we had sex. I mean she wanted to, it was probably her idea."

"What kind of sex?"

"Just straight old sex."

"Did you ejaculate?"

"Why the shit do you need to know that?"

"Did you?"

"Yes," Jason answered faintly.

"Then what happened?"

"We were just in the pool, then she got out and sat down. She had her crack pipe in her hand."

Gene looked briefly at Brown who responded by raising his eyebrows.

"I knew what she was going to do and I told her to put the crack away. I was sick of it. It's all she wanted to do anymore. She looked at me and laughed and said so what, you didn't buy it. And I said how'd you get it then? And she just laughed some more and drank her drink and told me to fix her another one. So when I got back from the pool house she was smoking the crack. I grabbed the pipe and threw it into the yard, over the fence. She went nuts and called me every name in the book. She put her bathing suit back on and told me to get the hell out of there. She could get crack anytime and could get laid anytime and she was tired of my bullshit and not loaning her money when she didn't have any. She was freaking out man."

"So what did you do?" asked Gene.

"What do you think I did? I left. I mean I said some lousy things, like you're just hosing the dealers now, that's why you don't need money and I'm not going out with a crack whore. Then she starting laughing and screaming and I just walked away. Got in my car and left."

"What about the cigarettes you bought her?" asked Brown.

"I forgot to give them to her."

Gene straightened in his chair. "What time was this, that you left?"

"I guess it was about eight or eight-thirty. It might not have been that late. There was still a lot of daylight." Jason leaned over and retrieved an empty Coors Lite can to use as an ashtray.

"How long were you there?"

"A little more'n an hour, I guess." Jason dabbed and rolled the lit end of the cigarette around the mouth of the can, his eyes focused on his undertaking. "I wasn't there long." His hand quit moving and he looked up at Gene. "I didn't kill her. I don't know what happened after I left. I just came back here, and watched TV and drank the beer I'd bought." He returned his attention to the beer can and cigarette.

"Did you drink at the pool?"

"Yeah."

"Coors Lite?"

"Yeah."

"Is that all you ever drank?"

"Yeah. Unless it was someone elses."

"What cigarettes did you buy her?"

"Virginia Slims. They're still in the car."

"Is that what she smokes?"

"Yeah."

"How'd you know to get them?"

"She's always out. No money. I just got `em for her."

"And your brand?"

"Camels, the filtered ones."

Lewis was now watching Gene intently as the investigator reeled off the questions.

"Where'd you throw the crack pipe?"

"I just threw it over the fence. It may have went in the bushes. I wasn't looking."

"What kind of pipe?"

"A little one. It may have been metal, at least part of it."

"It wasn't a homemade job, like a cut beer can?"

"No."

"The drink you fixed her. What was it?"

"Vodka and grapefruit juice."

"Did you see her Wednesday night?"

Jason looked up again. "I told you I didn't."

"You told me you didn't see her Friday, too."

"I was scared to tell you about Friday. Wouldn't you be? But I didn't see her Wednesday. I told you to ask Rita. Miranda was there with them that night."

"Does either Rita or Clyde smoke."

"You mean cigarettes?"

"Yeah."

"No. Well I've never seen it. I guess they don't."

"You told me last time we were here that she was seeing some of the boys in Lafayette. Do you know who?"

"No. I just suspected it."

"Did you go to any store, any place besides the Trading Post?"

"No. Well, there was that time we drove over to the Go Mart, or whatever it's called."

"Will you give us a blood sample?"

Jason eyes darted nervously between Roberts and Brown. "What for?"

"For DNA analysis. DNA will confirm your story about sex with her."

Jason dropped the cigarette into the can, causing a brief hissing noise. "I guess."

"I'll call you tomorrow to set up an appointment to draw the blood." Gene leaned over and added his cigarette to the can. "You don't mind driving to Lafayette Court House to have it done, do you?"

"No."

"Can I get those Virginia Slims from your car?"

"Sure. I won't smoke them."

Gene looked at Brown. "Anything else?"

"Nope," replied Brown.

"Alright. We're concluding this interview at three forty-eight." Gene picked up the tape recorder, switched it off, and put it in his coat pocket. "Thanks Jason," he said as he arose from the table. Brown stood, too.

Jason remained where he sat, peering vacantly at the makeshift ashtray in front of him.

* * *

The ride back to Lafayette Court House was quieter than usual, with Gene lost in his thoughts. Brown glanced at his boss several times but the questions on the tip of his tongue did not pass his lips. He was anxious to ask why Gene had not arrested Jason on the spot. What was Gene waiting for? If he himself had been handling the case he would have arrested Jason then and there. He looked at Gene again but said nothing.

Gene pulled another cigarette from his pocket. There was still something missing, like Miranda's whereabouts on Wednesday night, and the crack pipe that Jason had thrown over the fence. He wondered whether they had missed the pipe, or whether it had been one of the things Rita had taken care of in her own version of a sweep of the pool area, or perhaps, someone else had been there after Jason left, and the pipe had been retrieved. And then there was Jeff Smith. There were still too many unanswered questions and he was beginning to wonder how he could ever answer some of them.

* * *

Polly seated herself under the dogwood tree where Ev sat reading the paper. "Labor Day was given its name by a woman," said Polly.

Ev didn't have time to answer.

"Men relax and women labor."

Ev decided that prudence dictated caution.

"Do you hear them in there?" she asked referring to Will and Sam, "They're fighting over Pokémon cards. I've had it. They can just fight."

Ev attempted to chuckle.

"You're no help. I'll just go back in and referee."

The threat of burning the Pokémon cards quieted the two long enough for Polly to answer the telephone. The caller was Margaret Cross.

*Oh no,* thought Polly, *she's home.*

Without preliminary banter Margaret went to the purpose of her call. "Polly. I can't find my silver. Did you all take it to your home?"

Polly was speechless. She knew where this question was leading, and the thought of it infuriated her.

"I hid it before I left, and now it's not there," Margaret continued, without giving Polly time to respond.

Margaret always hid valuables when she went away, and this was not the first time she had been unable to remember where she had secreted something. Polly suspected that Margaret undertook these missions when she was drunk, leaving her confused not only as to where she had hidden things, but also about what she had hidden.

"Did you come over to check on the cats?" asked Margaret.

"Of course I did. You asked me to."

"Well I couldn't tell, they've messed everywhere."

*Of course they've messed everywhere,* thought Polly. The old woman had left the top of a shoebox filled with a couple of cups of cat litter as the suggested repository for her collection of felines. Upon seeing this farcical provision Polly had decided on the spot that she was not going to come over every day to empty the box top, replenish the litter, and then search the house for whatever piles the remaining cats had deposited. She had done that for the last two years when Margaret was away, and despite telling her mother-in-law that the box top was inadequate, the woman had persisted in the practice. A surge of guilt for having left the cats to their own scatological devices

78

momentarily humbled her and now she regretted her decision. "I fed and watered them," she answered again contritely.

"Well I can't find my silver. I've looked everywhere. Would you check your home, it just isn't here."

*Check my home!* Polly's brief tinge of remorse evaporated. She opened her mouth to deny the accusation and the request, but stopped with a hiss as the letter "I" died in her throat. There simply was nothing to be gained by arguing.

"Was anyone with you when you came over here?"

"Just the boys."

"Please ask them will you?"

"Ask them if they took the silver?"

Margaret, realizing the fatuousness of her demand, ignored Polly's question. "I've got to call Gloria about this." Gloria was Margaret's maid. "Goodbye."

Polly was embarrassed by the thought of Margaret accusing the black maid who had worked for her for twenty years, who was entrusted with a key to the house, and who was probably older than her employer. An accused family member, even an in-law, could get angry and defend herself; but she thought it pure evil to accuse a faithful domestic who counted as an invaluable part of her standing in her tiny world the fact that she was retained by 'Miz Cross.'

Ev appeared at the back door. "I ought to cut the grass but the damn mower is dead," he grumbled. "I'm not getting it fixed again. I'll buy a new one."

Polly decided that his remarks did not invite a response.

"I'm going to the hardware, do you boys want to go?"

Like victims of a hypnotist, neither boy took his eyes off the cards as each shook his head.

Ev looked at Polly for the first time since walking into the room. "What's the matter?" he asked.

Polly pursed her lips. It piqued her that Ev could now read her face. "Nothing."

"Well, something's the matter."

"No."

"Did my mother call?"

"It's nothing."

Ev sighed impatiently. "What is it now?"

Polly detected an impertinence in his voice that annoyed her, as it suggested that he would neither understand nor be sympathetic. Frequently he brushed off his mother's outrages as peccadilloes, not worthy of a response, or laid the incident at the foot of the bottle. "It's nothing," she repeated as she arose with an armful of the boys' clothes.

Ev shrugged his shoulders. "Okay. I'll be back later."

Polly walked into the narrow hallway leading from the kitchen to the two bedrooms and paused at the door to the boys' room in the vain hope that he would come back and ask her again.

It was shortly after two o'clock when Margaret called again. "Polly," spoke the dreaded voice. "Did Amanda talk to Ev last night?" Her delivery was vaguely lyrical, like that of an amateur actress getting her first chance on the stage.

Polly shuddered in a mixture of anger and regret, for the sing-song falseness was irrefutable proof that Margaret had been drinking. "No she didn't," replied Polly curtly.

"Well he needs to talk to her about what we're doing," said the lilting voice.

There was a secretiveness to Margaret's statement that immediately aroused Polly's suspicions. "I'll tell him."

"I can't believe she didn't talk to him. She told me she called. I just assumed that they'd talked about it."

Polly could not restrain herself. "About what?"

"About the house," answered Margaret sharply, her tone implying that Polly should know. "You know it's been getting to be just too much for me with Lucius gone. Anyway, Amanda and I decided we ought to sell."

"We...ought to sell," Polly repeated flatly, astonishment freezing her wits.

"Yes. It's too big and expensive to keep up and I don't want to spend another cold winter here. I always wanted Lucius to move to South Carolina after he retired, but he didn't live long enough."

Polly could not make a response.

"Oh. After I called Gloria, I found the silver. I had put it in the oven."

"Does Gloria know?"

"I'll tell her next week when she comes in. Of course there won't be much for her to do since I've already cleaned up after the cats."

Polly ignored the comment about the cats, wondering instead what Gloria would be thinking for the three days she had to live under a cloud of suspicion. "I'll tell Ev."

"Tell him to call Amanda. I just can't worry about this old place anymore." With that, she abruptly ended the call.

With the receiver to her ear Polly stood for several moments listening blankly to the dial tone. Jerking herself into action she laid the telephone down and walked slowly outside, interrupted Ev's mowing, and told him what his mother and sister had decided.

"Should you call Amanda today?" asked Polly after breaking the news.

He shook his head.

"Are you hoping this will go away if you ignore it?"

"No I'm not. I thought she was supposed to call me."

"Can we buy it?"

"I don't know."

Whenever they had discussed his mother's house in the past Polly had sensed that Ev would not bring himself to accept that he would have to buy it, yet nothing about Margaret suggested that she would give it to him. She suspected that he was as much hurt by his mother's, and Amanda's, abrupt decision as by the daunting sum of money the old house would fetch.

"Ev. Maybe you shouldn't worry about it. She was drinking when she called. It's probably just another passing whim. Or she'll forget she even mentioned it." After a pause, "Do you think you should call your mother tomorrow, before she gets into the sauce?"

"No. I'm not going to push it. Hints or not, I'm going to wait till she brings it up with me."

**CHAPTER 9**

Tuesday, September 8th

The day following a long weekend, especially a long hot weekend, always generates an endless stream of telephone calls and unscheduled office visits by those given extra time to drink, disagree, and fight, usually in that order. Ev had just finished hearing from Minnie Patterson when Linda Masencup paged him that he had a call from Oliver Farnsworth. Farnsworth was the senior partner in the Charlottesville firm of Farnsworth & Conte. He had, in the lawspeak of attorneys, a corporate practice, which meant that he handled business matters, an undertaking which entailed, in short, ensuring that people with money parted with as little of it as possible. Farnsworth had never defended a criminal case while Ev was prosecuting, so the only reason for the call would be Farnworth's Noble connection.

Farnsworth's secretary was on the line when Ev answered the call. "One moment Mr. Cross, Mr. Farnsworth will be right with you."

Ev drummed the fingers of his free hand on his desk as he rested the silent receiver against his ear with the other. He found it annoying that he should be the one to wait when Farnsworth had initiated the call. Then again, Farnsworth probably charged three hundred dollars an hour and most clients could ill afford to have him dialing his own telephone.

"Hello, Mr. Cross, this is Oliver Farnsworth," said a man's voice finally, his words hollow, as if they were coming from a tunnel, and Ev assumed that Farnsworth was using a speaker.

"Good morning."

"I have my associate, Paul Stankowski, on the telephone with me."

"Hello," came the other voice, more distant than Farnsworth's.

Ev greeted the associate as the phrase 'brief bag boy' came to mind, the moniker Wilmer Bledsoe used to describe the young lawyers big firm attorneys kept at their beck and call.

"I suppose your Labor Day in beautiful Lafayette County was as hot as ours in Charlottesville," said Farnsworth.

"It was a scorcher." Ev felt slightly silly for having responded in the vernacular.

"I'm calling you about Jason Thomasson. We've been retained to represent him."

A nervous tingle coursed Ev's stomach. The deputies had a habit of making arrests in serious cases without keeping their prosecutor informed. "Well, you're ahead of me Oliver. Have we arrested Thomasson?" There was a brief silence on the other end of the tunnel which Ev knew was the shock of disbelief. Corporate lawyers had no

82

conception of how the criminal system ebbed and flowed, accustomed as they were to keeping all the strings to a problem in their hands.

"Well, he's not under arrest. He's been questioned by your investigators. Also, your investigator asked him for a blood sample, for a DNA test. I would like to hold up on that as well."

*Not until old Paul can research all of that,* thought Ev.

"Are you in a position to talk about the evidence against Jason?" continued Farnsworth. "I know I've probably caught you at a bad time."

*Evidence against Jason? Something's happened.* Ev made a mental correction. Farnsworth was more adept at the criminal law than he had expected. He was following defense rule number one: give up nothing and ask for everything. "Oliver, I wasn't aware that we were at a point where we had evidence against Thomasson. I need to talk to Gene Roberts first. You probably know more about Jason's involvement than I do."

"I understand, perhaps we can chat about it after Roberts has talked to you. One more thing. Do you mind sending me copies of any statements Jason has made?"

*Paul has been in the books this morning,* thought Ev. "He's not charged yet, Oliver," he replied.

There was a brief silence in which Ev assumed that Oliver and Paul were communicating in sign language about whether to object to Ev's technically correct response about their client's statements.

"Okay," came Farnsworth's voice finally. "We look forward to hearing from you."

Ev hung up his receiver gloating over Farnsworth's use of the royal we, then remonstrated with himself for the covetous irrationality that always seized him when a big firm lawyer called the office. He turned his thoughts to Jason and the Miranda Noble killing and reached for the telephone to ring the investigators' office. He changed his mind before dialing the intercom number.

"I'm going to Roberts's office," he advised Linda as he walked by her desk.

Ev made his way to the rear entry to the sheriff's office, a set of narrow stairs leading from a door in the first floor corridor to the basement home of law enforcement. Finding the side door to the investigators' office locked, he walked to the front where the dispatchers plied their trade behind a scurfy plexiglass shield. "Where's Roberts?" asked Ev through the cluster of pencil-sized holes centered in the shield.

Willie Painter rolled his cigar to the corner of his mouth as he looked up. The cluster of holes was a foot above his lips. "They're all at the high school on the bomb threat."

"Damn," murmured Ev. Bomb threats had to be taken seriously, which meant all the deputies and a half dozen state police were combing the school for a non-existent bomb while the children waited in the bleachers. "Tell Gene to call me as soon as he gets in," he fairly shouted through the plexiglass.

Painter mumbled an unintelligible acknowledgement.

* * *

Roberts caught Ev in the parking lot as the latter was returning from lunch. "You wanted me?" asked Gene tersely.

"Yeah. Your friend Thomasson has a lawyer. Has something developed?"

"Sort of."

"When can we talk?"

"Right now suit you?"

"Sure," replied Ev as he watched Gene out of the corner of his eye. "My office?"

"If you don't mind. Let me go to my office, my work station that is, and get the file."

"Work station?"

"I'll tell you about that in a minute."

Ev was at his desk with the telephone at his ear when the investigator joined him with the file. Ev waved for the other man to sit down. "We won't drop the charges; we don't do that anymore," Ev spoke into the receiver. There was a pause. "I'm sorry the sheriff told you that. As I just explained to you, domestic assault charges are not dropped. All of them go to court." Another pause. "Thank you for calling." Ev dropped the receiver onto the body of the telephone. "Why does the damn sheriff tell people to call me? On top of that, why does he tell the complainant in these domestic assaults that I might drop the charges? I changed that policy four years ago."

"Who was it?"

"Dawn Grogan. I think Lester Snidlett was charged. So Jason has a lawyer."

"Yeah. Oliver Farnsworth. The firm that represents the Clyde Noble empire."

"Well, let me tell you what happened yesterday." Roberts recited the information Manfred Fitzgerald had provided and the new version of Jason Thomasson's story.

Cross listened in silence, his mind spinning the conclusions that this new evidence suggested. He did not respond immediately when Roberts was finished.

"What do you think?" prodded Roberts.

"What do you think?"

Roberts smiled wryly as he leaned back in his chair. "I say some things are still missing."

"Run them by me."

"First there's Miranda's whereabouts on Wednesday night. She must have been with somebody, and that means another potential witness we haven't interviewed. Then there's the question of how she got money for crack on Friday night. Based on Jason and Rita's statements, she was broke. I can't see her trying to cash a check if she already

84

had the stuff, and she was using too much to have the luxury of keeping a stash. There's the tear to the anus. There's the Bud can. There are three sets of prints with no match."

"No response from AFIS."

"Not yet. We didn't find the pipe Jason said he threw. There's the cigarette brand no one will claim. Smith won't talk, but I bet he saw her that night. And then there's DNA, which could generate another suspect without a name. Hell, the questions are endless."

"So, did Jason do it?"

"I don't know yet. If he's lying about killing her, then he's lying about some of this other stuff, too."

"Well, the plot thickens."

"Yeah," grunted Roberts.

"What's wrong with the lab? AFIS is computerized."

"I'm calling them again when we're done."

"Smith?"

"We're going to have to hotbox him, but we need something to prod with."

"Is the sheriff up to speed?"

"No."

"I'm not gonna touch that. What else is going on?"

"You'll probably start getting some calls about the burglaries in Lebanon Cove. Seven now."

"No suspects?"

"None. But Ronnie Snidlett visits Aaron Bota who lives up at the end of the cove road."

"Those names sound familiar."

"You've probably seen them in J&D court. But we haven't questioned them. I guess we're going to have to, but I don't have a thing on them. That call about Lester, Lester's Ronnie's brother."

"Anything else?"

"Do you need anything else?" answered Roberts as he arose from his chair.

"Oh, before you leave. What's this with the work station?"

Roberts shook his head. "Hank went to a sheriff's conference last week. The employment law speaker referred to our desks as work stations. I guess the big offices have such things. Anyway, that's his new word. And we're travelling incognito now."

"What?"

"Check out my car. I have an Albemarle county sticker on my windshield."

Ev laughed at the notion that another county's sticker would disguise a Ford Crown Victoria with three or four antennae protruding from the trunk lid. "Maybe that will help you with these investigations."

Roberts returned to his office and dropped heavily into his chair. He felt as if he could put his head down on his desk and sleep for days. Forcing himself from the lethargy that dogged him he picked up the telephone and dialed Clyde Noble's home number. Clara Wood answered the call.

"This is Investigator Roberts. May I speak to Senator Noble, please?"

"Just a minute."

Several minutes passed before the senator was on the line. "Roberts, this is Noble." His voice was sharp and impatient.

"Senator, I'd like your permission to search the pool area again."

There was a brief silence. "I'm tempted to ask why your people didn't complete the job two weeks ago. But I won't. I'm also tempted to ask you what is going on with Jason, but I doubt you'd tell me anything. Why do you need to search again?"

Roberts hastily considered concealing his purpose, then thought better of it. "I believe there's a piece of evidence near the pool that we might have missed, a crack pipe."

"When do you want to come?"

"This afternoon."

"Alright. Be here at four. But I want you to know that I'm going to ask Cross to turn this over to the state police. I've really had it with your screwing around with this investigation. If all you can come up with is Jason, then there's not a snowball's chance in hell that you're gonna solve it."

"State police assistance is always welcomed, Senator. Do you want to make an appointment so that we can go over what I've learned and what we're still looking for?" Roberts, seething, managed the answer and invitation in an even voice.

"I'll consider it." With that, Noble rang off.

The receiver clenched in his hand, Roberts sat for a moment absently listening to the dial tone. The remark about the state police was not surprising for he had heard the same line innumerable times in previous investigations. What bothered him most was Noble's attitude about Jason Thomasson. Roberts could not shake the notion that Noble was more interested in keeping Jason out of the picture than he was in finding out who had killed his daughter. Then again, Clyde did have to live with Rita. Finally he replaced the receiver and as quickly removed it again and dialed the intercom number to Cross's office. He received a busy signal. After finding a cup of rancid coffee and lighting a cigarette, he tried again. This time Ev answered.

"Ev,"

"What is this, mental telepathy?"

"Did you just get off the phone with Noble?"

"Yeah. I got my ear full. He wants the state police to take over."

"I'm about ready to grant his wish."

"Well, I agreed to ask them to help."

Roberts could not suppress the sense of betrayal the statement elicited, but he resolved to keep it to himself. "They could help here around the clock. Maybe I could get some rest."

"I told him you were still in charge of the case, that the state would not, as a matter of policy, take control of the investigation."

The caveat helped. "They won't under most circumstances, but a state senator has some pull. What did he say to that?"

"We'll see."

"Nothing we can do about that."

"Yes there is. The state police won't take over without my permission. At least I've never had it happen."

"Under normal circumstances. I get the feeling he doesn't care that much about the damn case anyway, as long as Jason isn't involved. I offered, again, to meet with him. You explain it to me."

"One word: Rita."

"Okay. Just keeping you posted."

Ev laid the receiver in its cradle. His stomach was still churning from the blistering he had received from Noble. The senator had made clear his distrust of Roberts's abilities and he had been almost as clear in conveying his lack of faith in Cross. Suspicious victims and victims' families, usually unsophisticated and marginally, if at all, literate, were an occupational hazard and more than once he had had to lay it out in plain English that he was the only prosecutor in the county and that he was going to try the case with or without their support. But he had not been as blunt with Noble and now he felt like a little boy who had sheepishly backed away from the class bully's challenge.

That afternoon Mervin McIntosh pulled a small wood and bronze pipe from beneath an azalea. He handed it to Roberts who sniffed the bowl once before dropping the pipe into a small paper bag.

"Cocaine?" asked McIntosh.

"Yeah," replied Roberts.

# CHAPTER 10

Thursday, September 17th

Wilmer Bledsoe pushed open the door to the coffee-copier room off the district court hallway. Ev was leaning against the counter with a styrofoam cup in his hand. "Mornin' Mr. Commonwealth," Bledsoe greeted him with a wide smile. "What do you want to do about Lester Hester Snidlett?"

"Snidlett?"

"You mean no reporter called you about Lester Hester?"

"Is that why you're here today? He was charged only two weeks ago, can't be set for trial this soon."

"Yeah. They got into a little pushing match and his woman charged him. I got the clerk to put the matter on the docket early because he's under a protective order and can't carry a gun."

"Deer season's a long way off, Wil."

"Don't ask me. I would've ignored his whining except that I've represented his old man for years. You know Roger Snidlett, has the cleft palette. Roger called me about it. 'Wil, iss id Woger. When can my boy gi' is guns back?' Now how could I refuse that?" Bledsoe laughed aloud as he poured himself another cup of coffee. "I got Lester Hester off on a burglary charge when he was a kid, but due only to the bungling police work of Hank Burke, back when he was assistant investigator, or whatever he was."

"This charge involves Sunny Grogan doesn't it?"

"Yeah. Sunny Dawn Grogan. I guess you won't consider taking it under advisement. You oughta know, Sunny is gonna say she can't remember what happened."

"Well, let her testify to that."

"Damn Ev, you're getting hard to deal with." Bledsoe put his cup to his mouth to conceal a wide smile. "What's going on with the Noble case? Been almost a month now."

"A month on the twenty-second, next week."

"I guess the Nobles are putting on the heat."

"I'll say. Rita Noble chewed me on Monday, sort of a weekly ritual. Half our problem is how damn slow the lab is."

"I'm glad it's your problem and not mine. Let's go in and see if Mary Jane will take our case. I've got to be in Charlottesville this afternoon."

The two lawyers passed through the crowded hallway and walked quietly into the courtroom, seating themselves in the back while Mary Jane Chandler finished ruling in the custody dispute she was hearing. "Do you all have something, Wil," asked the judge as the bailiff walked the litigants to the courtroom door.

"Just a little shoving contest. Won't take long."

"How often have I heard that?" responded Chandler. "Who is it?"

"Lester Hester Snidlett."

"Okay sheriff, call the Snidlett case."

The lawyers took their usual places in front of the bench as they awaited the contestants. Snidlett entered the courtroom first, his cowboy boots pounding the tile floor noisily as he shuffled indifferently to the front row of the gallery. He stopped at the railing which split the room and leaned forward on it, his muscular arms tense as if a show of force would somehow affect the disposition of his case. Several steps behind him followed Sunny Dawn Grogan, a buxom young woman whose dull blonde hair suggested ceaseless bleaching and whose thirty-something years wore heavily on her.

Bledsoe waved his client to a spot in front of the bench and began addressing the court over the clanking of Snidlett's boots. "We waive the reading of the warrant and enter a plea of not guilty. We also stipulate that the parties were living together and that the offense occurred in Lafayette County." He then motioned for Sunny Grogan to come forward as well.

Chandler swore the parties and then nodded to Ev. "You're Sunny Dawn Grogan?" he asked.

"Uh-huh."

"Tell the court why you took out the warrant against Lester Snidlett."

Grogan pursed her lips together and glanced at Snidlett before answering. "I really want to drop charges," she managed softly.

Ev looked at Bledsoe and shook his head. "Tell us what happened first."

Grogan looked down as if suddenly preoccupied with her feet. "We was just arguin' and callin' each other names. I don't remember how it started. But I hit him first."

"Where did he hit you?"

After a pause: "I don't know that he did. I was just mad and got the warrant."

"What did you tell the magistrate?"

"I don't remember. I didn't say nothin' about gettin' hit."

"The magistrate would not have issued an assault and battery warrant unless you said he hit you."

Grogan shrugged her shoulders as she continued her fascination with her feet.

"Well, you're under oath today, like you were with the magistrate."

"I done told you what I remember."

Ev looked at the judge and shook his head.

"Miz Grogan," interrupted the judge sternly, "do you expect the court to believe you can't remember?"

Grogan sighed and repositioned her feet.

"Well Mr. Cross," continued the judge, "There's not much I can do. Maybe you should investigate perjury before the magistrate."

Grogan glanced up at Snidlett who had not once taken his eyes off the judge during the brief testimony.

Chandler smoothed the copy of the warrant lying in front of her. "I have to dismiss the charge." When she had finished marking the warrant she looked toward the defendant. "I hope you're not in this court again on a similar matter."

"You can count on that judge," said Snidlett, his leer lamely disguised by a twisted smile.

Bledsoe whispered something to his client after which Snidlett turned on his heel and began his pounding exit from the courtroom. Grogan, still peering at her feet, quietly turned and followed him.

Chandler watched the duo until the courtroom door was closed behind them. "There's something scary about that young man."

"I think he was trying to impress you, judge," grinned Bledsoe.

"Not my type, Wil. Sheriff, call the next case."

* * *

The clerk handed Ev a note as he took his place in the back of the courtroom to await his other cases. The piece of paper read that he should call Roberts as soon as he was finished with court. An hour later Ev hurriedly made his way to the sheriff's department in the basement where he found Roberts at his desk, smoking a cigarette as he thumbed through a file. Brown was leaning against the wall. "Do you have something?" asked Ev without greeting the two men.

Roberts lifted his wan face and offered a vague smile before speaking. "Yeah," he said. "The AFIS report came back. Jeff Junior Smith's prints were on the vodka bottle. We've got Thomasson's on one can."

"So, can you put Smith there that night?"

"We might be able to. That would make him suspect number one."

"Thomasson?"

"He's not off the list, but he isn't the likely sort. Besides, it looks like he was there too early. And Smith has the connection with Alphonso Thornton's murder."

"There's something else," interrupted Brown. "We were re-interviewing some people, and Hector Lopez's wife, Juanita, says she saw a silver sedan turn into the drive that Friday night when she was on her way to the Trading Post. She didn't think anything of it because it stopped. She saw it in her rear view mirror."

Ev had not taken his eyes off Roberts. "And the significance?"

"Smith drives a silver Buick," answered Roberts. "I forgot to tell you that. We got that last night. Old Brown knows pretty good Spanish."

Brown continued. "What makes that important is she saw it at dusk. After nine o'clock. That would put him there after Jason and pretty close to the time of death. We thought he was driving something else, I've seen him in a red Volvo. But Mervin told us this morning that he always drives the Buick when he's dealing."

"What's registered to him?" asked Ev.

"Nothing," answered Roberts. "There're three cars in his grandmother's name, Anita Smith."

"How'd we miss this?" asked Ev, who immediately regretted sounding as if Roberts were at fault.

Roberts leaned back in his chair and looked at Ev evenly before replying. "Juanita speaks little English. I don't think she understood anything I was asking Hector and her the first time, at least that's the way she acted. The second time Brown directed questions to her in Spanish and out pops this."

"What's the plan with Smith?"

Roberts nodded toward Brown. "Lewis is going to round him up and try to set up an interview. We have something to work with now. With the prints and this business about the car. Also, Mervin has made a few crack buys with an informant. I filled Lewis in on that"

"Are you ready to move on Smith?"

"We're ready to put the pressure in him, see what we can pin down. I wanted to let you hear it first, make sure you didn't have any better ideas."

"No. Go for it." Ev looked at Brown. "Good luck, Lewis. This is a big one."

Brown glanced at Roberts and then pushed away from his desk. "I guess I better get on it." He stopped before leaving the room and looked back at Roberts. "Gene, don't forget to tell him about Tower." Then he disappeared around the corner.

"Tower?" asked Cross, perplexed.

"Different case. Lebanon Cove. But to finish, we've still got three prints that aren't Noble family and friends. One on the Bud can we found in the yard, one on the vodka bottle, and one on a Miller Lite. On the pipe Jason tossed, there was only Miranda's."

Ev sat down on the edge of Brown's desk. "I don't think I've ever had a case where prints were any use, and now they're running out of our ears."

"It is a little unusual. That gives us as many as three other people there, plus Smith, Thomasson and the victim. Of course some of these could be unrelated, maybe the Nobles forgot to give us some of the people who were legitimately there. And we always have the problem that these prints were left much earlier. Smith, for example, could have been there before Friday. But it's a start, finally. Another twist is that the real pipe was found over the fence, like Jason said. So it follows, or is possible, that the homemade job appeared after Jason left, maybe when Smith showed up."

"Tell me again the significance of the Bud can."

"Nobody saw it there before Saturday. It was in the yard by the driveway. Also, the cans in the trash were all Coors and Miller Lite. Thomasson drinks Coors. The Nobles kept Miller Lite in the refrigerator."

"You've got a ways to go."

"I know it. All we can do is squeeze Smith, and hope DNA narrows the field."

"What about the sheriff? Is he up on the news?"

"Ev, I tried to explain it to him, but he hears what he wants to hear. All he could say was push it, push it. So I said I would have Brown on it asap."

"What's this about the cove and Tower?"

"The mysterious blue pickup has been traced to Pup Tower."

"I don't understand."

"The residents have reported a strange blue pickup on the road. Lewis sat in the bushes a few evenings and spotted it. As soon as we get a report back on the prints comparison, we'll know whether to approach him."

"Prints again."

"Yeah, wild idn't it."

Ev laughed quietly. "Pup Tower stealing women's underwear. I wonder what he does with them."

"I don't want to know."

Ev nodded in agreement. "On Miranda, we're waiting on the lab for DNA?"

"Yep. At the least they can tell us how many different men she was with over the last few days."

"You don't sound too optimistic."

"I'm not."

* * *

Joe Lewis Brown felt a tingling of anticipation in his gut as he drove away from the courthouse. He was turning over in his mind Roberts's new found trust in his abilities. The sheriff, meeting him in the parking lot, had told him to go for Smith like a cur after a bitch in heat. That was a pretty clear marching order.

Where to find Smith soon supplanted the self-congratulatory musing. From the information provided by Mervin McIntosh, Smith was usually at one of three places: the Quik Mart, the Sand Lot, or his grandmother's. Brown glanced at his watch. Twelve-thirty—too early for the Sand Lot, he would try the Quik Mart first. At the edge of Lafayette Court House, just off the first exit serving the village, sat the Quik Mart, a dirty-white cinderblock convenience store, the front of which was nearly obscured by soft drink vending machines, and which included car wash bays, gasoline pumps and the best fried chicken available. It was a favorite night gathering spot for young people and in consequence the graveled parking lot usually contained more cars and trucks than were customers in the store. NO LOITERING signs were blithely ignored.

Brown quickly scanned the lot for the silver Le Sabre McIntosh had described as one of Smith's most likely means of conveyance. In the corner of the lot, partially obscured by a beer delivery truck, he spotted the Buick. Heady with his good fortune, the lieutenant parked next to the Le Sabre and sat for a moment as he contemplated what to do. He had been there only seconds when Jeff Smith rounded the corner of the store with a Pepsi Cola in his hand.

Brown quickly stepped out of the car. "Smith," he called.

Smith looked up languidly. "What's whitey's nigger want to bother me about today?"

Forgetting himself Brown dashed within inches of Smith.

"Oh no," continued Smith in a sarcastic, deliberate voice, "whitey's nigger boy gonna arrest me."

Brown drew a deep breath and stepped back a pace. "I don't need none of that shit." The words came out before he could think.

"Move out the way if you ain't got bidness."

"The business we need to talk to you about is Miranda Noble."

"We done talked about that once."

Brown felt a miserable sinking feeling mixing with his anger. He had lost control of the situation and Smith knew it. People like Smith who had experienced brushes with the law had figured out the limits and knew how powerless the police were when they needed information. "Why don't you come with me to the office? We can talk there."

"Ax me here. I ain't comin' in." He took a sip from his Pepsi.

Brown rapidly turned his options over in his mind. He had only one. "We know you were there the night she was murdered."

Smith looked at the officer briefly before replying. "That's a lie. Look, I ain't puttin' up with this." He began moving around Brown who stood between the Le Sabre and him.

Brown watched the Smith out of the corner of his eye as he moved by. "Your silver Buick was seen going into the Nobles."

"Okay. So I be the only dude in the world with a silver Buick."

"Does a vodka bottle help your memory?"

Smith kept walking.

"It should. Your prints were on it."

Smith stopped in mid-stride. "No they ain't," he said in a quieter voice.

"Come on with me. I'll show you the report."

"Who got it?"

"Investigator Roberts."

"Call him and tell him to come here with it. Y'all can talk to me here."

Brown sensed that Smith was wavering. "Best to go to the office."

"I ain't."

*Time to go for broke,* decided the lieutenant. "There's one more thing."

"Like what?"

"The Negative Retinal Image."

"Say what?"

"When a person dies the last thing he sees stays on the retina, like a photograph." Brown was impressed with his monstrous lie.

Smith shook his head cautiously. "How? Like…what you talkin' about? This image shit."

"I mean they have this Negative Retinal Image Machine, the FBI does. And when we get that report from the FBI on Miranda, who do you think the image is going to be?"

"Not me man." Smith's voice was faltering.

*I'm about two sentences from a confession,* Brown congratulated himself. *In about ten seconds.*

"Not me man," said Smith again.

"Au-ight. So let's talk in the car." Brown turned on his heel and began walking to his sedan. There was a sudden pounding footfall and Brown knew what was happening before he could spin back toward Smith. The latter was sprinting for the woods behind the convenience store; the Pepsi can rolling slowly behind him.

"Stop goddamit," yelled Brown, furious that he had allowed Smith the opportunity to run. Digging his toe into the gravel to take pursuit his foot skidded out from under him in the loose rock and he stumbled forward several steps before regaining his balance. By then Smith was out of sight. "Bastard," grunted Brown as he began quick stabbing strides like the ones that had served him as a cornerback. Reaching full speed Brown crashed through the briars and honeysuckle that had temporarily obscured Smith. Once within the tree line Brown could see his quarry running madly. Wild-eyed, Smith repeatedly turned his head to look over his shoulder.

"Stop!" Brown bellowed.

At the command Smith again turned his head, and heedless of what lay in front of him, crashed into a poplar sapling, spun to the side, and crumpled into a heap.

"Serves him right," murmured Brown as he slowed to a walk, gasping deeply, his eyes fixed on Smith's hands lest he should reach into his pockets for a weapon. "Hope you didn't hurt that tree, Jeff."

Smith, dazed, awkwardly raised himself to a sitting position and stared at the man approaching him.

"You ready to talk to me, now?" asked Brown.

"About what," mumbled Smith.

"The girl you killed."

"Look whitey's nigger, you ain't got nothin' on me. I ain't got shit to say to you."

"You gonna talk." Brown felt the anger surging again, the words whitey's nigger ricocheting around his brain. "You ain't got no choice…nigger," he growled, unaware that he had slipped into his prey's vernacular. He stopped just short of Smith and, reaching inside of his coat, produced his sidearm.

Smith glued his eyes to the pistol barrel oscillating several feet from his head. "No. Wait," he stammered. "I just went there to sell her crack. That's why she called me. She didn't have no money, so she give me a drink, you know, and I said that won't enough, so she does what every freak does."

"You had sex."

"Yeah."

"Before or after you smoked the crack?"

Smith's eyes narrowed as it occurred to him that Brown had no intention of harming him. His wits regained, he spat to his left for a response and moved as if he were going to get up. "I don't use the shit. Never have."

Brown bent over and patted Smith's trouser pockets. "What's this?" he asked as he fingered a lump in the right front pocket. "Give it to me."

"Don't touch me, Brown. I ain't under arrest."

Brown suddenly looked at the gun in his hand, and then at the driblets of blood welling beside the beads of perspiration on Smith's forehead. Every morsel of legal education Brown had ever received was cascading through his mind and he had followed none of it. He felt a panic sweeping over him and while his brain was still churning he heard himself speak. "Yeah you are. For murder."

* * *

Gene Roberts listened quietly as Brown recited the sequence of events leading to Smith's arrest. He then picked up the telephone and dialed Ev Cross's intercom number. When he received no answer he dialed the office telephone number. Linda Masencup answered. "Tell Ev I need him," he informed her without preliminaries. After returning the receiver to its cradle he looked back at the lieutenant. "Tell me about the gun again."

"I pulled it as I was approaching him. I didn't know what he might try after running from me."

Roberts rubbed his temples. "Did he make any moves?"

"No. He was just sitting there. I pulled it without thinking. It was just automatic."

"And you read him his rights when?"

"After I pulled the cocaine out of his pocket."

"Did you ask permission?"

"No."

"Did you know it was drugs when you touched it?"

"Figured it was."

"And is that when he said he ain't got shit to say to you?"

"Yeah, the second time he said it."

Roberts nodded his head. "Okay Lewis. You realize things didn't go according to Hoyle?"

Brown crushed his cigarette in the crowded ashtray on his desk. "I know," he said quietly. "Is that retinal image stuff a problem?"

"That remains to be seen. Pretty imaginative, though. No other statements?"

"After I put him in the car. Said that he didn't do it and wanted a polygraph."

"Call the state police and try to set one up asap, before he changes his mind. He hasn't requested a lawyer?"

"Not yet."

"Get a warrant for the cocaine, too."

"Magistrate's on the way, Gene," answered Brown as he seated himself at his desk.

"I'll be back shortly," called Roberts over his shoulder as he walked out of the room. He took the stairs to the first floor of the courthouse two risers at a time, cursing himself every foot of the way for having sent Brown to handle Jeff Smith. *He was too inexperienced,* he said to himself repeatedly. *Too young and inexperienced.* He met Cross in the hall outside of the treasurer's office.

"What's up, Gene?" Ev greeted his investigator.

"We've arrested Smith for murder."

Ev eyed Roberts cautiously. He didn't like the tone of voice accompanying the news. "Is that good or bad?"

"Let's go to your office."

The two men walked wordlessly up the stairs to Ev's second floor office. Roberts closed the door behind them and then, in measured tones, related Brown's narrative.

When he had finished, Ev, who was seated behind his desk, leaned back in his chair. "What's bothering you? The way he got the statement or the lack of evidence?"

"Yeah," said Roberts dryly.

"You're thinking he seized him without probable cause and forced the statements without first reading him his rights."

"It was natural for Lewis to chase him. And I might have drawn my gun, too."

"You're seeing the glass half full, Gene."

"Probably."

"Brown lost it. Maybe the racial stuff was too much for him. But look at what we've got. The prints and the car to begin with. Smith reacts to that by running. The police can lie to a suspect, so the Negative Retinal Image business shouldn't hurt us, probably helps. Brown drew his gun on a fleeing murder suspect. That should be okay."

Roberts rubbed his chin. "I ain't got shit to say to you sounds like he invoked his rights. To me."

"Maybe. DNA will cover the sex part. His statement was self-serving anyway."

"Except it put him at the murder scene."

"Brown's right. He was minutes away from a confession."

"Yeah, but he didn't get one. Maybe I sounded too convinced that Smith was our man; Lewis just reacted to what I said. But we've got a ways to go before we have our case put together, and this might have foreclosed some opportunities."

Ev laughed quietly. "Negative Retinal Image Machine. That would be funny as hell if this weren't so serious."

Roberts almost smiled. "It would be worth a laugh if it had worked."

"We can't just unarrest him."

"No. We have too much on him for that."

"Surely we have enough to convince the magistrate."

Roberts managed a smile. "Now tell me what magistrate is going to deny probable cause when the victim is Senator Noble's daughter."

"I guess you're right. We're going to have to dig ourselves out of this one on our own."

"By the way, Brown is going to get a search warrant for the car."

"Good."

Both men sat for a moment, each running down mental checklists.

"There's one more twist," said Roberts. "If he raped her first, then we could charge capital murder."

"Damn. But we don't have any proof of rape."

"He admitted sex, so he's stuck with that as part of his story. And there's the anal tear. But I know what you're thinking. We need DNA first. I'll get a search warrant for his blood and get that started." Roberts pushed himself out of his chair. "I've got to go."

"What about the press?"

Roberts sighed loudly. "Hank heard the first part of Brown's report and left the room to start calling. He ignored me when I asked him to wait."

"Then one of us better call the Nobles, both sets."

"I'll do that," said Roberts. "I'll fend them off with something about giving them a full report when we have time. Anyway, the press will start in on you any minute now." Roberts made his way to the door and opened it part way. "This is a helluva way to begin this horse race." He shook his head and walked down the hallway to the anteroom occupied by Linda Masencup.

Ev remained seated and gently drummed his fingers on his desk. Roberts's pessimism was contagious. The possibilities for disaster were endless. Smith's statement might be suppressed. The charge might be dismissed at preliminary hearing. If he made it so far, a jury could very well acquit. And every step of the way would be dissected by the press, the Nobles, Hampton Coleman—another endless list. Suddenly Ev felt nausea welling in his stomach.

# CHAPTER 11

Friday, September 18th

There were no calls from the press on Thursday, if the ringing which went unanswered at the Cross home that evening was not included. But Friday was different. The sheriff had unduly complicated matters by stating that a sexual assault might have occurred and that other charges were being considered. As instructed, Linda Masencup held off the incoming calls, but Cross knew that he could not hide behind his stalwart for long. Uncomfortable with how he must ultimately handle the reporters' requests, he decided to have one more conversation with Gene Roberts. He found Roberts alone at his basement desk.

"Well Ev, funny you should walk in," grunted Roberts.

"What now?" asked Ev, a sinking feeling intensifying his discomfort.

"The lab called me with the DNA analysis. Care to guess how many?"

"Just tell me."

"Three."

"Oh shit."

"Yeah. Oh shit."

Ev dropped heavily into Lewis Brown's chair. "That's three different men's semen?"

"Yep."

"How many days can that cover?"

"Up to three. But more than likely, about thirty-six hours. I'm not sure. Doesn't make a helluva lot of difference at this point."

Ev leaned back in the creaking chair and stared at the ceiling. "At this point," he repeated quietly.

"The results were all vaginal."

"So we still don't know anything about the injury?"

"DeWease can't say, so we have nothing. You know, those Marlboro Light butts we found at the pool don't make sense. We have questioned everyone, and nobody knows how they got there. They're like the Budweiser can in the yard."

"They're like those other goddam prints. They're like the squad of sperm donors."

"We need Thomasson's blood, that should eliminate one DNA source."

"Great."

"Look. Someone else was there. Who and when and what he did is the question. I've been through the file twice this morning looking for something that will point the way."

"I'll call Farnsworth on Jason's blood. I've been meaning to do it. Needing it for elimination purposes puts a whole new light on it."

"Good, because I was gonna suggest a search warrant." Roberts paused. "Well, there is one bit of good news."

"What? You actually have something good."

"The search of Smith's car. We got his little black book with the Nobles' telephone number in it."

"That's something," sighed Ev. "What do I tell the press?"

"Name, rank, and serial number."

"I wasn't in the army. Damn, damn, damn."

"One more thing. Smith invoked his right to an attorney a little later, after we talked. He made a call and then told us to forget about the polygraph."

"Then I guess he didn't tell you anything more yesterday."

"Nope."

"If Jason found her with crack, doesn't it make sense that Smith was there first?"

"If you figure she had no money, or extra coke lying around. But then there's the homemade pipe. That could have been made after Jason threw away her pipe and left...made later, when Smith showed up around nine. That explains the homemade job, and why the retinal image stuff scared him."

"Where did you find the homemade pipe?"

"In the trash. Mixed in with the stuff on top."

"That doesn't mean it was used that night."

"You're right."

"Besides the Lopez woman, how do we fix the time he was there?"

"I've got to talk to McIntosh about that."

Ev arose and stuffed his hands into his trouser pockets. "Like our potential witnesses against Smith won't remember Alphonso Thornton's fate. This is getting worse. We've got to have something else, either to clear him or hang him. And in a hurry. I presume he's being held without bail."

"Yes on all counts. I'll keep you posted."

"All counts? What the hell?"

"Murder and cocaine, Ev," answered Roberts with a smile. "That's all."

"Look Gene. We need a break. Like trout fishing."

"Pick the time."

* * *

Ev walked straight to his office and reached for the telephone. To his surprise, after wading through a receptionist and a secretary, Oliver Farnsworth was available to take his call.

"Oliver, Ev Cross here."

"Ev. How's the investigation? Cleared my man, yet?"

"We charged someone yesterday."

"And not Jason I presume."

"Not Jason. Anyway, my question is easy. Will you allow him to give us a blood sample? We need him for elimination purposes."

There was a brief pause. "I'll talk to my client and let you know."

*Which client,* thought Ev. *Clyde Noble?* "I need to know pretty quickly."

"I'll let you know promptly."

"Thank you." Cross rang off without any of the usual lawyer small talk. He walked back into the anteroom. "How many more?" he asked Linda.

"You're up to eight."

"Anybody else?"

"Someone from a lawyer named Isaiah Christmas. She said he's representing Jeff Smith. There're a few more that can wait."

Cross knew the name, although he did not know the man. Christmas practiced in Norfolk and had a knack for landing high profile cases which, win or lose, he always managed to leverage into maximum exposure for himself. He had a reputation for being able to guide the media around by the nose. He also had a reputation for being able to find, and exploit—at least in the press—a racial issue in every case.

"That's all the hell I need," mumbled Ev.

Linda Masencup looked at her boss questioningly and decided that she had better not say anything else.

At his desk Cross flipped through the pile of pink telephone messages before settling on the one with Christmas's name and number. *How is Smith affording Christmas?* he asked himself. *Or is this case too big for money to matter?* He flipped the piece of paper onto his desk and looked toward the window on the opposite side of the room. *No use putting these off,* he tried to convince himself. The telephone rang and he watched the face of the machine until the incoming line began to blink. "Damn it," he mouthed.

"Number nine. Arch Word, a reporter," said his secretary over the intercom. "Do you want to take it?"

Cross picked up the receiver without replying to Masencup's question. "Hello."

"Yes. This is Arch Word of the Post. I'm calling about the Miranda Noble case. Is this Mr. Cross?"

Cross briefly considered asking which Post, but thought better of it. "This is he."

"And what is your position?"

"Commonwealth's Attorney."

"Deputy, assistant?"

"Commonwealth's Attorney. I don't have any assistants."

"Oh good. Now your full name is Evers Cross?"

"Evander. Cross."

"As in the boxer's name."

"Yes." There was no use telling him the pronunciation was different.

"No middle name or initial?"

"No."

"Mr. Cross. We're following up on the charges placed against a Jeff Smith the third. We have that he's an African-American male, age twenty-eight. Is that correct?"

*The first question,* fumed Ev, *is race.* Moreover, he did not yet have copies of the warrants, and had no idea how old Smith was. "That's correct, except I don't have his age."

"How was the young woman killed?"

Ev opened his mouth to respond and then stopped himself. There were ethics rules which limited what he could say publicly about a pending criminal charge, rules which he had never had any cause to study carefully. With a foggy notion of what he could and could not say guiding him, he decided to tell Arch Word nothing. "I can't comment on the evidence."

"You won't be telling me anything new, I just needed to confirm our information. The reports indicate that the victim was asphyxiated."

"That seems to be the case."

"Is there some doubt?"

Ev gritted his teeth. He knew he could not win this battle of semantics. "I can't comment on the evidence."

Word fell silent for a moment. "Are you uncomfortable with the strength of your case against Smith?"

"Not...well...I can't comment on that." Instantly, Ev could imagine how that would appear in print. *The lone county prosecutor declined to comment on the strength of the charges lodged against the suspect.*

"I understand. Did Smith make an incriminating statement?"

"Mr. Word, I can't talk about that."

"About the incriminating statement?"

Ev propped his right arm on the desk and dropped his head into his hand. "I'm not permitted to discuss whether he made a statement."

The questions and the non-answers continued for several more minutes, turning from the facts in the case to when the first hearing would be held, which Ev did not know, to whether Smith had an attorney, which Ev acknowledged. The interview ended with Ev feeling like he had been a criminal defendant cross-examined on the witness stand.

Ev thought about the remaining eight reporters and considered whether he could simply ignore them. The notion was tempting, but he knew that the press, particularly the big organizations, could take a dislike to him that would spill into their coverage.

The possibility of a press conference to handle them all at once crossed his mind and was quickly jettisoned  since he would do nothing but stand in front of them and repeat 'no comment,' sounding more like an indicted Mafia don than a prosecutor.

His thoughts fumbled around for a few more minutes before he conceded to himself that he was better off just getting it over. By the third call he was prepared for the trick questions and had polished a brief disclaimer to explain the ethical considerations which limited his answers. After almost two hours he was finished. One call remained, and he had no script for how he would handle Isaiah Christmas.

Linda Masencup walked in while he delayed making the call. "Do you want me to get you a Coke and some nabs? Looks like lunch is out."

"No. No thank you," he answered without looking up. "I'll go to lunch later. He waited for her to leave the room before lifting the receiver and then listened to the dial tone for a moment before chastising himself for his hesitancy. Quickly he pressed the numbers on the dial pad and waited for an answer.

Finally, in a woman's voice: "Peoples Legal Rights Clinic. We serve the interest of justice. How may I direct your call?"

Cross marveled that a law office would answer the telephone in such a fashion. "Isaiah Christmas," he responded.

"I'll transfer you to Mr. Christmas's secretary," said the voice.

After a brief pause, another woman's voice: "Mr. Christmas's office."

"This is Evander Cross returning Mr. Christmas's call."

"Just a moment."

Another delay, then: "This is Monica DelGarde. How may I help you?"

"I'm trying to reach Mr. Christmas," said Cross, exasperation edging his words.

"And who is calling?"

"Evander Cross."

"And who is our client?"

"Jeff Smith."

"Just a moment."

Ev pulled the receiver away from his ear and glared at it as if the delay were its doing. "What the hell is this?" he said to no one.

"I'm sorry Mr. Cross, Mr. Christmas is in court."

Ev, having used the ruse himself, suspected otherwise.

"I am Mr. Christmas's executive assistant. We are in the process of being retained by Mr. Smith."

This, thought Ev, meant that the fee had yet to be received.

"Mr. Christmas was calling to advise you of this and to tell you that no one should approach his client without first contacting him. Also, we would like a copy of Mr. Smith's statements and the police report."

That someone's supernumerary was discussing a murder case with him after ten minutes of waiting left Ev seething. "Please put your requests in a letter as soon as you are retained," he replied.

"I should say that we are, in fact, going to represent Mr. Smith."

"In a letter, please."

"Should I tell Mr. Christmas you'll be responding?"

"It has always been my practice to respond to correspondence."

"Can we set the preliminary hearing now?"

"You'll need to do that through the clerk's office."

"We'll fax you the letter today. May I have your name, address, fax and telephone numbers?" Ev recited the information in a weary monotone. "Thank you Mr. Cross. Have a good day."

Ev rehung the receiver and then leaned back in his chair. He felt washed out, like he had been awake all night.

* * *

There had been no rain for almost a month and the fields surrounding the Cross home were a lifeless brown, the forests, save for hints of red and dirty yellow dappling, now a dull sullen green. The sun was a hot yellow in the western sky, yielding a dry heat strangely incongruent with the long shadows of the season.

Polly Cross was at the sink when Ev walked into the kitchen. "I don't need to ask do I?" she said without looking up.

"No."

"Linda told me about your calls."

"That's not the half of it."

Polly turned from the sink and looked at Ev. "What else?"

"The first DNA results are in."

"And?"

"Three men." He dropped heavily into one of the kitchen table chairs. "One must be Jason Thomasson, one must be Smith, and God knows who the other one is."

"You can't tell?"

"We have to have something to compare the results to. Blood for example, to type the DNA."

"What about Smith's lawyer?"

"He's some rabble rouser from Norfolk."

Polly walked to the back door and peered through the screen. "Did you see the boys when you came in? Sam got sick this morning and I had to pick him up from school. But he's recovered now, of course."

"No."

Polly did not move. "I hear a car coming up the drive." The car rounded the corner of the house and stopped. "It's your mother," said Polly tersely as she walked back to the sink.

Ev arose and walked to the door. "Hello mother."

"Ev. I didn't know whether anyone was home. I called several times this afternoon and no one answered."

Ev shot a glance at Polly who kept her eyes trained on her work. "You see what happens when I don't answer it," she retorted quietly.

He swung the door open. "We haven't been answering. Reporters have been calling about the Noble case."

"Well that's all right. I was a little concerned." She walked in carrying a manila envelope in her hand, which Ev eyed with a caution usually reserved for spiders. "I needed to talk something over with you." She glanced toward Polly before continuing. "Hi Polly. Where can we sit down?"

"Hello Mrs. Cross. Why don't you go into the living...room."

Ev followed his mother through the dining room. The envelope could only mean something unpleasant. The last such appearance had resulted in Margaret selling his father's fishing camp, a rough old cabin and almost a mile of mountain stream which to Ev was like selling one's soul. "It's too much trouble," Margaret had complained, although Ev had looked after it for two decades, and "it's just a financial drain," despite Ev's offering to pay the insignificant taxes and the minimal electric bill. The crux was that Margaret had never liked the rustic lodge, as Lodge was the moniker that Ev had devised for the place. Stretches of land along trout water came very dearly now, and Ev doubted that he could ever afford to replace it. Ev's Uncle E rescued the Lodge after which Margaret and her sister went to Europe for three weeks.

Margaret sat down on the living-den sofa and placed the envelope on her lap. She did not wait for Ev to join her. "Did Amanda talk to you about what had to be done with the house?"

*This is it,* thought Ev as he gingerly lowered himself to the edge of an armchair. "She hasn't called me."

"Well, I went to see someone about how much it was worth. You know it's just getting to be too much for me and I don't need all that space. And heating. It's just astronomical. Anyway, they said three hundred-fifty thousand. Can you believe that? I had them draw up a listing contract and I wanted you to look it over for me. They said fall was a good time to sell a place like mine." She began unfolding the clip that bound the envelope's flap closed.

Ev could feel himself wilting. *I can't deal with this now.*

"Do you have time?"

* * *

105

Polly paced the kitchen trying to decide whether she should join the conference in the other room. There was no doubt in her mind as to the purpose for the visit, and she did not for one moment consider that Margaret had come merely to discuss selling. Her mother-in-law did not operate that way. She would drop a few hints and then she would drop the bomb. Ev had said that he wanted Margaret to make the first move and now he had got his wish. Polly could not decide who irritated her more, Margaret for being oblivious to their interest in the house or Ev for pretending that the problem would simply go away.

She deliberated again what she could add to the discussion that would be remotely civil, and worried that if she did not intercede Ev would simply accept his mother's fiat and the house would be gone. She dropped the lettuce she was washing and reached for a dish towel.

"Mommy," came Sam's voice from outside. "Will's hurt." Will's vague wailing was now audible as he neared the spot where Sam was standing.

"Oh shit, not now," muttered Polly. "What is it, Will?" she called through the screen door in a practiced voice of concern.

"Sam hitted me with a rock."

"Did not," said Sam quickly. "It was a dirt clob."

Will rubbed a dusty clay-red splotch on his shirt. "Was too."

*Not now,* Polly repeated to herself. "Let me see," she said soothingly. She lifted his shirt and examined the red mark that would soon be a bruise. "You're okay. Sam. No more throwing anything at your brother." She turned to walk back inside. "You all go play."

"I'm hungry," said Sam.

"I'll call you when it's time to eat. Now go play."

Sam ignored the instruction. Polly opened her mouth to repeat the directive, but only a quiet sigh escaped her. *It's no use.* She walked to the door and let the two boys in. Margaret and Ev were in the kitchen by the time Polly entered.

"Hello boys," Margaret greeted her grandsons. Polly found the sweetness disgusting, having long ago decided that Margaret was the master of insincerity. "I'll wait for you to call, Ev." continued Margaret. "Goodbye."

"Go into the TV room while I make your lunch boys," said Polly. Will and Sam reluctantly obeyed. "Well?" she asked Ev.

"She wants to list the house for sale."

"I assumed that. What did you say?"

"What could I say?"

"Something along the lines that we want the house," Polly answered emphatically, her eyes firmly fixed Ev.

Ev sat down heavily in a kitchen chair. "She's been told to list it at three hundred-fifty thousand."

"What!"

"That's probably about right."

Polly turned abruptly and looked through the kitchen window.

Ev continued. "I asked her to wait, to give me time to see whether I could come up with the money. And to give me a figure she would take since there'd be no realtor commission if I bought it. Of course she'll call Amanda to decide that." After a pause, "this is not something I'm ready to deal right now."

"I should have started teaching this year."

"We can't do it all."

Polly turned around and crossed her arms. "Do it all? That's your family home. That's where you want to live. She can't up and sell it like it was a…a used car."

"I've got to have time to find a way, Polly. I wasn't prepared for this."

Polly crossed the kitchen and stood at the door to the dining room. "She's been dropping hints for months. You knew this was coming."

"Alright Polly. I knew. I'll deal with it."

"Three hundred-fifty thousand. What does she think she has? Tara?"

"Just look at the paper, Polly. Land in this county has sky-rocketed."

"But forty acres?"

"It's the house. Red brick, old, and a view of the mountains. The sky's the limit."

"So in another couple of years it will be a half million."

"I know. I just need some time."

Polly put the sandwich on a plate and left the room. Ev ate quickly, and deciding that Polly was in no mood to hear his voice, he said goodbye to the boys and walked to the Bronco. *This rattletrap won't be replaced anytime soon.* He could not focus his thoughts as he negotiated the cove road to the main highway. First Smith's arrest, then his mother's house, and now Polly's fury—each competed for his attention.

His Uncle Evander, known as E, had rescued the Lodge several years before, but Ev could not bring himself to ask the man to intervene again. For the elder Evander Cross, childless and long a widower, Ev had been a surrogate son. Many hours they had spent hunting and fishing, working cattle, or with Ev simply sitting in his uncle's study, absorbing stories from the old days and about his uncle's trials and the often humorous face of the human condition. For Ev to become a lawyer seemed a natural progression, even if it took some time for him to realize it.

Practicing alone was the biggest drawback to Ev's work. He had no one with whom to shadow box cases; he had no one to second guess strategies and offer suggestions. Most men refuse to confess errors or admit indecisiveness. They go their adult lives bumbling from decision to decision, knowing that other men are in the same boat, and all of them pretending just the opposite. Ev was no different, except with his uncle. The older man knew the legal business, he knew prosecution, and he knew politics. There would never be a conversation where Ev laid his soul bare. That could not happen, except with Polly every once in a blue moon, but he could outline the problem with his uncle and the latter would fill in the details, and questions, on his own.

Even E could be of little help with this one, or ones. The framed admonition in E's study came to mind. Duty Is the Sublimest Word in the English Language. The name R. E. Lee appeared below. Ev's thoughts returned to the office and what he would face when he got there, and the knot in his stomach twisted tighter.

* * *

Polly was refereeing the boys' dinner when Ev trudged into the kitchen for a Jack Daniels refill. "I'm going to see my mother about a lower price."

There was a pause which Polly concluded called for a response. "Okay," she replied, keeping her attention on the two boys.

"I think we should offer her three hundred thousand."

Polly thought the sum would never fly, but tonight was not the time to debate the point. "Whatever you think we should do."

"What do you think?" he asked tersely.

Polly recognized the tone of voice, the one that was inviting an argument. She wanted the Cross home, but loathed the idea of handing that much money to Margaret Cross since she had no doubt most of it would find its way to Amanda and Amanda's children. Moreover, Polly was certain that Margaret would consider any reduction in price a gift, and remind Polly of it until one of them died. On the bright side, Margaret would probably move to South Carolina and her calls were bound to all but cease given that she would have to pay long distance tolls. Concluding that Ev was not going to leave the matter be, she gave her opinion. "I don't think she'll take that."

"Probably not, but it's a starting point. We can manage more if that's what it takes."

"When does this undertaking start?"

"I don't know. Soon When I can be civil. It will take her a while to settle on a price."

*Yeah, Amanda can be pretty slow making up her mind.*

"But I'm not going to commit to this until this Noble mess is straightened out."

"Ev, why are you worried? Nothing is going to happen to you."

"I don't need that house to worry about right now. I don't need to be contending with banks right now."

108

"We'll make it work Ev. I can go back to teaching. I don't have to wait till Will's in school."

"Great. Plan B is to simply start over."

"Ev," she tried again. "Everything is going to be fine. Quit second guessing yourself."

"I'm not. This is a big case and we're stumbling. And a fall comes easy in a big case." He turned on his heel and walked into the dining room. He paused just past the threshold. "We buy that house and private school for the boys is out. And I've got to replace the Bronco. I didn't intend for us to live like this." He then continued back to the living-den.

*Me either,* thought Polly. Just today she had read her alumnae bulletin, a mistake she had vowed once before not to repeat. But she had, drawn to her class notes to read about the friend who was now a vice-president—a real vice president —at Wachovia Bank, and the classmate who had just returned from three years in Paris to manage the east coast's main office for some kind of advertising firm. For a crowning blow her roommate and her roommate's husband had sold their dot-com and retired. Age thirty-seven. Retired.

She walked to the refrigerator to retrieve another gallon of milk. The dead sole interior light was salt in the wound. *We don't even have a functioning refrigerator.* Her former classmates were somewhere counting their money and she was hoping for a refrigerator. It was enough to make her want to take up cigarettes again.

A half hour passed before Ev reappeared. He started talking as if he had never left the room. "Why do you think she won't take three hundred?"

"I just know her Ev." She regretted having been honest with him.

"Well maybe I ought to say that's it, final offer."

"You can't do that. You'll have to play her game."

"I'm in too many games right now."

Polly poured a glass of wine and walked to Ev's side. "We'll make it work. Go see her and get it behind you." She put her arm around him and squeezed gently.

# CHAPTER 12

Monday, September 21st, a.m.

"Did you see the news Friday night?" asked Linda Masencup when Cross walked into his office on Monday.

"I missed the first run. Glenn Apperson called and told me about it, so I watched the eleven o'clock version." Apperson was Ev's childhood friend.

Linda watched Cross carefully. "I was right angry that Anita Smith said this charge was a racial thing. Do you think somebody put it in her head?"

"I wondered the same thing. At least I wondered if Isaiah Christmas put it in her head to mention it to a reporter. Part of the interview was on the news channel, too…you know, a five second blip with the words 'racially motivated' in it. And just listening to her, I doubt she's ever used the word motivated before. Maybe they should interview Lewis Brown. But he's a cop. Black cops are just white people masquerading as black."

Linda shook her head in agreement. "Your files for this morning's sentencing are on your desk."

"Thanks," Ev mumbled as he walked to his office. He again wondered how Jeff Smith could afford Christmas. No two-bit drug dealer could afford to hire a lawyer; they always waited for court appointed counsel, so maybe Smith was really in the big leagues. Or perhaps Christmas took the case because he glimpsed free advertisement; Clyde Noble was involved, and national press, free national press, anyway, usually only attended notoriety. Any publicity, even bad publicity, was good advertisement for a lawyer. The telephone rang, interrupting his musing, and he listened as Linda answered, assuming the call concerned Smith. Bits of small talk were discernable, and Ev sighed audibly in relief that the call was not about the murder. He opened the first file in the stack and began reading the pre-sentence report on the man who had forced himself on little Quanisha Graddy.

Linda Masencup walked in before he was finished. "I forgot. Did you read what the sheriff said?"

Ev looked up swiftly "No. What paper?"

"The Charlottesville paper. That was my sister calling about it, which is what reminded me. He was interviewed about the race thing and Hank said race was being floated as a defense since the murder would probably end up a death penalty case."

"Oh, for Christ's ….goddam it. The fool."

Linda nodded approvingly. "I thought you'd need to know that," she added quietly as she walked toward the door.

"That's it," growled Ev under his breath. "This is going to stop."

The telephone rang and this time Linda buzzed Ev's intercom. "Ev, it's Isaiah Christmas."

Ev stared at the blinking light on his telephone for a moment, his thoughts jumbling Hank Burke and Isaiah Christmas. Finally, he lifted the receiver. "Hello."

"Mr. Cross, Isaiah Christmas, I represent Jeff Smith." There was a melody to his deep delivery. "I talked to my client yesterday and, of course, this prediction by the sheriff of capital charges was the main topic."

*That and what else?* thought Ev in the momentary pause while he seined for a response. He realized that he had not decided how to handle Christmas, whether openly as he would the Bledsoes and Dicksons, or cautiously, as he would a reporter. "I've made no decision on capital charges." He managed, thereby electing the latter approach.

"What would it be based on, rape before the killing?"

"At this point, I need to review that with the sheriff and investigator." Cross seethed in the knowledge that Burke's babbling put him in the posture of appearing to have no grasp on a major case.

Christmas paused too, while he attempted to analyze his new opponent. "I haven't been in your county, so my first question is your file policy."

"I have an open file, except for my own notes."

"From what Jeff told me, I think you've got problems with his statement to your officer—"

"Brown."

"Yeah. Brown." The melodious ripple had disappeared from Christmas' voice. "I'll move to suppress that. You know, at gunpoint, and that lie about the retinal machine or whatever your officer called it. Also I told him flat out to forget the polygraph. I take it you got physical evidence, semen and so forth?"

"We do."

"On Jeff, DNA?"

"We just got his blood last week."

"Well, my assistant will be scheduling a hearing. But would you let me know what you decide about the capital charge? There appears to be a lot going on with the case."

"I'll do that." Ev wondered if Christmas's last remark suggested the racial twist.

"He's pleading innocent."

"No surprise there."

"Your jail is something else." Christmas' voice lightened as he mentioned the seventy year old two story jail designed to house twelve prisoners.

"Low security," answered Ev glibly.

"I'll say. The female guard just let Jeff walk into that main room where the entrance is. He coulda knocked us both over and bolted through the doors."

"It's one of the pleasures of rural practice." Ev felt his tension easing as the call turned from the murder. In the lawyerly camaraderie, Ev put the question that had been on the tip of his tongue. "How'd a Norfolk lawyer end up with a Lafayette case?"

Christmas laughed in response. "Jeff's uncle was a client of mine. He called and, well, it sounded like a good one."

*Maybe the uncle has the money.* "Plenty of free press, too."

"Oh yeah, never hurts. Well, I've got court. Goodbye." He rang off without awaiting a response.

Cross slowly laid the receiver in its cradle as he pondered how little Christmas had asked about the case. For a usually loquacious defense lawyer to nibble at the edges in the early going meant one of two things: that he had a potent defense or that his client was dead in the water.

The telephone rang before Ev could leave for the sentencing hearings. He walked down his office's hallway and waited at the door until Linda waved him away. She mouthed the word "reporter" as she wrote down the caller's name and telephone number.

Ev found Roberts, in uniform, sitting in the bailiff's customary chair as he entered the courtroom. The other players—judge, clerk and defense lawyers—had not arrived. A few blank faces peopled the gallery.

Roberts cracked an almost wicked smile as Cross approached him.

"Why are you here Gene? Nothing better to do?" Ev was always amazed, and annoyed, that Hank Burke would ever use his best cop to babysit the courtroom.

"I guess you haven't heard?"

"What?"

"Alfred Sawyer, goes by Mickey, died Friday."

"Oh, a funeral," groused Ev.

Roberts shook his head. "More than that, an honor guard. Sawyer's granddaughter asked the sheriff for six uniformed pallbearers. So two shifts worth of deputies are there."

"The sheriff actually agreed?"

"He was more than happy to oblige, over my objection of course. Please a couple of living voters and one dead one."

"That's the damnedest thing…well, another damnedest thing." Cross sat down heavily in the chair beside Roberts. "We've got to talk to that bastard today. What the hell is he doing giving interviews about a capital charge we haven't even placed? What the hell is wrong with him?"

"I guess I should have called you about that."

"When did you find out?"

"When I read the paper this morning."

Ev sighed, staring aimlessly across the room toward the massive windows and dark oil portraits interrupting the stark white of the opposite wall. "When's the funeral?" he asked after a minute's silence.

"At ten."

"Okay, after these hearings, we go to him. He should be back by then. I'm gonna put it on the line. He quits ad-libbing about my cases or else I will unload on him at the election. I don't have any pull, but he probably doesn't know that."

"Just stick with politics, that's all it will take to get his attention."

Jim Crawford entered the room in the quiet that followed. Ev moved to his customary counsel table and informed the judge that the first case would that of Quanisha's abuser. Following a few minutes testimony from the probation officer and a tearful incoherent statement from the mother still more loyal to her man than to her daughter, Crawford sent the defendant to the penitentiary for five years.

* * *

Hank Burke, slouching in his swivel chair with his feet propped on his desk, was talking to Okra Alexander when Roberts and Cross entered the tiny room used by the sheriff as an office and having space only for his desk and two chairs.

"I'd offer you a seat boys," smiled Burke.

Roberts reached outside the door and pulled in a battered ladder-back chair. "This will do. Okra, could you give us a moment?"

Okra raised his chin in acknowledgement and ambled out of the room.

Burke's eyes narrowed almost imperceptibly. "Sit down Ev."

Ev took the proffered chair and leveled his eyes on the sheriff while trying to keep from his own face the anger he was suppressing. Throughout the sentencing he had been turning over in his mind how he could broach this subject with the sheriff without arousing the other man's ire even before the heart of the matter was reached. He could not settle on the precise language he would use, and now he opened his mouth hoping that the words would simply come.

"Sheriff, we've got a real media and political hot potato."

"You're right about that," answered Burke quickly.

"That's what I need to talk to you about. If this goes south, you and I could be retiring next fall."

Burke grimaced at hearing what he had been thinking about for weeks. He lowered his feet to the floor and straightened in his seat.

"Now let's face it. If Gene and I, and Brown, can put this together, you get most of the credit. You end up looking good. If we flub it, you're tagged. Now what

I want to tell you is this. This is a serious damn call, but the man has been charged, so it's mine now. Everything that gets out, if it's wrong, gets repeated in every newscast until trial. I'm going to put this straight, all cards up. If I lose this case because the sheriff's department screws it up, I'm going to have to say so. I can't go down the tubes for somebody else."

Burke nodded his head slowly as he cast a dark glance toward his investigator. Roberts knew that the sheriff was already deciding whom to blame for this little tutorial, but he was past the point and the age of worrying about it.

Burke drew a breath. "I probably jumped the gun on talking about a death penalty charge." His voice was even, confessional rather than apologetic.

"Hank," continued Ev, "it's more than that. First you called it an accident, then you started talking about people being cleared, like Jason Thomasson, then the capital charge interview. How does that make us look, from an accident to a capital case? I can tell you what Rita Noble would say, half-witted inbred redneck buffoonery." Ev paused, pleased with his description, to let it sink in.

Roberts eased his chair back onto two legs and toyed with an unlit cigarette as he carefully watched Burke. He found himself taking a twisted pleasure in the exchange.

"But maybe the most important thing is what happened with Lewis Brown," continued Ev.

Burke pursed his lips tightly. Cross was warming to the subject.

"We weren't ready Hank. We've got three sources of semen with this woman, and haven't identified a one. Fingerprints everywhere. We're still pinning down that Thomasson was there before Smith. We had work to do. You know how hard it is to get information after a charge is placed."

"You're telling me you've got problems with this charge?" Burke leaned forward in his chair. "You're not sure Smith's the right one? I mean, he all but confessed when Lewis came up with that bit about the eye machine."

"Sheriff," Roberts quietly interrupted, "you didn't let me keep you fully informed. We do believe Smith's the one, but we're not sure we can prove it. Maybe Lewis felt a little pressure from you. I know what your pressure means, Brown apparently doesn't."

Burke exhaled audibly, his eyes darting from Roberts to Cross as a gray pallor clouded his face. Knowing that he had set the hook Ev pushed quickly forward. "Obviously I don't want any bad blood at the next election. You let us handle the case and I'm not going to be a problem for you. In fact, I don't think anything we do will do anything but help you. Just work the public. Leave the rest to us."

Burke leaned back heavily. "What do you want, have Gene handle the interviews?" he asked, resignation clear in his voice.

Ev glanced at Roberts. "No," answered Roberts, "let's just coordinate. My thought is that we never comment on charges that aren't filed, not without clearing it with Ev."

"I'm okay with that," said Burke. After a pause, "I sure am worried about what y'all think of the case. And what's this stuff about race?"

Ev, fresh from having brought the sheriff to heal, simmered anew at the notion that Burke was just now asking about the racial allegations after having given an interview about them the day before. "Look Hank, we don't know. And for now, all we can say for public consumption is that nothing has been provided to law enforcement that suggests any involvement of race in this case."

"That sounds good to me," said Roberts. He lit his cigarette and arose from the chair. "We've got work to do."

Outside the sheriff's office Roberts motioned Ev to follow him to the rear steps. "Just so you can say you kept your promise to Noble, I called the state police, actually I called R. C. Hawkes. He's damn good and has helped me before. He's due here later today for a briefing so that we can divide some of the work."

"You didn't take my promise personally did you?"

Roberts smiled wearily. "I'm no neophyte. I know the games we've got to play."

"Did you think we got to the sheriff?"

"I'd say so. At least for awhile."

Ev started up the steps to the first floor hallway. "I just hope we weren't too late."

"I'm going to see the Nobles. Rita set today for our meeting."

"I'm sorry."

"Don't worry," grunted Roberts, "you're next, fellow buffoon. That's a good word. Buffoonery. Bet the sheriff doesn't have the slightest notion what it means."

# CHAPTER 13

Monday, September 21$^{st}$, p.m.

Hector Lopez was repairing a board fence in one of the fields along the drive to Noble View. The window was down in Roberts's Crown Victoria, letting in the warm September air, as he slowed to a stop in the road leading to the house. The way was lined with Bradford Pear trees, their leaves already hinting at their autumnal purplish red. He looked into his rearview mirror contemplating how much Mrs. Lopez could have seen of the silver car she said had turned into this road the night of the murder. Then his thoughts turned to the meeting awaiting him.

The Nobles made him uncomfortable. Their blustery arrogance and impatience were not the reason, for Roberts had long ago learned that people of some wealth or some importance, or both, especially new wealth or new importance, were fully capable of such behavior. As far as he had been able to discern he was in the same league with filling station attendants and waitresses, a factotum who was expected to do what was necessary…quietly, quickly, and efficiently. There was something else about the Nobles. On Rita's part, she unabashedly disliked the family's public connection with the crime, and Clyde Noble was cold, not in the sense that he was indifferent, but as if his every move were somehow calculated.

Accelerating slowly he eased along the drive until he reached the wide circle in front of the house. Roberts, eyeing carefully the configuration of the road, wondered where Smith and Jason Thomasson had parked. The east and west portions of the circle were open leaving unobstructed the view of the home on one end and the Blue Ridge Mountains on the other. On the north and south sides of the circle copses of white pines and reddening dogwoods offered ample opportunity for concealing an automobile. Roberts turned to the right as he entered the loop.

At the house on its south end was a more narrow drive leaving the circle which appeared intended for a service entrance. As he passed this road he saw a small car parked at the end which he assumed belonged to Clara Wood. The Nobles' Mercedes and Suburban were parked in front. He passed them and parked just beyond, on the north end of the house where the Budweiser can had been found. The pool's privacy fence, barely visible from the spot, lay some one hundred fifty feet from the circle, north and to the rear of the dwelling.

Rita Noble opened the front door while Roberts was still ascending the portico steps. "Come in Gene," she greeted him crisply.

It was the first time Roberts could recall her having addressed him by name, any name. While responding he noticed that her smooth blonde hair was shorter—a Dutchboy cut—which failed to make her look as young as she must have intended. She was thin to a fault, like a bulimic model, and her cheeks vaguely suggested a hollowness which emphasized the little wrinkles inexorably gaining ground under her eyes. Roberts had no doubt but that she punished herself daily with fasting and an exercise regimen in perpetual preparation for the office of United States Senator's wife.

Rita forced a frosty smile as she guided him into the living room, a smile that did nothing to soften her features, leaving Roberts curious whether her face were capable of being genuinely pleasant. She directed Gene to a chair and left the room. In a moment she returned with Clyde Noble.

Noble's polo shirt was ill-suited to hiding his paunch, and together with his slight shoulders and thinning hair, he looked more like a tire store service manager than the usual photogenic candidate for senator. Noble, after shaking hands, seated himself on the sofa opposite Roberts. Rita, though standing beside the sofa, moved to another armchair. They were situated so that Roberts could not observe both at the same time and he automatically wondered whether that was their intention.

Rita sat with her legs crossed, the crossing leg swaying in abrupt motions, and watched her husband intently as Noble and Roberts talked about college football. Noble's casual conversation was not what Roberts had expected given his last few conversations with him; he wondered what to expect now.

Noble abruptly stopped the small talk. "Well you can imagine the questions the reporters are asking, a capital charge, racial overtones. That a young woman is dead is starting to sound like a detail in the way of the real story." An edge was coming in to Noble's voice and all the insignificance of his physical presence was suddenly eclipsed. "I've tried to keep out of your way," Noble cast a swift glance at Rita, "but I feel like we're the last to find out anything."

Roberts simmered. He had called the Nobles the day of the arrest to find that the Senator was in New York, and Rita had set Monday afternoon for their meeting. More irritating though was that Roberts had had no control over the utterings of either Anita Smith or Hank Burke.

Noble continued. "I don't understand how there could be a question about the charge when Miranda was murdered almost a month ago to the day. Sounds to me like somebody jumped the gun on this. I mean, did you all get Ev Cross's approval on charging this Smith man?"

Roberts's thoughts were racing ahead of Noble's accurate assessment. His natural reaction was to defend himself, and the blameless Cross, too; but that would mean laying the blame on his protégé Lewis Brown and on his boss the sheriff. In Roberts's analysis of unprofessional conduct, disloyalty was barely second to incompetence. But Clyde Noble was no simpleton and a smear of eyewash would serve only to magnify his doubts.

"Ev was informed Senator. Unfortunately, we can't always control events. Smith ran when Lewis Brown tried to talk to him, right after Lewis told him about a few pieces of our evidence. I don't think Lewis had any choice but to seize him then."

"Why wasn't someone with more experience put on this?" asked Rita.

"He and I were working it together. R. C. Hawkes of the state police is assigned as well."

"That's good to hear," said Noble. "What's going on with the race motivation accusation?"

*I bet this is the heart of it. The only time he wants to think about race is when he's addressing the NAACP.* Roberts replied, "We don't have any idea why Anita Smith brought it up, except that it's not unusual when the defendant is black and the victim is white."

"That's it?" asked Rita, her tone dripping incredulity.

"That's all we have now. We have to wait for his attorney to flesh it out, if he's got something."

"Who's the attorney?" asked Noble.

"Isaiah Christmas, from Norfolk."

"Well," huffed Rita, "I'm obviously no lawyer, but when the sheriff is asked about race he says there might be the death penalty. It doesn't take much imagination to wonder if the death penalty comes up if the man charged is black."

"That's not it, Rita," said Noble, impatiently, "but what is the basis, rape?"

Roberts knew this question was coming, and the answer, any kind of answer, was going to reveal just how premature Smith's arrest had been. "Rape or similar sexual assault could be the predicate offense to a capital charge."

Noble leaned forward. "Well?"

Roberts kept his eyes fixed on his inquisitor. "As I told you after we got the autopsy, she'd had sex, and there was a small tear at the anus."

"Oh my God," interrupted Rita. She looked at Noble. "You knew that?"

Noble winced but did not look away from Roberts. "Yes."

"Smith has admitted to sex. But there are three sources of semen. We haven't positively identified any of them yet."

"Three!" repeated Rita. "God … this is…." She sputtered to a halt.

Roberts turned his attention to Rita. "Smith admitted to sex, as has your brother. So we're working on the third source."

Noble abruptly arose and walked across the room, placing himself beyond and behind Roberts's chair. "I'm not sure how much more I want to hear. A beginner is sent to question a capital murder suspect, you haven't nailed down who had relations with my daughter and I haven't heard one thing about motive. I didn't expect this to be easy, but if I was on a jury, I'd be wondering what the hell is going on in your department."

"And my God, the reporters," added Rita. "If those other men are both white, it will look like you charged Smith because he was the black one."

"Mrs. Noble," began Roberts.

Clyde Noble interrupted. "We all know that's not it, Rita. But what of motive. Why would he kill my…my daughter?"

Rita suddenly turned her eyes toward her husband. Roberts could see no trace of sympathy on her face; rather disgust and anger seemed to blend in her piercing gaze.

Roberts replied to the voice behind him. "We don't know the motive."

"You don't know," said Noble quietly. "How about, he demanded sex, she resisted, and she ended up dead? But trials aren't guess work, are they."

Roberts had permitted himself to serve as a punching bag for as long as he thought necessary. "There are things we need to pin down, and I need your help. First, I'd like to point out that Jason's lawyer has cut us off and won't agree to a DNA test."

"He's not the murderer," said Rita curtly.

Roberts ignored the interruption. "Jason has helped us nail down some time frames, and if his DNA is a match, we'll have one of the sources verified. We're already having Smith's DNA checked. Also, I'm still trying to determine Miranda's whereabouts on Wednesday night."

"I've told you we don't know," answered Rita.

"Was she seeing anyone in Lafayette County?"

"Obviously she was," replied Rita.

"Leave it be Rita," said Noble. "I'll talk to Farnsworth. If he says Jason can be tested, then we'll see to it. I wasn't here Wednesday. I left that morning, didn't return until evening. Miranda was gone by then."

Roberts, who had kept his eyes on Rita, saw her lips tighten at the mention of Farnsworth and Jason. "What can you tell me about that Wednesday, Mrs. Noble?"

She looked back at Roberts. "Well, she left around midafternoon, I think. She didn't say anything. I saw her driving away."

"Three, four o'clock?"

"Fourish."

"Do you know where she was going?"

"No. We…we hadn't spoken that day." She glanced at Noble when he was not looking.

"What about the Snidletts?" asked Gene.

"They came around eight and left just after noon," answered Rita. "That was it. And that was enough. I can't stomach that young one. He struts around like he thinks he's God's gift. And leers at you. He's a foul human being."

"They won't be doing anything in the yard again Rita," said Noble evenly.

"Did Miranda know him, the young one?" asked Gene, his interest piqued.

Noble answered. "I can't see how. That was the only time they've been here this year. Except for Jason, I've never seen her even speak to another male."

Gene drummed the arms of his chair with his fingers. "One of my concerns is her whereabouts on Wednesday night. She told her mother that she was here Wednesday night. She told Jason the same thing. Maybe it doesn't matter, but I don't know."

"I'll get Clara," said Noble. "Clara and Miranda were pretty close."

For several moments the room was silent. Roberts kept his eyes on the sofa in front of him, all the while watching Rita from the periphery of his vision. She sat rigidly still in her chair staring at nothing. Finally, she spoke. "Miranda and I didn't get along. The drugs and drinking were bad enough, but the sex. I caught her here once with Jason, in bed. I wouldn't have it. Not in my house. Clyde just wouldn't say anything. I had to." The sound of approaching footsteps silenced her.

Roberts rose as Clara Wood walked in, her eyes glued to the floor. "Hello Mrs. Wood."

Clara looked briefly at Roberts and responded with a quiet "Fine, thank you."

"I was curious about the Wednesday Miranda was here, before she…before her death. Did you all talk?"

"Just friendly talk."

"Do you know when she left?"

"I don't remember, in the afternoon."

"What kind of friendly talk?"

"Oh, you know, about her Mom and goin' back to school. She wanted to go back to school."

"Did she say what her plans for Wednesday night were?"

"No."

"Did she make any phone calls?"

"She might 'uv. She was down to the pool, there's a phone there."

"Did she see anyone?"

"No. No one was here but me and Mrs. Noble and the chil'ren, after the senator left. And them tree cutters."

"The Snidletts?"

"That's them."

"How was she, happy, sad?"

Clara looked up again, this time a hunted look was in her eyes, or perhaps, thought Roberts, they were pleading. He quickly answered his own question. "Just normal?"

"Yes sir," she answered quietly, "just normal."

"Well, thank you, Mrs. Wood."

Clara Wood left the room looking at neither Noble nor his wife as she went.

"Anything else?" asked Noble.

"Not today. Thank you for seeing me."

"Call me with whatever you need," replied Noble. Roberts detected a sincerity that had not been present either today or in their prior conversations.

Roberts nodded toward Rita and began walking toward the hall. Noble followed. Once outside, he spoke again. "I'm getting a sense of what you're up against. I'm at your disposal."

Roberts thanked him, shook hands, and walked to the car. He slumped into his seat and breathed deeply against the exhaustion suddenly enveloping him. *I'm just getting too damn old for this.* Glaring toward the pool fence, he saw the stump the Snidletts had left. *I wonder what the Snidletts could see that day? One more rabbit to chase …again.*

Roberts made the rest of the circle. His mind automatically started darting from one snippet of evidence to another. Diffidence did not plague Roberts, at least not very often, but he was not comfortable with this case, which meant he was not comfortable with his own efforts. He had to admit that some of Noble's criticism was justified. The pieces were not falling into place and the investigation was not smoothly accelerating; rather it was jumping with fits, starts, and reversals, like a hurried switching engine in a rail yard.

* * *

Ev was at his desk reading the incident reports for the burglaries in Lebanon Cove when his intercom rang. He picked up the receiver.

"Ev, this is Lewis. I've gotta weird situation. Horace Seay picked up Pup Tower on another domestic last night. Pup's cooling his heels in the jail. He called Horace and told him he had some info on the Noble murder. If we wanted it, he wanted a deal on the domestic, including his bail."

Cross pulled off his glasses and laid them on his desk. "What kind of info?"

"He won't say. Said he would only talk to you."

"Hell," mumbled Ev. Talking to defendants could get him into ethical trouble; stool pigeons needed to talk to the police first. But this was different, and Ev did not want to give Tower a chance to change his mind.

"What's his bond?"

"Five thousand secured."

Ev doubted that Tower's girlfriend had the five hundred in cash to pay a bail bondsman to post a five thousand dollar bond, but some family member probably had real property that would suffice. He had no time to delay for once Tower was free on bond he would lose interest in talking.

"What do we know about the charge?" he asked.

"Horace said it was run-of-the mill pushin' and shovin'. A few bruises, no blood. Tower was blind drunk."

"Okay, you bring him over. Don't tell dispatch he's in my office."

"You're the boss."

Ev returned the telephone to its cradle and immediately picked it up and dialed dispatch on the intercom. Willie Painter answered with his customary "Yeah?"

"Patch me through to Gene's mobile phone," said Ev. There was a delay. Then Painter was back on the line. "No answer."

"Okay, tell him to come to my office when he signs back on."

"Au-ight."

Ev gathered the burglary reports and piled them on the mound of files growing at the end of his desk. Nothing short of a jury trial set Cross's stomach churning like the prospect of a snap decision on inadequate facts. Snap decisions left too much room for error, and error resulted in angry victims and grinning defendants who bragged freely to fellow scofflaws that they had "got off." He put his glasses on and waited for Brown and Tower.

Within minutes Brown appeared at his door with Pup Tower in tow. Tower was not in the usual orange jail garb, rather he was still wearing his jeans and a dirty tee shirt with the Lickety Split Trucking logo. Gaunt yet hard-muscled, Tower was every bit the angry young man hell-bent on finding the next opportunity to test the settled limits of polite society. Bored indifference was the most tolerable of his traits, an indifference which rarely succeeded in veiling the mean undercurrent nourished by an existence he had neither the initiative nor the insight to alter.

Ev did not rise. He motioned to Brown and Tower to take a seat in the chairs opposite his desk. "Mr. Tower, I understand you want to talk to me."

"Un-huh." Tower's answer was as vacant as his face. He stroked his mangina beard as if to convey his indifference.

Ev looked at Brown. "What's this about Lewis?"

"Mr. Tower says he has information about the Noble murder."

"What sort of information?"

Brown looked at Tower expectantly. Tower, sitting with his arms crossed, said nothing.

"What do you have?" asked Ev, directing his question to Tower.

Tower unfolded his arms and leaned forward with his elbows on his knees. "First, I want out of jail. I don't want no jail time. Then I reckon we can talk."

"I can agree to a personal recognizance bond. What do you mean about jail time?"

"I don't want no time for pushin' Dawn after she slapped me. It won't me that done it first, so I want off that."

"I can't talk to you about what happened last night. What I need to know before I can give you any…agreement on your charges is what kind of information you've got. It might be something we already know."

Tower wet his lips and leaned further forward. "You know who she was runnin' with?"

"We know several."

Tower's eyes darted toward Brown before he responded. "I mean, who she was screwin'."

Ev pushed back in his chair. "When are we talking about? Any particular month or week or what?"

"Try Wednesday night before she got killed."

Brown shot a glance at Ev. The Commonwealth's Attorney remained motionless. "Okay, we'll take your charge under advisement, same thing as last time. But I can't do it again. That's what I'll do only if everything you tell me is the truth. If we find out you were untruthful, the deal's off. Are we clear?"

Tower slowly pulled his shoulders erect. "Same as last time. No jail. And I get out today."

"That's right."

"Au-ight. I seen her and Lester Hester Snidlett at the Quik Mart on Wednesday night. He was buyin' beer and smilin' and winkin' and shit and pointin' his head to his truck where she was at."

"What time?"

"I dunno. After work. Not long after work 'cause we stopped just after leavin' work."

"Who's we?"

"Me and Danny Bota. I was givin' him a ride home."

"What else?"

"I seen Lester at the wood yard on Thursday. He was braggin' about it, how much he got and all. Said they won't done. Told me not to let on to his old lady. Told me that his story was that he was playin' cards all night with me and Danny."

Brown shifted in his chair so that he could face Tower. Ev picked up a pencil and started making notes.

"And?"

"That's it."

"Have you seen him since that Thursday?"

"I've seen him. Maybe early the next week."

"What did he say about Miranda Noble?"

"The girl. He said he was awfully sorry she was dead. He said the crack was probably what caused it."

"Caused it?"

"That's what he said."

"What did he mean?"

"I don't know. He didn't say nothin' else. Changed the subject. Told me not to talk about it. He didn't want cops snoopin' around because his old lady would get him in court again. Said she'd bust his ass and he'd get the blame."

"Get the blame for what?"

"For Sunny Grogan jumpin' on him. Said she started it last time and then charged him."

"Have you seen him since Jeff Smith was arrested?"

"Naw. We're haulin' from another job now, so I ain't been at the Quik Mart or wood yard."

"Heard anything on the street?"

"What?"

"Has anyone else talked about Miranda's death?"

"I ain't heard nuthin'. I never seen her but the time at the Quik Mart."

"Then how do you know that was Miranda Noble?"

"Lester said so. Said he wouldn't be surprised if Clyde Noble's wife didn't need a real man, too. Shit." Tower grunted a laugh for emphasis.

"Was she a blonde, very pretty?"

"Oh yeah. She was some kind of pretty."

"Was anyone with them?"

"With Lester Hester and her? No. I mean, he didn't have need for nobody else for what he had in mind."

Ev looked at Brown. "Anything you need to ask?"

"Did he say how they met?" asked Brown.

"Naw."

"So you've told us what you know?"

"Uh-huh."

"Okay," said Ev, "we might need to talk again. I'll call the clerk and get the judge to change your bond."

"How long will that take?"

"Not long. I'll do it now." He reached for the telephone.

Brown stood, and Tower, after a pause, joined him. "Come on Pup, let's go." The two of them left the room as Ev explained the new bond to the clerk.

He was still on the telephone giving the standard non-answers to a reporter when Gene Roberts walked in. Roberts settled into a chair and lit a cigarette while Ev struggled to end the call.

"I'm sorry. I can't comment on the case." Pause. "I'm not permitted to discuss those things." Pause. "No decision has been made on upgrading the charge to capital murder." Pause. "I can't comment on that either." At length Ev finished and wearily laid down the receiver. "Did you see Lewis?"

"Yep. I'm going to pull together what we've got on Snidlett, prepare before going to see him."

"This Snidlett thing gives me a bad feeling. His comment that cocaine probably caused the death came early on, while Burke was telling the world it was an accidental drowning."

"Sounds like he was there doesn't it?"

"Looks like we have our third sperm donor, at the least."

"That's some consolation."

Ev looked at the clock on the desk. "I've got a short trial in a few minutes. You can call me later or at home. How was the ordeal?"

"What I expected. Rita hasn't softened. It's clear she's blaming Miranda for all this. And Clara Wood was scared to talk. So I will see her tonight, if I make it that long."

"What's wrong?"

"Out of steam. I'm exhausted. But what the hell. I'll check with you later."

Ev followed Roberts to the front of his office.

"Want to put any money on Sunday's race?" Roberts asked Linda Masencup.

"No thanks. My mama taught me not to gamble."

Roberts laughed his response as he left the room.

"Ev, Gene looks bad," said Linda.

"He said he felt tired. I guess I hadn't noticed it."

"Well, he looks sort of gray." She handed Ev two pink message slips. "Paula Noble called while you were busy. So did Oliver Farnsworth."

* * *


Polly Cross almost enjoyed Monday. With Sam at school there was one too few boys to support a fight, at least not until after she retrieved him. Her mother-in-law had not called even once. But the greatest relief came from Ev's having gone to the office, taking most of his gloom and impatience with him. He had been insufferable through the weekend, grousing about the Noble case, fuming about his mother, and cursing the telephone. Sick of reporters he had demanded that no one answer the telephone. Polly ignored him. Then on Sunday he went to see Margaret.

The first thing Polly did Monday morning was call the telephone company and request Caller I D.

Polly knew what to expect on Monday. Sometime in the afternoon, after the highballs had started to work their black magic, Margaret would call Polly to complain about the offered price. It was bad enough to have to hear it, it was worse to hear it a second time since she had already rehearsed in her thoughts what Margaret would say. Her summations were right on the mark.

Margaret's affected voice was satisfactory proof that she had been indulging. She fussed for a moment about the weather and complained that her electric bill would never go down unless the heat abated, then she got to the point. "Did you know Ev came to see me about the house?" There was an edge of suspicion in her voice, as if she should be the one to break the news.

"We discussed it."

"Well, I don't know what to think. His price is so much lower than what it's worth. What do you think?"

*Phase one is in motion. She wants to blame me for the price offered.* Polly took a deep breath. "We thought it was fair since you wouldn't need a realtor." She loathed making excuses to Margaret.

"I just don't know. Lucius paid a lot to have the heating and air conditioning redone nine years ago. And I imagine homes are cheaper in Chatham."

Polly could only wonder what her hometown seventy miles away could have to do with anything. She had not thought of a response before Margaret plowed into phase two.

"Amanda thought three hundred fifty thousand was a good price. She said it was a steal compared to Richmond."

"Richmond is hardly a fair comparison to Lafayette County."

"Well, Amanda keeps up with that sort of thing. I can see this is going to be difficult for me."

Polly wanted to tell her to sell it to anybody who would buy it, and then to go to hell, which she hoped Margaret would share with Amanda. She bit her lip. "You and Ev will have to work that out Mrs. Cross. You know how he can be."

"And he doesn't want to do anything till his trial is over. Todd Kidd said that October was the best month to show it. I don't want to miss the best time."

*Forty years in that house and suddenly a couple of months are an imposition.* Polly knew Todd Kidd the realtor as well as his wife and she was surprised that Kidd had not told Margaret that tomorrow was the critical day. Maybe Tonya Kidd couldn't hold off until October to buy her newest Volvo. Tonya thought herself some sort of princess, but the alliterative names—Todd and Tonya—were enough to irritate Polly.

"I've got another call, so I've got to go. Bye," said Margaret.

Call waiting, or whatever it was called, normally irritated Polly, but in Margaret's case it was a blessing. Polly rehung the receiver and swept a lock of hair from her face with the back of her hand. Ev deserved to hear about the conversation, but she thought better of it. *Let them both smolder.*

By six o'clock, when Ev's Bronco pulled into the driveway, Polly had already promised herself two dozen times that she would ignore his ugly mood.

Ev paused at the door and studied the canopy of dark clouds veiling the sky. "I guess we're going to get some rain," he announced as he walked in. "Where are the men?"

Polly wondered if an imposter had entered her home. "In their room, I hope," she answered over her shoulder. She turned from the stove to face him. "Long day?"

"Pretty long."

Ev's light mood speared her two dozen promises. "Linda said something was up with the sheriff."

"Yep. I think I got his attention. It had to happen. He couldn't keep running off at the mouth and interfering with investigations."

"That's good."

"Plus we found out where Miranda was on Wednesday night."

"I didn't know that was a question."

"Maybe I forgot to tell you. Anyway, she was servicing some ruffian named Lester Hester Snidlett. We should have all our DNA accounted for, or will. Of course we have another suspect."

"With Jeff Smith charged?"

"That's why we went to see the sheriff. Rein some of this mess in before we get embarrassed any more. Roberts'll figure it out." Ev laid the mail on the kitchen table and left the room.

She shook her head and turned back to the stove. *I wonder if they're all that way.*

# CHAPTER 14

Tuesday, September 22nd

It was almost two o'clock when Ev left court and returned to his office. In his stack of pink telephone slips was a note that Roberts needed to speak to him. Ev found Roberts at his desk surrounded by three large black notebooks, several file folders, and a full ashtray. R. C. Hawkes was at Brown's desk with the telephone to his ear.

"What's up Gene?" asked Ev.

"I've spent most of the morning trying to run down a set of prints on Snidlett. You know he was charged with burglary ten years ago. Well guess what. No prints in the file. Another investigation handled by Hank Burke. I pulled the domestic file from a couple of weeks ago and guess what. No prints. Some of Wimpie Carson's usual work."

Neither coaching nor intimidation by Roberts had changed Carson's work habits. Sixteen years as a deputy had not made much difference either. Moreover, there was no indication that Carson had a neck: his head sat on his shoulders like a bowling ball cradled on a stack of paper napkins, and he was short. So short that a local tart, Rhonda Gooden, swore that he kicked up dust when he farted.

Roberts continued. "I was pulling all Carson's files, all ten or twelve of them, to see whether he had put Snidlett's prints somewhere else. And guess what. They were in a file for Lester Stanton. Twelve files and he can't put them in the right folder."

Ev laughed and pulled up a ladder-back chair. "So what's new? He did lock himself in the back of his car."

Carson, alone on a drug stakeout, had positioned himself in the backseat of his patrol car, forgetting that it was designed for keeping prisoners from escaping. When he couldn't get out, he called Willie Painter in dispatch who did not hesitate to inform the sheriff, over the radio, to which every scanner in the county was tuned.

"Damn his time," groused Roberts.

"And guess what. Horace Seay still hasn't gotten the photographs developed. I told him to do that the very next day. He's probably lost the damn film. R. C. is taking Snidlett's prints to Richmond to the lab. That's who he's on the phone to. I'm not taking a chance on a fax. I think we'll have results in the morning."

Hawkes replaced the receiver as Roberts was speaking. "The lab said to bring 'em on," he answered in a loud voice. A heavy set man with a short, steel-gray flat top, Hawkes gave little indication that he had played noseguard for N.C. State.

"Good. Have you met R. C., Ev?"

Ev arose and introduced himself to Hawkes. "He's pretty entertaining isn't he," said Ev, motioning to Roberts.

Adjusting himself in Brown's noisy chair Hawkes smiled broadly. "The last time I saw him happy was when we were on a helicopter leaving Da Nang."

"I didn't know you were in Vietnam Gene," said Ev.

"We were over there together in the early days," said Roberts without looking up. "Two privates with no damn clue except how to watch the calendar. Anyway, that was another lifetime," he added quietly. "Look, I'm going to catch Clara Wood this afternoon. Lewis is in Lebanon Cove. You can guess why. R. C. and I figure to corner Snidlett tomorrow when we have the print info back."

Ev nodded his head. "Farnsworth called yesterday. He'll let Thomasson donate some DNA. He said you could handle the scheduling. No questions though. He's not ready to allow that yet."

"I guess Senator and Mrs. Noble got some of my message on that," said Roberts grimly.

"Paula Noble wants a meeting, too," said Ev. "I told her I would arrange one with both of us."

"Okay. After tomorrow." Roberts piled the notebooks on the corner of his desk. "One of the first things I do under the new deal with the sheriff is ask him for the authority to send some of these lard asses home for a few days, without pay."

* * *

Clara Wood lived with her sister in a neat white frame house just outside the spot on the Norfolk Southern rail line known as Red Springs. Red Springs had once been a stop for the railroad, and two cold storage buildings, a general store and a post office had sprouted near the passenger station. The shipment of apples by rail had long ago ceased and the passenger station was a boarded paintless remnant. The village had withered on the declining railroad vine. Only the post office stirred with activity, and very little at that.

Roberts passed through what was left of Red Springs and turned onto an unpaved road which wound to Wood's house. Clara and her sister were on the porch when he pulled into the yard.

"Hello Mrs. Wood." Roberts called out in a voice more pleasant than he thought he could muster.

"Hello Mr. Roberts," replied Mrs. Wood.

"Hello," added her sister as she arose from her rocking chair. She looked at best twenty years older than Clara, and Clara was at least sixty-five.

Clara remained seated. "She's goin' in. I thought you'd be comin' to see me."

Roberts walked onto the porch as the sister retreated behind the screen door.

"We was just enjoyin' this cool weather, after that nice rain last night. Makes everything look fresh scrubbed," she continued. "Sit down."

Roberts sat in the rocking chair just abandoned by the sister. "I didn't frighten your sister did I?"

"No. She's real shy. She can't hear too good, so she doesn't like to be around folks cause she has to yell to hear herself."

"How'd you figure I'd be back?" asked Roberts.

"You knew when you was at the Nobles. I could see you had more questions."

"Well, I do. That Wednesday, how was Miranda acting?"

Clara rocked gently for a moment. "I knew Miranda when she was real little, I sat for her, before the first Miz Noble moved away. I knew her real good. She was the sweetest child. I liked the first Miz Noble, too."

Roberts pushed gently back on his rocking chair. He knew Mrs. Wood had something she needed to tell him and he had no choice but to let her wander to it.

"I didn't see her for the longest time. 'Cause I didn't sit for them anymore. But when Mr. Clyde, the senator…the new Miz Noble said I'm s'pose to call him the senator. When he got his new wife and she had children, they hired me to work full time. By then Miranda was bigger. But she quit coming. It was years before she came back. That was this spring. She just showed up.

"We talked a lot, when Miz Noble won't around. And that poor child was so sad. She said she'd never had a daddy. Stuff like that. The senator didn't seem to mind her coming. But Miz Noble. Sweet Jesus forgive me. Miz Noble just out and out hated her. But at first she acted like she didn't want to let on. Miranda knew. Maybe that's why she drank so much. I don't know. I don't touch it. Satan's spit. She came right often. Spent some nights. Mr.…Senator Noble and her would talk and she liked that. But when he won't around Miz Noble just acted like she won't there. Then that Jason showed up. Now there's a boy what I don't have no use for. He was like poison. He got Miranda to sneakin' around. That's when Miz Noble caught 'em."

"Were you there?" interrupted Roberts.

"No. My day off. But Miz Noble didn't keep it no secret. She told the senator Miranda had to go. Called her awful names. The senator just mostly ignored her, and Miz Noble stayed fit to be tied. And Miranda, why, she kept comin' like she wanted to show Miz Noble up. And Miz Noble would get on the 'phone and tell that Jason to stay away from her. Said the girl was on drugs."

"Was she?"

"I think so. I can't tell. But, you know, things would happen. She got so she never had money. Sometimes she'd sleep by the pool all day. Not eat one thing. But that Wednesday. The senator left and she was up to her room asleep. Miz Noble just bust in there and yelled at her. Told her to get out. I couldn't listen but I couldn't help it. And the awful names. Names I never heard out of a woman's mouth. Then she slammed the door and wouldn't be in the same room."

"What did she say when she told her to get out?"

Mrs. Wood folded her hands and stared into her lap. After several minutes silence she sighed and continued her narrative. "She said bitch, get out, don't come back. Whore, don't come back. Your ass is finished if you do. And something about a will"

"A will?"

"Something like that. It's been a hard place to work at this summer. Everybody always mad. I heard Miz Noble fuss about the will to Mr. Clyde. But I don't understand that stuff."

"What was Mrs. Noble saying about the will?"

"Said Miranda didn't need to be in the will. School cost enough money. Child support. That was more'n enough. Think of his own chil'ren."

"What happened after the yelling on that Wednesday?"

"Miranda, she finally got up and when I saw her she was crying. She said she didn't know what to do, but she wasn't leavin' just because Miz Noble told her to, only her daddy could do that. Then she called her some awful names. Mostly the same names. Then she said she ought to go back to school, cause her Mama wanted her to. Then she went to the pool and stayed till that afternoon. I just tried to stay out of everybody's way."

"So she didn't speak to you when she left?"

"Not a word. Just left. I never saw her again" Tears collecting on the lens of Clara's glasses began to dribble down her cheeks. She fished through her apron until she found a tissue and dabbed it at the rivulets. "That poor child."

Roberts fidgeted with the buttonhole of his blazer as he allowed Mrs. Wood to regain her composure. As gently as he could, he asked, "why didn't you tell me this in August, when I came to see you?"

"I don't know. Didn't seem to matter. We thought she drowned. Miz Noble called me and said she'd drowned. Wanted to know whether she was there when I left on Friday. Of course she won't."

"Did she ask if anyone had called for Miranda?'

"I think so. I was so upset. I forgot to tell her about Jason."

"And you knew nothing about Jeff Smith."

"No. Oh I've heard of him. But not about Miranda."

"What do you think happened?"

Mrs. Wood lifted her head and looked at Roberts evenly. "I don't know. I don't know why anybody would smother that sweet girl."

"Has Rita Noble told you to keep quiet, not tell me about what happened that Wednesday?"

"She don't know I heard her yelling at Miranda. She didn't hear Miranda tell me about it. She thinks I'm there like a chair, like a stick of wood." She managed a wan smile. "But that's my name idn't it? Wood." She looked away,

"Why were you afraid to tell me this in front of the Nobles?"

"Afraid? Not afraid. I didn't see a reason to hurt Mr. Clyde again. I knew him when he was little, knowed him all his life. He didn't need to hear those things from me."

Roberts sat quietly for awhile, listening to the soft creaking of Clara Wood's rocker and staring ahead at nothing. Finally, he arose and faced the diminutive woman beside him. "Thank you," he said quietly.

She nodded, but kept her eyes riveted to the front of her.

* * *

It was after five by the time Roberts returned to Lafayette Court House. Seeing Ev's Bronco still in the parking lot the investigator walked to the court building and up the steps in the rear addition. He met Cross in the hallway. "You got a few minutes?"

Roberts sank down in one of the chairs lining the wall in front of Linda Masencup's desk. "I've got a motive."

Ev sat down a few chairs away. "Well I be damned. Why'd the bastard do it?"

"There's a small problem."

"Then maybe I don't want to hear it."

"I've got a motive for the wrong person."

"Snidlett or Thomasson."

"Neither."

"Okay Gene. What's happened to us now?"

Roberts pulled a cigarette from his blazer pocket. "Rita Noble." He lit the cigarette while speaking.

"That doesn't help the cause."

"She hated Miranda. She issued an ultimatum Wednesday morning, a threat. And there's a will involved somehow. Clara Wood didn't know how the will figured into it."

"Forget the will. Rita was with her husband in Richmond when the girl died. Is there some massive conspiracy here that we've got to untangle" A murder for hire? A cover-up—"

"Look," Roberts interrupted him, "I don't like a new twist anymore than you do."

Ev pursed his lips and thought for a moment. "The will isn't hard to figure. Noble was going to leave Miranda in for a share and Rita wanted everything for her

132

own children. It's a story a few generations removed from Cinderella. The Stepmother Syndrome. Anyway, we knew there were problems between them. I don't see how it changes anything."

Roberts rubbed his eyes before speaking. "A basic rule in investigating murders is to work from the inside out. Rita is certainly inside, and she's got the motive. That really bothers me."

"Rita has been pretty up front that she didn't like Miranda, or at least made no credible efforts to hide it. Second, most families hide dirty laundry. But you've got me nervous. What do you think?"

"I don't know. I'm just reporting it. I'm going to closet myself at home with the file and think this thing through without distraction. As soon as we've talked to Snidlett."

"Well, the evil stepmother didn't kill Cinderella, and Cinderella lived with the woman. Our problem is why Smith did it, unless it's so obvious we're just overlooking it."

"I've got to get up with Mervin. See what he's dug up on Smith. Has a preliminary been set?"

"Not yet."

"Well try to buy us some time. The DNA analysis can be pretty slow."

"Okay." Ev took off his glasses and examined the lenses. "How'd we get into this fix?"

"We just did. Anyway, I've got retirement to look forward to."

"I don't. At least I hope I don't."

# CHAPTER 15

Wednesday, September 23rd

General District Court had begun its regular Wednesday session by the time Ev left his office. The hallway outside of the courtroom was filled with people awaiting their cases. Ev walked into the courtroom where he found the benches packed as well. A state police officer and a fat young woman stretching her shorts and tee-shirt beyond their capacity were at the bench. Ev concluded that it would be sometime before the court was finished with the unrepresented defendants. He was almost to the stairs to return to his office when Wilmer Bledsoe called his name.

"Ev, got a few?"

"Sure."

Wil led Ev into the coffee-copier room. "Let's get rid of some of these, Ev. I gotta drunk driver who had the foresight to wear his Budweiser tee shirt today. He'll plead."

"Okay," answered Ev smiling. "That was easy."

Wil ran off a few more cases that would be guilty pleas, thus narrowing to a handful the cases they would have to try to the judge. With the negotiations behind him Wil poured himself a cup of coffee without paying the required quarter.

"What's going on with the Smith case?" he asked.

"Plugging along," said Ev.

"That Isaiah Christmas. Now he's a piece of work. Stays in trouble with the Bar."

"That's nice to know."

"He's black, you know."

"I knew that."

"When he's not acting the wild man, he's pretty good in court. We've referred a few cases to each other."

"I guess I'll get to learn the old fashioned way."

"Yeah. It's a lot easier to try a case against someone you know. You know what to expect. You know where their weaknesses are."

"Just for future reference, what are mine?"

Wil laughed. "You don't have any. But I wouldn't tell you if you did."

"Thanks Wil."

"Back to Smith. What's all this business about race?"

"I haven't the slightest idea."

"Everybody's a victim. Charge a black and it's because he's black. Charge a woman and it's PMS that made her do it. Convict a murderer and it's because he didn't have money enough for a real defense. Charge a president and it's because he's a liberal. Wonder how old Clyde is taking all this? I bet he's fartin' marbles worrying that the black vote will turn on him."

"They haven't been fun to work with."

There was a knock at the door.

"Yeah," answered Wil loudly.

"Judge is ready for the represented cases."

Wil and Ev made their way to the courtroom. Upon reaching the bench, Wil dropped his files on counsel table and approached the judge. "Okay judge. Let's dispense with some justice."

Lincoln pretended that he had not heard the remark.

When the cases were concluded the bailiff, Okra Alexander, informed the judge that Elwood Smoot was ready to be brought over from the jail. Smoot, commonly called Gooseneck, was the village's principal drunk. Gooseneck had been in court for public drunkenness so many times that the bailiffs had begun bringing him in last after all the litigants had departed, primarily because he liked to address the judge on a first name basis. Gooseneck, when sober, was a genial sort, talented with the harmonica, and generally harmless. As he had grown older, however, drinking elicited a mean streak and the village merchants lost whatever tolerance for him they once had.

Wil elbowed Ev when he heard Smoot's name mentioned. "We might as well stay for this. Free entertainment. I got him social security disability a few years back. Back when being a drunk was a disability. He hasn't worked a day since."

Within minutes Wimpie Carson opened the door and led Gooseneck in. Smoot's head, as his moniker implied, sat perched on a long thin neck. The rest of him was gangly as well and he walked toward the bench like a stork with stiff knees. With Wimpie just behind him the two could have passed for a Laurel and Hardy routine.

"'Lo Abner," Gooseneck greeted the judge. He was thoroughly sober, having been in jail three weeks awaiting trial.

"Well Elwood, you're back. I told you last time not to come back," replied Lincoln, who had given him the same directive for several years. No one addressed Smoot as Gooseneck as he failed to appreciate the nickname.

"I know."

"You're charged with public drunkenness and indecent exposure."

"I had to go."

Lincoln sat back in his chair. "What's the plea?"

Gooseneck put his elbows on the bench. "I reckon the same as usual."

Lincoln shook his head and pursed his lips against his mirth. "Guilty, I take it," he finally managed.

"But I had to go," continued Gooseneck.

"Elwood, you said you had a place to live in Charlottesville. That's why I let you out last time."

"I did. I was just passin' through."

"To where?"

"To Charlottesville."

"Why not just stay there?"

"Made a bad decision, I reckon."

"You know Elwood, you've made a lot of bad decisions in your life."

"You're right. But when you're drunk you've got a lot more options."

Lincoln lowered his head and laughed quietly. "Where you going if I let you out?"

"Charlottesville." Gooseneck turned to address Wimpie Carson. "You can give me a ride can't you?"

Lincoln shook his head. "They can't run you around the state."

"I'll just hafta walk."

"After sixty days."

"Sixty? For gettin' drunk? In the warm weather?"

"On the indecent exposure. You've pulled most of it already."

Gooseneck shook his head as Wimpie tugged at his arm. "Piss in my pants next time," he mumbled as he turned away from the bench.

Everyone in the room broke into laughter when the door closed behind Elwood and Wimpie.

"You know judge," said Wil, "all we need now is for Porky Pig to jump through the clerk's door and yell "Tha- Tha- That's all folks.""

"Wil, just let me be Daffy Duck," said Lincoln.

Ev was still grinning and shaking his head when he returned to his office after General District court.

"Must have been a good morning," Linda Masencup greeted him.

"Gooseneck," Ev began to explain as he took the telephone slips Linda handed him.

"Mr. Christmas has set a bond hearing for this afternoon," she interrupted him.

"What! Lot of notice he gave me." Cross spun on his heel to walk to his office. "And what a waste of time. Abner Lincoln isn't going to set any bond."

Linda shrugged. "I told his person, Monica Del-something, that you might not be available, and she said call by one if you weren't."

"Who set this, the clerk?"

"Yes."

"Why didn't she call me first? Why didn't she tell me when I was in court?"

"I don't know."

Ev patted his foot several times before starting down the hall. *He could have called me, given me a day or two notice,* he thought. *What a son of a bitch.* He toyed with the idea of calling the Peoples Legal Rights Clinic and telling Delgardo that he was not prepared for a bond hearing. What difference would another week make since Smith had no chance of being allowed bail? Ev took a deep breath and dropped into his chair. Christmas was bound to know the effort was futile, then why was he doing it? The reason, he finally concluded, was the same as with every other defendant. Smith, and every one of his kinsmen in the Commonwealth, were probably clamoring for a bond; people in his boat always did. Defense counsel routinely asked for hearings just to get their clients off their backs, and to cover their flanks against a future bar complaint. Criminals had a habit of filing complaints with the State Bar accusing their lawyers of allowing them to be convicted.

"Has anyone come from his office to review my file?" Ev yelled to Linda from his office.

"No," came the answer from down the hall.

*He's covering his ass. That's all it can be.* Ev decided to let the hearing go forward. "What time?" he yelled again to Linda.

"Three-thirty. Minnie Patterson called. I put her off. But she wants to see you."

"About cats?"

"Of course."

"When should we get the first frost? Soon?"

"Yes, a couple of weeks."

"Maybe her tomatoes will be dead before I have to see her."

* * *

R. C. Hawkes did not appear at the sheriff's office until eleven, which was no surprise to Roberts. Gene maintained that the state police did not go to work until ten. While Roberts waited, he listened to Lewis Brown's update on the Lebanon Cove burglaries.

"What did they find?" Roberts greeted Hawkes as he entered the investigators' office.

Hawkes smiled at Roberts and looked at Lewis Brown before answering. "Is he always in this kind of bust-your-ass hurry?"

"Oh yeah," replied Brown. "He'd ah created the world in four days and then fussed about it for three."

"What did they find?" repeated Roberts.

"Snidlett is a match on the Budweiser can."

137

"That could have rolled out of his truck when he was there cutting this tree," groused Roberts.

"The Nobles, Clara Wood, and Hector Lopez said it wasn't there Thursday and Friday," said Brown. "It was only a couple of feet from the driveway. They'd have seen it."

"They could be wrong," replied Roberts dryly.

"I wasn't finished yet," said Hawkes.

"You sure fooled me," said Roberts.

"He matched that other print on the Vodka bottle."

"Damn," breathed Roberts. "When was he there? How'd she have time to service all three?"

"He had to be there didn't he?" said Brown.

Roberts stared at the ceiling silently before speaking again. "You say Pup Tower is driving that blue pickup the people up there have reported."

"Yeah. He gives Danny Bota a ride sometimes. Bota lost his license on a second DUI."

"So you're back to nothing."

"I guess. At least the burglaries have stopped. Been a week now."

"No help with the prints?"

"I haven't got anything back yet."

"Well, that's something. Call the lab and raise hell."

"Yes sir boss."

Roberts looked at Hawkes. "I oughta get the teacher of the year award. Appear on the Disney Channel."

"Who taught you Gene?" asked R. C.

"Can't remember that far back. Okay, here's what I propose. Lewis and I will go track down Lester Snidlett. My information is that they're cutting a tract of wood near Morgan. R. C., you and Horace Seay go see Sunny Grogan. Pin her down on Friday night. Stay vague. Pay attention to any cigarettes and beer cans you see."

"Damn Gene," said Hawkes, "I did read the file."

Lewis Brown could barely hide his relief at being asked to rejoin the Noble investigation. Following the Smith arrest, Roberts had said almost nothing to Brown regarding the murder. Brown would have preferred a thorough chewing. Police work was like football; if the coach quit hounding you, it was because he had given up.

Lebanon Cove was his purgatory. Sitting for hours in the bushes and honeysuckle staring at the Cove road, he had ample time to think about his handling of Smith. The Cove task began to feel like a sentence rather than an assignment, and like every man sitting in prison he tried to convince himself that he was innocent. After all, both Gene and the sheriff had all but said to go for the juggler. Then he would go home, read the newspaper articles covering the Noble case, and wince at the mess that was jelling.

Brown lived alone, so his thoughts stayed bottled up in his head, careening around and leading him to wonder whether he ought to be looking for another job, perhaps as a junior varsity football coach. Nobody cared if your team won, the good players were pulled up to varsity, and he would get paid ten grand more a year. But the thought of quitting while he was behind was about as inviting as the notion of wearing lipstick on the gridiron. He put it behind him and patiently served his time in the bushes.

* * *

Roberts said very little as they drove to Morgan. The old mill village—the grist mill had been torn down by a firm in the business of selling antique wood—lay in the flood plain of a mountain river and was surrounded abruptly by the Blue Ridge Mountains. Acres of pastures, hayfields, and apple orchards spread from the river to the mountains' base. People from the city were mesmerized by the valley and lined up to buy a piece of it.

Roberts pulled his car into a heavily traveled farm lane and drove to the wood's edge.

"Well, I can see they've been here," observed Brown. "How'd you know where they were?"

"Called the sawmill," answered Roberts. He stopped the car and got out. "Let's walk in. The road's too rough. Lester's the cut-man, logger's lingo for a sawyer. His father runs the knuckleboom and drives the truck to the mill. They have another guy who runs the skidder, when he's sober."

Brown wanted to ask how Roberts knew all this but decided not to show his ignorance again.

"In case you're wondering," added Roberts, "I got that from the same call."

Brown laughed in spite of himself.

They had not walked far when the groaning of a truck engine met them. Within moments an old Chevrolet piled three times its height with logs rounded a curve on the rutted road. The truck slowed and Roger Snidlett leaned through the window spitting a stream of tobacco juice into the honeysuckle before speaking. "I weckon y'all want to thee my boy."

"Yes sir Mr. Snidlett," answered Roberts in the same tone he would use with a judge.

"He've up yonder cuttin'. I tole him nat woman would be hith undoin'." He pressed the accelerator and wormed the truck forward. "I gotta go," he yelled over the engine, and spat again.

Gene waved at the old man as the truck pulled away. "Roger was adamant that Lester could not have seen Miranda that day they cut the maple. Just goes to show you have to question everything someone tells you. And Roger is honest, a pretty sorry businessman, but honest."

They continued to walk, Brown a step behind, making their way toward the whining of a chain saw. Roberts soon halted and after he heard the thunderous crash of a felled tree he walked quickly to the stump where Lester Snidlett was mopping his forehead and eyeing the forest for the next victim of his machine. Snidlett turned after seeing his visitors from the corner of his eye.

"Hello Lester," Roberts greeted him above the puttering of the idling chain saw.

Snidlett nodded his head in acknowledgement. Then he turned his face away loudly hocked from deep in his throat and spat a globule of resulting phlegm and dust at least ten feet. That done, he shut off the saw and set it on the ground.

The impudent crudity was not lost on Roberts.

Brown looked away, pretending to survey the cut-man's work. Several acres in the midst of the forest looked as if a World War One movie were about to be filmed.

"What's she said I done now?" asked Snidlett pointedly. "I wish the bitch would just go on back to her husband."

"We're not here about Sunny Grogan. I'm Investigator Gene Roberts. This is Lieutenant Lewis Brown."

"I know you." Snidlett sat down on the stump he had just created. "And he went to school about when I did," he said, referring to Brown without looking at him.

"We played football together," said Brown dryly.

"I've heard you were seeing Miranda Noble," continued Roberts.

"Yeah?" Snidlett pulled a pack of Winstons from his tee-shirt pocket and started patting his skin-tight blue jeans for a lighter. "Where'd you hear that?"

Brown knew why Snidlett was patting his pants but was in no frame of mind to accommodate him.

Roberts put his hand into his blazer pocket. "Wednesday night. August nineteenth. You spent the night with her."

Snidlett smiled, revealing even white teeth, the only part of him that was free of grime, crud, and sweat. "I did. I guess you want to hear all about it." He continued to fumble with his pockets.

Roberts pulled out his Zippo and handed it to Snidlett.

Snidlett studied the Zippo for a moment before lighting his cigarette. "I like this Roberts. Oughta get me one." He pitched it back when the task was accomplished.

"I don't need to bother you for long," continued Roberts. "Just need some details. First, you had sexual intercourse with her. That Wednesday."

"That's a nice word for it. A real shame she's dead."

Roberts took a breath and ignored Snidlett's commentary. "Second she was with you all night."

"Yeah. I went home around four. She…well, me and the old man has a huntin' cabin over behind Onan. She stayed until she left, whenever that was." He spat again without the preliminary hocking.

"Did you go to the Nobles' home on Wednesday?"

"No."

"What about the tree you cut?"

"Oh yeah. To work, not to see her."

"You saw her there."

"Yeah. Look, I seen over the fence. I spoke to her. She said to meet her at the Quik Mart. That's all."

"Didn't go to the pool house?"

"No." Snidlett drew the word out.

"Drink anything. A beer, vodka."

"No." He drew the word out again. "I just talked to her over the fence, and got an eye full. And I guess she musta liked what she saw too." Snidlett smiled again.

"Did she take her car with her to your cabin?"

"Yeah. After we rode around awhile. I took her back to the Quik Mart and she got it and followed me."

"What about Friday?"

Snidlett's eyes narrowed. "I thought you had that…had somebody locked up for that."

Brown shifted his feet. Roberts darted a cold glance at him which Brown correctly took to mean that he needed to keep quiet. "Friday?"

"Just saw her that Wednesday night. We didn't make no plans."

Roberts pulled a cigarette from his blazer pocket and lit it with the Zippo he was still holding. He exhaled slowly, then, "look Lester. I can put you at the pool Friday night."

"The hell you can. I was home Friday night. Drunk. And I don't drive around drunk."

"You were home Friday night and didn't go out?"

"Oh I may have went out. To pick up beer or something."

"So you went out before you were drunk."

"Yeah. Ask Manfred Fitzgerald. I prob'bly went there." Snidlett crushed his cigarette with his boot and stood up. "You finished? You got your dee-tails. I gotta work for my living."

"You want to think about Friday night a little bit more?" asked Roberts.

Snidlett responded by spitting a third time.

"One more thing. Did she use crack cocaine Wednesday?"

"Yeah, but she had it. Didn't come from me."

"Do you know Jeff Junior Smith?"

"The only Jeffs I know of race cars."

"Well, Jeff Smith is no race car driver."

"Then I don't know no Jeff Smith."

"Did she have a pipe?"

"Yeah, she had a pipe. I'm finished answering questions."

"Did she use that pipe Friday?"

Snidlett glanced at Roberts briefly before responding. "What kind of fool would I be goin' over to Clyde Noble's at night? If she wanted me she'd drive to me."

Roberts dropped his cigarette and ground it carefully with the toe of his shoe. "Just one more thing. You've heard of DNA?"

"Yeah," replied Snidlett, his eyes narrowing yet again.

"We'd like you to come to the health department and give us some blood. We know you had sex with her. We can use DNA just to wrap that part up."

Snidlett leaned over and picked up his saw. "Y'all know how to git back to your car. I'm busy." He yanked the starting cord on the saw and gunned the engine several times as he walked to another tree.

Snidlett studied a large red oak while Roberts squatted and pulled from his breast pocket a small envelope. Flipping it open, he placed it by Snidlett's cigarette butt and popped the butt into the envelope with a small twig. He smiled at Brown, stood up, and started back down the logging road. "More than one way to skin a cat," he said quietly to Brown.

Brown smiled. "Pretty sharp, Gene."

"A crude bastard wasn't he."

Brown grunted. "I'm glad he's white, cause if he wasn't he'd sure give black people a bad name."

Roberts smiled briefly. "Now why did he deny Friday night? He's making me suspicious."

"Why didn't you just tell him about the fingerprints?"

"I want to hear what R. C. and Horace found out. Anyway, he'll stew about it. Something will pop out."

"As long as it ain't no more wads of spit."

"Remind me to call McIntosh when we get to the car. I'm still waiting on his reports on the drug operation with Smith. He's so damn slow. By the way, what's happening to your English?"

"No one else we deal with knows the language. I guess it's rubbing off."

"You saw the cigarette brand?"

"Yeah, Winston."

"Those Marlboro Lights don't have an owner. Maybe Smith. Hell, maybe Miranda, since she couldn't buy her brand Friday."

"Smith don't … doesn't smoke. I searched him and his car. Not a trace of tobacco."

"Caught yourself didn't you," said Roberts.

* * *

Mervin McIntosh was sitting on Gene's desk with a styrofoam coffee cup in his hand when Roberts and Brown returned to the Sheriff's department.

"Damn Mervin," said Roberts, "I'm sorry there's no room for your feet."

Mervin scratched his head before standing. "You wanted me?"

"Yeah."

"To talk about Smith's dealing?"

"Yeah."

"Good timing. Poochie Essex is here to see me."

"Who's Poochie Essex?"

"My informant. The black girl that's been working with me at the Sand Lot."

"Is that the young woman sitting on the bench in the hall?"

"Yeah. I thought you might need to talk to her."

"Isn't very wise to bring an informant around the sheriff's department, Mervin."

"Look Gene. She swears she saw Jeff Junior Smith the night of the murder. She's got a cousin or something who saw him at the Sand Lot too."

Roberts and Brown exchanged quick glances. "Why am I just hearing this now Merv?" asked Gene icily.

"She just told me today. Wednesday's our day to meet. But word is the Sand Lot's closed for business with Smith in jail. Anyway, I haven't seen her since before the arrest. Wasn't much use, with Smith out of commission."

Roberts walked around Merv and dropped into his chair. "I don't believe this crap. What do you think Lewis?"

"Let's hear her out."

"Is she straight, Merv?" continued Roberts.

"She doesn't do drugs. I got her to help by offering her a break on a grand larceny. She's got money problems. That's all I know of. She's worked the Sand Lot and bought off Smith with a state policeman right beside her."

"Then you trust her?" asked Roberts.

Mervin nodded his head. "She's got no reason to lie."

"Okay. Bring her in. She knows you. You ask the questions. No need for her to feel like she's in the Star Chamber."

"Star Chamber?" asked Mervin.

"Go get her," Brown interceded.

Mervin set his cup on Roberts's desk. After he was out of the room, Roberts grabbed the cup and dropped it into the trashcan. "They won't learn, will they?"

"Remember what I said about home trainin'," chortled Brown.

Mervin led Poochie into the room and seated her against the wall midway between the two desks. Most of her face was hidden behind large dark sunglasses and a bandanna covered much of her tightly braided hair. Slender almost to emaciation she looked every bit the part of a young woman living on crack cocaine, and probably did, Mervin's simple faith notwithstanding. Mervin made the minimal introductions and then sat down beside her.

Roberts nodded gravely while Brown smiled and said "hello Poochie."

"Poochie," began Mervin, "you and me talked about Jeff Smith."

"Yeah," answered Poochie.

"And you know who I'm talking about."

"Of course I do. Jeff Junior Smith. Who don't know him?"

"You made some buys from him for me?"

"Yeah."

"What can you tell me about that Friday night that the Noble girl was murdered?"

"I seen him at a party in Hogantown."

"How do you know?"

"I was there."

"I mean, how'd you know it was the same night?" asked Mervin.

"Cat told me. After he was arrested. Cat said he was at the Sand Lot. She was at Hogantown at the party. It all came back to me. He couldn't be no two places at once."

"Well, he was at the party and at the Sand Lot, that's two places."

"I mean he couldn't be at Onan and at the party, and he couldn't be at Onan and the Sand Lot. That's the two places I'm sayin'."

Gene slumped back in his chair and glanced at Brown. Listening to Mervin struggle with a witness was like watching paint dry.

"You're cousins, right?"

"Some kind. Cat's daddy and my mother is double first cousins."

"What is double first cousins?"

"All right. Look. My granddaddy and his sister married….brother and sister married brother and sister. That's double first cousins. Say you and me brother and sister. Your sister married my brother, and we had children. They double first cousins. Your brother married me."

"Even though you and I are sisters, I mean brother and sister?" Mervin scratched his head again.

Poochie shook her head and laughed. "No. Look, you gotta sister and I gotta brother. Say me and you were married. You gotta sister and I gotta brother, right. They got married. We had children. Double first cousins."

"The children?"

Gene leaned forward and sniffed loudly. "Let me step in here, Merv. Your cousin, or whatever, Cat, was at the Sand Lot on Friday night, August twenty-first?"

"Yeah."

"How does she remember the date?"

"Her boyfriend and her went over there…will she, you know, like get into trouble?"

"Absolutely not."

"They went over there for crack. It was his birthday. Jeff gives a twenty-dollar rock to someone on their birthday. Says it's good for business. They come back to the party at Hogantown and I saw her and asked where'd she'd been at and she said over to the Sand Lot. I told her she better not be goin' there."

Gene leveled a piercing glare on Merv. "Did you tell her why?"

Poochie shifted in her chair. "I said…I said she could get caught and go to jail."

"That's all?"

"That's all. She younger than me. She told me it was free 'cause of her boyfriend's birthday. She said him and Jeff was buddies and Jeff got everybody to sing Happy Birthday."

"So you saw Jeff at Hogantown at a party?"

"Yeah. Early. Like eight or nine. Then he left. He likes to get to the Sand Lot around nine. Mervin and me figured that out."

"She's right about that," said Mervin.

"And then Cat saw him at the Sand Lot?" continued Roberts.

"That's what I just said."

"And when did you see Cat the second time."

"You mean when she come back. I don't remember. Ten or so. Like they just went over there and come right back."

Gene picked up a pencil and appeared to study it carefully. "You saw him at eight, maybe nine. And Cat was with you at the same party."

"That's right."

"Then he left, around eight. Later Cat left and came back at ten."

"Ten or eleven."

"And she saw Smith at the Sand Lot."

"Yeah."

"How do you know these times you're giving me?"

"I'm on probation. Merv said I had to be home by midnight. So I sorta watch the time."

Merv raised his eyebrows and shot a quick glance at Roberts. "That's what I told her," said Merv.

Gene laid the pencil down and straightened in his chair. "Anything else Lewis?"

"Heard any talk about Smith and the murder? From people who know him," asked Lewis.

"Yeah. They talkin'. Said he was framed 'cause he's a drug dealer…and black. That kind of stuff."

"Okay."

"Thank you Poochie," said Gene. "You can go back in the hallway. Merv will be out in just a minute."

After Poochie left Gene turned to Merv. "Get all the names from her she can remember, of the party guests, and give 'em to Lewis. Also, no more buys with her. Not for now. Get your reports to me so we can decide the charges."

"Gotcha," answered Merv as he got up to leave.

With the two of them alone Gene looked at Lewis for several minutes, his brain churning. "Lewis. You interview some of that bunch on the list Merv is making. Let's corroborate Poochie's story. Check out Poochie too. But I've got an awful sinking feeling."

Brown did not respond immediately. When he did, his voice was low, as if he were speaking to himself. "You think you do. Shit."

Willie Painter opened the door connecting the investigator's office with the dispatch room. "Gene. R. C. Hawkes is ten seventy-six to here, about ten minutes."

Gene laid down the incident reports he was scanning and looked at Brown. "Why do I think that didn't go well?"

"Hadn't been our day."

Hawkes walked into the office exactly ten minutes after Painter's message. Horace Seay was a step behind.

"Any luck?" asked Gene glumly.

"Hell no," answered Hawkes as he sat heavily in the chair Poochie had earlier occupied. "She wasn't at the trailer. We waited, drove around, went back, waited. She didn't show. This Snidlett fellow came in while we were driving past for the tenth time, he was in a hurry, so Horace and I decided to retreat and regroup."

Roberts leaned back in his chair and looked at the ceiling. "I guess he left the woods right after we finished with him. To get home and get Sunny's story straight."

"That ought to be pleasant," said Lewis. "Wonder what he's going to tell her?"

"What?" asked Hawkes. "Did he deny being at the pool?"

"Yep," answered Roberts. "Just said he was drunk and might've gone out for beer…before he was drunk, of course."

"Did he admit sex with her," continued Hawkes.

"Wednesday night. Denied Friday," answered Gene.

"Guess we'll see how true this love is," Lewis said with a chuckle. "He said he told her he was playing cards on Wednesday."

Roberts leaned forward and looked at Lewis. "You and R. C. go back there until you get her alone. I've got Mr. Thomasson coming in to give blood tomorrow. Then I'm going to Richmond to hand deliver his blood and Snidlett's cigarette butt. I don't want any delays on the analysis."

"You got Snidlett's saliva on a butt?" asked Hawkes.

Brown nodded his head. "We coulda got a pickle jar of it if we'd had a pickle jar."

Gene arose and picked up his blazer which was draped over the back of the chair. "Lewis. Fill R. C. in on the Poochie story. I'm beat. I'm going home."

* * *

At three o'clock Ev gathered his file, a legal pad, and his calendar into a neat pile on his desk. He wondered whether Christmas would come to his office before the hearing. Most out-of-town attorneys came up to introduce themselves when they were new to the Lafayette courts.

Ev walked to the window and looked at the courthouse lawn. Dabs of yellow and red fringed the maples. Soon the ashes would be turning their lemon yellow and the dogwoods would be in their glory; already their red berries were gracing the gnarled branches like tiny Christmas ornaments. *Time to go fishing,* he thought, the sight of a crisp tumbling trout stream dancing in his mind's eye. Turning, he stared at his desk for a moment, the brief wistfulness gone. Doubts were beginning to challenge his earlier conclusions. *Christmas must be up to something.*

Once Ev was downstairs and in the hallway leading to the front of the courthouse any question in his mind disappeared. A phalanx of reporters and cameramen were waiting outside the entrance to the circuit courtroom and the only way the press could have known about the hearing was through Christmas.

Ev briefly greeted Varney Mitchell who looked more disheveled than usual and a few other reporters whom he had met in the past. "Is it in here?" asked Mitchell pointing to the circuit courtroom.

"No, upstairs," replied Ev.

The troop of newsmen followed Ev up the steps to the district court. The reporters started filing into the courtroom while the three cameramen took seats on the benches in the hallway. Cameras were not permitted in the courtroom, no small blessing in Ev's estimation.

Angela Keating, reporter for the Charlottesville television station, pulled Ev aside before she entered the courtroom. "What kind of hearing is this?"

"A bond hearing," answered Ev, already uncomfortable and reticent simply because the press was present.

"Oh," she answered. "This isn't the preliminary thing."

"Nope."

"Thanks." Keating went in and joined the others.

Through the door Ev saw a cluster of black faces and decided that they were Smith's family. He stepped in far enough to see that no one was seated at defense counsel's table.

Ev turned and walked into the clerk's office. Mary Thornton, the clerk, turned to a man seated on the far side of the small room. "This is Mr. Cross, Mr. Christmas."

Christmas quickly arose from his chair and walked toward Ev. He was a big man, bordering on corpulent, with gray flecked hair and a broad smile. He extended a large hand as he introduced himself. "Nice to meet you. I'm Isaiah Christmas."

"Ev Cross," said Ev as he shook the massive hand.

"I'm sorry about the notice. My office was suppose to call you yesterday."

Ev nodded as he wondered whether Christmas was lying.

"This is a beautiful courthouse," Christmas continued.

Ev agreed.

"Can I see my client a minute before the hearing?"

"He's on the way now," said Mary Thornton.

"Good," replied Christmas. "I guess you know Wil Bledsoe, don't you Ev."

"Oh certainly," replied Ev, wondering if Christmas was ever without something to say. *He must be a Norfolk version of Bledsoe.*

Wimpie Carson stepped inside the clerk's door with an orange-clad handcuffed Smith at his side. "Here he is."

"Hi Jeff," Christmas greeted his client as if they were old friends. "Where can we talk?" he asked Ev.

Ev pointed to a door leading to a tiny file room situated between the clerk's office and the courtroom. Carson walked the defendant through the clerk's office to the door and let him in.

"We're ready in a minute, Ev" said Christmas as he followed Smith through the door.

Ev stared at the door for a moment, letting the whirlwind settle, and then walked into the hallway to enter the courtroom through the public's entrance. Abner Lincoln, having left his tiny chambers, was a few steps ahead.

Everyone took his place and waited for Christmas and Smith to join them. The courtroom was silent.

Five minutes passed and the defendant and his attorney had not yet exited the side door connecting the courtroom with the temporary conference room. Lincoln looked at his watch and then turned to the bailiff. "Tell them we're starting."

Christmas responded immediately to the bailiff's message, briskly walking to the bench and introducing himself. Smith followed behind him at a casual pace, throwing back his head in greeting to his following seated in the middle of the gallery. He was short and of medium build and in his orange jump suit looked younger than his thirty-one years.

"Come on up here," said Christmas as he motioned for his client to stand in front of the bench.

Lincoln shuffled the papers in front of him. "We're here on your motion requesting a bond," he announced in a firm voice.

"Yes sir," replied Christmas, his voice much louder than the near whisper lawyers usually employed when huddled with their clients at the bench.

Ev looked from Christmas to Lincoln and back to Christmas. Christmas was going to make sure the press corps could hear him. Lincoln was going to be stiffly formal for the same audience.

"Is the Commonwealth ready?" asked Lincoln.

"Yes judge," answered Ev quietly

"It's your motion Mr. Christmas. Please proceed."

In the routine bond hearing defense counsel called his client as the first witness and asked him about his job and living arrangements. Christmas proceeded altogether differently.

"Your honor we ask that a reasonable bond be set in this matter and I have several reasons. First, I will be filing a suppression motion today for any statements my client might have made. Quite simply, as the result of an unfortunate exchange of names between deputy Brown and Mr. Smith, racial slurs and such," here he paused very briefly for emphasis, "the deputy ran Mr. Smith down, drew his service weapon, his gun, and at gun point, interrogated him without any advisement of his rights. And, the officer provided my client with false information about a test being conducted."

Ev pursed his lips. This was supposed to be a bond hearing he thought ruefully. Christmas sounded more like he was arguing his case to a jury and he had conveniently omitted, for the benefit of the press, that Lewis Brown was black.

"Second, your honor, Mr. Smith is a lifelong resident of Lafayette County. He has a few minor traffic infractions. He will be living with his grandmother and is employed."

*At the Sand Lot,* thought Ev.

"But last, and very critical, is the strength of this case. I have three witnesses, so far, who are in no way related to Mr. Smith, who will place him miles away from the crime the entire evening of August twenty-first."

Lincoln glanced at Ev from the corner of his eyes.

Ev was not surprised that Smith was able to round up some crack heads as alibi witnesses, but he was surprised that Christmas would bring it up in a bond hearing. *He has a plan,* Ev told himself. *What's the plan?* He looked briefly to the left and saw that the reporters were hunched over their notepads busily scribbling Christmas' every word. *That's the plan.*

"I should add," continued Christmas, "that DNA will not be dispositive in this case. It is my understanding that DNA from three different people have been connected to the ... to Miz Noble's death."

*How the hell did he know that?* wondered Cross.

Christmas, who had inched his way closer to the judge as he talked, now paused and stepped back. "I have his grandmother here who can testify where he'll be living at, your honor, if you want to hear from her."

"Is that all, Mr. Christmas?" asked Lincoln.

"For now, yes sir."

"Mr. Cross," said the judge.

Ev turned and faced the judge. Like an old warhorse straining at the first whiff of gunpowder, Ev was anxious to let go his salvo. "I didn't come prepared to try the case your honor. Probable cause has been found by the magistrate and this isn't the preliminary hearing, Mr. Christmas can try to prove his case later. For now, we have a murder with which the defendant is charged. He's a flight risk, he ran from Lieutenant Brown—who, as the court knows, is also black—at the mention of his possible involvement with the killing. There is no alternative for an accused murderer, no safe alternative but jail. As for his employment, our evidence points to something else. We haven't even been told what his employment is—"

"Landscaping," muttered Smith.

Ev stopped speaking and looked briefly at the judge. Unemployed local defendants always claimed one of three lines of work: landscaping—mowing lawns—hanging sheet rock, and cutting pulpwood. If everyone who claimed to cut wood actually did so there would not have been a tree standing in Lafayette County. Ev, reading the judge's mind, let Smith's statement speak for itself. "I ask that bail be denied," concluded Ev.

Christmas moved closer to the bench. "Your honor, house arrest would—"

Lincoln waved his hand. "I don't need to hear any more Mr. Christmas. The Commonwealth is right. I'll be glad to review his bail status after the preliminary hearing."

Smith, who had been studying the floor throughout the exchange, jerked his head up and looked toward the ceiling.

"I'll see you in a minute, Jeff," Christmas whispered as Wimpie Carson led the defendant away. The Smith family entourage went out first, fussing quietly among themselves, followed by the reporters who wanted to be well-positioned to snag the departing lawyers.

Ev picked up his papers and walked to the defense table where Christmas was packing his brief case. "Let's set the preliminary hearing date while you're here. How about November eighteenth."

"I'd like it sooner than that," said Christmas. "It's got to be Wednesday right? How about mid-October?"

Ev was not sure how long the balance of the lab work would take, but three weeks seemed too soon. "I've got lab reports outstanding," began Ev.

"I'll stipulate you found Smith's semen, along with two others."

The proposal made Ev uneasy. "Let's just take it up with the judge."

The two lawyers wrangled about the laboratory results for several minutes before Lincoln split the baby and set the hearing for October twenty-first.

"Who are these alibi witnesses?" asked Ev.

Christmas looked at his adversary and smiled. "Can't tell you that. Alright if I look at your file while I'm here today?"

Ev was too stunned to answer. The unwritten rule in his experience was that defense counsel provided alibi evidence and certain other information if the prosecutor permitted the examination of his file. He finally found words. "Our local practice is reciprocal discovery."

The smile faded from Christmas' face. "You didn't tell me that when we talked on the phone the other day. You said you had an open file policy."

"I do. With the understanding you'll give me what the rules would allow me with formal motions."

Christmas studied Ev for a moment before replying. "I'll have to think about it. I probably don't need to see your file right now anyway. Just give me the exculpatory stuff."

They shook hands and Christmas left the courtroom. Although Ev knew the reporters were waiting they were far from his mind. Maybe in Norfolk the informal rules were different; he had no idea. Maybe Christmas was trying a sucker punch. Regardless of the niceties of Christmas's motivations Ev also had the queasy feeling that he was going back on his word to the other man.

In any event the exculpatory evidence would include, at the least, the fingerprint and DNA analyses that showed other playmates had been at the Noble pool. And Ev would have to surrender Jason's conflicting statements. The Supreme Court required him to give this information to Christmas and that might be all the defense needed. Keeping secret the alibi witnesses was a big advantage as Christmas could spring them at trial without Cross having had the benefit of his investigator learning beforehand their every closeted skeleton.

*I'll sort this out later,* he decided.

The reporters were busy with Christmas, cameras whirring, when Ev entered the hallway. Angela Keating pulled away from the cluster and motioned her cameraman to follow. "Can I ask you about the DNA evidence?"

"I really shouldn't talk about it."

Angela shrugged before responding. "Okay. We'll just get a shot of you leaving. Any problem?"

"No problem," Ev answered softly. From the corner of his eye he saw all three cameras trained on him as he made his way to the top of the stairs. He wondered what the voice-over would be on the evening news. "Evander Cross, the Commonwealth's Attorney, could not speak to us following a dramatic hearing in which the defense attorney claimed that DNA from at least three people was connected to the murder." The bigger problem was that the voice-over would be absolutely correct.

# CHAPTER 16

Thursday, September 24th

Polly sank into a lawn chair to breathe the coolness of the autumn morning while her cat Jasper rubbed against her legs. Ev's semi-retired Pointer, Chief, circled, lay down, and slept. Polly didn't question for a moment the pressure the Noble murder was putting on Ev, but she had trouble following the twists and turns the case was taking and she assumed that Ev was not telling her everything. Ev was usually sparse with details about his cases; his foul mood made him even more tight-lipped about this one.

Aside from the gloomy atmosphere—Ev reminded her of a cartoon character walking around with a dark cloud over his head—she was hurt that he wouldn't take her fully into his confidence. Her mother said it was a man thing and attempted no further explanation. Polly distilled the problem to a single cause: she had not married a modern man, that new breed found in the movies and magazines who are openly sensitive and vulnerable. The pre-modern man didn't know what he should safely reveal so he revealed as little as possible about everything.

Moreover, Margaret's timing could not have been worse. Margaret took little interest in local affairs—she was much more concerned with what her sister and nephew were doing in Georgetown, South Carolina—and probably did not understand that Ev was facing a difficult murder trial.

The ringing of the telephone interrupted Polly's musing. She jumped from the chair and ran inside hoping that the call had not awakened Will. Margaret Cross's name was the caller I D. Polly sighed as she lifted the receiver.

"Polly, an absolutely awful thing has happened."

A knot of fear tightened in Polly's stomach. Were Sam and Ev okay?

"Something has chewed an ear off Kitty Carson," continued Margaret without a pause, her voice faltering.

Kitty Carson was Margaret's favorite cat, favorite dead cat anyway. Kitty, deceased eight years, had been so dear to Margaret that she insisted that he be stuffed upon his demise. The preserved Kitty was eternally engaged in his favorite pastime: sleeping. Lucius Cross had suggested that Kitty be left performing his other pastime, but Margaret saw no humor in the proposal and declined to respond. Comfortably curled, Kitty had been resting without interruption on his preferred sofa in the living room.

Except for a trail down his back left by Margaret's occasional caress, Kitty had grown dusty as the housekeeper Gloria refused to touch the cat or anything else dead and that included using either a vacuum or a feather duster and Margaret, who had never used either, wasn't starting now.

Polly didn't know what to say.

"Polly, are you there?"

"Yes. I'm here. That's terrible," she finally managed. Polly detected no lilt in Margaret's voice; it was early even for Margaret to be drinking, but she was no stranger to early starts.

"He was fine yesterday. Just lying there peacefully as always and then this morning…."

"How did it happen?" asked Polly, unsure what else she could ask.

"I don't know. Maybe mice."

"With seven cats living inside?"

"Oh no, I guess that can't be it," said Margaret quickly. "I'm wondering if Gloria vacuumed his ear off. He's so brittle you know."

Polly discounted Gloria as the culprit since it was no secret that she avoided Kitty. She avoided the living room if she could manage it. "I just don't know Mrs. Cross."

"It's just one more thing. Poor Kitty Carson. Just when I was so worried about selling."

*Please no,* thought Polly. Will appeared in the kitchen rubbing his eyes as she waited for the other shoe to drop.

"I'm so worried about my finances. I don't know if I can accept your price."

"It's not my price, it's Ev's," said Polly reflexively.

"I'll probably want to buy a condo in South Carolina. And prices there are outlandish now. I wish we'd bought land there when my sister did. I told Lucius we should. He just wouldn't listen."

Polly wondered if Margaret had heard her response.

"You know," said Margaret, "I really haven't considered whether Amanda might want this home. She was telling me how much she liked it the other day and I realized I hadn't even asked her."

*Please God,* thought Polly.

"I just don't know what to do," said Margaret.

"Mommy, I'm hungry," said Will.

"Okay, okay," whispered Polly as she waved him toward the closed porch where the toys were housed.

"Mrs. Cross. Will just got up and I need to take care of him."

"He ought to fix his own breakfast. Amanda's children do."

"I've really got to go Mrs. Cross."

Margaret finally rang off after lamenting one more time the fate of Kitty Carson's ear.

* * *

Linda Masencup greeted Ev with a handful of pink message slips.

"A couple of lawyers and more reporters Ev," she said as she handed them to him. "Remember that you have Paula Noble coming in at noon. And Gene called and said he couldn't be here."

Ev glanced through the slips as he walked to his office. Christmas had done a fine job of exposing the Smith case weaknesses to the world and the local television stations had been generously accommodating with their airtime. Judging from the pink slips some of the out-of-town media were following up.

Cross knew that Roberts was scrambling to gather the loose ends in the case and Roberts usually kept to himself when he was in the thick of an investigation. Knowing his investigator's routine did not ease Ev's anxiety. The charge against Smith had taken a decidedly southward turn and that cat was out of the bag. And what was he to say to Paula Noble? She had not pestered him about the case and he felt a little guilty for not having called her first. The televised difficulties with Smith's charges would be the inevitable focus of their meeting.

The first Mrs. Noble appeared promptly at noon and Linda Masencup brought her to Ev's office. Ev rose to greet his poised and attractive visitor. "Mrs. Noble, I'm sorry it's taken this long for us to meet," began Ev.

"Please call me Paula. I know you're very busy Mr. Cross. Gene Roberts has kept in touch with me."

"And call me Ev," he responded. Ev felt awkward and wasn't sure how to begin their meeting. "Where do we start?" he finally managed.

A wan smile brightened the dark circles under Paula's eyes. "When I made the appointment, it was to find out what I needed to do…how I could help you in the trial. Now I'm confused after last night's news."

Ev leaned forward and rested his arms on the desk, clasping his hands together. "The DNA and so forth?"

"Yes."

"Paula, our evidence is that Miranda had sexual relations with three different men close to or on Friday night."

"Oh my God," breathed Paula. "Gene called me last week to tell me something like this was developing. So that's what Smith's lawyer was talking about."

"Yes."

"I take it Jason is one of the three."

"Yes."

"And Smith?"

"We're all but certain."

"Who is the third one?" she asked weakly.

"That we're not sure of. We believe it's a man named Lester Snidlett."

"Snidlett? Who is he?"

"A logger who was at Nobles, at Clyde Noble's home on the Wednesday before."

Paula pulled a tissue from her blazer pocket and wiped beneath her eyes. She tried to smile as she spoke. "I've been carrying these with me lately. I apologize."

"You needn't. I'm sorry I can't find a better way to tell you this."

"Well. What does this mean?"

"It means Smith will point to the DNA and say it could have been one of the other two who were with her."

"The DNA can't tell you when they were with her?"

"No. Not really. Of course we'll look at that."

"Jason?"

"Nothing suggests he did it."

"Why would this Smith do this?"

Ev felt the muscles in his chest tightening. A layman with no understanding of either DNA or criminal law was picking apart the case that Lewis Brown had prematurely initiated. "That's still not clear, but it could have to do with drugs."

"How did all this happen without me seeing it?" said Paula quietly, as if to herself.

Ev wanted to turn the conversation away from the weaknesses in his case. "Was she asking for money?"

"No."

"Was she saying anything about her father, about the Nobles?"

"No. Well, she said sometime before, mentioned, how difficult Rita was. They didn't like one another. I don't know why Miranda persisted in going over there."

"Were you and Miranda close? I mean, did she confide in you?"

"Yes. But not as much when she quit school. She was, she seemed different, distant. I thought she was worried about that. Sorting things out in her mind. I didn't press her. I guess it's clear she wasn't confiding." Tears suddenly spilled from her brimming eyes. "I should have been asking, asking."

Ev leaned forward until his chest was against his desk. "This wasn't your fault, Paula."

Paula wiped her eyes again and then balled the tissue in one hand. "Gene told me about Jason. I'm telling you Ev. He's changed his story and I don't trust him, he's up to something. And I've heard Rita's lies firsthand. She can lie to your face without batting an eye. He can too, I bet. I'm not comfortable that he should be written off." Paula's voice was strengthening and the tears had stopped. "I know better than to tell you how to do your job. And Gene Roberts certainly knows what he's doing. But I can promise you that Rita will spend every dollar it takes to shield her brother." Paula looked toward the wall when she finished speaking. "I needed to tell you that," she said in a softer voice. "Especially after what I heard on TV. Rita will play everyone she needs to. And she'll use Clyde to help her."

In the ordinary course Ev would have discounted an ex-wife's suspicions about her replacement, but his own experience with Rita Noble gave credence to Paula's warning. Nervousness boiled in the pit of his stomach; it was time for him to admit to himself that the Smith charge was unraveling.

"Gene and two other officers are working on this non-stop," said Ev. "I've got confidence that he'll make some sense of it."

"There's no sense to it," replied Paula.

They concluded their talk with a discussion of the trial procedures. Paula was anxious about her daughter's promiscuity coming out in the trial and Ev had no choice but to tell her that nothing was sacred once witnesses started testifying. It was clear that she didn't like what she was hearing but she held her tongue. For Ev that was some relief, as it was not uncommon for victims and their families to blame the prosecutor for the hard edges of a criminal trial.

"Miranda will be painted as the bad person won't she," said Paula.

"The defense will probably try something like that."

Paula shook her head and then arose. "I've taken enough of your time. Please stay in touch with me. I don't want to learn about things from the news."

Paula tried to force a thin smile, then she walked quickly out of his office. Ev attempted to follow but she was down the hall and leaving the reception area by the time he was through his door.

The press, Hampton Coleman, Rita Noble—all the things that had kept him tense and irritable were now far from his mind. Paula's visit had washed them away, and left in their place a clear sense of the obligation he owed Paula and her dead only daughter. He was filled with an urgency that he could not relieve; he had to let Roberts gather the pieces, but then the fight, Paula's and Miranda's fight, would be his.

* * *

Lewis Brown was at his desk early Thursday morning re-reading his Lebanon Cove notes when Hank Burke walked in, a styrofoam coffee cup in hand.

"See the game the other night? Braves were awful," said Burke.

"No. Missed most of it and didn't feel like watching the end," answered Lewis.

"Yeah. I fell asleep in the eighth," said Burke. "Any luck in the Cove?"

"Not much."

"I think it's them boys Ronnie Snidlett and the Bota kid."

"I can't seem to put it on them," replied Brown, still trying to focus on his notes.

"That Dillon Cobb or Klobb or whatever it is cornered me about it at the Quik Mart. Wanted to know where we was at."

"I'm on it boss," answered Brown.

Burke was the sheriff so it was appropriate that he have little or nothing to do, but his effort to keep himself entertained meant bothering everyone else. Brown much preferred the mornings when the sheriff was at a breakfast meeting with the Ruritans, the Senior Forum, or one of the other of the multitude of civic groups that seemed to meet for breakfast every other week.

To Brown's relief R. C. Hawkes appeared an hour earlier than was his routine.

"R. C. How's it shakin?" said Burke loudly as he shook Hawkes's hand as if the election were the following week.

Brown laid down his file. "Let's hit it, R. C.," he said, anxious to get away from Burke's confabulating.

"Where you boys off, too?" asked Burke.

Brown was uncomfortable in telling Burke anything. He had heard an earful on the importance of confidentially from Roberts the day before while on their way to talk to Snidlett. "Another interview on the Noble case," he finally replied as he headed for the door.

"Who's this time?" continued the sheriff.

"Sunny Grogan," replied Hawkes.

"How's she involved?" asked Burke, the cup almost to his lips.

Hawkes glanced at Brown's retreating back before deciding an answer was up to him. "That's what we're trying to figure out."

Burke drained his cup and waved his hand as Hawkes followed Brown through the door. He set the empty cup down on Roberts's desk and walked to the dispatchers' door. He opened the door slightly and poked his head inside the tiny room. "Willie, did ja see that game the other night?"

"What's going on with the sheriff?" Hawkes asked Brown once they were out of the sheriff's department parking lot.

"Aw, you know. The usual stuff. Been talkin' to the press too much."

Hawkes laughed. "That's his job isn't it?"

"I guess," replied Brown quietly. Roberts's rule about loyalty had suddenly come to mind.

"The news last night didn't sound too good. Alibi witnesses and three sources of DNA."

"Yeah I heard," answered Brown.

"It gets under your skin when every Tom, Dick and Harry knows as much about the case as we do."

Lewis pulled a cigarette pack from the dash. "Always a problem. I don't care what we do. Someone is blabbing."

The two men fell silent until reaching the driveway of Lester Snidlett's trailer. A faded blue Honda Accord was parked near the front steps. The baying of a half dozen penned hounds greeted them.

"That Honda should be hers according to Horace Seay," said Hawkes.

Lewis got out of the car and straightened his tie. As he mounted the steps Lewis could see through the window that Sunny Grogan was sitting in front of the television set, still in her bathrobe, a cigarette protruding from the corner of her mouth.

"What do you wont?" she said brusquely when she opened the door. The robe did a poor job of hiding her ample cleavage and the butterfly tattoo on the rise of her generous left breast.

Lewis introduced himself and Hawkes while the talk show on the television continued unabated. "We'd like to talk to you for just a few minutes."

"What about?"

"Can we come in?" asked Lewis.

"I guess." Sunny opened the door and turned to walk back to her chair. She picked up the cigarette she had momentarily abandoned while answering the door and drew on it before crushing it in the ashtray. Crossing her arms, she faced the officers. "Okay, you're in. What is it?"

Lewis glanced at Hawkes before deciding to take the plunge. "Lester Snidlett lives here with you, doesn't he?"

"Y'all oughta know. You've been here before."

"Well, I haven't. But he does, correct?"

"Yeah. It's his trailer."

"I want to ask you about Friday, August twenty-first."

Sunny shook her head. "Look, Lester said y'all were asking him about that girl's murder. He couldna done it. He was here."

"How do you remember that?"

"He works and he comes home every night. Don't go nowhere, except maybe to the store. That's not five minutes."

"Every night?" asked Lewis. "For how long has he been doing that?"

"I don't know when he wasn't here. Maybe huntin' season. They camp during huntin' season."

"Ten months ago?"

"Something like that."

Lewis paused, running through his mind whether to ask about the Wednesday night Snidlett spent with Miranda. Apparently Lester had left that little snippet out of his report to her of the afternoon before. What would Roberts do in this situation? Lewis decided to avoid a decision for the moment. "Lester drink every night?"

The television talk show was interrupted by a commercial for feminine napkins.

"Yeah, probably. I mean he gets his cereal from a can. But, you know, I don't follow him around. But on Friday and Saturday. I know for sure he does. One reason he don't go out, to keep from gettin' a ticket."

R. C. Hawkes had been carefully studying the room while Lewis dueled with Sunny. Near the refrigerator he saw a Budweiser twelve pack carton. "I guess that Budweiser is his?" he asked, gesturing toward the refrigerator.

Sunny looked in the indicated direction as if that corner of the trailer were new to her. "Yeah," she answered slowly. "Anything wrong with that?"

"Nope," answered Hawkes. "Anyone else live here? Children?"

"No. I mean my children visit sometimes, but they live with their deddy. Anyway, they won't here at all in August."

Lewis used the interruption to determine his course. Like a defensive blitz on the football field, the object was to disrupt the other team's play. Nothing he had learned about Snidlett the previous day suggested that Sunny Dawn Grogan was going to take her man's womanizing lightly.

"Sunny, it's been a long time, but do you remember the Wednesday night of that week. The week the girl was killed."

Sunny's brow wrinkled. "Not a thing. Why would I? Days run together."

"You don't remember that Lester came home about four in the morning. That would've been Thursday morning?"

Flush crept into Sunny's checks. "I went to bed early. Most of the time I do. I'm not for sure."

"But he was out that evening?"

"I don't know that," she said, her voice now devoid of the earlier defiance. "Who told you that?"

"Lester told me that."

"Told you what?"

"Didn't he tell you he played cards at the cabin all night?"

"He might 'uv."

"So he wasn't here."

"Look, I don't know. He's plays poker sometimes."

"Maybe strip poker?" asked Brown.

Laughter erupted on the talk show and Hawkes bit his lip to keep from joining in with the well prompted audience

Sunny glared at Brown and then Hawkes. "What are you gettin' at?" Suddenly her tone was acerbic.

"You remember, then, that he wasn't here?" continued Lewis.

"I don't know what I remember. What's this got to do with the girl gettin' killed?"

"We're just trying to put all the pieces together."

"Well he was here that Friday night, so that's one piece you don't have to look for."

Brown smiled. "Okay. Thanks for your time."

Sunny unfolded her arms and walked to the door. "What did you mean about strip poker?" She watched Brown and Hawkes from the corner of her eye as they followed her.

Brown stopped and looked squarely at Sunny Grogan. "Lester was with Miranda that Wednesday night."

"That son of a bitch. He told you that?"

"He did."

"Why were you beatin' around the bush about it?"

Hawkes paused at the door and looked at Brown. Brown had not moved. "We wanted to know whether you'd be truthful."

Sunny opened the door, and walked back to the sofa where she had been when Brown first knocked. "Close it behind you," she said without looking back.

The two men showed themselves out and returned to the Crown Victoria. Brown hurriedly reached for a cigarette while turning the car around.

"That Snidlett fellow's got his hands full," said Hawkes with a wry laugh. "I wonder why he thought he could get away with not telling her about Wednesday night."

"Well, I don't know what he told her. He had to cover Wednesday and Friday. I think he got to bragging about Wednesday with us before thinking it might get back to Sunny. He's probably in the woods right now dreamin' up a lie to tell her about that."

Hawkes rubbed his eyes with the heel of his palms. "Did you notice the cigarettes?"

"Sure did. Marlboro Lights. Old Lester must have been in too big of a rush to stop by the Trading Post on Friday night." The Onan Trading Post flashed by on the right just as Lewis finished speaking. "He passed right by it," added Lewis.

"You think he was at the pool Friday night?"

"Yep."

"Some fingerprints and those cigarette butts are all we have, Lewis."

"Maybe they went as a tag team, Thomasson, Smith and Snidlett."

"Yeah," answered Hawkes sarcastically.

Lewis pulled a sheet from the file at his side. "Merv acted pretty fast for a change. This is the list of names from the Hogantown party. Do you want to try and find a few of them?"

"Might as well."

"Some of these are high school kids. Let's start there. Cat's a senior. She was at the Sand Lot too."

"That's encouraging. A murder case resting on what high school students have to say, which is usually not the truth."

"It's all uphill from here R. C."

* * *

Brown and Hawkes had the usual luck with the high school students on Mervin McIntosh's list. Of seven, one was absent. Three, twisting in their seats and looking wild-eyed around the guidance counselors' office where they were being interviewed, denied ever having been to the Sand Lot or the Hogantown party. Three, uneasy and red faced, admitted their presence at one or the other and generally confirmed Poochie Essex's story. Brown expected several sets of parents to call the sheriff complaining that their children had been interviewed, but that wasn't his problem and it would give Burke something to do.

The two men brought Roberts up to date at the end of the day. Roberts listened, stared at the ceiling, and kept his thoughts to himself. Brown went home hoping that he might be left alone to watch the Thursday night football game on television.

The telephone rang in the first quarter. "Lewis, this is Reggie Williams. You gotta another burglary over in Lebanon Cove."

*I've got one?*

"Stu and Mary Linda Kemper. They live at—"

"Marilyn. I know where they live," said Brown. Between his watch from the bushes and his regular trips up and down the Cove road he had memorized every inch of the Cove.

"They expectin' you," said Reggie. "You need the numbers?"

"No. I'll take care of it." Brown rang off and repositioned his tie. He drove to the Kemper home where he heard the familiar tale that the two working occupants had come home to find their back door forced and guns and money, and panties, missing. In Marilyn's case, the panties were pretty big.

* * *

162

There were times in Gene Roberts's twenty-eight years as a policeman when he thought that he couldn't take one more day of inefficiency and incompetency. He had almost called it quits on so many occasions that he had lost track, and he had quit even thinking about quitting, not because he was slowly making progress in his efforts to improve the sheriff's department, but because he was too close to retirement. The sheriff established the goals and set the pace for a department and the last two sheriffs he had served, Hank Burke and Conway Lawson, set only one goal: re-election, and the pace was designed to keep the waters calm, ruffling as few feathers as possible including the feathers of inadequate deputies.

The Noble murder presented a different problem. The problem was not foot-dragging deputies, the problem was that he had not been able to determine who killed Miranda Noble and that was his job. He had spent every night of the last week trying to convince himself that Smith was the culprit and every day he found something else suggesting that the wrong man was charged. Most evenings he spent sitting on his deck, looking at the mountains without seeing them, turning over in his mind the pieces of the puzzle he had and the pieces he was still missing. Just what evidence would pin down which of Miranda's playmates had been the last one with her? The conundrum was more than a professional challenge, it also pricked his professional pride, most pointedly since a man was charged and sitting in jail while Roberts struggled to convince himself as to the identity of the murderer. If Roberts couldn't convince himself that Smith should be sitting in jail then he certainly ought not be tried, at least not on a murder charge.

While Roberts thought himself immune to criticism, the immunity was not working now. He knew Rita Noble would be insufferable if the charge against Smith were dropped. Being accustomed to hearing people complain didn't always make the bitter pill easier to swallow and a dismissal of the charges would play right into Rita's constant harping that the local cops couldn't handle the case.

At the heart of it was Brown's mishandling of the arrest which had hamstrung the whole investigation and Roberts blamed himself. He should have provided Lewis with precise guidance. In fact, he chided himself for not having handled Smith himself. He knew he had a hundred balls in the air all the time, but he wasn't about to offer that for an excuse. Whining was on the same level with disloyalty and incompetency and Roberts's Trumanesque advice to himself was the same as to the deputies: if you can't take the heat, get out of the kitchen. Getting out of the kitchen was out of the question; he was going to solve this riddle.

**CHAPTER 17**

Friday, September 25th

For what seemed like the thousandth time Brown turned the Crown Victoria onto the Cove road and followed it to its dead end at Danny Bota's house. Brown had been to the house before; he had interviewed Bota and everyone else in the Cove. Bota had been or seemed to have been as clueless as the rest of the Cove's residents.

Bota lived in a small frame house, once a farm tenant's quarters, that could not have had more than four rooms and what paint remained suggested that it had once been white. In the narrow space between the road and the sagging front porch sat two Pontiac sedans of the same model, both on cinderblocks and missing their wheels and tires, futilely awaiting a merger of their parts into one functioning automobile. If he hadn't known better Brown would have thought the place abandoned.

Brown stopped on the side of the road in front of the house. Aaron Bota and Ronnie Snidlett had been loitering on the porch the day Brown questioned Danny Bota about the burglaries, but questioned wasn't the word, he had only asked if Bota had seen anything unusual. Aaron and Ronnie, overhearing the question, each responded with an insouciant shrug.

The boys seemed the likely burglars, but Brown had not one iota of evidence. *Snidletts,* he thought, *my luck to be investigating Lester and his brother Ronnie at the same time. I guess God put Ronnie here to prove his older brother wasn't an accident.*

* * *

Roberts was a witness in Ev's burglary trial on Friday morning so when he saw Ev he had time only to tell him that they needed to talk. Ev set their meeting for two o'clock. Roberts spent the rest of the morning sitting uselessly in the witness room enduring the half-drunk rambling of the other witness while awaiting his turn to testify.

After playing his part in the trial, Roberts walked down the steps to his desk in the sheriff's department and began glancing through the incident reports that had accumulated over the last few days while he had been occupied with the Noble case.

Brown and R. C. Hawkes were out trying to find more of the Sand Lot witnesses Mervin McIntosh had listed. Cocaine customers were not generally known for their veracity, but they couldn't be ignored if enough of them would talk and had the same story.

"You got time to talk to me about a burglary in Morgan?" interrupted Horace Seay as he dropped his hat on Brown's desk.

Roberts leaned forward and aligned the pile of incident reports. "Not now. Cross is due here any minute. Monday okay?"

"That's okay." Seay picked up his hat and walked toward the door. He stopped at the threshold. "That Smith case is getting kind of screwy, isn't it?"

Willie Painter opened the door from the dispatcher's room before Roberts could answer. "Lab on line one for you Gene."

Roberts picked up his telephone and Seay, realizing that he wasn't going to get an answer, pulled on his hat and left.

* * *

Roberts was sifting through his mail when Cross walked in.

"What happened in your trial?" asked Roberts.

"Acquitted. My so-called victim got everything confused. Was he drunk?"

"You should have been breathing the air in the witness room. It's a wonder I'm not."

Ev seated himself in the chair behind Lewis Brown's desk and took off his eyeglasses. "Well, your invitation had an ominous ring this morning. What's happened?"

"Then or later?"

Ev smiled and shook his head. "Okay. Unload."

"The lab called. Man number three is Lester Hester Snidlett. Man number two is Thomasson, like we thought."

"I guess we expected that for Snidlett."

"For Wednesday, yes, which he admits. But his semen still in her by Saturday, that's somewhat of a stretch, but not impossible. Probably more important, we've got six kids who saw Smith in Hogantown and at the Sand Lot between eight-thirty and eleven that night."

"How would they remember? He's selling every damn night."

"There was a big birthday party. Mervin's informant is one of the people. She's the one who alerted us to this. Hawkes and Brown are out rounding up a few more customers. So now the times aren't jiving. Smith must have been there earlier. Before Jason."

"Hell, I'm lost," said Ev leaning back in his chair.

"Think of this. Miranda goes to buy cigarettes and cash a check. She has no money. Manfred Fitzgerald won't take the check. Jason has put an end to his contributions. She calls Smith figuring she'll barter something. Smith arrives, say five or six, gives her cocaine and gets laid for the trouble. Jason shows up later. She

165

services him. She smokes crack again and he throws the pipe over the fence, which of course, we found. She puts her bathing suit back on and he leaves."

"Didn't you find the pipe later?"

"Yes. You're right. Could've been placed there, could have been there from some other time. And while you're poking holes, the homemade pipe in the trash could've been from another night, too. But my guess is the homemade pipe was made and used that night after her real pipe was tossed."

"Why believe Jason?"

"No particular reason, except instinct."

"Snidlett could've showed up, maybe helped with the new pipe and things get a little rough. He uses force and smothers her in the process."

Ev stood up and walked across the room to Roberts's filing cabinet. "So we're back to square one."

Roberts chuckled as he lit his cigarette. "I'm not sure we've made it to square one."

"Maybe Jason was there earlier than he says."

"Manfred says differently. And I checked with Jason's employer. His story checks out for when he left work. He could've been there later, but not earlier."

"What about the silver car the Mexican woman saw?"

"I don't know what the hell to make of that, except it's probably connected with the killer."

"Jason's car?"

"Green."

A tightening sensation was enveloping Ev's entrails, as if someone with a giant greasy hand were slowly squeezing his guts into a tiny ball.

"Snidlett's car?"

"He drives a big wheel pickup. Sunny's car is blue. Snidlett denies being at the Nobles Friday night and Sunny Grogan is backing him."

"Shit shit shit," mumbled Ev.

"So what do you think?" asked Roberts.

Ev walked from the filing cabinet to the dispatcher's door and leaned against it. "Are you sure about this Gene? Because if you are, I've got to cut Smith loose now. I can't leave him in jail over the weekend if I think he's innocent."

Gene reached for his telephone receiver. "Let me see whether I can reach Lewis. See what they've got."

"How'd you get the DNA analysis so quickly?" Ev asked while Roberts was dialing.

"I had to plead with a few of my friends in Richmond."

Only Roberts could have pulled that off thought Ev. His next miracle would be more challenging.

"Lewis," said Roberts into the receiver, "What do you have by way of alibi people? The Commonwealth Attorney and I are talking. No names."

Roberts listened quietly for a moment, then, "Okay. See you in thirty." Roberts dropped the receiver loudly into its cradle. "They've talked to seven. Four admitted they were there and claim Smith was at the Sand Lot. Covers nine to eleven-thirty."

The poison of indecision was seeping into Ev's thought process. Uncertainty of the proper course was an habitual professional burden, but indecision promptly transformed a lawyer into a legal eunuch. For a lawyer who lived in the courtroom, and especially a prosecutor, decisions were made at a furious pace; he who hesitated was lost and he who decided wrongly was soon in a seminary or working as a claims adjuster for an insurance company.

"This gives me a bad taste, Gene. We're relying on high school kids and crack heads for a decision."

"That's about as good as we get in this business, Ev. When was the last time you had a priest or a Shakespeare scholar for a witness?"

"Could he have slipped away between the times these people saw him, and then returned?" Ev knew the answer but wanted to hear it anyway.

"From Hogantown or the Sand Lot, which is near Oak Grove, it's about twenty-five minutes to Onan. That means at least an hour. Now Smith is the only person selling at the Sand Lot. Merv says he doesn't delegate which makes sense. If he left his stash with one of that crowd, the stuff would get used on the spot. But I'll ask Lewis to provide me the times he has. We can check for an hour plus gap."

"I doubt any one of them was checking his watch, Gene." Ev paused, and tried again. "If the likes of Miranda Noble wants to work a little swap, don't you think he'd skip an hour of sales?"

Roberts shook his head. "Maybe in 1960. But in these progressive times, he's probably got a string of good lookin' crack whores."

Ev didn't need examples. He had interviewed undercover officers who had observed young mothers drop to their knees in front of a dealer, watched by a score of crack toasted hangers on, in order to perform her end of the agreed consideration—for a tiny rock of cocaine.

"Alright Gene, what do you think?"

Gene leaned back in his chair and put his hands behind his head. "Let me start from the back end. We can't get a conviction. Ten alibi witnesses. Two other sources of semen. Can we get by preliminary? Yes. Because Christmas won't put on any evidence. Do I think he did it? I'll tell you. I don't know who the hell killed that girl and I don't know why."

Ev pushed away from the door and walked to Brown's desk to retrieve his glasses. "What else can you get me? Pretty quickly."

"Details from Lewis and R. C. Otherwise, probably nothing."

"You're not going to tell me whether I should cut him loose are you?"

Roberts grinned for a response.

"Call me after you've talked to Brown and Hawkes." Ev walked to the door and paused at the threshold. "This puts Jason back on the hot seat."

Roberts leaned forward and snuffed his cigarette. "I've got some angles to work, Ev. I'll call you as soon as Lewis gives me his report."

* * *

The telephone was ringing when Ev walked into the anteroom of his suite. "It's Wil Bledsoe," said Linda Masencup with her hand cupped over the receiver. "Do you want to take it?"

"I guess so," grumbled Ev. He walked into his office and picked up his telephone.

"Well, Mr. Commonwealth," said Bledsoe, "glad to see you're working on a Friday afternoon. I hope a few voters see you in the office."

"I hope they don't" said Ev grimly.

"Come on Commonwealth. No use being there if somebody doesn't know it."

"Why are you so chipper, Wil?"

"Just lovin' it Ev. I just had a little college chickadee in here with more knockers than sense hiring me on a reckless driving. I thought about asking her to try and touch her elbows behind her back and I'd waive my fee, but I decided she might have more sense than I suspected."

Ev was glad he had taken the call. Bledsoe could lift spirits in a funeral parlor. "She's getting you primed for Friday night."

"Not much chance of that. Have you noticed how these young girls talk now?"

"Isn't that where yadda yadda yadda comes from?"

"Maybe. But I've been studying this awhile. These girls all talk fast and high pitched and it's damned near unintelligible. The words come right off the roof of their mouth, from right behind their upper incisors. I call it the Disney Dialect." Bledsoe gave his rendition of the chatter.

"That's pretty good, Wil."

"I finally figured it out. All these girls have braces on by the time they're twelve or thirteen. They don't like rubbing their lips over those braces so they talk without moving their lips and half of it comes out the nose. Has to, to be heard, because you can't talk from the back of your throat like you're supposed to with your lips not moving. And girls are lemmings. Once a few of them do it, then all of them are doing it. And then it hit the Disney channel. In one generation, we've got a Universal American Accent, at least for girls whose families can afford braces."

"So the underprivileged don't do it?"

"Nope. Listen next chance you get. But that will change, too."

Ev chuckled at Bledsoe's newest social observation. "So this is what you called to tell me?"

"Naw. Just wondering what you'd allow me on an eighty-two in a fifty-five. Poor little thing was driving to Charlottesville from Sweet Briar. With a set like she's got, I'm sure some young fella at UVA was glad she was in a hurry."

"I can't give anything on speeding tickets. Where would it end?"

"After this call, Ev."

Ev laughed aloud. "Tell her to wear a tight blouse at trial. Abner might give her a break."

"Don't worry. She'll be there. Abner is definitely a bosom man. I don't think Mary Thornton could've ever got the clerk job without her set."

Ev could hear a woman's voice in the background. "Is she there with you?" asked Ev, certain that Bledsoe would have no hesitation in talking as he was with the client sitting right beside him.

"No. Just Marcie." Marcie was his receptionist. "She said I had a room full of nappy heads waiting to see me. She also said to get my mind off boobs. Thanks anyway." In the background Marcie's laughter was clearly discernible.

Linda walked in while Ev, staring at the window, was trying to decide how Bledsoe got away with all his peccadilloes.

"Reverend Johnson would like to see you," she informed him in a whisper. John Henry Johnson Senior was the minister for Walnut Hill Baptist Church, the perennial secretary of the local NAACP Chapter, a county Democratic Committee member, and dump truck driver for A. E. Henderson and Sons.

"Okay. Show him in," said Ev. He wasn't in the mood for the Reverend, but he knew he shouldn't turn him away.

John Henry Johnson appeared in Ev's office about every six months, usually to plead for a miscreant communicant but sometimes to talk politics and ask how Margaret and E were doing. The Reverend seemed to assume that his position on the Democratic committee required that he periodically check on the local officeholders.

In deference to Reverend Johnson's position in the party, his Walnut Hill Church was the first Ev visited when he was seeking the Democratic nomination for the job as prosecutor. Located in an isolated part of the county and accessible by a narrow rutted gravel road, the small white frame building dating to 1887 was set under two ancient walnut trees on a small knoll. Air conditioners protruding from several windows were whirring against the heat of the June morning.

The candidate arrived five minutes before eleven, spoke hurriedly and self-consciously to the deacons standing at the door, and went inside. Ev sat and waited.

And waited. Women and children drifted in and out. Women over thirty, to a soul, were wearing hats. The drummer moved instruments around while choir members chatted, walked about, and sometimes left the room altogether. People he'd never seen walked into his pew and welcomed him.

Then suddenly with no hint it was going to happen Reverend Johnson strode into the sanctuary from a side door, ceremoniously mounted the one step to the pulpit, and loudly proclaimed, "Welcome brothers and sisters. Let us pray."

The choir and drummer promptly broke into song and accompaniment at the end of the prayer and everyone stood and joined the singing, swaying and clapping in unison with the choir. Not a single hymnal was to be seen. Ev stood too, listened to the hymn he'd never heard and wondered just how obvious his presence was. In stark contrast to the scripted quick-paced Episcopalian liturgy in which Ev had been raised, there was a comfortable informality throughout the Walnut Hill gathering. He quickly reached a conclusion: Episcopalians come to worship God in the beauty of holiness, and black Baptists come to enjoy the beauty of His presence.

Reverend Johnson then looked at Ev. "Today we also have Mr. Ev…I think it's Everett, but we all know him as Ev Cross. He's running for office this year and I know he have a few words for us."

Cross had not realized that he would be called to speak. He wasn't sure whether to remain in his pew or to walk to the front. He had no version of a standard stump speech; local campaigns were one long question and answer session and he had polished plenty of answers which wouldn't make much sense unless a question preceded them. He decided against walking to the front. All eyes were on him as he rose to his feet. In the expectant silence seconds felt like hours as Ev tried to form a smile as cover for his frozen tongue. Finally, "Good morning."

A scattering of voices responded with their "good morning."

Ev then looked at Reverend Johnson. "Thank you for having me as your guest." Ev paused, looked into several of the attentive faces, felt a tingling in his feet, and then proceeded. "I hope to have an opportunity to meet all of you this fall." His effort sounded stupid, fall was a long way off, and the faces were still watching, but he sat down anyway.

There was another silence. Finally Reverend Johnson spoke. "We have seen two unusual things today. A lawyer what don't have much to say and a politician what could open his mouth and a lie didn't come out."

There was general laughter and a few amens all of which seemed to Ev like a favorable response.

Following another hymn unknown to Ev Reverend Johnson took his position behind the pulpit and grasped it firmly with both hands. He surveyed the room, letting the quiet set the stage for his sermon. When all the shuffling ceased the minister leaned forward and in even modulation began reciting the Genesis story of

Joseph which quickly progressed to Onan, who had gone in unto his brother's widow, which was against the law. But Onan had spilt his seed which apparently created another problem, and God slew him.

For his part Ev well remembered Onan's difficulties. He had undertaken as a boy to read the Bible beginning to end, and failed to finish…three separate times. He had got as far as Joshua twice and into First Samuel on the third try. But each time he had started with Genesis. Salacious verses were not easily forgotten, especially when read three times.

Onan and his fate had a special application to young teenage boys and Ev's friend, Glenn Apperson, said the passage meant that self-stimulation invited instant death, or a least blindness. Besides worrying about these Draconian consequences, Ev wondered why someone had named a little crossroads in Lafayette County after a man whose only claim to fame was spilling his seed, and he also wondered what people thought when they saw the sign proclaiming Onan Post Office. Then again, most people had not read Genesis three times.

* * *

Ev greeted John Henry Johnson at his office door and invited him to sit down. The reverend was a small man with graying close-cropped hair. A gold tooth was prominent in his smile.

"I guess you right busy lately," said Johnson.

"Pretty hectic," agreed Ev.

"How's your uncle doing?"

"Doing to suit himself."

Johnson laughed softly. "I oughta go see him. He don't have a thing to do I bet." He hung his A. E. Henderson & Sons baseball cap on his left knee before continuing. "There sure is a lotta talk 'bout that Smith boy."

Ev knew this was coming, and though he dreaded the topic, he also was curious what was circulating in the county, the black part of the county. Ev could converse light-heartedly with Johnson, but he could also discuss more serious topics when necessary. The Reverend's immersion in politics did not exclude room for personal loyalty, and though Ev kept a reasonably safe distance, he did not have to walk on eggshells as was the case with the Hampton Colemans of the party.

"What do you hear?" asked Ev.

"Word is a lotta people saw him somewhere else."

"Have you talked to anyone who saw him, or is that the scuttlebutt?"

Johnson shifted slightly in his chair. "No. None said it to me. Just I heard it from several, you know. I figured you needed to know, if you haven't heard."

Johnson was choosing his words carefully and Ev decided the other man's statement was really a question, one that he ought not try to avoid.

"We've gotten wind of that," said Ev, "but more specifics would really help."

Johnson nodded his head as he looked at his hands, a reaction which Ev took to be Johnson's decision not to be the one to provide the specifics.

"What else is floating around?" ask Ev.

"This and that, just talk how he won't the one."

The ever-present venom of politics—race—was lurking somewhere in what was unspoken. Race usually reared its head when the victim and defendant were not the same color, and Ev didn't have to ask about it, for someone else could be counted on to beat him to it. Yet today Johnson was not going to broach it and Ev wanted to know what the street talk was. He decided that this time he needed to broach the subject first.

"Do people think Smith's race has anything to do with his being charged?"

Johnson looked up, a hint of satisfaction in his eyes. "Some have said that. Some say it's 'cause he's a black dope dealer."

"People can't seriously think we'd charge a man because of his color."

"I know that. But you can't stop talk."

"Do people know that Lewis Brown made the arrest?"

"Oh yeah. But you know what they say. He just doin' what somebody else told him."

"And the somebody else is white?"

Johnson raised his eyebrows but didn't respond.

Ev leaned back in his chair and took off his eyeglasses. "You know I can't make decisions on charges because people have the wrong notions. I mean, if people disagree with me, they'll just have to disagree."

"That ain't it zactly. They know you fair, like your Uncle and Daddy was fair. So I wouldn't tell you what the voters gonna do. What I'm telling you is they watchin' *how* you do what you gonna do."

Ev understood the reference to voters. Johnson meant black voters. "Well, I assure you. We're working on every rumor. If people have information, they ought to contact Lewis or Gene Roberts."

"I'll keep my ears open."

Ev looked through the window beyond Johnson and studied the changing colors of the trees. He switched the subject to the neutral topic of the weather and let Johnson ramble for a few minutes. The telephone intercom cut the conversation short.

"You a busy man Mr. Cross, I won't take no more of your time," said the Reverend as he arose.

Ev rose as well and nodded to Johnson as he left, then he picked up the receiver.

"Ev," came Gene's voice. "We've got it pretty well mapped out."

"What's your conclusion?"

"Nine people have him at that party and the Sand Lot. They aren't sterling witnesses, but there're nine of them. Two said he wasn't driving the silver Buick. One said it was in the shop."

"In the shop?"

"Yeah, I want to look into that. That might nail it down."

"Then I guess we've got to wait."

"You still have a cocaine charge."

"This gives me a bad feeling."

"I'll let you know as soon as I have something."

"Have a nice weekend Gene."

"Thanks … pal," Gene laughed.

Ev laid the receiver in its cradle and stared again through the window. It was four o'clock and he knew he wasn't going to accomplish anything else. Defying Wilmer Bledsoe's admonition he picked up his coat and bid Linda a good weekend. He left the courthouse through a side door and walked around the front of the original courthouse, pausing for a moment to look at the white arcade.

Flanking the doors under the arcade were two plaques, one listing the county's losses in World War I, the other with a longer list of those killed in the Second World War. The quiet of the grounds, together with the lawn's rich green in gentle contrast to the old court building with its tarnished plaques, was a stark reminder to Ev of his mortality. The names on the plaques were vanished links to the past. The old gentry—Thorntons, Dicksons, and his own great-uncle Thomas Cross were there—as well those of lesser circumstances: the Grogans, Essexes, Burkes and Ricketts; and providing most of the names were the yeomanry: the Campbells, Clodfetters, Masencups, and Sneads. The feeling was both humbling and encouraging, one that imbued Ev with the sense that he was playing some part, but for only a very brief, fleeting piece, of the timeless whole.

To the right of the arcade near the front of court square stood the Confederate monument, a life size granite soldier frozen in a posture of patient waiting. Ev had been present at its dedication in 1965. Lafayette was surely the last county in the South to erect a monument to her rebel heroes. The high school band had played Dixie and a senator and governor had posed in Confederate kepis holding a young Ev Cross. A picture of the trio was run on page one of the *Lafayette County Times*, and still hung in the living den.

Ev turned the corner to make his way to the parking lot behind the courthouse. From the corner of his eye he saw a young heavyset black woman waving from the street.

"Hello Mr. Cross," she shouted, "I'm behavin' myself. You don't have to worry 'bout me!"

Ev waved in return. "That's good," he called in response. He had no idea who she was.

# CHAPTER 18

Sunday, September 27th

Brown called Ev Cross Sunday morning. "I've got some bad news, Ev," said Lewis. "They took Gene to the hospital this morning. Heart attack. A bad one."

Ev could find no words; the news paralyzed him just as it had when he learned of his father's fatal heart attack.

"That's not all. Merv McIntosh was shot last night. But he's going to be okay."

"Dear God," Ev finally managed. "What happened?"

"Merv was responding to a domestic. He was approaching the door when Carl Littleton popped out, pulled a pistol and fired."

"Who is Carl Littleton?"

"I don't know him. Apparently he's never been any problem. Anyway, Merv tried to jump out of the way. The bullet caught him in the shoulder. If he hadn't jumped, it would have hit him square in the chest."

"So he's okay."

"Yeah. Twenty-five caliber."

Ev leaned against the hutch. "Didn't he have backup?"

"Okra pulled in as the shot was fired. He yelled and Littleton ducked inside and yelled back that he'd shoot him too, and fired. Okra called for help, then he saw Littleton's wife and her two boys running from behind the trailer so he headed them off and Littleton shot at them too. But he got them away from there. Gene got there and talked Littleton into surrendering or else the sheriff would have blown the place away. Gene had ice water in his veins Ev."

"How long did this all take?"

"Probably not an hour from start to finish."

"What about Gene? What do you know?"

"Not much. He was taken in about an hour ago. Reggie Williams just called me. Said he was unconscious when the squad got there."

"That's not good. Do you need me for anything on this Littleton bastard?"

"No. He's being held without bond. He ain't going anywhere."

"I'm afraid to ask, but, is there anything else?"

"Roberts gave me some info on Smith. On Saturday. More of the same."

"Are you going to be in the office today?"

"I'm fixing to go in now."

"Alright," concluded Ev. "I'll probably see you later then." He slowly replaced the receiver. These men were not just the people he depended on, partners he saw almost everyday, but were friends, too, who shared ribald or silly stories about the untoward problems which were theirs to handle and made light of the danger intrinsic to every instance when an officer confronted another human being.

And while he knew it was a selfish reaction Ev could not stop himself from wondering how he would prevail in the difficult cases, the Noble murder looming largest of all, without Gene Roberts. Ev felt a surge of guilt. He, like everyone else, piled work on Roberts, depended on him to sort through the deluge, and expected him to unravel the abstruse knots fastened by human frailties

Ev walked back outside. "Polly," he said, "my troops had a bad weekend."

"What happened now?"

"Merv McIntosh was shot and Gene Roberts had a heart attack."

"What! Killed!"

"No. Injured. Lewis said he'd be okay. But Gene must be in pretty bad shape."

Polly arose and walked toward Ev. "Who shot Merv?"

"Some guy named Carl Littleton."

"One of Sam's schoolmates is a Littleton. Joshua Littleton. Ev. Is Gene okay? Are you okay?"

Ev stared at the pasture beyond the fence. "I'm okay." He sighed heavily. "I'm going to the courthouse. I don't know how Gene's doing."

Polly put her arm around Ev's neck and hugged him tightly. "I'm sorry Ev. I hope Gene will be alright."

Ev patted Polly on the small of her back before pulling away. "I need to go in."

The sheriff's department was uncharacteristically quiet, even for a Sunday afternoon, when Ev arrived. Brown was sitting at his desk when Ev entered the room. Neither spoke. Ev continued across the room and stopped near Gene's file covered desk. He picked up a half filled cup of cold coffee and dropped it in the wastebasket.

Brown pulled a cigarette from the pack lying on his desk. "I'm gonna quit these. Take a week's vacation and quit. I sure as hell can't quit while working around here."

"Any word?"

"No. The sheriff and Okra left a little while ago to check on him."

"And Merv's okay."

"The sheriff's already been to see him. They might release him today."

"Thank God crooks use small calibers and are bad shots."

Brown grunted in response.

Ev moved to the wall and settled into a ladder back chair. "Do you know why Littleton shot Merv?"

"Drunk. Pissed off. Angry with his wife. He said she was screwing someone else. He confessed to everything, started crying and blubbering. Said if we hadn't come, he was gonna kill her and himself."

"Damn domestics," muttered Ev. "The most dangerous thing y'all do happens every day."

Brown rolled his cigarette along the lip of his crowded ashtray. He managed a weak smile. "Gene actually complimented us."

Ev pulled off his eyeglasses and made a pretense of studying them. "What did Gene find out on Smith?"

Brown leaned back in his creaking chair. "He confirmed that the silver LeSabre was in the shop. Ronnie Gibson's Exxon. Then he said he touched base with a few informants he keeps on the string. They pretty much agreed that Smith was at the Sand Lot."

"Who are those guys?"

Brown smiled. "You know Gene. He made a point of not telling me."

Ev pursed his lips. "So what did you decide?"

"He said we'd flattened this cat enough. But he wanted to go see Snidlett again. He was gonna call me on that today." Brown snuffed his cigarette in the piled ashtray. "Guess that won't happen," he softly added.

Ev stood up and walked across the tiny room. "Well. It's our baby now. Maybe I should say it's your baby." He remained where he stood peering at the Bridgewater College diploma behind Gene's desk.

Brown had been grappling with that same conclusion all morning. He had been at his desk, smoking cigarettes, shuffling files, and trying to come to terms with the immutable result that he was going to have to carry the ball—alone. The sheriff had said as much between trips to the two hospitals.

"It seems I've got the wrong man in jail," continued Ev. "Unless you say something to convince me, I probably should go up and call the judge and get the bastard out."

"Lieutenant, the sheriff's on line two," interrupted Willie Painter from the dispatch room.

Brown answered and then listened. After he put the receiver back in its cradle he spoke evenly but with an obvious tone of relief. "Gene should pull through. Everything is looking okay. But he's out of commission for a while. Maybe permanently."

Ev shook his head. *Thanks be to God*, he thought. He turned to face Brown. "That's good news. By the way, I like how the employees are being trained. Addressing you as lieutenant."

"Ain't that some shit," laughed Brown. "Boy I feel better. Shoulda known Gene was too tough to kill on the first try."

A pall had been lifted and with it the sloth of indecision and doubt.

"If Gene wanted to talk to Snidlett, then he must have had some lingering question about Smith. What do you think?" asked Ev.

"I'll track him down today. I've got another thought. On Lebanon Cove. I gotta bounce this stuff off somebody."

"Well go ahead. But I'm no cop."

Brown explained his proposal. "I was thinking of parking that old undercover car up near the Botas. Put one of our seized rifles in the back seat and lock the car. Leave the hood part way up."

"Let them steal a gun?" asked Ev, his reticence undisguised.

"It'll be disabled. Anyway, we'll be watching."

"Do you think they're dumb enough to try to break in the car? It'll have trap written all over it."

"I'm fresh out of suggestions. The fingerprints don't have a match in AFIS."

"Worth a try. Back to Smith, let me know first thing in the morning how things go with Snidlett. If we don't have something solid pointing to Smith, I'm cutting him loose."

"You're the boss," answered Brown.

"Did Gene say anything more about Snidlett?"

"He had said something about whether Snidlett was lying and if he was, then what was his motive in killing the girl. His brain was churning Ev, and you know how he is when he's like that, he doesn't say much."

Ev felt uneasy getting too specific with Lewis yet he harbored misgivings whether the young man had the experience and skill to bring the investigation to a conclusion. He hoped that Brown's skin wasn't too thin since Ev had no choice but to keep careful watch over his progress.

"I suggest you review the whole file. Who knows what Gene has stuck in there that we don't know about?"

"Okay."

"Let's talk about where we stand in the morning."

"Sure."

"What about Hawkes?"

"He's supposed to be here tomorrow afternoon."

Ev bade the lieutenant good luck and left. Brown pulled another cigarette from the pack and toyed with it unconsciously. He had a general notion of what Ev was thinking and he had no intention of taking one step without Cross's approval. He decided to wait for the sheriff and Okra Alexander to return before he paid a visit to Lester Snidlett. Alexander would do fine as a second during the interview. Sunday was not the preferred day to make a business call, but he had his marching orders. He read Roberts's notes on the Snidletts as he waited.

The blue Accord and Snidlett's pickup were parked at the trailer when Brown and Alexander arrived. The hounds were baying in unison as the two men stepped out of Brown's patrol car and Snidlett, alerted by the barking, opened the front door before they reached the steps.

"Whada y'all want?" he demanded brusquely. He was clad only in tight blue jeans and a pair of cowboy boots. The pearly white of his torso clashed incongruently with his sun weathered face and neck. He drained the Budweiser in his hand and pitched the can beside the trailer.

"Lester," began Brown, his advance halted by Snidlett's demand.

"Look," interrupted Snidlett, his voice hard, "I'm watchin' a game. Why don't you just get in your little po-lice car and get the hell outa here."

"Okay," Brown said evenly, "Where will you be tomorrow? I'll come see you then." He knew coming on Sunday was a bad idea.

Snidlett bared his teeth before answering. "Don't come fuckin' around when I'm working either."

"Well, it's now or later," said Brown.

Snidlett was turning to close the door when Sunny, her bathrobe hanging loosely on her and her arms akimbo, appeared at his side. "What do they want?" she asked.

"To fuck with me," answered Snidlett.

Sunny Gorgan turned to the two officers. "What do y'all want?"

Brown was ready to tell her the precise reason they were there, but Snidlett's head jerked at her question and he decided to wait a moment.

Snidlett stepped onto the narrow stoop and glared at Brown. "Okay goddamit. I don't wanna be bothered again." He pushed past Sunny and stomped down the wooden steps to ground level, then stopped and looked at her. "Go inside Sunny."

"Why?" she asked sharply.

"Go on, just let me handle it."

Sunny's eyes narrowed and her lips twitched, but she didn't' respond. She pulled the bathrobe closer covering the butterfly on her breast and slammed the door.

"Au-ight," grumbled Snidlett.

Brown quickly glanced around for a place to sit while they talked; sitting was a Gene Roberts rule. Several white plastic lawn chairs sat under a pine tree nearby. "Can we go over there to talk?"

Snidlett's eyes darted toward the trailer. Sunny was standing at the window.

"Yeah," he answered as he begun walking heavily to the suggested place. He sat down and watched Brown and Alexander carefully as they joined him.

"I'm gonna keep this short and to the point," said Brown.

"That's the first fuckin' good idea you've had today," replied Snidlett.

Brown nodded toward Okra. "This is Deputy Alexander—"

"I know him," grunted Snidlett.

"We know you were with Miranda Noble the day she was killed," said Brown.

Snidlett leaned forward, placed his elbows on his knees, and intertwined his fingers. Facing the ground he opened his mouth and released a trail of sputum. Then flexing his powerful biceps, he answered. "How many times do I have to tell you the same goddamned answer? Ask my old man. He lives right up the road." Snidlett gestured over his shoulder with one hand.

"We've got your fingerprints on a vodka bottle from the pool and a beer can from the yard near the driveway," continued Brown.

"Big fucking shit," murmured Snidlett.

"And your DNA was in Miranda Noble."

Snidlett slowly sat up, his eyes bloodshot and sullen. "You're lying."

"We got one of your cigarette butts. They can type your DNA from a butt. And you matched up."

"Ask my old man. I wasn't there that day."

"How about that night?"

"I won't there."

"Will you take a polygraph?" asked Okra.

Brown liked the question and wished that he had asked it.

Snidlett sat erect in his chair. "Damn right I will. I won't there. I seen her Wednesday. That's it."

Brown responded. "Then I'll set it up and call you."

Snidlett looked from Brown to Alexander and back. "Set it up? So you get to come back here and fuck with me some more? Tell me right now when to be there and I'll be there."

"I've got to schedule it with an examiner. I don't know what's available."

Snidlett looked at the ground and shook his head. "Call my old man. I ain't got no phone anymore. He'll tell me when."

"When did you lose it?" asked Brown.

"A month ago. Sunny run up the fuckin' bill sittin' on her ass and I couldn't pay it."

Alexander glanced at Brown and then spoke. "Just so we'll know. Where's your father gonna say you were that Friday?"

Snidlett shook his head again. "I don't have an idea where I was except I was with him. We're workin', I'm with him. I don't keep this shit wrote down in case some fuckin' cop comes along and wants to know." He looked at Brown before continuing. "Where the hell was you on some Friday night in August. See. That's what I mean. You don't know neither."

Brown leaned back slightly. "Were you working that night?"

Snidlett looked up. "Huh?"

"You asked us about Friday night."

"You asked me about Friday night."

"I just wanted to make sure we understood each other."

Snidlett stood up suddenly. "Get off my ass. You got one boy in jail for killing that girl. What do you need, a spare?"

Brown stood too followed quickly by Alexander. He let the 'boy' remark go. For a moment he pondered suggesting the Negative Retina Image Machine, then thought better of it. "Okay," said Brown. "We'll call your father. Sorry we had to bother you today."

A grunt was Snidlett's response.

**CHAPTER 19**

Monday, September 28th

Ev arrived at the office Monday morning with the Smith dilemma foremost in his thoughts. He was waiting for Brown's call when Linda Masencup paged him. The caller was Lewis Brown.

"Ev. Okra and I went to see Lester Snidlett yesterday."

"And?"

"He's sticking to his story that he wasn't there Friday night. He's agreed to a polygraph. And I'm tellin' you. He's a class one asshole."

"We'll see what comes of that…the polygraph request."

"He told us to talk with his father, that he was always working and he'd have been with his old man. So we went up there. The old man, Roger Snidlett, is nothing like his son. So I believed him when he had trouble remembering what he was doing on August twenty-first. He said Friday's the day they finish hauling the wood they've cut during the week. Makin' the week he called it, and then after that they get parts and work on their equipment and that kind of stuff. Then he asked was that the same week he cut the tree over at Nobles. And when I said it was, he said they weren't cutting timber that week on account of the skidder and the knuckleboom being broke down, that's why they did the Noble job. So that Friday morning he was going after some parts. He left Lester working on a truck. Didn't see him again until about midnight."

"Whew," whistled Ev. "Why midnight?"

"Well get this. Roger went down to the trailer 'cause Sunny called him and said Lester was bustin' up the place. Blind drunk. Roger got him quiet and he passed out."

Ev let the information sink in before responding. "And Sunny didn't remember any particular Friday night. Seems like she'd remember that night, unless it happens every Friday."

"Sunny Dawn is a piece of work herself. She must be lying, but I can't figure why."

"Get your polygraph set up fast."

Lewis laughed. "You know the state police. It will be at least two weeks."

Ev took off his glasses and shut his eyes. "Tell them it's got to be this week. If you can't get them to act, call me. I'll get somebody's attention."

"You're the boss," said Lewis. "Farnsworth scheduled an interview for Thomasson, with Gene. Are you going to be in on that?"

"Let me think about it. What do you think about Smith?"

Brown hesitated before answering. "I don't think we can put him there, not when she was killed."

"I've got a bad feeling about him, especially considering who these alibi witnesses are. But I don't know how we can refute them. What about Snidlett? Are we overlooking the obvious?"

"I've done the what if game in my head till I'm dizzy," answered Brown. "He's got an excuse for his DNA, but not his prints, and no alibi, except Sunny's half-ass statement. Smith was there, he said so. Jason was, too. What if Jason got angry and killed her because of drugs and Smith?" Brown paused and thought a moment. "Maybe Jason got hot because she was having sex with a black man."

"I wondered the same thing about Snidlett, but their interest in the girl was recreational sex. I doubt either cared. Like Smith. Why kill her? But it's a thought. There's got to be a motive somewhere. And if race were a motivation, I'd pick Snidlett. If old fashion jealousy is the reason, I'd say Thomasson."

"I'm getting dizzy again," grumbled Brown.

"We need more. We just don't have enough."

"Hawkes's due any minute. I'll pick his brain."

Ev sighed. "Well. I'm calling Abner Lincoln and tell him what I'm doing with Smith. Then I've got to call Christmas."

"Look," said Brown, "I'm sorry I put you in this spot."

Ev appreciated the apology but accepted his own part in how the debacle had begun. "Don't blame yourself, we all had a hand in it. Anyway, Smith acted guilty as hell, running when you mentioned the prints and retinal images. He's guilty of something; it just doesn't seem to be this murder. You don't disagree with me do you? Is there anything you can dream up that points to Smith?"

"I think he's out of the picture. At least for the murder."

"I can't come up with anything. I've got to bite the bullet and turn him loose. We can always charge him again if the right facts spring up."

Ev sat staring at the window after Brown's call. He had resolved that he had no choice but to drop the murder charge against Smith, but the thought of it made him weak-kneed. The thought of leaving in jail a man he didn't have the evidence to convict was worse. He was reaching for the telephone to call Lincoln when the intercom hummed with Linda Masencup's voice telling him that Wilmer Bledsoe was on the line.

"Mr. Commonwealth," boomed Bledsoe. "Watching those fools in Washington reminds of the three things that motivate mankind: sex, money, and power. Easy to forget that when we regularly see drunks, idiots, and sociopaths."

"Where did we go wrong?" laughed Ev.

"Speak for yourself. Anyway, speaking of Washington, Fago Henderson was in here bright and early to talk about his trial next week, for raping Debbie

Washington. You probably won't be surprised to hear it's the first time he's come in. I care about what happens more than he does. For what it's worth, he says if anybody got raped, it was him, since she's twice as big as him. Anyway, Fago has a pretty high opinion of his desirability in the eyes of womanhood. Have you got any room on this or are we gonna have to put it on?"

"The victim won't budge."

Bledsoe laughed. "Victim. Debbie Washington a victim?" he laughed again. "Do you know where Henderson's name came from? El Fago Baca?"

"I don't have a clue."

"El Fago Baca was a character in some shows in the fifties or early sixties. A Zorro type character. It was spelled differently than Henderson's version, of course, which is no surprise. Can you imagine saddling a kid with a name like that? Almost as bad as Wilmer Dale. Anyway, I should've asked for a jury, but that would just waste twelve peoples' time. So think about and let me know."

Ev stared at the telephone a moment before redialing. He spoke briefly to Abner Lincoln, explained his decision on Jeff Smith, and then replaced the receiver. Finding the Peoples Legal Rights Clinic's number in the Smith file he dialed again.

"Peoples Legal Rights Clinic. We serve the interest of justice. How may I direct your call?"

"Here we go again," groused Ev. "Isaiah Christmas please."

There was a pause occupied by a woman's throaty recorded voice. "Have you been injured in an auto accident, or on the job? Do you have a disabled love one who has been denied social security benefits? Are creditor's hounding you day and night? The Peoples Legal Rights Clinic can help you. Our staff…."

A voice interrupted the message. "Mr. Christmas's office."

Ev asked for Christmas knowing he would not hear him answer.

"Just a moment."

During the pause, the recorded message continued. "Six experienced professionals are available to assist you in protecting your rights. We…."

"This is Monica Delgarde. How may I help you?"

"This is Evander Cross. I would like to speak to Isaiah Christmas about Jeff Junior Smith the Third." Ev wondered whether the task of five of those professionals was to page each other on the intercom.

"Mr. Smith is our client?" responded Delgarde.

"Yes. Should I just leave my number?" Ev assumed that Monica was not about to connect him directly to Christmas.

"Perhaps I can help you."

"I'll just leave my number." Then in the hopes of speeding the response, he added, "I think Mr. Christmas has been awaiting this call."

The other end of the line was silent for a moment.

"Please hold," replied Delgarde stiffly.

The throaty voice returned. "When you need legal assistance, you need the best. Call, day or night...."

Then, "This is Isaiah Christmas."

"Evander Cross here."

"Yeah, Cross. How are you? What kinda good news do you have?"

"We're dropping the charges against your man."

"Before I get to do any fine lawyering?"

"You did your part. We interviewed Smith's friends and associates. Seems he wasn't around the victim at the right time. But he is a witness."

"What about the cocaine charges."

"I'm dropping that too. But we've got other drug charges that will probably come down later."

"That's not much encouragement to a potential witness. But I'll let him know. Hey, thanks Cross. I enjoyed my visit to Lafayette."

"Our pleasure."

The call ended and Cross was slow in replacing the receiver. It was not eleven o'clock, yet he felt listless, and washed out, as if he had been in front of a jury all day. He took a deep breath and reached for the telephone again. Now he had to call Paula Noble and the Senator.

* * *

Sam was at the kitchen table with his practice sheet homework in front of him. He couldn't progress a line without asking Polly for help.

"Don't you have a book that goes with that, Sam?"

"I do, but it bees at school."

"What!"

"It is at school," Sam said carefully.

Polly rubbed her forehead and bit her lip against chastising the boy. The telephone rang just as she had calmed herself enough to answer his question.

"Why me," mumbled Polly when she saw the name on the called I D. "Hello."

"Polly. It's Margaret. Is Ev home?"

"He's still at the office."

"Well, I'm not going to bother him there—"

*So bother me instead,* thought Polly.

"so would you have him call me. I've settled on a price."

Polly's lower jaw dropped involuntarily. She had heard it; it was in keeping with Margaret's attitude toward her daughter-in-law; and still she could not believe Margaret's impudence.

"Polly, are you there?"

"Oh yes. I'm here," said Polly quietly.

"Have you been to the Douglases' antique shop lately?"

"No," answered Polly. *Now I get to hear what she bought herself.*

"I found the cutest love seat there. It needs recovering, but that's all. It will go well with Amanda's living room furniture. I couldn't pass it up. Do you know who does recovering?"

"We haven't had anything recovered so I wouldn't know," responded Polly sullenly.

"I hope it doesn't cost much but things need to be just right in their home…for Richard's position. You know with entertaining for Richard's business, and teas."

"Teas?"

"Well, whatever they do. Tell Ev to call. Goodbye."

Polly rehung the receiver. She felt overwhelmed and trapped, as if the walls were closing in and the lights dimming. Sam's voice, sounding detached and distant, wound its way to her consciousness. He had pushed the work sheet away and was looking at his mother.

"Yes Sam," she said wearily.

"My teacher told us the national symbol."

"She did."

"The…some kind of eagle."

"Bald Eagle."

"You know it too?"

"I know it too. Now finish the work sheet."

"It's on the quarter. It's on lots of things.

"Good."

"Mama. Is the mermaid the Mexican's national symbol?"

Polly looked away from the wall which had kept her attention following the conversation with Margaret "The mermaid. I don't think so. Why?"

"You know. On the back of their trucks. We see 'em at the store. They have those silver mermaids."

Polly looked at Sam quizzically, trying in her mind's eye to visualize what he had seen. Many of the migrants drove pickups studded with extra running lights and festooned with beads and trinkets within. Then she realized what Sam was describing. On superfluous mudflaps or affixed to the corner of the rear glass many of these pickups sported the chrome profile of a seductively reclining busty woman. Polly began to laugh, laughter both of mirth and relief.

It was Sam's turn to wonder why his mother was reacting so. "Mama?"

"Sam. It's not a mermaid. It's a woman. It's just a…decoration."

"Why?"

Polly wondered the same things herself and concluded that it was the international symbol of male wishful thinking. "I don't know why. Some men just like that sort of thing."

"Do women put silver men on their cars?"

"Not that I've ever seen," laughed Polly. "Now get back to your homework."

Polly heard the Bronco in the driveway while she answered another question about the work sheet. She had flashlight in hand peering into the recesses of the dark refrigerator when Ev walked into the kitchen. The light interlude provided by Sam had passed upon her renewed frustration with the failing refrigerator. A scowl on her face was her greeting and she didn't care that his mood mirrored hers.

"Okay Polly. What is it?" Ev asked as he tousled Sam's blonde head.

"Your mother wants you to call her," Polly answered icily as she closed the refrigerator door.

"About what?" he managed after a pause.

"About her house she's selling to you. She apparently didn't think I needed to know."

"I'm sorry Polly."

"I don't know what sorry has to do with it."

"What else do you want me to say?"

"Would you please just call her so she won't keep calling here?"

"I just walked in, Polly."

Will appeared at the dining room door. "Mama. Jasper went pooh pooh in there." He gestured over his shoulder.

"That damn cat," said Ev.

"He must be sick. He doesn't do that," rejoined Polly testily.

"I guess I'll get a vet bill out of this," Ev murmured.

"I didn't say he needed to see the vet," said Polly.

"Mama. What's this mean?" asked Sam, waving his work sheet above his head.

"Just a minute, Sam," replied Polly.

"It looks like a mud puddle," said Will.

"I might as well be at the office," Ev grumbled as he walked briskly toward their bedroom containing a second telephone.

Will snatched the fluttering work sheet from Sam's hand. "Lemme see."

Sam promptly smacked Will on the head which elicited a wail of dismay from the latter. "Moron," said Sam, "give it."

Will turned on his heel and sped into the dining room with Sam a step behind him.

"Give it, Moron!" yelled Sam.

"Okay, okay, OKAY!" shouted Polly as she followed the two into the dining room.

She was an arm's length away when Sam throttled Will by the collar. The smaller boy gurgled another yelp as he swung his arm away from Sam and released the work sheet. The paper floated out of Will's grasp, each end rhythmically taking turns in leading its descent, like a maple leaf floating to the ground on a windless autumn morning, until it finally touched the floor, face down in the brown puddle left by Jasper.

"Let go!" yelled Will as he struggled against the immediate prospect of another blow from Sam's free hand.

Polly grabbed Sam's unencumbered arm, which was already in motion, and pulled him toward her; Will involuntarily followed. Once in her grasp she pulled Will to one side and Sam to the other where she clutched them tightly to her legs. Sam, watching his work sheet transform into the same brown color as the puddle beneath it, began to sob quietly.

Polly released Will and with the same hand that had restrained him she smacked him on the arm before he could effect his escape. "Go to your room William Cross," she ordered as Will, who had burst into tears, dashed around the corner into the living den.

Ev's heavy tread announced his presence in the dining room. "I can't make this urgent call you demanded in all this mayhem."

Polly straightened without letting go of Sam. "This is my world and welcome to it."

"I won't get recess," moaned Sam.

"We'll take care of this Sam." Polly said quietly, keeping her back to Ev. "I wonder what the teacher will think when she reads my note that Sam's homework fell into cat shit."

Ev caught sight of the work sheet and decided to leave the room without further comment.

"I hate Jasper," said Sam.

"It wasn't his fault Sam," replied Polly.

"Then I hate Will."

"You mustn't hate your brother."

"Then who can I hate?" Sam had quit crying.

"Nobody. I'll take you to school in the morning and get another work sheet."

Sam, appeased by the offer, slid out of Polly's arm and walked back into the kitchen. "Can I go outside now? I don't have no more homework."

"You don't have what?"

"No more homework."

"You don't have any more homework."

"Any more homework. Where's Will?"

"He'll be out later. Go on."

Polly eased into the kitchen table chair that Sam had neglected to push back into place and waited for Ev. From the corner of her eye she caught sight of Will peeking around the corner of the door to his room.

"Come in here Will," she called softly.

The boy darted back into his room, then slowly walked out. "I've been a bad boy," he said meekly.

"Just leave Sam's homework alone. Okay?"

"Okay," answered Will, his eyes fixed on the floor.

"Now go outside."

Will hurried out of the room slamming the porch door behind him.

Polly could hear Ev's muffled voice but could not make out what he was saying. The call seemed to be taking a long time, especially since Ev's telephone conversations with his mother were always brief. Margaret saved her long-winded harangues for Polly.

Presently the muffled voice ceased speaking yet Ev remained in the bedroom. Polly twisted in the chair and debated whether to join him. She felt a little silly, waiting like a scolded child while the future of her home was being plotted in the next room. The notion that she had to stand inconspicuously on the sidelines struck her as not only unreasonable but also demeaning and the thought turned her impatience into disgust. She was rising from the chair when Ev entered the hallway.

"Well what did the two of you decide?" she asked in a voice laden with sarcasm.

Occupied with his thoughts Ev was oblivious to the tone of Polly's question. "Three fifteen," he answered. "She'll finance fifty thousand for one year, essentially the down payment, to give us time to sell this house. She won't finance the balance, she plans to buy a place at the beach. I guess Richard and Amanda were her advisors."

"Well?"

"It will be a stretch."

"So she knocked off twenty-five thousand."

"Thirty-five. About what she would have paid in realtor fees."

"Wow," deadpanned Polly. She walked to the cabinets and retrieved a wine goblet. "How much better would we have done if we were strangers?"

Ev didn't respond.

"Screw it," said Polly. "Just screw it. Let her sell it." She lifted an opened bottle of red wine from the counter.

"Polly—"

"Don't Polly me. You're just gonna do whatever she says." Polly turned up the bottle impatiently and filled the goblet with a glub-glub stream of wine. "I don't know why I have to put up with this."

Ev breathed deeply before replying. "The first question is whether you want the place."

"Does my opinion count on that?" She had no idea why she was arguing that particular point for she very much wanted the old Cross home. Remonstration with herself at this juncture was useless, however, and she was disgusted that Ev didn't have the sense to stop asking questions.

"Well, she wants a decision. So what is it?"

"Oh, by all means. Right now. This minute. Well run in there and call her with your decision. I'll just busy myself with cleaning up the cat shit."

"Forget it Polly."

"Oh no. Don't get mommy pouting. Run in there and do whatever she says. She can treat me like shit but that's okay."

"I'm sorry she's that way."

"Well, sorry doesn't cut it. You're not here all day."

Ev's jaw twitched. "Look. My office is no pleasant place."

"You said you'd rather be there."

"I said I might as well be there."

"Will you just quit yelling at me."

"I'm not yelling at you."

The telephone rang, almost as if to signify the end of round one.

"You answer it," said Polly in a low growl. "She probably wants your decision."

Ev looked at the called I D. "It's unavailable. Probably a reporter. I cut Jeff Smith loose today."

"Aren't you going to answer it?"

"Hell no Polly."

Polly jumped to her feet. "I'll answer it."

"Can't you just let it ring? Have you ever let it just ring?"

"Just leave me alone."

"I'm leaving. I'm not here," said Ev.

"Fine. You're the one with the options. Hello." Polly's voice suddenly reverted to its normal tone. "I'm sorry. He's not here." Pause. "I'll tell him you called, but I don't know when to expect him." She hung up the receiver. "See. That was simple. Now they won't call back."

"They. More than one." Ev could not pass up the opportunity to pick at the English major's miscue.

"She. She. Does that satisfy you?"

"Okay Polly. I'm going out to rake some leaves." He walked out slowly, as if expecting Polly to respond.

She didn't. Polly took a gulp of her wine and stared in the opposite direction. She remained where she stood even after the screen door closed behind him.

* * *

Ev didn't come back inside until dark. The boys had eaten and were in their room playing, for the moment, quietly. Polly was at the kitchen sink which seemed, Ev admitted to himself, to be the only place she occupied when awake. He wanted to discuss the house but decided he wasn't the one to bring it up.

"I guess you want to eat," said Polly.

"Whenever you want to."

"I'm not eating. I'll fix yours in a minute."

Ev retrieved a beer from the refrigerator. *It's going to be one of those nights.*

"It would sure be a lot easier on me if you ate with the boys," said Polly.

"I'm sorry" almost slipped out before Ev caught himself. "Okay," said Ev. He wondered why he ever tried to apologize. Polly never apologized. She would calm down and usually act like nothing had happened, even try a little extra attention, but no apology. It had to be a feminine characteristic.

"Do you think you should make a counter offer?" asked Polly.

"We did. This is the counter to our counter offer."

"You're right. And it would probably make her angry and she'd blame me and either torture me or just put it on the market. Right?"

"Something like that."

"Then tell her yes. At least we can put one thing behind us."

"I'll call her tomorrow."

Polly ceased her efforts in the sink. "Call her tonight, please."

"She might be drunk."

"Call her tonight. Then call her in the morning. Say you forgot something. Say all the appliances stay."

Ev chuckled at the suggestion. "Okay."

Margaret was drunk. She wavered on the appliance request, which Ev decided to mention right away because Amanda might want them, but eventually she capitulated. She gave every indication that the burden of her existence had been lifted.

"Okay, Polly. I've taken care of it. Are you happy?"

Polly walked in the hall and listened to the boys. "Good," she said.

"Polly."

"Yes."

191

"Is shit your favorite cuss word?"

Polly looked at Ev for a moment. "Like I curse all the time. Curse, Ev, is the word."

"Where'd that come from?"

"My daddy. He hated it. So it was my little rebellion. What would you have me say? Fuck?" Polly blushed slightly after speaking.

"I can think of times," answered Ev.

"You're disgusting," replied Polly.

Ev did call Margaret the next morning. She was amazed that Ev asked whether the appliances would come with the house, but agreed after a moment's contemplation.

# CHAPTER 20

Tuesday, September 29th

Gene Roberts had never been an avid television viewer, excepting car races and football, and in the last two days he had decided that his emotion about the machine was not simply one of indifference but of downright disgust. Even with his own television off Gene was subjected to the noise and endless commercials of the box serving the man who was sharing the room with him.

The other man was ten years younger than Gene, which gave the latter a perverse sense of relief, and had been stricken with his heart attack while changing a truck tire. He was divorced and remarried, had three children by the first wife, one of whom was a minor league catcher, had been changing tires at the same tire store for twenty three years—following his discharge from the Navy—and followed the NASCAR competition with religious fervor, all of which Gene heard about in exacting detail during the frequent interludes when the tire man was not watching the country music television channel. Gene had always thought that strenuous physical activity was the great preventative for heart attacks, but acknowledged to himself that the tire man's near three hundred pounds had probably more than offset the salutary effects of his physical labor.

Having spent Sunday in the intensive care unit Gene missed the day's stock car race, a happenstance he regretted all the more since he had to hear from tire man a lap by lap recap on Monday covering all five hundred of them.

Regardless of his diversions, both voluntary and involuntary, Gene's thoughts repeatedly returned to Miranda Noble. The thought continuously nagged him that he was missing something, that something was right under his nose, something obvious.

Lewis Brown visited Gene Monday evening with the intention of assuring his boss that the sheriff's office was running smoothly. Their conversation inevitably turned to the myriad investigations Brown was juggling.

"What about Lebanon Cove?" asked Roberts.

Brown explained his plan to use the old car as bait.

The investigator smiled weakly. "It's sort of like that greeting card that has on the front, open only in an emergency. You believe they just won't be able to resist."

Brown laughed before answering. "Look. They took Marilyn Kemper's panties. And hers were big enough for a pro tackle. Plus, if it's Aaron Bota like I think, he won't have sense enough to smell a trap. If he had two heads, he'd be twice as dumb."

"Okay," said Roberts. "Can't hurt." After a pause, "What about Horace's burglary in Morgan? I was supposed to talk to him about it yesterday."

"We talked. It was a storage shed at that model's house. Lydia McDonald. The problem he was having is that the victim decided she didn't want to pursue it. One of her witnesses, I guess the only witness besides herself, is some guy named Rich Garrison. Sounds like she didn't want anybody to know he was there. I guess it dawned on her he'd hafta be a witness in court."

"The thief must have interrupted some extra-curricular activity."

"Yeah," answered Brown. "They were in the hot tub at ten in the morning on a Monday."

"Nothing like getting caught with your pants down. What did you tell Horace?"

"See the C. A. Horace already had the warrants issued. It's up to Ev, not Miz McDonald."

"Damn I'd like a cigarette."

"You want me to leave you a few?"

"That's probably a felony in Charlottesville."

"Don't worry boss. I left 'em in my car."

"With the motor running?"

"No Gene," laughed Brown.

Roberts maintained a serious demeanor. "Cops always leave their patrol cars running."

"Damn Gene. You keep worrying about things like that and you'll never get out of here."

"You're right. So tell me about the big one. What did y'all do?"

Brown explained his meetings with the Snidletts and Ev's decision to drop charges against Jeff Smith. Roberts received the information without comment.

"Jason's coming in tomorrow," concluded Brown.

"Think outside the box with him."

Roberts knew he had missed the mark when he saw the quizzical expression on Brown's face. "What I mean Lewis, is ask about anything you can think of. What cars were there when he was there? Did the phone ring at the pool? Just get as much about other things covering those three or four days, or weeks, as you can. That boy, or whoever it is, isn't gonna come in and confess. It's all the other stuff that might be helpful."

"Do you think…never mind."

"Think he did it? I can't rule him out…yet." Gene intertwined his fingers and stared at them, in thought, for a moment. "Maybe we've been overlooking someone."

Brown had asked himself the same question. "But who else can it be, unless it's a stranger. That is, assuming it isn't Snidlett or Jason."

"I'm not writing Snidlett off either. But who else that we know of could have had a motive?"

"Beats me."

"What about Rita Noble?"

Brown laughed nervously, then grew serious. "You ain't shittin' me are you?"

"Not one turd, lieutenant."

"Come on boss. She was in Richmond."

"Think outside the box."

"How big is this damn box anyway?"

"Big enough to include Richmond."

"What's on your mind? What Clara Wood said?"

Roberts nodded approvingly. "Glad you read the file. The bit about the will and the fact that Rita was furious about her sorry brother servicing Miranda at her home."

"Kill her over that?"

"Where there's a will, there's a relative. Usually a greedy one."

"Won't there enough to go around?"

"There's never enough. It's just a thought. Expand the box. And while you're at it, something else bothers me. If she's using crack, why did she pass out?"

"Got me." Brown stood to leave. "Anything else?"

"Solve it before I'm released."

"I hope you're well quicker than that. Anyway, what are you gonna do? Retire and play golf?"

* * *

Ev was fond of saying that Gene loved crime. Roberts knew what was intended, he did enjoy unraveling a case and putting it back together so that there was no way out for the bad guy. Losing at trial was for Roberts the same as for a lawyer: utter devastation. But he could get over it. Worse was not being able to solve a crime. It simply lingered there, suspended in front of him, absorbing his efforts, distracting his concentration; then he would go home and sit and think it through until he was sick of being a prisoner of his mind, trapped there with some implacable enemy. Now he was doubly trapped: trapped in a hospital room and trapped with the Noble case. He slipped into a light sleep while turning the maze over in his thoughts.

The telephone awakened him.

"Investigator Roberts, this is Ev."

195

"You checking on me, too?"

Ev laughed. "As a matter of fact, yes. I hadn't wanted to bother you. But I figured you'd get insulted if I didn't do something. I decided flowers weren't appropriate."

"Thanks pal. How's Brown doing?"

"He's being careful. Goes over everything with me."

"Good." Gene paused. "Are you going to sit in on the interview with Thomasson?"

"I hadn't planned on it."

Gene paused again as he mulled Ev's decision.

"Is that okay with you?" asked Ev.

"Yeah. He needs to restore his confidence. And Thomasson's there with a lawyer. There won't be anything earth shattering. Let him do it."

They talked for a few more minutes before Ev rang off.

Roberts stared at the ceiling. *I wonder if I'll like golf. I hope Brown thinks outside the box. Screw golf.*

* * *

Brown caught Ev in the sheriff's department parking lot that evening. "You want an update?" he asked the prosecutor.

"About Thomasson. Sure."

"First. He didn't confess."

"That's news."

"Yeah. Anyway, it was the same stuff as first. Then I just started with off the small questions. I asked whether the telephone rang at the pool. It did. Miranda answered it. Now I'm pretty sure the pool phone has a separate number from the house. Jason asked who called and Miranda said it was nothing. His words were, 'she said, don't worry about it.' I asked him whether any cars were there. He said only the Suburban and Miranda's car."

"What's the significance?" asked Ev, his mind already churning.

"Well the call, it wouldn't have been on the caller ID memory. I don't think. I need to double-check that, though. Second, Gene –has he told you this—he said we couldn't exclude Rita Noble."

Ev spinning new scenarios in his thoughts, was only half listening. "I guess we can't exclude anybody."

"Well, here's a thought. Juanita Lopez saw a silver Buick-like car. Maybe it was a gold Mercedes."

"Lopez works for the Nobles," responded Ev, doubt clear in his response. "Wouldn't she know her boss's car? And besides, Rita was with her husband in Richmond, one hundred miles away."

Brown thought about Ev's observation a moment before answering. "I guess you're right. It just seems to add a twist. Two twists with the telephone call."

"Well. Don't ignore them. Follow them through." Ev looked at the ground after speaking. "I guess Gene wouldn't be raising the question if he didn't smell smoke."

Brown was crestfallen, but he tried to disguise his reaction. "Add 'em to my list. There's probably no way to know who called anyway. Unless somebody admits it."

Ev continued in the direction of his Bronco. "Keep beating the bushes Lewis."

Brown slowly turned to walk toward the sheriff's office entrance. Gene was blowing hot, Ev was blowing cold. *We don't have shit, unless Snidlett confesses*, he argued to himself. *There's nothing to do but work them…when there's time.*

Ev backed the Bronco to the sidewalk Brown was trodding. "Polygraph for Snidlett?"

"Next Tuesday."

"Damn."

"Best I could manage."

"Okay."

Ev pulled away while Brown watched unconsciously as he fished for a cigarette in his coat pocket. A coaching job, maybe in the recreational league, never seemed more appealing.

CHAPTER 21

Monday, October 5$^{th}$

Debbie Washington and her daughter Tomika Jones were sitting in the gallery of the old circuit courtroom, alone except for the bailiff Okra Alexander who was leaning against the railing cordoning off the clerk's desk. Parallelograms of October morning sunlight, their paths fluid with dancing dust, cast a natural spotlight on counsel table used by the Commonwealth.

Ev walked into the courtroom, nodded to the two women sitting in the gallery, and laid his file on the illuminated counsel table.

"Hello Commonwealth," said Okra.

Ev returned the greeting as he walked toward the door at the side of the courtroom. The door opened into a narrow corridor leading to the judge's chambers and the jury and witness rooms.

"Wil's in there with Fago," added Okra.

Ev entered the side door corridor where Wilmer Bledsoe sat, along with Fago Henderson, in the chairs along the wall.

"Good morning Mr. Commonwealth," boomed Bledsoe. "Hey, Fago why don't you wait in that witness room."

Fago Henderson got up and shuffled to the witness room. "Okay. Hey Ev," he mumbled pleasantly as if they were passing on the street.

Bledsoe brushed a leaf off his boot. "I've talked to Debbie. On this alleged rape she'll take a misdemeanor and thirty days in jail, that and the two hundred dollars he owes her."

"Two hundred?"

"Look. Fago is happy with that."

"Maybe I ought to hire you as my assistant."

"Oh well. Hey. On another light note, did you see the toilet in the hall by the clerk's office?"

Jim Crawford entered the hallway before Ev could answer.

"I was just telling Ev," continued Bledsoe. "There's a damn toilet sitting outside the uni-sex bathroom with a large sign on it saying Do Not Use. I looked in there and damned if there wasn't what looked like a turd of shit layin' there."

"Oh come on," said Ev.

"I want to see this," said Crawford.

The three men walked to the main hallway and followed it to the lavatory near the clerk's office. Sure enough an object bearing all the indicia of a corn-mottled length of feces lay at the bottom of the dry bowl. Okra Alexander joined the three before anyone could comment.

"This looks like a serious offense deputy," said Bledsoe.

"Yeah, the sheriff dropped that Babe Ruth in there. He's been hanging around all morning so he'd be the one to tell the janitor someone ignored his sign."

Crawford rubbed his left temple as he shook his head. "Now what in the world would someone from out of town think if he walked in and saw this damn stool in the hallway of the courthouse?"

Bledsoe grinned slyly. "Excluding present company of course, maybe they'd decide not to move here."

* * *

"Lewis wants you to call," Linda Masencup greeted Ev when he returned to his office. "As soon as you're free."

Ev walked to his office and dialed the lieutenant's number.

"Lester Snidlett broke western last night," answered Brown. "Beat the tee-total hell out of Sunny."

"That probably shoots the polygraph."

"That's not why I'm calling. She's down here now. She's given us an updated version of the Friday night."

A nervous tingle seized Ev. "And?"

"Lester won't at home. Look. I think you oughta come talk to her. Make sure we're not missing something."

Ev paused. He didn't like the idea of becoming the lead gumshoe, but Brown was being cautious and Ev decided this was not a time to push the fledgling investigator out of the nest. "I'll come right down."

Sunny was sitting on the bench in the sheriff's office hallway hugging her arms to her chest. Beneath her eyes were dark purple swatches, as shiny and slick as grease paint, and the hazel iris of one eye was surrounded by red. Blue bruises were sprinkled over her arms and chest. Brown was not exaggerating.

Brown with Horace Seay behind him walked out of the investigator's office before Ev had time to speak.

"You know Mr. Cross don't you Sunny?" said Seay.

"I know 'im," she answered dully.

At that moment Miss Dora Temple of the Lafayette County Historical Society entered the hallway from the outside door, a large paper bag in one hand. "The nuts have arrived," she announced in tinkling tones, a smile further creasing her wrinkled face. "The sheriff and Mr. Brown ordered some."

Ev sighed before speaking. "We'll be in my office, Lewis. Hello Miss Dora." Motioning to Sunny, he instructed, "Please follow me."

199

Brown made no effort to disguise the resignation in his voice. "I'll be up in a minute, Mr. Cross." Brown had adopted Gene Roberts's protocol of addressing Ev formally when in the presence of the public. "I've got to pay for these...nuts."

In his office Ev studied again the damage done to Sunny, who with Seay was seated in front of him. "Have you been to the hospital?" he asked.

"I went. Nothin' broken."

"Snidlett's in on a ten thousand dollar bond," said Seay. "His daddy refused to post it, for now."

Ev looked at Sunny a moment longer before continuing. "Lieutenant Brown tells me you have something to tell us about the Friday night before Miranda Noble was..."

"Yeah, I do," interrupted Sunny. She sighed quietly and studied her hands a moment before continuing. "I lied to y'all. To cover his worthless ass. I ain't sayin' he done it. But I lied."

"Go on," said Ev. "What happened that night?"

"He come in around seven or so and set down in front of the TV with his usual beer. Later on the phone rang and he answered it, which was funny 'cause he don't ever answer the phone. Then a little later he said he was outa beer and needed to check with his daddy on any money comin' to him and he left."

"What time?" asked Ev.

"I don't know. Wasn't payin' attention. After eight. He didn't come right back, so I got suspicious. He had went out all night on Wednesday. I lied about that too. I guessed he had him a girlfriend. Wouldn't be the first time. That's why he beat the shit out of me last time." Sunny looked up from her hands and blinked against a tear.

Ev leaned forward at his desk and rested his chin atop his interlaced fingers. "What happened next?"

"Oh he came home."

"When?" asked Ev.

"Ten. Ten-thirty. I'm not sure. But it was eleven when I called Roger, his deddy. I know 'cause Roger said why you callin' here at eleven? See, we'd already been fightin'. I just asked him right up. Who you screwin'? And he went apeshit. Throwin' things. Broke the broom on the counter. I called before he tore up the whole trailer. He woulda just started on me next."

"How did he answer your question?"

"None of my F-ing business. He'd screw who he pleased and please who he screwed. We won't married. Move out if I don't like his hours. That kinda crap."

"How'd he react when Miranda was killed?"

"I mentioned it Saturday to him after he finally woke up. Somebody told me, I guess it was Manfred at the store. Lester looked strange. Didn't say a word. I don't know. He didn't talk about it. And I didn't even know if he knew the girl. Then he rushed home after Lewis Brown and Roberts talked to him in the woods. Said don't say shit about that Friday. Say I was home. They think I killed that girl. I didn't and I can't prove it. He was sweatin' bullets. He even started cryin'. Shit. I fell for it."

"What happened last night?" continued Ev.

Lewis Brown walked in and quietly seated himself while Ev was speaking.

"He was nervous about that lie detector test," continued Sunny. "So I just ask him, it's about the girl isn't it? See, he wouldn't say before, when Brown come over that Sunday. Just said they were framin' him for some stealing, which I didn't believe. And he lost it. He was half-drunk anyway. F no. F no. I'm gettin' framed. And then he started in on me. You're gonna F me over, turn me in. The more he yelled, the more he hit me. I ran out and got in the bushes, then snuck up to Roger's and called nine-one-one. Wimpie called me after they arrested him. Said he was just sittin' on the steps. Drinkin' a beer and smokin' a cigarette. Stood up and held out his hands for the cuffs."

"Did he ever say anything specific about Miranda Noble? About seeing her?" asked Brown.

"No. I mean, it was like it was on the tip of his tongue. But he wouldn't say anything. Just stuff like they think I did it and I can't prove I didn't and they're framin' me. And cuss, cuss, cuss."

"Any strange calls, or a call from a woman, from that Wednesday to that Friday night?" asked Brown.

Sunny shook her head. "That I know about? Just the one I told you. And I don't know who that was."

"Where will you be staying?"

"At my mama's. I'm through with him. I'm gettin' my stuff out this morning, what he hasn't broke, and that's it. All she wrote."

Ev mulled his next question before asking it. "Has Lester ever gotten angry about sex?"

"What'd you mean?"

Ev was uncomfortable with this topic but forged on. "When you turned him down. Or wouldn't do something he wanted to do?"

Ev might have been uncomfortable but Sunny answered without hesitation. "Look. I'm not gonna lie. That wasn't one of our problems. I could wear him out."

Ev felt his face turning red.

A hint of merriment brightened Sunny's bruised eyes when she caught sight of the color in Ev's cheeks. "He said I was a nympho. I'm not one of those thirty year old women who just up and don't like sex anymore. So that's got something to do with the murder?"

"We're covering all angles," managed Ev.

"Well he thinks he's the king stud. But I showed him a thing or two, taught him that is. I mean what else do you need to know. I'll tell you. I sure as hell don't care."

Ev pretended to ignore Sunny's invitation. "I guess I'm getting at force."

"There wudn't any need."

Ev, his composure returning, looked from Seay to Brown. "Anything else?"

"He sure didn't mind force last night." said Seay.

"That's different. We were fighting. If he wanted sex, well, he could be real nice."

"How about the Wednesday before?" asked Brown.

"He won't home till morning, said he was playing cards. Yeah. I mean, he coulda done me." Sunny's face had fallen again.

Seay patted Sunny on one of her trembling hands. "Come on. I'll walk you back down."

Ev and Brown sat quietly until they heard the door at Linda's desk close.

"Okay Lewis," began Ev. "What do you propose?" Roberts's Socratic Method came automatically.

"I think we go confront him. He's in jail and probably sober by now."

"Tell him we know everything?"

"Yeah. He's not stupid. He'll know where it came from. He'll either come clean or dig a deeper hole."

"Or invoke his rights. Do you believe her?"

"Yep. She doesn't know everything. If she was setting him up, she could've done a much better job. And you could see she's already having second thoughts about leaving."

Ev studies his interlaced fingers before continuing. "Who's going?"

"I thought Horace and I would handle it together. I don't think Lester Hester likes me too much."

"Black man with a badge?"

Brown smiled. "That, and I was faster than him in football. Used to piss him off. So he was usually my blocking back. As far as I remember his football was a lot better than his grades."

Ev laughed softly as Bledsoe's mob management theory came to mind. "Poor bastards. The high point of their lives ends with high school sports."

"Unless you count his nights with Miranda Noble."

Ev shook his head. "You'll report as soon as you can."

"Oh yeah." Brown smiled. "I ain't chargin' nobody till I talk to you."

Ev followed the lieutenant to Linda's desk. "Good luck, Lewis" said Ev.

"Thanks," replied Brown dryly as he let himself out.

The door closed, Linda leaned toward Ev as if she might be overheard. "Do you think we've got enough this time?"

Ev was always amazed at what Linda could hear through closed doors. "We're close, at least closer, this time."

"Lord I hope this is it," she said, almost to herself. "By the way, Minnie Patterson called and said not to worry about the cat messing—not her words – in her garden."

"We haven't had a frost yet, or did I miss it?"

"I don't think that's what she meant. She said she took care of it and it wouldn't be a problem again. I didn't ask how. Didn't want to."

"Good," replied Ev. "'Cause I don't want to know."

* * *

Lewis Brown waited in his office smoking one cigarette after another while Horace Seay retrieved Lester Snidlett from the drunk tank of the jail.

Snidlett walked in, his hands cuffed in front of him, disheveled and looking as if he were on his way to the gallows. Seay pointed to the chair against the wall and then seated himself in the chair behind Gene Roberts's desk.

Snidlett eyed the coffee machine in the corner. "Can I get a cup of that?" he asked, looking at Seay.

Brown responded first. "Sure."

Seay handed the prisoner a styrofoam cup of black coffee. Bringing the cup with his tethered hands to his mouth, Snidlett blew on the coffee and took a sip. "This is a whole lot better than that cold shit you give us over yonder." He jerked his head in the direction of the jail.

Brown glanced at Seay and gave a brief nod of his head.

As Seay leaned forward in his chair, Snidlett spoke again. "Y'all got a smoke I can borrow. I'm out."

Brown arose and walked over to Snidlett with a cigarette and lighter. Snidlett lit the cigarette with one hand while holding the cup at his chin with the other.

Then Seay spoke. "I have a few questions."

"I hit her," interrupted Snidlett. "The bitch."

"Just wait a minute," continued Seay. "I'm gonna record this." He pressed the record button on a tape recorder. "It's twelve-twenty-six p.m. on October fifth. Now first I have to read your rights to you. You have the right…."

"I know 'em," said Snidlett, "Ask your questions."

Seay and Brown had briefly discussed their strategy minutes before. Seay would begin by going right to the heart of Miranda's murder. Brown would interrupt if he felt the need.

"Okay, you know Miranda Noble, right?" asked Seay.

Snidlett looked at Seay, his resigned demeanor replaced by a quizzical expression. "What's this shit? I told Brown and them others about that." His eyes narrowed. "What did that bitch tell you?"

"We know about the Friday night now," said Seay.

Snidlett grunted. "I said I'd take the lie detector. Where is it?" His scowl bespoke the return of a surly defiance.

"Machine will be here Tuesday. That Friday. Did you go over there?"

Snidlett flicked his cigarette ash on the floor. "Yeah. Yeah, I went." He took a deep breath. "I didn't kill her. She called. I went. She wanted it and I didn't see no need to say no. She was lit up, man. Then she dranked some and smoked some more and sorta passed out. She was on that pool thing, that lays out. So I figured I might as well leave. So I did. That's it."

"A pool thing?" asked Seay. "A recliner, lounge chair type thing?"

"Yeah."

"How close to the pool?"

"Over by the pool house."

"So when you left she was passed out on the lounge chair. Naked?"

"Had her bottom on."

Brown and Seay exchanged glances.

"Where was the top?" asked Brown.

"Laying on the ground beside the lounge chair. I think. That's where she was at when she took it off."

"A towel, shirt, anything on the lounge chair?" asked Brown.

"Just her," answered Snidlett.

"What did you do before you left?" asked Brown.

Snidlett studied his cigarette as he answered. "I told you. Screwed her. When she was awake."

"Vaginal intercourse?" asked Brown.

Snidlett looked at Brown before answering. "Yeah Brown."

"Was she on her back or stomach when you left?" asked Brown.

Snidlett's eyes narrowed. "I don't have no fuckin' idea. I was drunk too."

"Did you do any other things, sexually, with Miranda?" asked Brown.

Snidlett's eyes remained trained on Brown. "What's this bullshit? Where's the lie-detector?"

"Did you?"

"No. She passed out. Look. She drowned didn't she? I figure she got up and fell over in the pool. After I left."

"If you thought she drowned," asked Seay. "Why didn't you just tell the investigators that up front?"

Snidlett put the empty coffee cup on the floor and dropped the spent cigarette butt into it. "Cause you know and I know somebody's ass has gotta be burnt. She was a rich girl and her rich daddy ain't gonna listen to nobody say it was a accident. Somebody's ass'll fry no matter what. So now it's my ass. Frame my ass and Noble'll be happy. I know how this shit works. See any rich boys over'n jail? See any rich white boys over'n jail?" He looked squarely at Brown as he uttered the last sentence.

Brown met the steely gaze. "What's your point? Should there be any particular rich white boy over there?"

"How about that Noble woman's brother?"

Brown's mind burrowed through the mass of details it had absorbed from the Noble file. He could recall nothing to suggest that Snidlett knew anything about Jason Thomasson. "What do you know about him?"

"He called the girl while I was there. I know 'cause she cussed him over the phone. Said not to bother her. She didn't need his…him. I thought it was pretty funny so I asked her and she said it was that asshole Jason or Josh or somebody, and then started griping about his sister and what a bitch she was and that both of 'em had called, worryin' the shit out of her."

Brown resisted the sudden urge to bolt up right in his chair.

"Said he was as big ah shit as her. That's when she poured down a full glass of gin or vodka or something and smoked crack out of a beer can contraption. Won't long after that she passed out."

Brown was reeling. Snidlett had put a name to Jason's freshly remembered incoming call while exposing, once again, Jason's careful prevarication. "She was talking about Rita Noble, her stepmother?"

"That's what she said. I don't know. Girl was drunk as a fart, on something."

Seay's jaws were twitching. "The girl's name was Miranda. Did you know that?"

Snidlett looked at Seay. "Yeah. Miranda."

"You've got a pretty good recollection of all this," said Brown.

Snidlett shrugged his shoulders.

"What time did you leave?"

"Damn if I know. I got there it was still dusky day. I left it was dark. I was there an hour or two."

"What cars were there?"

"I didn't pay no attention. The gir…Miranda said she was alone. Why should I?"

"Now why'd you leave?" asked Seay.

"She passed out. Hell. I thought she'd come around. So I was waitin' and drinkin', drinkin' and waitin'. Thought I'd get it again, and damn I thought I heard a door slam—"

"A door slam?" asked Brown, unable to conceal the surprise in his voice.

"I thought, shit, I'm outa here."

"Car door? House door?"

"I don't know. I left. A light come on that brick deck. A lotta light. I didn't look neither when I got to my truck. Got on away. Had to get home and catch shit from that whore I live with."

Brown lit a cigarette and stared at the wall behind Seay. "I think we could use a break." He handed Snidlett a cigarette. "Why don't you take him back over to the jail, Horace?"

Snidlett, saying nothing, took the cigarette and arose as Seay walked around the desk.

"One other thing," asked Brown. "She didn't drown. She was smothered."

Snidlett stuck the unlit cigarette in his mouth. "Well Mr. Po-lice man. I didn't fuckin' smother her. Ain't no man alive with something in his pants gonna cut hisself off from *that*."

"Jesus, Lester, that's enough," growled Seay. "Let's go."

With the room to himself Brown twisted from left to right in his creaking swivel chair, his thoughts careening from one speculation to another. Snidlett was so forthrightly disgusting in his answers that Brown found himself believing him. The telephone calls injected a twist that was turning all his earlier theories to one big question mark.

A door slam? A light on the terrace? Was someone at the house? Jason? Work from the inside out. Think outside the box. Roberts's directives were roiling together. "God almighty," muttered Brown, "What the hell went on?"

# CHAPTER 22

Tuesday, October 6th

Brown was jotting down notes to himself when Tim Whittle arrived. Special Agent Whittle of the State Police was the officer detailed with operating the polygraph.

Polygraph results are not admissible in court, but suspects, usually unaware of the niceties of the rules of evidence, seemed to believe that the bravado of asking for the test would convince the police of their innocence. While the general public had a notion that the polygraph could work magic, the kind of magic it worked was not what was generally believed. Suspects, once seated in front of the machine, feared the contraption so that most confessed to their misdeeds before being tested. Of the ones caught in a deception by modern technology, most threw in the towel and admitted their guilt. Defense lawyers uniformly advised their clients not to subject themselves to a polygraph examination. The defense bar did not fear the inadmissible results, they feared their client would talk too much before and after the test. Talking was admissible.

The examination itself was not a far ranging inquisition. To the contrary, when the preliminaries were concluded the meat of the interview was composed of several short, straightforward questions. The preliminaries were required to allow the operator to ascertain how the polygraph responded to a suspect's truthful, and untruthful, answers. Truth was easy. Untruthful, however, required a near certainty that the examinee was going to lie in response to a query. The fun was in figuring out a question that would elicit a lie. No ground was more fertile than sexual peculiarities.

"Lewis Brown," Whittle said loudly, "We're still on?"

"Yep. You can set up in the witness room." There was no quiet privacy in the sheriff's department. The witness and jury rooms in the courthouse offered the only secluded spaces for lengthy interviews.

"Got your questions?"

"I'm revising them now. Our guy gave us some new things to consider." Brown reworked his list. To being at the pool on Friday night and having intercourse with Miranda, Snidlett had already admitted. The obvious last question was whether Snidlett had killed Miranda. He also wanted to know if Snidlett had attempted, or completed, anal penetration. The telephone call from Jason was highly suggestive and Brown wanted to make sure Snidlett had not invented it for cover.

Brown walked out of his basement office and entered the courthouse. He paused at the toilet; noticing that the Babe Ruth was missing he surmised that the janitor had finally come upon the ruse.

In the witness room Whittle had his mysterious machine in place. They discussed the questions and reviewed Snidlett's latest revelations so that Whittle could redraft Brown's proposed queries, then Brown left to retrieve Snidlett. Snidlett, the lone occupant of the two cell drunk tank, was sitting on the edge of the lower section of the steel-framed bunk bed staring at the concrete floor.

"Let's go Lester," said Brown.

"'Bout time. This place stinks." The two cells had a perpetual odor of Pine Sol, vomit, and stale cigarette smoke.

Horace Seay and Brown took seats in the chairs along the witness room wall as Whittle connected various wires to Snidlett. Motionless, Snidlett could not take his eyes off of the lie detector and watched it as if it were Whittle's pet Black Widow.

The preliminaries lasted more than an hour. The test questions evolved into the sordid and Brown renewed his commitment that he would never subject himself to the humiliation of a polygraph examination. By the time Whittle had established his baseline for registering a falsehood the questions about Miranda seemed almost innocuous.

"Did you attempt anal intercourse with Miranda?"

"No."

"Did you penetrate Miranda anally with any object?"

"No."

"Did Miranda receive a telephone call from a person named Jason while you were at the pool with her?"

"Yes."

"Did you kill Miranda?"

"No."

Whittle leaned back in his chair when the four questions were completed. Snidlett wiped the perspiration from his brow and stared at his inquisitor.

"Horace, take Mr. Snidlett into the hallway," said Whittle.

Snidlett was wide-eyed, no longer surly and threatening. "Well?" he asked.

"We'll talk to you in a minute," answered Whittle.

Horace guided Snidlett out of the room and closed the door. Brown's stomach tingled with anticipation.

Whittle peered at his results and rubbed his chin. "Mixed bag, Lewis. Deception on the first two, truthfulness on the third, and inconclusive on the fourth. And he's mighty nervous."

"Damn him," said Brown. "He's still lying."

"On the fourth question, it's real close to truthfulness. You know, some examiners might register it as truthful."

"I guess we grill him then."

Horace brought Snidlett back in and pointed to the chair opposite the polygraph. His sun-browned hands now trembling, Snidlett sat down and resumed his careful observation of the machine.

"Alright Mr. Snidlett," said Whittle. "Let's talk."

"About what?" answered Snidlett evenly.

"Well, let's start with the first two questions," said Brown brusquely. "You lied."

Snidlett's broad shoulders slumped forward. "Shit," he mumbled.

"What did you do to her?" asked Brown.

Whittle eyed Brown but kept quiet.

"Well. Just tell us," said Brown.

"She was passed out," said Snidlett. "And I got tired of waitin'. She won't comin' around. And that just pissed me off. So I…yeah, I tried it. Woulda done it, but I heard that door slam."

"You were forcing yourself on her while she was passed out?"

"Yeah. She wouldn't ah knowed. Then that damn door."

"You must've tried pretty hard. She had an injury down there."

"I meant business, but I didn't aim to hurt her."

"What'd you do? Just leave her there, undressed?" Brown was leaning forward now and Snidlett's eyes were glued to the polygraph.

"No. I pulled her bottom part back on. Then I got the hell outa there."

"She was on her stomach, then, when you put her bottom on?"

"Maybe, shit. I guess so."

"Was that light on the terrace on when you got there?"

"I don't know. The door slammed, I looked around, and seen the light."

Brown leaned back and breathed deeply. "We got problems with the last question, too."

Snidlett jerked his eyes level with Brown's. "You can just have a problem Brown. I didn't kill her."

"The machine doesn't exactly agree with you." Said Brown.

"Fuck the machine."

Brown twisted in his chair and looked at Whittle, it was now or never for pressing Snidlett. "Sounds like you got pissed off, couldn't force yourself in, so you just killed her,"

"Hell Brown. That's bullshit. I told you I thought she fell in and drowneded."

Whittle returned Brown's glance. "May I?" he asked.

"Sure."

"She was smothered," said Whittle.

"Y'all told me that. And I sure as hell didn't smother her."

"You just left," said Whittle.

"I just left."

"Anything else?" asked Whittle, looking at Brown.

"That telephone call. That was just before she passed out?" asked Brown.

"Yeah. I mean, how the hell did she answer it passed out?"

"How long between the call and the time you left?"

"Half hour. Hour. I won't watchin' a clock."

"Did you see any additional vehicles in the drive when you left?" asked Brown.

"I was lookin' to leave, not take no damn inventory."

"That's all I have. Take him to the jail Horace."

Brown spoke after Snidlett and Seay were out of the room. "Do you think he's worried that she drowned, regardless of what we tell him?"

Whittle nodded his head. "He ain't no rocket scientist. And despite the fact he doesn't have a decent bone in his body, it might be he's thinking he shouldn't have left her out cold by a pool. Sorta blaming himself."

"I think he's telling the truth. He's added some things that changes the picture."

Whittle pursed his lips. "A phone call and a light and that silver car, and a door slamming. You got yourself one Lewis."

Brown arose and walked out of the witness room absently thanking Whittle as he departed. Snidlett had set loose another horde of rabbits that needed chasing.

The sheriff met him in the basement hallway.

"Havin' any luck?" asked Burke.

"Snidlett was there. But he denies killing Miranda."

"Sounds like he's the one."

"I don't think so."

Burke rocked back on his heels. "We gotta put this one to bed. What else you need?"

"A lot. I'll bring you up to date later this week."

"I'll check with you later," said Burke over his shoulder as he left the hallway. "Have a good one."

Brown walked into his office and dropped into his creaking chair. Then he hit the desk with his fist. "Why didn't we just ask him if he'd smothered her?"

# CHAPTER 23

Wednesday, October 7th

A parade of people always decided they needed to see Ev just before the ten o'clock docket in General District Court. Deputies, state troopers, and lawyers were as guilty as the rest, darting in to ask a question about a case or explain why a charge should be dismissed.

Brown appeared at nine-thirty "You gotta minute?"

"I doubt it will be that brief. What's up?"

"What's up fits just right. Snidlett." Brown then explained the developments from the previous day's session with Lester Hester Snidlett.

Ev, listening quietly, leaned back in his chair and toyed with his eyeglasses. "So you believe Snidlett enough to think we've got to look elsewhere? Now what do you do?"

Brown had already spent Tuesday evening trying to answer the same question for himself. "Find a silver sedan. Try to figure out the Noble's telephone system. Go to Richmond. Talk to Thomasson."

"So Roberts convinced you?"

"Yes and no. I've got to assume Snidlett's telling me the truth just to verify it one way or the other."

"Validate what he's saying and put this back on some Noble, or prove him a liar. That means putting some heat on Jason and Rita doesn't it?"

"Yeah. Tip 'em off and I think they could shut me down. Jason will cover for Rita or Rita will cover for Jason or whatever."

"Keep me posted, Lewis. I've got court."

* * *

The crammed docket ended well after two o'clock. Robbie Fleming followed Ev out of the courtroom.

The rumor that Fleming might run for commonwealth's attorney came to mind. Ev thought a moment about the possibility as they walked. If anyone in Lafayette County could mount a serious challenge it was Robbie Fleming. His father was the dean of the local bar and his mother the daughter of an old-time country doctor who was still affectionately remembered though he had been dead twenty years. Robbie, to top it off, was an excellent lawyer.

"Abner appointed me to represent this Snidlett character," said Fleming. "He can't make bond, what's your position?"

"He can sit in the can."

"I'll see him this afternoon and convey your regards."

Ev chuckled before continuing. "I hear you might want to take over my high-paying job."

Robbie looked at Ev and smiled. "That's what I've heard, too."

Ev wondered if he was going to have to settle for the evasive answer.

Robbie continued. "Some of the Republicans have asked me. I told them I'm not interested. To tell you the truth, I don't envy your lot."

Ev wasn't sure whether to be relieved or insulted.

"You've got Rita and Clyde Noble to deal with," continued Robbie. "Thank God I don't."

* * *

Brown called Gene Roberts as soon as his district court case was concluded. Roberts was home now and his recuperation was supposed to be work-free, but the sheriff's staff seemed unable to function for more than an hour without calling the investigator for guidance. Roberts fussed about being bothered with the minutiae no one was capable of handling and then sat near the telephone looking forward to the next call.

"What do you need, lieutenant?" growled Roberts when Brown called.

"Hep. I need hep," laughed Brown.

"You and the rest of those clowns."

Brown explained the new developments and then listened to the silence on the other end of the line.

Finally Roberts spoke. "You're just muddying the waters, lieutenant."

"I know."

"Snidlett's such a sorry bastard that he's got you believing him. That little snot Jason has lied to us. And another tidbit suggests someone else was there. A number four. We've run out of sperm to match up. So what do you propose?"

"Talk to Jason again. Then try to figure out if one of the Nobles came home that night."

Roberts didn't respond.

"Boss?" asked Brown.

"I should've checked out the Nobles right up front," replied Roberts in measured words. "You've got a plan, I hope."

"Sure do," answered Brown while at the same time hoping Roberts would not ask for the details he had yet to formulate.

"Okay, get with R. C. and go to it."

"Slight problem. R. C.'s on leave."

"State police," murmured Roberts. "Do your best. At some point we've got to look like we know what we're doing."

Brown remained at his desk for several minutes, toying with a cigarette and staring at the Miranda Noble file piled in front of him. He wasn't thinking about "we;" he was thinking about "I." He didn't need either the press or a veteran like Roberts to remind him that the investigation, regardless of the difficulties, cast a grim reflection on the department, and more pointedly, now, on the lieutenant.

He wondered about Hank Burke. Brown didn't try to fool himself; he was convinced that his murky position as assistant investigator—lieutenant—was a sop to Burke's black supporters. It was all politics. How Brown got his job was a product of the netherworld of vote-grabbing. What he did with it was something else.

If he failed to solve Miranda's murder, he would be blamed in some fashion: youth, inexperience, race, political appointee, or just plain small department incompetent. "I guess it doesn't matter what reason they want to use," mumbled Brown. "I've got my chance."

Brown pulled Horace Seay's report from the file hoping that there was something in his initial report that would explain Snidlett's claim that a fourth person had been at the Nobles. A single line at the end of Seay's narrative caught his eye. "This officer took photographs of the general area shortly after arrival, film being held for processing."

Brown pawed through the file looking for a large brown envelope containing the photographs. Finding none he returned to Seay's report. At the bottom of the page was Roberts's neat penmanship: "Film to be processed."

"Damn," blurted Brown aloud. "Horace hasn't done his yet." He pulled a pad from his desk drawer and in bold letters instructed Seay to produce the roll of film, immediately. He tore the sheet of paper free and walked out of his office into the hallway where the deputies' in-boxes occupied a corner.

* * *

Brown crossed Scott's Mountain amid the lemon-yellow poplars and crimson dogwoods and began the tortuous descent into the broad valley which cradled Onan. At the foot of the mountain, left of the straightening road, bulldozers pushed grizzled apple trees into piles just beyond a large sign proclaiming "Copperhill, A Planned Community." He reached the entrance to Noble View and turned in slowly. Now he was having second thoughts about appearing at the door without having first called for an appointment. The element of surprise seemed like a good idea when he was walking out of the sheriff's department, but as he turned the potential line of questioning in his mind while driving there, the prompting possibility of quick

213

success fizzled. There were still seemingly innocuous questions about the telephone system he reminded himself.

Clara Wood answered the doorbell. "Lewis Brown," she greeted him brightly. "How are you? How your mama and daddy?"

Clara Wood was related to his mother, but Brown could not remember the degree. They chatted at the threshold for several minutes before the lieutenant could manage to address the business at hand. "Are the Nobles home?"

"No. They on a trip. For two weeks. Left Monday. Come in."

He followed Clara to the cavernous kitchen where they sat at the kitchen table. Clara poured two cups of coffee.

"When you gettin' married, boy?" asked Clara.

Brown smiled and evaded the topic. "Savin' that for another day. Maybe you can help me with something since the Nobles aren't here."

"About my poor little Miranda. I'll do my best."

"That phone in the pool house. Does it ring on the number to the big house?"

"No. They different."

"Is there an answering machine on it? A caller I D?"

"No. Just a regular phone. None of this modern stuff. Mr. Clyde said he didn't want to be bothered at the pool."

"Does this place have a burglar alarm?"

"Oh yes."

"Who knows the code?"

"Mister…Senator Noble and Miz Noble and me. And Miranda did too, for a while."

Brown felt a tingle of anticipation. "For awhile?"

"Yeah. But Miz Noble and Miranda had an awful fight…I told Mr. Roberts…and that next day Miz Noble changed the numbers."

"Next day. Thursday?"

"Yeah."

"You didn't give the numbers to Miranda?"

"Lawd no. That's Mr. Clyde's business. And I didn't see her after Wednesday. Didn't talk to her."

"Could Miranda get in without the code?"

"This place? A silverfish couldn't get in here. And I double-check every door and window when I left Friday. If something was to disappear from here, Miz Noble'd blame me."

"How about the children?"

"I doubt it. I'm keepin' them this week. And when we get home from their school they ask me to unlock the door 'cause they can't remember the numbers."

Brown twisted in his chair, gazing through the floor to ceiling windows overlooking the terrace, and sipped the coffee. "They went to Richmond the Friday Miranda…died."

"That's right. Early. They took that Mercedes to the shop."

Brown leaned forward. "To the shop?"

"That's what Mister…Senator Noble said. To leave it off."

"They took just one car?"

"That's right."

The next phases of the plan suddenly jelled amid the jumble of questions Clara's story was prompting.

"Do you know where?"

"No. I just know he bought it there."

"Where they'd stay?"

"At a hotel. The numbers over at the phone. I'll get it." Clara walked to the telephone, wrote the number on a piece of paper and handed it to Brown.

Brown finished his coffee and arose from the table. He walked to the window and looked at the terrace. "Can we go outside?"

"Of course." Clara joined him and opened the door.

Outside Brown found two brass carriage lamps on either side of the two sets of French doors, one serving the kitchen and the other the dining room.

"How do you cut these on?"

"There's a switch in the kitchen and over there in the dining room."

Brown studied the doors and then turned and surveyed the pool. Then, "How's it been here? Since Miranda died?"

"Well Mister Clyde fusses a lot. He's busy with the campaign. And he wants whoever did it caught. And Miz Noble just gets angry. She just doesn't want to hear the girl's name. Keeps sayin' put it behind us. Move on. Let the police handle it. I think they went on the trip to get away from it all."

"Well. Thank you for the coffee. I'll just walk out around back."

"Not superstitious?" asked Clara.

"No. Not me. In one door and out the other."

"Goodbye," said Clara. "Good luck."

Brown walked around the side of the house nearest the pool. In front he walked to the Mercedes which was parked beside Clara's car in the service drive. He pulled out his notebook and wrote down the name of the dealership appearing on the rear of the automobile.

The next step in the plan was to go to Richmond, but that would have to wait until the following week. There might be time to squeeze in a session with Jason early in the week. Brown guided his sedan down the driveway, wondering whether Oliver Farnworth would let Jason meet with him again.

# CHAPTER 24

Tuesday, October 12th

Columbus Day—the real one—had broken cool and clear with dew so heavy that the blades of grass and spent wild flowers bent under its weight, the droplets glistening in the morning sun like a mature field of diamonds awaiting harvest. Puffs of cottony clouds drifted in the deep blue sky and the slopes of hardwood rising quietly from the narrow valley where Ev and Polly lived were engulfed in yellows and reds so perfectly dappled that they seemed artificial, like the scenery carefully manicured by a grown man for a toy railroad.

The pastures proved irresistible to Polly and as soon as the dew had mysteriously vanished she and Will took a long walk with Will asking a thousand questions and Polly trying to answer. Chief ran ahead crossing left and right hoping to find a quail. As they neared their home on the return Will slipped his hand into Polly's.

"Mommy," said Will quietly. "I don't wanna move."

Polly looked at their little red brick house and then at the top of Will's blonde head. On days such as this she had difficulty finding words to convince him otherwise. Her two boys had been babies in the house; her thoughts filled with memories of Christmas mornings and crisp autumn evenings by a fire, of walks in the snow and the patter of little feet running into the kitchen. Tears welled at the corner of her eyes as she squeezed the little hand that had sought hers.

"At the new house you'll have a big bedroom all to yourself," she managed.

"I don't won't to be by myself. I like Sam in my room."

Polly sighed quietly. "Oh, I bet you'll like it."

"Can we come back and live here someday?"

"Maybe," Polly answered. "Maybe you'll buy it someday."

Polly climbed the wire fence bordering their yard as Will crawled beneath the lowest strand.

"Can we take walks at Granny's?" asked Will.

"Even longer walks. And Uncle E has cows. You and Sam will have to help with Uncle E's cows like your father does."

"I'm scared of cows."

"Are you scared of the cows that live here?" Polly gestured toward the pasture through which they had been walking. No cows were in sight.

Will nodded his head.

"You won't be when you're bigger."

"Sam says I'm too bigger now to be scared."

"Well, we'll see," said Polly as they neared the side door, freshly painted by Ev over the long weekend in preparation for putting the house on the market. She could hear the telephone ringing as she opened the door. *It's about time for Margaret's daily harangue,* she told herself. Polly, to her dismay, was correct.

"Polly, where have you been? I've been calling all morning."

"We were on a walk."

"Oh. Well. I went to town yesterday. I just had to get out. The thing with Kitty Carson has upset me so. So I started my Christmas shopping today."

"You did," answered Polly. She suspected that Christmas shopping was a ruse. Margaret was probably out of vodka and she refused to buy one dram of alcohol at the local ABC store.

"The reason I called was to talk about my furniture."

The old Cross home was filled with antiques, almost all of them from the Cross family, since Margaret's mother had died with little of value and six children to fight over it. Polly had given no thought to the possibility that Margaret would fail to take every stick with her when she moved and now she wondered if she should dare hope that some of the furniture would be left behind.

Margaret continued. "I thought you might want the cherry sideboard in the dining room."

The cherry sideboard was a prize and Polly was breathless with her good fortune. "Mrs. Cross, we'd love it."

"It's too big for any room except one like my dining room. Amanda said she couldn't use it."

Polly's warm feeling drained away. "Oh." She paused. She knew she really didn't want the whole story, but like a bird mesmerized by a swaying snake she couldn't resist her curiosity. "And what did Amanda want?"

Margaret didn't answer and Polly knew her mother-in-law was frantically trying to devise a prevarication.

"Well," Margaret finally said, "I told Amanda to make a list of what she wanted…when we were talking about what I should take with me. And I think that's fair, since you're getting the house."

Polly could find no couth words with which to respond.

"I'd like to move after New Year's," said Margaret.

Polly ignored the diversion. "Mrs. Cross. We are buying the house. Is Amanda buying the furniture?" Polly couldn't believe she let the question slip. In all likelihood, Margaret would now decide that Ev and Polly should buy the sideboard.

"Certainly not!" came Margaret's icy response. "I thought you'd be pleased with the sideboard." Click.

Polly kept the telephone to her ear listening to the dial tone and trying to suppress ruminations of mayhem and murder.

She was still seething when Ev arrived for lunch.

Ev saw the set jaw and kept his thoughts to himself since he was going to hear about the cause sooner than later.

Polly dropped a sandwich in front of him as Will climbed into a nearby chair. "Guess what she's done now."

Ev shook his head. "I wouldn't know where to start. Hello sport," he said to Will.

"She told Amanda to make a list of what furniture she wanted. Amanda gets furniture since we're getting the house. What do you want for lunch Will? As a consolation prize, we get the cherry sideboard."

"It's not worth worrying about," said Ev. He didn't want to think about it either.

Polly brushed away the hair that had fallen over her left eye. "I cannot, just cannot wait, until January first. When she moves." She handed Will a plate with his sandwich, never having heard his response.

Will eased from his chair and went into the enclosed porch where he settled in front of Dexter's Lab.

"The Appersons' party is next Saturday. Evelyn called today," continued Polly. Evelyn Apperson was Polly's best friend, and like Polly, she was from somewhere else and was married to a native, Ev's friend Glenn. "Is that date alright?"

"Sure. All I've done this fall is work on this place. Nothing else planned."

"Live here ten years and you finally get around to fixing all the things that needed it. We should sell our house more often."

"I guess this is the Appersons' beautiful people party." The Appersons had begun to move in a new circle—the Jet Set was one of Ev's terms.

"Oh Ev." Polly crossed her arms and leaned against the counter. She spoke to Ev's back. "It will be fun. You know what else? She said Rich Garrison and Lydia McDonald were having an affair. And apparently Carole Garrison doesn't know."

"I got wind of that."

"You what? Why didn't you tell me? Evelyn didn't know any details."

"It came up in a criminal matter. I didn't feel comfortable talking about it. Plus, it slipped my mind."

Polly squeezed her arms a little tighter, buckling her blouse and exposing her bra-less cleavage. "I wouldn't tell anybody. You know that. How could you forget a tidbit like that?"

Ev explained how Garrison and McDonald were entertaining each other in the hot tub when a burglary occurred on McDonald's property. "Horace said she was probably going to call me to drop charges, but she hasn't yet."

Polly was quiet a moment. Then, "Ev. She's at best ten years older than he is. Poor Carole. And Carole's the one with the money."

"I suspect that's why Lydia asked Horace about dropping charges. It would all come out in court."

"Oh I wish I could tell Evelyn."

"You can't."

"I know. Will you drop the charges?"

Ev turned his head to answer. "I don't know. I guess I'll decide if she calls. It's not my place to break up a marriage." He caught sight of the buckled blouse.

Polly was looking at Ev, her thoughts racing about the fabulous morsel of gossip that she could not tell. She saw Ev's eyes drop and recognized immediately The Look. "Behave yourself," she said as she fastened a button on her blouse.

"Interested in a brief diversion?"

"No Ev. Will is in there." It was her renewed conclusion that men always had sex on their minds: libidinous minefields that could be set off by any one of a thousand trip wires.

"We could always walk out to the shed."

"Ev. No." How could his timing be so ridiculous? First she had been driven to murderous thoughts by his mother and then he had belatedly told her the gossip of the year and she couldn't mention it.

"Rich Garrison must have had the same problems with Carole," mumbled Ev.

"Well that's his problem. Your problem is that you thought about Rich and Lydia and got it on your mind."

"Your blouse got it on my mind. Your open blouse."

"You're envious of Rich."

"I imagine Rich is envious of me."

That helped, but Polly was not swayed. Margaret's face kept appearing in her thoughts and Ev's mouth was too much like his mother's for Polly to look at him, with interest, at the moment. "You go on back to work. Maybe later tonight." She wouldn't see Ev's mouth in the dark.

"Sex delayed is sex denied," said Ev as he arose from the table.

* * *

Defying human nature's fixation on routine Ev always parked in a different spot and used any one of three doors to enter the courthouse. Today he decided to walk past the front of the oldest part of the building to reach a side door near the rear.

In the anteroom of his office sat Lewis Brown. "Thomasson and Farnsworth are on their way Ev."

Ev walked into the small conference room that also served as his library. Dozens of bound volumes of Virginia appellate court decisions lined the shelves and beside them were ancient treatises and thick obsolete books of the Virginia Code. Some of the old volumes carried the name of William Cross, Ev's great-great-grandfather. The room was half library and half museum. Ev took off his blazer and laid it across a corner chair.

Brown settled into a chair at the library table. "I'm glad you're gonna be in on this one Ev. I mean, this is interview number five, and I'm wondering just what Jason is holding back."

"Or why," said Ev.

"That too."

Ev heard the door open in the anteroom and walked out to greet Farnsworth. Behind Farnsworth was a smaller black haired fellow in a dark blue suit who looked as if he wasn't old enough to shave. Bringing up the rear was Jason Thomasson.

Farnsworth introduced the small man first. "This is Paul Stankowski, an associate in my office." In keeping with Bledsoe's observation that associates were brief bag boys, Stankowski carried a briefcase, one as new and unscarred as its owner. Paul stepped forward and pumped Ev's hand vigorously.

"Nice to see you," said Ev. "We met over the telephone some time ago."

Farnsworth introduced Thomasson as well. Jason's handshake was limp and moist and reminded Ev of the way Hampton Coleman shook hands. Thomasson barely made eye contact before returning his gaze to the floor.

The four joined Brown at the table. On one side sat Ev and Brown, on the other was Jason flanked by his attorneys.

Farnsworth cleared his throat and assumed what he seemed to believe was a commanding demeanor. "Gentlemen. We were just here for Jason to talk to the lieutenant. I was hesitant to agree to this second interview, but we are trying to cooperate."

*Okay,* thought Ev, *you've made your speech for your client.* He glanced at Stankowski and wondered why the neophyte associate was tagging along, perhaps the billable hours at Farnsworth and Conte needed an injection. The cost for the two of them just to drive to and from Lafayette Court House would be at least eight hundred dollars. The interview itself would probably cost less than that.

Brown looked at Ev. "You start Lewis," said Ev.

Brown leaned forward. "Thank you for coming. Again. Look. We keep learning things. And when we do, I find out Jason hasn't told us something."

"I've told you everything," said Jason with whinny petulance.

"Well try this Jason. Why did you call Miranda after you left the pool that Friday night?"

"Do what?" Jason glanced from Brown to Ev.

"We know now you called her later that night. Say about nine-thirty."

"Look Mr. Brown. I told you someone called her, when I was there. I forgot about it until two weeks ago, when I told you."

Brown folded his hands in front of him. "We'll get to that in a minute. Now you called her. I don't know why you'd keep that from us, unless after the call you went back to Onan to see her."

"Uh-uh," said Jason quickly, shaking his head. "I didn't go back there. Anyway I thought I was cleared, or whatever."

Brown leaned forward. "Nobody's been cleared. And that includes you."

Farnsworth was watching Brown intently. Stankowski was scribbling away on a yellow legal pad.

Ev took his glasses off and leaned back in his chair. "You've talked to us four times, and each story has been different. We're beginning to worry you're not being straight with us." That was the understatement of his career, but Ev didn't want Farnsworth jumping in to deflect their efforts.

"I guess we can get your phone records," said Brown. He could get the records, but they wouldn't contain local calls, and Charlottesville to Onan was local. He was gambling that television crime shows—in which the cops could get records of anything overnight—might have mislead his listeners, especially the two lawyers who spent most of their professional time sparring over other people's stocks and bonds.

"Well get them then," said Farnsworth.

Ev glanced at Brown. He wondered whether the lieutenant was on the level with his statement, and he wondered if Farnsworth, who seemed to be playing along, knew something that Ev didn't. He decided everyone at the table was bluffing.

The mind games ended with Jason's response. "Yeah I called her. I mean, I felt bad about what I'd said. I called to apologize. And she just like sorta sang an answer. Go to hell. I don't need yours. And hung up. So I said screw her and watched television." Jason was watching his hands.

Farnsworth glared at Jason but said nothing.

"So nine-thirty sounds right?" asked Brown.

"I don't know. After I got to the apartment. So I guess that's about right." Jason looked up. "I called a girl in D.C. right after that, too. I didn't go anywhere."

"Get the records," said Farnsworth, with a sarcastic edge to his remark.

Brown looked at Farnsworth without responding. He was trying to decide himself which one of them had been trapped. "Okay. Now. The first call."

"Yeah."

"Who was it?"

"Well, I mean, you'll get those records too." Jason's narrow frame seemed to be shrinking. "It was Rita."

Farnsworth's eyes widened and his mouth fell ajar, but only for a flash. He pressed his lips firmly together and looked at Jason.

Ev was watching Farnsworth's reaction carefully. Jason's answer had touched an exposed nerve and Farnsworth was rapidly on his way to having a crippling conflict of interest with the wife of his firm's biggest client.

"What was that about?" asked Brown.

"Miranda laughed it off. Said Rita was calling to see whether she was there. And to see if I was there. And Miranda…I can't believe this…Miranda told her we were both there and she'd just finished fucking my eyes out. Miranda hung up and that's when she got the crack pipe. I mean, you know, she was like angry and upset at the same time. So, then we argued. And I cussed her for telling Rita I was there. Then we started arguin' about the crack and I threw the pipe. And. Well. I told you that. You got it on a tape."

"What else did Miranda say Rita said?" asked Brown.

Jason shrunk still further and sighed. "She said—"

"I think I need a few minutes with Jason, Ev," Farnsworth interrupted.

"I don't think he's hurting himself right now," answered Ev as evenly as he could manage. He had no doubt but that Farnsworth was about to stumble on a slippery ethical slope, the slope separating Jason's interests from those of Rita Noble.

Oliver Farnsworth looked at Ev briefly; it was obvious his mind was churning the dilemma Jason had created for him. "We won't be but a minute," said Farnsworth.

Ev arose abruptly and motioned for Brown to follow. An anger born of frustration was quietly rising within him, tightening his chest muscles and making his stomach queasy. Jason might be able to fill in some blanks, maybe exonerate himself, unless Farnsworth told him to quit talking. And the only reason Ev could devise for advice of that sort was Farnsworth's desire to shield Rita. How, he asked himself, could Farnsworth commit an ethical lapse of that proportion? Jason was his client in a murder investigation. What did Farnsworth know about Rita? Or was Jason the one after all?

Once in the anteroom Brown tried to speak but Ev waved him off.

Evander Cross was trying to control himself, to think through the thoughts he'd just had and determine whether he was being irrational. He, like every other prosecutor, worried that a big case would go south, leaving the commonwealth's attorney looking flabby and ineffective and giving the public an excuse to elect new blood. Many elected prosecutors forgot, or never learned, the other half of the equation, the half that balanced and focused hard-nosed prosecutorial zeal: perspective.

Perspective. The subjective evaluation of the relative significance of one person's transgressions with those of others necessarily trenched an inherently gray area. One guy might get a break and the next, no quarter. It required the prosecutor to consider each defendant as an individual and to acknowledge that there was, sometimes, another side to the story. And it was crucial to maintain the distinction between big cases and the ninety-seven per cent that weren't big.

Prosecutors without perspective also came to distrust defense lawyers almost as much as they did criminals: guilt by opposition. Trust was the sinew of professional etiquette. Lose trust and perspective went with it, leaving lawyers who wouldn't discuss cases candidly and who made little effort to find mutually tolerable resolutions. Without perspective and trust, the twin virtues, everyone fought, called each other names—under the breath—and battled relentlessly in the trenches. The adversarial process degenerated from a boxing match with rules to a messy street fight to the death.

A prosecutorial zealot in a big city or sprawling suburban county, devoid of perspective and shielded by a phalanx of assistants, was a step removed from the public he served and had less reason to worry that the voters might get nervous and remove him. And only God or a change in the oval office could undo a federal district attorney. The political existence of a rural state prosecutor is governed by a slightly different set of rules. Get tough on crime means get tough on the other guy's crime; not my son's, not my driving, not trespassing at the Quik Mart's rear service entrance at two in the morning to screw my sister-in-law in the back of her car. And when the citizenry started grumbling about the prosecutor, it was because he had lost, or never had, perspective, and grumbling could flush out a contestant for the job in the blink of an eye.

It was easy to go rigid and irascible about minor offenses, always demanding maximum sentences and refusing to enter plea agreements for fear of looking soft; fussing about the judges who failed to jail every miscreant and fuming that the Constitution was constantly being twisted to thwart the police: the entire system perverted to hobble those trying to stop the bad guys. It was a comfortable, self-indulgent, holier than thou affliction that replaced judgment and clouded memory. For zealots—Wilmer Bledsoe called them Nazis—forgot they had bought booze for their underage college buddies, or smoked some marijuana in the dormitory, or most assuredly engaged in intriguing varieties of sexual fun that were forbidden under Virginia law, and had not been caught. They forgot that even stellar citizens occasionally make a mistake in judgment.

Ev examined his reaction. Was he assuming Farnsworth would end the interview for the wrong reason? Couldn't he have a legitimate reason? Would it be original sin for Farnsworth, if caught off guard, to try to look out for two clients at once?

Ev walked into the hallway outside his office. The School Board, the lavatories, and the water fountain shared the rest of the floor with his office. The voices of a man and woman were clearly audible from Ev's position at the fountain.

"On top of that, Ferrell's daughter is pregnant and she just won't tell nobody. And Jesse is still out of work and my mother goes in for more cancer tests Friday." The despondent voice was that of the school superintendent's secretary.

The man, whom Ev didn't know, responded. "It gets right rough sometimes. Seems like you get to the point that you wouldn't have no luck if it wasn't for bad luck."

The secretary laughed lightly. "I bet that country music singer they made the movie about, what's her name, hasn't been through all this stuff. But I guess other people get in the same boat at some time. Though I swear, I've about decided I've gone crazy from it all."

"Well, if you're crazy, you're in the right county," said the man. County came out as 'canty'.

"Isn't that the truth," said the secretary as they both laughed.

Ev smiled. *Down home philosopher, this one with a Stoic influence,* he told himself. He walked back to the anteroom after a few sips at the fountain. He was not going to assume that Farnsworth would do something unethical. The tension in his chest was gone and he was ready to contend with whatever curve Farnsworth planned to pitch.

"Where's Brown?" Ev asked Linda Masencup.

Linda answered that the lieutenant was in Ev's office.

Ev found Brown smoking a cigarette and staring through the window.

"What do you think?" asked Ev.

"Damn man, it's like being right at the edge of a cliff and not being able to look over."

"You know what's happening don't you?"

"I know his lawyer looks like he's going to shut him up."

Ev sat on the edge of his desk. "Give me a cigarette, if you don't mind."

Brown turned on his heal and looked at Cross. "I didn't know you smoked."

"My wife and I quit eight years ago."

Brown handed him a cigarette and lighter. "Never really quit, do you?"

"Stop maybe, but never quit." Ev lit the cigarette and drew deeply before continuing. "You might need some background. Farnsworth's firm represents Clyde Noble and his business empire. That's how Jason ended up being represented by him. And I can assure you, he ain't cheap. You can guess who's paying. When old Jason mentioned that Rita was the caller, Oliver obviously didn't know about it, so he found himself trying to figure out what to do. He smelled the same rat we do. If he lets Jason serve up Rita, he's going to lose one big damn client."

"Who's his client, then?"

"That's what was getting under my collar. He's got himself in a bind. Helping clear Jason hurts Rita. She's a client of sorts, just not in this investigation."

Brown smiled. "I see you're coming around a little bit, about Rita."

"I'm not going that far. Yet. I just want the whole story." Ev walked toward the door and paused. "Have you wondered why Miranda was so anxious to answer the phone at a house where she wasn't supposed to be?"

"Well, I guess I'm wondering now," answered Brown.

"It's like she was expecting a call. Smith? But he'd been there once, and he tried to call her at the main number long before that. Snidlett? Or, God forbid, was she expecting a number four?"

"Doesn't make sense," said Brown sullenly.

"And another thing. Why was Jason holding back on Rita's call? He was covering something. Something was said."

Linda Masencup appeared at the door. "Mr. Farnsworth's ready," she whispered.

"Alright," said Ev. "Let's go see what the hole card is."

Farnsworth was standing at the library table beside Jason and Stankowski, who were still seated, as Ev and Brown filed in. The brief bag toter was staring at his yellow pad, though Ev doubted that the young lawyer was reading what he had earlier written.

Farnsworth's hands were resting on the top of his chair. "I've advised Jason that the interview is over."

Ev felt his body stiffening. He had just spent ten minutes convincing himself that Farnsworth would not use Jason to cover for Rita, or whatever he was covering. Farnsworth was a respected lawyer, the senior partner in a top-notch law firm, a big fish in a big pond who had served on a half dozen bar committees. Ev tried momentarily to tell himself that Farnsworth must have legitimate reasons for cutting Jason off, but the effort failed. It was Rita. Stankowski did not move. He wasn't even blinking. *The brief bag boy knows,* thought Ev.

Ev leaned over to pick up his legal pad telling himself to let the trio go without his saying something, for anything he said was going to be taken as a personal affront by Farnsworth. His effort at restraint faltered. "Well that's certainly Mr. Thomasson's right," Ev said in a low voice, "but it seemed to me he was not telling us anything that implicated him."

Farnsworth was motionless. "That was my advice, Ev," he repeated.

"If anything, he was exonerating himself."

Jason, a quizzical expression on his face, looked up at Farnsworth.

"This is not a matter for debate," replied Farnsworth as he tapped Jason on the shoulder.

Jason pushed his chair back with Stankowski quickly following suit. Brown was watching Ev.

"Who should we contact if we want to talk to Jason again?"

"My office, of course. But I think we're done."

"He's not charged, we really don't need your permission."

"It was my understanding that your people wouldn't try an end run like that."

Ev swallowed and tried to suppress his anger. "Oliver. I perceive a conflict of interest here, and it's putting all of us in a bad spot." He had sugarcoated the accusation as best he could.

Farnsworth reddened quickly while Stankowski, wide-eyed, was watching. "I am amazed that you'd suggest that. We are finished here," said Farnsworth.

A bewildered Jason followed Farnsworth into the anteroom. Stankowski arose and carefully placed the legal pad in his briefcase. He glanced at Ev as if to speak, then looked quickly away while closing the briefcase.

Ev's eyes followed Stankowski's retreat and when the three were clear of the anteroom Ev spoke. "Shut the door Lewis."

Brown closed the door to the library and turned to face the prosecutor.

"Fuck that son of a bitch," said Ev slowly, emphasizing each word. "He just killed our best shot at figuring out what that fucking Rita was up to. He just blew our chance of sorting out why Jason's playing games. I ought to make a complaint to the bar on that self-righteous sanctimonious bastard."

Brown had never seen Cross in this light. It was akin to happening upon a Baptist preacher drunk at a whorehouse.

Ev continued. "We've got three suspects. Snidlett, who could have stayed and done it. Jason, who could have come back and done it, or Rita, who could have got pissed and come back and done it. I don't think there's a mystery fourth. That bitch Rita called the pool, and said something, and she called Jason the first thing next day when she got home. I doubt she called if Jason knew Miranda was dead, so either she was grilling him or getting her alibi in place. That little shit Jason knows enough to sort this out."

"You think Farnsworth had no idea about Rita?" asked Brown.

"Hell no. Jason caught him off guard. When he sees his meal ticket about to disappear…what I mean is, the Nobles would blame him for Jason spilling the beans. And if he represented his client right, he'd know he needs to clear Jason and that means implicating Rita. Screw him."

Brown lit a cigarette. "I don't know your ethics rules. But if we don't have much on Jason, and all Jason can do is hurt Rita, is it wrong to protect them both?"

"Look at it this way Lewis. You're being questioned about a murder because you were there and had opportunity. You hire a lawyer. While you're being questioned, you start telling things that might point to someone else as the murderer.

Your lawyer shuts you up because the other suspect is also a client of his in some other matter. So information that would help clear you is kept from the police. Would you be happy with that lawyer?"

"I don't know, Ev, Farnsworth was on the spot too." Brown was cautious with his statement.

"I was on the spot with Smith. I might've had some patience with Farnsworth if he'd just gone ahead and said he had a conflict. He knows he's got a conflict and still he's covering all the bases. So he just decides to hell with Jason's exposure. Now he'll run back to Charlottesville and start scrambling to protect Rita. Money is everything. So much for the silk stocking assholes who look down their noses at prosecutors and country lawyers and guys in one-horse practices."

"Ev. Did you have to decide to cut Smith loose on the spot with his lawyer sitting across the table from you?"

Ev eyed Brown for a moment. *Out of the mouths of babes*, he chided himself. "Okay. You've gotta point." He suddenly felt foolish for his outburst.

Brown crushed his cigarette in an ashtray on one of the bookshelves. "By the way, I've been thinking about taking up coaching."

**CHAPTER 25**

Wednesday, October 14th

Wednesday morning had come again although to Ev it seemed like he had just walked out of General District Court. He could not shake Oliver Farnsworth from his thoughts and between flashes of anger he contemplated buying a pack of cigarettes. It was not yet nine o'clock and the telephone was ringing incessantly. Ev could hear Linda dutifully deflecting the callers until he was back from court. Then his intercom buzzed.

"It's Dillon Klobb, Ev. Do you want to take it?" asked Linda.

Klobb, besides being the self-appointed citizen co-coordinator for the Lebanon Cove burglary investigation, was vice chairman—vice chairperson as Klobb styled it—of the Lafayette County Democratic Committee. Ev did not want to listen to Klobb; he knew that Klobb was going to complain that the sheriff's department hadn't solved the Cove crime spree. "Hello Dillon," answered Ev.

"Ev. Thank you for taking this call. I'm sure you're aware of the burglaries in the Cove. There was another last night. We can't seem to get the sheriff's department to take the problem seriously. I want to know what you're going to do to help us."

Succinct and to the point: When are you going to stop beating your wife. A rhetorical question couched as a demand. Klobb had lived in Lafayette County for twenty-five years, been active in politics for the last two decades, and still didn't understand that the commonwealth's attorney could not order the sheriff's department to do anything.

"Dillon. I know they're working on it. I've reviewed it with Lewis Brown. The problem...."

"We've talked to Lieutenant Brown. But he hasn't returned my latest call."

"The problem is that one deputy's recovering from a gunshot, the investigator's recuperating from a heart attack, and Brown is essentially doing two men's work. But I'll remind Brown he needs to get this resolved as quickly as he can." Ev was not going to say anything critical about the sheriff's department that Klobb could repeat, but he was irritated that Brown had not followed through with his bait and trap plan.

"I was wondering how these things were prioritized. How your office handled that."

Ev tapped his desk with a pencil. "I can't make the sheriff's office do any particular thing. I can only ask. The sheriff is independent, a constitutional officer."

"Yes. Of course. I just wanted you to know how concerned we were. That perhaps we were being overlooked."

228

Ev acknowledged the problem and promised to push Brown; he could think of nothing else to do, and there was no use blustering.

"Please remember the committee meeting tonight," added Klobb, suddenly changing the subject. "We want to adopt a formal endorsement of Clyde for senator. A little spark early in the campaign for the nomination."

"I'll try Dillon, but I can't promise to be there." Ev clenched his jaw at the canard. *Right Dillon,* he thought, *jump into Clyde's campaign while investigating his wife.* And besides, Lafayette County's influence on statewide politics was about equal to a stadium janitor's contribution to a Southeastern Conference football game.

"It's important to have all the county's elected Democrats endorse Clyde. I'm sure you understand the significance of this for all our office holders."

"Makes sense," said Ev, thinking at the same time that there was the unmistakable odor of blackmail in Dillon's statement. "No more calls," Ev called to Linda after Klobb rang off. He made a note to himself to badger Brown so that he could honestly say he had tried. Then, deciding not to delay, he dialed Brown's extension. Receiving no answer he called dispatch.

"Oh. He's in Richmond today," advised Willie Painter. "He went down there with R. C. Hawkes."

Ev gathered his files for district court as he pondered what Brown was looking for in Richmond. He also wondered whether Brown had previewed his plan with Gene Roberts.

Varney Mitchell, his tie askew, appeared at the door before Ev could depart. "Hello Ev," he said.

Ev laid the files on the corner of his desk and sat down. "Come in Varney."

"Just checking," said Varney as he settled into a chair opposite Ev's desk. Varney wore a Harris Tweed jacket over a rumpled tattersall shirt. His glasses were sliding down his nose as he spoke. "Nothing new on the Noble case?"

"There's always something new, it just doesn't seem to get us anywhere," answered Ev.

"Any suspects?"

"Several."

Varney pushed his glasses back into place. "I don't guess you want to tell me, do you."

Ev smiled as he rocked back in his chair. "Not yet. But I'll make sure you have a first shot at the story, if we ever get there." Ev received at least one call a week from some reporter digging for the same information. It would be poetic justice to allow the local weekly the scoop.

"I guess you're hobbled without Gene Roberts."

"Lewis Brown is filling in well," answered Ev, although he wasn't certain he believed what he was saying.

"What about the attempted capital murder. That guy who shot Mervin McIntosh. Littleton, I think."

"The preliminary is next week. Robbie Fleming is the defense attorney. I imagine that will be a plea. At trial."

"Yeah, that's good. I'll come for that. Oh. There's a rumor floating around that Conway Lawson wants to run for sheriff again. Heard that?"

Ev laughed. "I guess he didn't get the message before when the voters filed a petition for his removal."

"I heard he's saying that Burke's handling of the Noble case isn't any better than his handling of Alphonso Thornton's murder."

"That's a hell of a campaign platform."

Varney shrugged his shoulders. "Who knows."

"You don't remember Ossie Goines do you?" asked Ev.

"No."

"Back in the sixties Ossie ran for sheriff in the Democratic primary. He was probably six-five, and no more than a hundred-twenty pounds, and made a little money dabbling in real estate, and bootleg whiskey. He got three votes, two were his and his wife's. The next day my uncle saw him at Bishop's Esso, the Exxon now, and Ossie had a forty-four revolver strapped around his waist. Uncle E asked him why he was wearing a gun and Ossie said any man with no more friends than he had needed to carry a gun."

Varney's laughter started his glasses back down his nose. "I might need to do a story on that one."

"Would be more interesting then rehashing Conway Lawson."

"Well, keep me posted. I know you've got court."

Ev waved his farewell to Mitchell. The hint of an opponent for next year's election was certain to send the sheriff into apoplexy, even an opponent with little or no chance. But sheriffs were the prototypical political creatures and Hank Burke would react by ceaselessly pressing his deputies to solve crimes promptly and allow him to announce arrests to the press regardless of whether there was enough evidence to secure conviction. Ev had a sinking feeling that the arrangement he and Roberts had backed the sheriff into accepting not two months before would be conveniently forgotten.

* * *

Lewis Brown had forgotten how euphoria felt. He had decided that nothing would ever equal beating a nationally ranked opponent, heretofore unbeaten by his school, while he was playing football in college; the morning's events had proved him wrong.

Brown took the liberty that all cops do—except Roberts—and hurried back to Lafayette Court House twenty miles over the speed limit. An hour and fifteen minutes after leaving Richmond he was standing in Ev's office, too excited to sit.

"You must have something Lewis. You're grinning like the Cheshire cat."

Brown took a breath and then sat down. He pulled his cigarettes from his blazer and offered one to Ev.

"Why not," said Ev, taking one.

Brown lit his cigarette and leaned forward. "I went to the Mercedes dealership. Got it off the nameplate on Noble's Mercedes. He dropped his car off Friday morning and they gave him a rental unit. A silver LeSabre. They turned it in Saturday morning. Of course they didn't charge him anything, but someone marked the mileage in and out anyway. Care to guess?"

Ev was motionless. "Tell me Lewis."

"Two hundred sixty-one miles."

"Damn" muttered Ev.

"We went to the hotel they stayed at. Roberts said to check for security cameras. The parking deck had 'em at the elevator. Mrs. Rita Noble got out of the elevator at seven-thirty-eight and got back in at eleven-fifty-one"

"You have the tape?" Ev lit the cigarette.

"Of course."

Ev blew a stream of smoke across the room, his gaze fixed on the window behind Brown. "Say two hundred miles round trip, Richmond to Onan. Almost two hours each way, maybe an hour and a half if she's flying. She's there around nine until ten, ten-thirty. Shit Lewis. She killed her."

"What about this Ev? What if Jason did it and Rita knows and is covering for him. You know. Went there and found the body and figures it was Jason's work. If she'd gone there and thought anybody else had done it, she'd have reported it."

"That other possible somebody being Snidlett?"

"Yeah."

"Thanks Lewis. Muddy the waters right up front."

"How do we sort that out?" asked Lewis wearily.

"We've got to pin down Clyde. How could he miss his wife for that long? And phone records. Rita and Jason. Jason said something about a call to D.C. Another one of his late-breaking revelations. That would be on the phone bill and would take him out of the picture. Then we zero in on Rita."

"This all sounds simple," deadpanned Brown as he ground the cigarette into the ashtray while shaking his head.

"We need some poop on the Nobles' doings that Friday night. We need that before we talk to either of them." Ev was starting to write jerky sentences on the pad in front of him.

"That's a good job for Gene," said Brown. "He can do that on the telephone from home. Especially since he knows damn near everybody in the state."

Ev stopped writing. "First thing is go see Jason."

Brown straightened and shoved his hands into his pockets. "I take it we don't invite Mr. Farnsworth."

"Screw him."

Brown grinned. He was beginning to enjoy the smoking and profane Ev Cross. He looked at his watch. "If I go now, I'll be waiting for him when he gets home."

"That's if he doesn't have some little teenager he needs to service."

Brown walked to the door and paused in the threshold. "I'll call Gene and let you know tomorrow about Jason."

Ev had returned to jotting notes on the pad. "Good." He looked up. "I'm assuming Jason will have already tossed his phone bill. If so, get the company name and whatever else you need."

Brown nodded and walked away. He stopped at his basement office to check for messages. Horace Seay, seated at Roberts's desk, was completing a report. Several styrofoam cups edged the area of his endeavor.

Brown clucked his tongue and then spoke. "Roberts is gonna kick ass if he comes in and finds all that trash on his desk."

"Not my stuff," said Seay.

Alerted by the voices Hank Burke peered into the room from his tiny office as Brown scanned the pink message slips on his desk. "What the hell is going on at Lebanon Cove? Y'all ever gonna take care of that?"

"I'm doing my report now. I worked that burglary this morning," answered Seay.

"I'm not talkin' about no goddam report," spat Burke. "I mean catch the bastards and put an end to this. The people up there are burnin' my phone up." The sheriff slammed his door without awaiting a reply.

"Sweet Jesus," said Brown, quietly.

"You wanna set up the trap tonight?" asked Seay. "He's gonna stay on us till we solve this."

"Late. Yeah."

"It's gotta be late. Or after the bus runs tomorrow."

Brown scratched his chin. "Let's do it tomorrow. I've got too much on my plate today. What's his problem?"

Seay smiled. "Conway Lawson's talkin' about running for the Democratic primary."

"That explains it."

Seay pulled a small valise from the floor beside him. "I got those photos. Plum forgot. I'm sorry."

"Anything exciting?"

"Doesn't look like it."

Brown walked over to Roberts's desk and took the manila envelope from Seay. Inside were six eight-by-ten color photographs. "Damn," said Brown, "there're people milling around all over the place."

"I took the pictures before I cleared them."

"Probably a good mistake. Now we know who all was fartin' around the pool when you arrived."

Brown studied each picture carefully. The last photograph mesmerized him. "Horace. Look at this one." Brown handed the sixth photograph to Seay.

"Yeah. What about it?"

Brown walked around the corner of the desk so that he could see the photograph as Seay held it. "Look. That's the lounge chair. And look beside it. Her bathing suit top. And Rita's standing behind the lounge thing with a towel in her hand."

Seay's brow furrowed as he looked at the picture.

Brown whipped through the other five pictures. "Here, you might have taken this one a few minutes later. Rita's walking toward the trash can with the towel folded and there's something in her hand."

"The bathing suit top. I didn't see her do that, pick it up."

Brown gathered the pictures and walked back to his desk. "I bet that towel was the murder weapon," he said quietly.

Seay looked at Brown a moment before speaking. "So she's the suspect now?"

"Sort of." Brown was suddenly uncomfortable discussing his thoughts outside of the triumvirate of Hawkes, Roberts, and Cross.

As if he were reading Brown's thoughts, Seay replied quietly. "Don't worry Lewis. I'm not talking. Not around here." He nodded in the direction of the sheriff's door.

* * *

Brown watched Jason Thomasson get out of his car and walk to his apartment door. The lieutenant waited for the door to close before tracing Jason's steps. His knock went unanswered and Brown surmised that Jason had seen him through the peephole and was exercising his constitutional right to be uncooperative. Brown knocked again and again there was no response. "Jason," called Brown. "I know you're there. I saw you go in. And I'm not here to arrest you." If Jason's neighbors heard him, so be it.

The deadbolt clanked in immediate response and the door swung partly open. "Shit man. Do you have to tell everybody? I don't have anything to say."

The door was closing when Brown stuck his foot over the threshold. *Just like TV,* he thought. "It's time to come clean and clear yourself Jason."

"What about my lawyer?" asked Jason, a plaintive edge to his voice.

"He doesn't have to be here. Anyway, you know from the other day he wasn't doing you any good."

Jason pulled the door open and walked toward the dining room card table, his head and shoulders slumped like a little boy being sent to stand in the corner. "Why won't all of you just leave me alone. I don't have anymore to tell you."

Brown entered the room and closed the door soundlessly. A cloying unpleasant odor of cigarette smoke, stale beer, and perfumed deodorant greeted him. "Yes you do. Sit down and get it over with."

Jason dropped into a chair and began talking before Brown could put a question. "That damn Rita. God. She told Miranda she was on her way and Miranda's ass and mine better not be there. Miranda laughed. I mean she was messed up. Nothing Rita could say was going to bother her. We argued about the drugs and she called me a pissant coward."

"Did you hear Rita say that, about her coming?"

"Yeah. When Miranda said she'd fucked my eyes out, I was getting a beer, and I grabbed at the phone and pulled it away from her ear so I heard it, too. Rita was screaming. She was…she was out of control."

*Fucked his brains out is more like it,* thought Brown. "Hear anything else?"

"No. That's when Miranda jerked the phone away and hung up."

"Let me get this straight. The phone rang and Miranda answered. Wait. I want to record this." Brown pulled his tape recorder from his pocket, set it on the table, pressed record. "Let me get this straight Jason. Rita called the pool house at what. Seven? Seven-thirty?"

"Probably seven-thirty. I'm not sure." Jason's voice was nearly inaudible.

"Speak up. And Miranda answered?"

"Yeah."

"And you walked in the pool house to get a beer while Miranda's on the phone."

"I sorta followed her. And she covered the mouthpiece and said it's Rita and she wants to know if you're here. And before I could say anything, she said yes I'm here, meaning me, and she'd fucked my eyes out. Then she laughed. That's when I grabbed the phone and heard what Rita said."

"Which was?"

"I'm on my way there and your ass and his ass better not be around when I get to that fucking pool."

"And then Miranda hung up?"

"Yep."

"After you got back here, you called Miranda?"

"Yes."

"Anybody with her?"

"I don't know. She didn't say."

Brown took several aimless paces as he thought through what Jason had just said. "Now when did you talk to Rita again?"

"The next day. Midday, two. I don't know. She called and said Miranda's drowned. Was I there when it happened? And I said hell no. I heard you were coming and left. And she said she didn't come, she'd said that to scare Miranda. Then she said I better be careful, keep quiet, because the cops might think I'd done it, meaning me." Jason dropped his head into his hands. "She said the bitch is dead and still causing her trouble."

"What about your call to D.C.?"

"I called Tamara Harding. I dated her some last year. Figured I better line up somebody else. Plus I was pissed at Miranda. We talked about ten minutes and she basically said to go to hell."

Brown walked back to the table. "You got your phone bill?"

"Yeah. In the kitchen. It's late." Jason arose slowly and walked to the kitchen. He returned with the statement and showed Brown the entry for his call to Tamara.

"Nine-forty-one?" asked Brown. "That's the one? You talked fifteen minutes?"

"Yeah. I told you. I couldn't have killed her."

"Who did?" Brown's eyes were riveted to Jason's.

Jason turned his head. "You think Rita did it."

"What do you think?"

"Oh God. I'm afraid Rita did it. She keeps telling me to keep my mouth shut. You'll fuck up everything. If you hadn't gone there, Miranda wouldn't be dead. It's all your fault." Jason lowered himself into the chair and burst into tears. He tried to speak but the words came out as unintelligible blubbering.

"Just get hold of yourself," said Brown softly. He waited for Jason to calm himself before continuing. "Has Clyde Noble talked to you?"

"No. Well yes. Just to tell me to go see his lawyer. Which I did. That's it. Look, like I've been staying clear of them. I mean, I don't need Rita's crap."

"So Rita's hounding you and you think she's hiding something."

Jason looked at the lieutenant before answering. "I guess. Look. She's my sister. I'm not dropping the dime. Cause I don't know anything but what I told you."

"You've got an excellent track record for rememberin' new stuff, Jason."

Jason rubbed his nose and chin. "I know man. I was scared. But I'm outa new stuff. Like, there's nothing else. I didn't do it, I don't know who did, and Rita's whacking out."

"Why did she tell you Miranda wouldn't be dead if you hadn't gone there?"

"I asked her what she meant, you know, sounded like she was accusing me, but she wouldn't answer, just told me to keep my mouth shut; I'd caused enough trouble for her."

Brown pulled out two cigarettes and handed one to Jason. "Keep your mouth shut?"

"Yeah. I figured she meant for me to just…not tell you anything. She keeps saying it was a drowning and you hillbillies will give up after awhile."

Brown smiled at the characterization. The only black hillbilly he could think of was a country music singer from the seventies. "Have you talked to Rita since the last interview?"

"No." Jason tapped the table twice with an empty Pepsi can. "What's gonna happen next?"

Brown was mulling the same question, but from another angle. He was wondering how quickly Rita would squeeze out of Jason the extent of his revelations. But for the Nobles being away she probably would have talked to her brother two days ago, but that was assuming Farnsworth would and did inform her of the interview's suspicious turn. If Brown could keep Rita in her blissful state— the state of believing the hillbillies would eventually give up—he could pursue his investigation much more effectively. Either Jason or Farnsworth could tip the scale and there was little he could do about it. "We just keep working on it, Jason. You know, the less you say to Rita, the better. She damn near got you charged."

"You don't have to tell me."

"Look. If anything comes up, just call me. I don't wanna see you in any trouble." Brown added the last sentence without knowing why.

Jason nodded his head. "I'm not talkin' to that lawyer either."

# CHAPTER 26

Friday, October 16th

Brown and Horace Seay sat side-by-side on two bales of hay peering through the cracks in their hiding place, an old tobacco barn. The old car, its hood open and battery missing, was parked directly across from the barn on the side of Lebanon Cove Road. A Martin thirty-thirty rifle and leather jacket were lying in the back seat. The school bus was expected any minute.

Brown's mind was elsewhere. Like a jogger pounding a treadmill his thoughts were turning the Noble case. Brown called Gene Roberts from home Wednesday night after returning from the interview with Jason. Following his recapitulation of the events in Richmond and Jason's latest disclosure, Roberts had his customary response: a brooding silence. Brown waited.

Finally, "What next Lewis?"

"I was hoping you'd tell me."

"What'll you do when I retire?"

"Call you on the golf course."

Roberts grunted a short laugh. Two weeks of sitting at home had convinced him that he wasn't ready for retirement. Two weeks at home led his wife to the same vocal conclusion "Come on Lieutenant," he grumbled.

"Interview hotel staff, get the statement for the room and hope Rita called from the room phone."

"Yeah."

"Ask you to call some of your buddies in Richmond and find out what Noble did Friday night."

"Me?" Roberts feigned an incredulous tone even while he began plotting the undertaking.

"I sure don't know nobody in Richmond."

"Nobody."

"Just testing you."

Roberts leaned back in his recliner and raised the footrest. "Then?"

"Then interview the Nobles."

"That's where this is all going. An interview. That'll be tricky. Together? Separate?"

"I've been thinking on that myself."

"We'll cross that bridge when we get to it," said Roberts. "Odds are they're gonna figure out where we're heading, so an interview will be scripted or they'll just refuse to talk. Still I don't believe Clyde Noble knows what's going on. It just doesn't strike me that he'd cover for Rita, or anybody for that matter. Have you heard from them recently?"

"I've never heard from them."

"I can't figure those damn people."

"That's because you're a hillbilly."

The churning of a diesel engine interrupted Brown's musing and refocused his attention on the crippled car.

"That oughta be it," said Seay.

The school bus passed, slowed and just around the bend above the barn came to a stop. Within minutes the bus passed again on its way out of the Cove. The two men waited another fruitless hour.

"Whatya think, Lewis?" asked Seay.

"I don't know. I don't want to sit here all day. And I'm not leaving that rifle there, even if it is useless." Brown was already devising what he would do next with the Noble case. Cross had not been impressed with Jason's latest story; he wanted more evidence and the places to look were on an ever shorter list.

# CHAPTER 27

Thursday, October 22nd

"Did you watch the game Sunday Lewis?" asked Linda Masencup.

"Half of it."

"Half was too much," said R. C. Hawkes.

"Go on back. Ev's in his office," said Linda nodding her head in agreement.

Ev was in his chair reading Wimpie Carson's report on a malicious wounding. "Hello gents. Let me tell you. If you ever want to see the many ways the English language can be murdered look at one of Carson's reports. But he doesn't get much practice; I get about one a year."

"I know," answered Brown. "The affidavit on his annual DUI arrest began with the words 'I had came up on a car driving erotically.'"

"Maybe it was, to him," said Hawkes.

Cross looked at the ceiling and laughed quietly before speaking again. "Where you been Lewis? It's been a week. You're getting as bad as Roberts, just disappear for days at a time. By the way, today makes two months since the murder. Any good news?"

Hawkes and Brown seated themselves across from Ev's desk.

R. C. spoke first. "We've had a little luck."

Ev leaned forward. "Anything to connect to what Jason told Lewis last Wednesday?"

Brown spoke next. "The hotel required a search warrant before they'd give up the Noble bill. There was a phone charge on the room and we finally matched it to the pool number."

"Damn," muttered Ev, "that's a start."

"Called at seven-thirty-one," added Brown. "She didn't waste a minute leaving the hotel."

"That helps, but…."

"Hold on. There's more. Roberts pieced together Clyde Noble's itinerary. He was at a teenage alcohol conference on Friday afternoon. That night he went to a presidential defense fund fundraiser, without Rita. Began at seven. Went to about ten. After that there was a cocktail party at some Democratic honcho's house on the river. We don't know when he left, but it was late."

Ev leaned back in his chair. "Hard to imagine Rita Noble missing all that elbow rubbing. How the hell did Gene get that stuff anyway?"

R. C. smiled. "The son of a bitch can turn more tricks than a twenty dollar hooker."

"You can't place her at Onan though," continued Ev.

"I ain't finished," said Brown. "Lester Snidlett called me Monday. Said he forgot something. He stopped that night for beer at Onan Trading Post right at closing, which is ten o'clock."

"That's convenient," said Ev dryly. "How'd he suddenly invent that?"

"He said Manfred fussed at him about his tab at the store this past Sunday and handed him a cash register ticket. That's when he remembered rolling in there right at closing, drunk and with no money, to buy beer after he left the Nobles."

Ev opened his mouth to speak but Brown stopped him with the wave of his hand. "Look. I figured it was bullshit too. But Lester had the receipt. Nine-fifty-six p.m. on August twenty-first. So I went to see Manfred and sure enough he had given the cash register ticket to Lester, with date and time. He had written Lester's name across the top. His accounting system consists of a bunch of these things in a cigar box. He'd just run across it last Saturday."

"Lewis," said Ev, "you must be livin' right to have that kind of luck."

"Luck my ass. Hard work," laughed Brown.

"I take it Snidlett made bail."

"His old man finally went his bond," said Brown. "Let him sit there a week first."

"What's next?" asked Ev.

Brown looked at Hawkes before responding. "That's what we've been discussing. Went over it with Gene, too. Might as well go for broke. Go see Rita. When they get back."

"It would sure be nice to talk to Clyde and Rita separately."

"That's my thought," said Hawkes.

"Mine too," said Brown, "but we take what we can get. If he's there, he's there."

"Confront her?" asked Ev.

Brown pulled a cigarette pack from his coat pocket. "No. I mean unless one of us is Perry Mason, she'd just say no and leave the room. We thought we'd ask about what we know. The call, the threat, where she was, that kind of thing. See where it goes."

Ev nodded his head. "Pin her down. The more lies, the better. Every little lie will be priceless at trial. And she's going to lie if she opens her mouth."

"Sounds like you're convinced," said Brown, a gleam of devilment in his eyes.

"I sure am close," answered Ev. "But I have to be sure. What about Clyde?" The possibility that Noble would cover for his wife was so farfetched that Ev hadn't considered it.

"All we can figure is that he doesn't know about any of this," said Hawkes.

"That's the only sensible conclusion," Ev said quietly. He wondered if Paula would agree. She had called Friday to ask about the progress in the case. Ev answered her with generalities, feeling as shameless and evasive as a husband caught with another woman's lipstick on his collar. Paula, seeming to sense that something was afoot, persisted politely with her questions. Each vague response he gave made Ev uneasy, but there was nothing else for it; the investigation had to run its course. "When are the Nobles coming back?"

"I thought this week," answered Brown, "but Clara Wood says now it will be Sunday or Monday. They decided to extend it."

"Three weeks," said Ev. "How does anyone leave young children for three weeks?"

Hawkes snorted and then answered. "You can figure that out when you're rich."

"One more thing," said Ev, "it would be helpful to know exactly what was in the will that set Rita off. I'd like to know whether it was executed, or just under consideration."

Brown looked at Hawkes. "Anything else?"

Ev answered. "Smith. We've got to figure out what to do with him. We're going to need him as a witness and Mervin has those cocaine buys we need to do something with."

"How do you want to deal with that?" asked Hawkes.

"I've got to think about it," said Ev. "That will get messy."

"Well let me know," said Brown.

"What about Lebanon Cove?"

"We set the trap last Friday. No takers. So we brought the car back in. I'm back to square one."

Ev pressed his lips before speaking. "Well…shit. Keep me posted. And let Dillon Klobb know you're still working on it."

"I know. I know. Sheriff's on me like a duck on a junebug."

Linda Masencup brought Ev a pink message slip as soon as Brown and Hawkes were gone. "A Lydia McDonald called, so I set her an appointment at three. You'll be out of J and D by then."

Wilmer Bledsoe called before Ev could leave the office. "Mr. Commonwealth. Romey Bryant just retained me on that malicious wounding Wimpie Carson took out."

"I just read the report, Wil, what report there is."

"I bet Wimpie didn't put in there what it was about, so I'm calling you so you can be thinkin' about it. Rhonda Gooden caused the fight between Romey and your so-called victim Skeeter Hawkins. Now Rhonda could have been a model, or at the minimum, a rich man's second wife, if her father hadn't been a bootlegger and she'd been born mute."

Even in her mid-thirties Rhonda turned men's heads, at least until she opened her mouth. When Rhonda spoke every word came out with a hard R, or missing a G, or simply mispronounced, and the voice delivering it was loud, nasal, and annoying. Horace Seay swore he had heard her at the Quik Mart cursing while he was standing, a half mile away, at the sheriff's department's door. Her profanity could peel paint from a wall and her insults entertained everyone except the intended target. It will be remembered that she saddled Wimpie Carson with the fart kicking up dust description. For former lovers her cuts were particularly personal. After a short-lived tryst with Lester Snidlett she was fond of saying that if his organ were as big as his mouth he could run a three-leg sack race by himself. She did not, however, maintain the subjunctive in her vocabulary.

Ev grasped the tenor of the fight as soon as Rhonda's name was mentioned. "That tells me a lot, Wil. Just answer this. Was your man the new boyfriend, or the guy on the way out?"

"Well get this Ev. It was a *menage a trois*."

"Right."

"Yeah! Romey said Rhonda had given up on one man doing her any good, and wanted two at once."

"Well I don't believe you or Romey Bryant," said Ev, chuckling at Wil's story.

"Hey Ev. You can't make this stuff up. They were all drunk and Rhonda suggested it."

"Gooseneck was right. When you're drunk, you've got a lot more options. But how did that start a fight?"

Bledsoe was beginning to laugh between words. "After a few minutes of the great experiment, Rhonda told Skeeter that he could go on out of the room, that Romey could more'n handle it for both of them."

Ev leaned back in his chair and stared at the ceiling, still trying to decide whether Bledsoe was on the level.

Bledsoe continued. "Skeeter took offense at that. I mean, can you imagine that hump shouldered redneck being disgraced like that. So when Romey came out of the room, Skeeter cussed and carried on till they got into it. Romey whipped him and left. Meantime somebody called the cops. When Wimpie got there, Skeeter was too embarrassed to tell the truth. So he just said Romey beat him."

"Skeeter needed ten stitches on his chin and had a broken nose."

"Romey said Skeeter cut his own self by accident."

"Sure Wil. I guess you're gonna call Rhonda as a witness at preliminary hearing."

"Hell yes. Ain't it great? We get paid for this."

Ev joined Bledsoe in his laughter. Said Ev, "I'd say you're making it better than it really was, except I've been in the courtroom before."

"I betcha Skeeter will be happy to let this go on accord and satisfaction."

"You're probably right. Get his doctor's bill and avoid hearing testimony about the size of his hooter."

"Maybe you should interview Rhonda, Ev."

"Thanks pal."

* * *

Lydia McDonald, still model thin and as wrinkle-free as modern medicine could manage, was waiting in the anteroom when Ev returned from J & D Court. From Polly's intelligence reports Lydia was nearing fifty and had changed her name from Harriet Holsapple when she entered the world of modeling. She and her daughter—there had never been a Mr. McDonald or any other mister—had moved to Lafayette County eight years earlier when age and gravity had brought Lydia's career to a conclusion. Ev saw Lydia from time to time at the few parties he and Polly attended and knew her well enough to speak to her on a first name basis.

"Hello Ev," said Lydia pleasantly as if the purpose of her coming were to deliver Girl Scout cookies.

Ev handed Linda his J & D files as he replied. "Lydia. Sorry you had to wait. Court ran over."

Once seated in front of his desk Lydia became pensive and spoke very quietly. "I'm sure you know what happened at my house."

Linda walked in and handed Ev the file while Lydia was speaking. "I do," he answered.

"I talked to Sergeant Seay, and he told me you were the only person who could…do something with this charge. I don't want that person to think he can get away with it, but I, you know, it could all be embarrassing."

Ev wondered whether she was aware that the word about Rich Garrison and her was already out. "Yes, I understand," he answered.

"Is there some way this can get through the court without that…other person being involved? It's probably not in the report, but we were in the hot tub together when it happened. We weren't in a position to just jump out and yell at the guy. I think you know what I mean."

Ev had no need for further detail. "It's not that I need him as a witness. But the defense attorney will see Seay's report. Questions might be asked in the courtroom. I can't give you any assurance."

Lydia looked at her hands lying limply folded in her lap. "I really don't want to go through with this. Rich certainly doesn't want to, either. I just don't know what to do."

"What if I allowed the defendant to plead to a misdemeanor, say trespass, and wheedled a few months in jail?"

Lydia looked up but remained silent for a moment. Finally, "That would be good."

Ev leaned forward slightly. "I'll work something out."

"Well, I leave that to you. Whatever you think best. I just…this just can't be broadcast in the courtroom. But we aren't seeing one another now. It was just one of those things that happen. Blip, and it's over." She forced a smile.

This time Ev noticed that her perfect teeth had a faint blue tint, no doubt the result of repetitive bleaching, which reminded him of the false color of the dentures that his grandmother faithfully soaked in a glass of Polident on her bedstand every night.

"I don't think I'd want this job," she said.

"There're times when I don't want it."

Lydia laughed. "How about Polly? How is she? I just never get to see her."

*The Jet Set,* thought Ev. "She's fine, trying to hold her own against two little boys."

"Well tell her hello for me, and I hope I see you two soon. Do lunch maybe. And God, not like this." Lydia arose abruptly and lightly, as if a millstone had been removed from her neck. "Thank you for squeezing me in."

Ev arose and watched Lydia leave the room. As he returned to his chair, he wondered what possessed people to tell him so much about so many private things. It was if his office were some sort of confessional.

# CHAPTER 28

Saturday, October 24th

Painting was an undertaking that Ev loathed. He managed to paint the kitchen and dining room when he and Polly first bought their home. Listing the house had been stronger incentive and now Ev was working on the boys' room, covering their small faint hand prints and their names scrawled in crayon. Polly, her eyes moist, avoided the room while he worked; she couldn't bear the sight of memories losing their tiny palpable threads.

"I forgot to give the gossip update," Ev called to Polly.

"On what?" said Polly from the kitchen.

"Lydia McDonald and Rich Garrison."

Polly instantly appeared at the door, her maudlin mood eclipsed. "What is it?"

Ev explained Lydia's visit to his office.

"I wonder if they'll both be at Evelyn's party next Saturday," said Polly. "Maybe the question is whether both Richard and Carol will be at the party."

"I don't think a little fornication here and there is going to interfere with the Jet Set."

"Oh Ev," replied Polly, the ring of the telephone cutting her short. "Hello."

"Polly, isn't it just special outside today." Margaret's use of the word special was proof that the vodka was already flowing.

"It is a beautiful day," Polly managed.

"I've been walking and wondering why I'm moving away. It really is special." Margaret's voice became quieter. "Lucius loved these October days. It's lonely without him."

*Oh no. She's on a sentimental drunk.*

Margaret was quiet a moment, then she resumed. "I wanted to remind you that Amanda gets the chandelier in the old dining room."

"I'm sorry?" answered Polly in disbelief.

"I told Ev. And I know you'll want to get one to replace it. So I thought I should remind you."

Polly felt a tingling at the back of her neck. She bit her lip against a response that would be, at best, uncivil, and she couldn't wait to confront Ev with this perfidy.

"You know that chandelier was originally made for gas. We had it wired when we moved here. Amanda has always loved it."

"Yes ma'am," said Polly, knowing that Margaret would quickly run out of things to say if her listener interjected no change of subject.

"Are you still painting?"

"Yes ma'am."

"Well. I know you've got a lot to do. I remember when Amanda had her house repainted. All those people underfoot. At least you don't have that to deal with."

"Yes ma'am."

Margaret described an abscess bothering one of the cats and then abruptly rang off.

Polly rehung the telephone and walked quietly to the boys' room. "Well Ev. Thanks for telling me your sister was getting the chandelier."

Ev lowered the paint roller to his side and looked at Polly. "Was this something I was supposed to know?"

"Your mother said you knew."

"Well I didn't."

"Don't we have a say-so about anything? She's just stripping the place. I mean, we are buying it. This is beyond belief." Polly crossed her arms and glared at Ev. "Well?"

Ev shook his head. "It's not worth a fight."

"Not worth…. I'd say a couple thousand dollars is worth saying something about. I can't believe those two."

Ev looked from Polly to the partially painted wall in front of him.

"And she just had to mention that Amanda hired people to paint her house. What's your problem? Are you adopted or something? What did you do? What did I do? I put up with her drunken shitiness and no one else has to. No one else would. This is too much Ev. This is just over the line. We're not buying the place if this is going to continue. She'll be stripping the wallpaper out of the hall next. That's valuable too."

"I'll go over in the morning and sort out what's staying."

"You'd better go first thing. She starts bright and early on Sunday unless she goes to church. And what do you mean? What's staying? We have a deal. Everything's staying." Polly spun on her heel and left the room.

Ev decided that he had made a poor choice of words.

# CHAPTER 29

Wednesday, October 28th

R. C. Hawkes rumbled into Brown's office at eleven. "What's the plan with the Nobles? You call 'em?"

"No. After we talked, I decided we'd just show up. May get lucky and catch Rita cold."

"Important people don't like us just popping in. My boss'll probably get a call from the senator. Good thing I'm near retirement. I really don't give a damn."

Rita Noble was not pleased to find Brown and Hawkes on her doorstep, and she made no effort to disguise her irritation. She led them into the living room and took her seat in one of the armchairs, folded her arms, and waited.

Not having been asked to sit Brown stood in the middle of the room, feeling clumsy and uncomfortable. Hawkes showed no reservation, he settled onto the end of the sofa nearest Rita.

"Please have a seat, too" said Rita coolly to Brown. "Now what can you ask me that hasn't already been asked."

"Just working on tying up loose ends, Mrs. Noble," said Brown. He wanted to add that hillbillies of all colors were fascinated with loose ends.

"Well please work fast," replied Rita, "I have an engagement at two."

By pre-arrangement Hawkes was going to start the questioning. "We were interested in a call Miranda got at the pool."

Rita reddened noticeably beneath her tan. "Yes. I thought so."

That was no surprise to Brown. Oliver Farnsworth had beaten the cops to the punch.

"Could you tell us about that?" asked Hawkes, his words soft and measured.

"Of course. I called to see if she was here. I suspected she might be, with one of her male friends. She's certainly done it before. I should've told Roberts that before. It didn't register with me that it was important."

A well-coached response thought Brown.

"Were you angry?" asked Hawkes.

"I lost my temper."

"Because Jason was here?"

"That didn't help matters."

"Did you threaten to come to the pool from Richmond?"

"No. I said something to the effect I should."

"Any comment about hitting…or kicking Miranda?"

"Most certainly not. Why would you ask such a thing? Surely Jason didn't tell you anything like that." She straightened ramrod stiff as she spoke, but her posturing left Brown with the sense that it was calculated.

"I take it, then, you didn't come here, to the pool?"

Rita snapped to her feet like a private seeing his first general. "I do not have to be subjected to this."

"I take it that means no?" asked Hawkes.

"No. I did not come here that day, or that night." Rita's words were hard, edged, and cold.

"Where'd you go Friday night?"

"The senator went to the meetings without me. I was tired. And I'm getting very tired of this." She walked behind the sofa. "You're treating me like a criminal and I will tell you, I am disgusted."

Brown decided that Rita was only breaths away from telling them to leave. He had to move quickly. "What about Miranda's bathing suit top at the pool?"

"What about it. You have it don't you?"

"Where did you find it?" said Brown.

"Where did I…that's quite enough. You may leave."

Brown and Hawkes arose simultaneously.

"The appropriate people will hear about this," continued Rita.

"Thank you Mrs. Noble," said Brown. "By the way, where'd you go when you left the hotel?"

Rita stared hard at Brown, and the lieutenant was certain that she was trying to guess how much the police knew.

When she answered her voice was low and menacing. "I do not have to account to you people for every meal I eat and every store I visit. Now, again, leave."

"Thank you, Mrs. Noble," said Brown.

Hawkes nodded his head toward their hostess.

Brown promptly lit a cigarette upon entering Hawkes's car. "Testy won't she," he said.

"I wasn't sure your theory would hold water. But I gotta say she took care of my doubts."

Brown looked at his cigarette watching the smoke curl from the burning end. "She was pretty careful, left herself some room."

"She denied going there. That's good stuff."

"Yeah. But we can't put her there. The camera, the call, the mileage, Snidlett seeing the lights come on. That doesn't put Rita there."

"I don't know that we can."

* * *

"Damn a full moon," grumbled Ev as he hung up from a call from one of his crazy regulars who now was certain that her former son-in-law had implanted a tracking device in her nose and was scheming to cheat her out of her half acre of land. He was staring at the ceiling when Brown and Hawkes walked into his office. "Holmes and Watson, come in." he greeted them.

Hawkes laughed as he sat down. "Maybe that's who we need on this one."

Brown reached for his cigarettes as he began describing Rita's interview. Ev took an offered cigarette and then sat pensively after Brown was finished.

"Well?" said Hawkes.

Ev leaned back in his chair. "Okay. So maybe we can put her there, maybe. But we still have nothing on the murder."

"She was there at the right time," said Brown

Ev drew on the cigarette and tapped it in the ashtray. "She's got three people to pin it on. Smith, Jason, and Snidlett. Tell me a jury is going to believe Smith and Snidlett over Mrs. Clyde Noble. All these little time frames are going to get foggy when we put those losers on the stand."

"We've got her in a half dozen lies" said Hawkes. "We've got a motive. We've got opportunity."

"Are these lies or half truths?" said Ev. "She left some gray areas. And maybe Snidlett bought beer and went back to the Nobles. His wife can't be certain about the time he got home. And Jason. With his evolving story, he's still a wild card. And what if she is covering for him?"

Hawkes leaned back in his chair and looked at Ev. "We're running out of places to look. And I can tell you she ain't gonna sound as good as she looks in front of a jury."

Ev could see the impatience on Hawkes's face. Resisting the police was never an easy task. The effort always cast Ev as overly cautious or fearful of a difficult trial. Left unsaid was that he, and not the police, had to try the case. The experienced officers usually accepted his decisions gracefully, but without concession.

Ev responded. "We need more. Checked her driver's history, criminal record? Talked to Smith? We just don't have enough pieces. You know the game. Knowing it and proving it are two different animals."

There was a brief silence, then Hawkes pressed his palms together and leaned forward. "Okay Lewis. What about Smith?"

"I guess the time has come," answered Lewis. "Who gets him?"

Ev had been turning this same question in his mind. The tag-team approach was out as Smith would resist if outnumbered; and in any event he was not going to open up in front of a white state trooper. Brown had proved that he could get under

Smith's skin, literally as well as figuratively. Moreover, Ev was certain that Brown was itching to redeem himself. "He's your baby, Lewis."

* * *

In anticipation of the assignment Brown already had the benefit of Mervin McIntosh's intelligence on Jeff Junior Smith the third. The Sand Lot was out of business and the informant Poochie Essex had nothing to suggest that Smith was still retailing cocaine. Rather, Smith claimed to have a job in Charlottesville, but Poochie didn't know where or with whom. Smith still made stops at the Quik Mart, usually around six o'clock, but Brown wasn't comfortable with risking a replay of his earlier confrontation with Smith in the Quik Mart parking lot.

Brown leaned back in his chair and lit a cigarette. Why play cat and mouse? He would call Smith's grandmother and leave word for Smith to call him. Brown was dialing Anita Smith's number when the sheriff walked in.

The threat of political opposition was keeping Hank Burke busy. No funeral, Rotary breakfast, or high school football game would occur without his presence. Burke kept a bag of plastic Junior Deputy badges in the front seat of his car, badges that also displayed the phrase Hank Burke Sheriff, which he gave to every child he met. The campaign was time intensive and there were not enough hours in the day. As a result his department was functioning, more so than usual, on autopilot.

Burke stopped in front of Brown's desk and began speaking before the lieutenant was finished dialing. "That Cobb fella has called me again about Lebanon Cove. What are y'all doin', Lewis? I thought y'all had that about wrapped up."

Brown laid the receiver in the cradle without listening for a connection. Dillon Klobb had called him as well. "We set a trap Hank. It didn't work."

"Well something better work. What about fingerprints. Can't you get a alnysis on them?" Despite his years in law enforcement Burke had never mastered the word analysis.

"We tried that. Whoever's doing it isn't in the data bank."

Burke planted his hands on his hips before responding. "Well this ain't no Boy Scout merit badge contest. Y'all get on this and get it solved. And another thing. What's going on with the murder? Nobody telling me nothin', but I see you and Hawkes fartin' around."

"Still chasing leads, sheriff." Evasiveness with the sheriff didn't come to Brown easily.

The sheriff spun on his heel and began a circuit in the small space between the two desks. "I haven't been pushin' you, but I ain't no mushroom you keep in the dark and feed shit to. Where's this one goin'?"

250

Brown looked Burke in the eye before responding. "Everything's pointing to Rita Noble."

The sheriff's pacing halted abruptly and he stood motionless, as if time had stopped. After a pause, "The senator's wife? This sure better be no half-cocked rabbit hunt. I mean you don't just rare back and accuse someone like her. What d'ya got?"

Brown began explaining the evidence supporting his conclusion, but the sheriff was impatient and interrupted the lieutenant before he could finish. "Now wait a minute. You got three jacklegs who were givin' her dope and beer and screwin' her all on the same night, and Mrs. Noble just runs on home from Richmond and kills her and heads on back."

"That's right," answered Brown.

"Well you better run this by Roberts," said Burke.

"He's in the loop."

"And Cross, too."

"Cross wants more evidence."

"I guess he does. You guys screw this deal up and me and Cross'll be lookin' for a new job. You too probably." Burke resumed walking and headed toward the door to his office. "Another thing, round up the radars. These damn road deputies need to spend their time solving crimes and quit runnin' up and down the road tryin' to get a speeder. That's what the state police are for."

"Yes sir," said Brown to the closing door. Rounding up the radars was a traditional election year tactic, and while Brown knew the purpose was to prevent a fast-driving county voter from retaliating against the sheriff at the ballot box, it did have the beneficial effect of forcing deputies to put more time into their investigations. And every case not reaching his plate would allow Brown more time to manage Rita Noble and Lebanon Cove.

The sting of Hank Burke's uncharacteristic remarks began to take effect, quickly chasing radars from Brown's thoughts. Second guessing his efforts and wondering whether he was fooling himself about Rita Noble, doubt reared its head, and insulted and deflated, Brown told himself he should resign. Resign to do what? Coach junior varsity?

**CHAPTER 30**

Thursday, October 29th

Gene Roberts arose early, dressed in a blue blazer and red tie, loaded five empty pasteboard boxes in his cruiser, and drove to the sheriff's office in Lafayette Court House. An exasperated Lewis Brown had called the night before complaining of the sheriff's chewing and cataloging his doubts about the progress of the Noble investigation.

A foot tall stack of papers awaited Gene on his desk as well as several styrofoam cups of long cold coffee and a full ashtray. He suppressed a smile at the familiar sight; finding the desk neatly arranged as he had left it would somehow be an inappropriate homecoming. Roberts cleared the mess and straightened and moved the paper stack to the desk's left corner. He then walked to the filing cabinet behind Brown's desk and removed the three Noble investigation notebooks from the top drawer. At his desk he opened the first notebook and began scanning the first page. He was midway through the second notebook when Lewis Brown arrived.

"You're here just in time for brunch, Lewis," Roberts said gruffly. "You're picking up the bad habits of the state police."

Brown smiled broadly. "I figured if I came in late long enough, you'd come on back to work." Roberts could fuss all he wanted, Lewis was relieved beyond words to have the older man seated behind his desk.

"And I appreciate my desk being used for a dumpster," continued Roberts.

"Hey man. I told those numb-nuts not to trash it."

"It might interest you to know that a Mountain Dew can was among the litter."

"And you're assuming that's mine."

"Work from the inside out."

"Okay. I'm probably guilty."

"The trash can is full. Does the janitor ever darken the door?'

"Did you think things were gonna change just because you weren't around? I haven't seen the janitor in here in my career. Anyway, he knew you were out." Brown settled into his creaking chair. "Couldn't stay away could you?"

"I've seen enough baseball and football and NASCAR and crime shows for three lifetimes." Roberts switched mental gears without looking away from the notebook. "Horace has all the physical evidence doesn't he?"

"I hope so."

"Nothing like certainty in a murder investigation. Tell Willie I want to see Horace this a.m. What are your plans?"

"DMV and criminal history on Rita Noble. Smith. The loose ends."

"No one's run a history yet?"

"I get the message." Brown opened the door to the dispatchers' room, leaned in, and asked Willie Painter to print Rita Noble's criminal and driving history. "Horace on duty?" he asked Painter.

"Yeah," answered Painter.

"Tell him Gene wants to see him."

"Uh-huh."

Brown shook his head at the diffident response and pulled the door shut. "I've gotta question Gene."

"What's that?" replied Roberts without looking up.

"You sign your name C. R. Roberts. What's the C. R. for?"

Roberts looked up and automatically reached into his blazer pocket for a pack of cigarettes. They weren't there, as he hadn't smoked since the heart attack, but the reflex of reaching for them was hard to break. He pulled his hand out and retrieved a pencil from the desk instead. "Now what brought that on?"

"Looking at reports in old files while you were away. Never really noticed it before."

"Never really read 'em before, did you?"

Brown laughed quietly.

"Right there on the diploma." Roberts pointed over his shoulder with his thumb. "Staring you in the face for two years."

"Three." Brown walked over to Gene's desk and looked at the Bridgewater College diploma. "Carroll Robins huh. How'd you get Gene out of that?"

"I didn't."

"Okay."

Roberts tapped the pencil on the desk. "My older brother thought Carroll was too much like a girl's name, so he started calling me Gene."

"He just came up with it?"

"Yep. Maybe he'd just watched a Gene Autrey movie."

"I guess Robins, or Robin, wouldn't cut it either."

"I guess not."

"Well, there was a Robin Hood."

"Shit Lewis."

Brown laughed as he walked back to his desk. "I called Anita Smith's number last night and got an answering machine. What are the chances Smith will call me?"

"Your guess is as good as mine."

Willie Painter opened the dispatcher's door and waved the computer print-outs Brown had requested. "Nothing on the criminal," he said to Lewis. He nodded his head in Roberts's direction and rolled his unlit cigar from one corner of his mouth to the other. "I reckon he couldn't stand not bein' here no more."

"Hello Willie," said Gene.

Brown laid the driver's history on his desk and flattened the sheets. "Sweet Jesus," he muttered. "She got a ticket in Albemarle County on August twenty-first. That's the day idn't it." Brown arose involuntarily from his chair in his excitement.

"That's it," said Roberts, not taking his eyes off the notebook. "Brilliant police work. What are you gonna do?"

"Damn," said Brown; he hadn't heard Roberts's question.

"Even a blind hog finds an acorn in the forest occasionally," said Roberts.

"Damn," repeated Brown.

Horace Seay entered the room at the same moment. "Didn't trust us did you?" he said to Gene.

"Now you know that's not so. There're two or three of you I trust. What are you gonna do Lewis?"

"I'm going to Charlottesville. Get the summons. It's a state police ticket. Find the officer."

"Good. And?"

"And?" repeated Brown.

"Find out what she told him."

"I know that," said Lewis.

"What about R.C.?" asked Roberts.

"He's got a trial in Appomattox today."

"What's going on?" asked Seay.

"Our girl got a speeding ticket in Albemarle on the day of the murder," answered Roberts.

"Miranda?" asked Seay.

"No. Rita Noble," said Roberts. "Also, Lewis, call Pittsburg P. D. Some of these states are the late-comers to the world of computers. It's worth a shot."

"Right," said Brown as he left the room.

"I find the exuberance of youth refreshing," deadpanned Roberts.

"He's been working hard, Gene."

"Yeah. I know it. What I needed from you is the physical evidence."

"There's a lot of it. Crammed in the evidence room."

The evidence room was one in name only. Situated off the narrow waiting area of the sheriff's office, the room was little more than a walk-in closet. It had been the janitor's storeroom until commandeered by Roberts a decade ago and still retained a faint Pine Sol aroma.

"Where can we spread it out?" asked Roberts.

Seay thought for a moment. "Well, unless we take it to your house, the jury room is the only place I can think of."

"Call the clerk and make sure it's free. It's time to put this one to bed." Roberts reached inside his blazer and grimaced at the re-discovery of the empty pocket.

* * *

Brown obtained a certified copy of Rita Noble's traffic summons from the Albemarle County General District Court. Trooper J. M. Gregory had stopped her at ten-twenty-one p.m. She prepaid the fine and did not appear at court. Brown called the regional state police headquarters and had the sergeant page Gregory. Gregory and Brown met at a Citgo station at the edge of Charlottesville, near the interstate.

Gregory was a young officer, spit polished and crisp, ambitious, and black. He and Brown had never met. Gregory stood stiffly erect when he shook hands with the lieutenant. There was no preliminary small talk. Brown explained the purpose of their rendezvous and Gregory promptly retrieved his trial folder from the trunk of his car. Brown looked on anxiously.

"Clocked her at eighty-two in a sixty-five," said Gregory. "Gave her a break to keep her out of reckless. I wrote her for seventy-nine. She said it was a rental car and she was so nervous I thought she was going to start crying."

Brown moved closer to Gregory so that he could read the officer's copy of the summons. "A silver 1996 Le Sabre. Where'd you stop her?"

"Just south of the Crozet exit."

Brown nodded his head at the information. Had Rita been traveling from Onan, she would have used the Crozet interchange to access the interstate. "What's your note say?"

"Late for political event with husband in Richmond. Driving rental. Car in shop."

"What'd she look like?" asked Brown.

"Blonde, very thin, sorta pretty. But she was so nervous she looked kinda gray. If you don't mind, why your interest in a traffic ticket?"

Brown ignored the question. "Did you recognize her?"

"No."

"She's Senator Clyde Noble's wife."

"She didn't say so. That's real unusual. Most people with connections let me know right up front. Like that matters. So is she complaining or something?"

"Anything else you remember?"

"No. She had her rental agreement. I mean, she was so nervous I thought she might be a mule." Mule was police terminology for someone transporting narcotics. "But, you know, she didn't look like the type."

"Profiling, trooper?" smiled Brown.

255

Gregory did not flinch.

"May I get a copy of that?" asked Brown.

"Sure. Can I mail it to you?"

"Yeah." Brown handed the trooper his card. "This woman's a murder suspect, that's why I'm interested."

"Noble," said Gregory softly. "That girl in the pool.  I never connected the two."

"Don't worry. We were awhile connecting them ourselves."

"Wish I'd ask to search the car now." Gregory was crestfallen, obviously disappointed that he hadn't been the one to nab a murder suspect while performing routine duties.

"Thank God you pulled her. This ticket is going to be worth its weight in gold."

"Well anything I can do, let me know," said Gregory as he returned the folder to the cruiser's trunk. "You like it up in Lafayette?"

"Place is okay."

"I wouldn't mind being assigned there. Eight hours on the interstate, day in, day out, gets endless."

"And you don't know when someone's goin' to take a shot at you."

Gregory smiled for the first time. "Yep." He pulled the brim of his Stetson service hat down close to his nose. "Nice meetin' you lieutenant."

* * *

Seay pointed to the trash can sealed with red evidence tape. "I'm not sure you want to open that thing in the jury room. It didn't smell too good two months ago."

"You went through it didn't you?"

"Yes."

"Well leave it for now. But a second visit is likely. There're five cardboard boxes in my car. Do you mind getting them?"

"Sure."

With Seay on his errand Roberts absently studied the shelves lining the three walls of the evidence room. Guns of every description occupied one side of the room. Too many of the deputies neglected the paper work required to dispose of them properly. Most of the weapons were worthless; the better weapons had a habit of disappearing after a few months. It was no secret that Wimpie Carson regularly took one home with him. Roberts complained about the pilfering to Hank Burke, but nothing was done, in part because Burke was now in possession of a fine Italian rifle that he had claimed for his own before he was elected sheriff. Much of another wall contained evidence from unsolved cases: a lone boot, several dozen knives, two baseball bats, a decapitated Teddy bear, spent shotgun shells, pieces of clothing, and an assortment of brown paper bags taped shut, the contents long since forgotten.

Roberts and Seay placed the Noble evidence in three of the boxes and carried them to the jury room on the first floor. The jury room was situated next to the judge's chambers; windowless and poorly lighted. The room seemed to have been designed to make jurors' deliberations as unpleasant as possible, thereby speeding the conclusion of their mission.

"Okay, let's spread this stuff out," said Roberts.

Most of the items were sealed in brown paper bags. Once arranged on the table, Roberts slit the red tape sealing the paper bags, and unfolded each bag so that he could see the contents within: liquor bottles, cans of Pepsi, a plastic Dr. Pepper bottle, ashtray, Miranda's bathing suit and clothes, cups, glasses, and multiple plastic bags holding cigarette butts, pool sweepings, empty beer cans and bottles, the homemade crack pipe, a hair brush, and sundry other items found at the pool. "Merv got everything there didn't he?" asked Roberts.

"Just about. I mean, he left pool chemicals and brooms and that sorta stuff," answered Seay.

"Everything fabric?'

"That's what he said."

"What do you notice about this stuff on the table?"

"There's a whole lot of it."

"Yeah. But what's not here?"

Seay peered into the bags on the table. "Got me. I give up."

"Towels," said Roberts. "There's only one." He picked up the bag holding a folded large towel. "Why only one? You'd think the pool house would have a stack of towels. The Noble's pool house anyway. Maybe Mervin left the ones that hadn't been disturbed. Call him. I want him over here."

Seay left the room to find a telephone.

Roberts, while he waited, seated himself in one of the chairs lining the wall. *One towel,* he thought repeatedly.

Roberts was still seated when Seay returned.

"You told me something about Mrs. Noble and a towel," said Roberts.

"That's right," answered Seay. "She was folding a towel when I got there. I even got a picture of it."

"Then it was this one. Look at your evidence list. Where was this found?"

Seay flipped through the list McIntosh had prepared. "On the table beside the pool."

"So that's got to be the one Rita was folding," said Roberts quietly. "And it's beige. Like a bathroom towel. Not striped. No designs." Roberts pulled on a surgical glove and lifted the corner of the towel. "It's monogrammed. With an N. This is from inside the house." He walked back to the chair he earlier occupied and sat down. If the discovery was significant, then once again he had taken too long in realizing the importance of a clue. "You took your sweet time getting those pictures developed."

A quizzical expression formed on Seay's face and he did not respond immediately. Finally, "I know." After a pause, "Do you reckon there's any chance of hair or DNA on that towel?"

"Same question crossing my mind, Horace. Of course, what would that prove? It's Rita Noble's home, her towel, and you'd expect Miranda to have used it, especially if it was the only one down at the pool. What has me even more curious is how it got down there."

McIntosh, his breathing labored, entered the room abruptly.

"Damn Merv," said Gene. "Just because that bullet didn't kill you doesn't mean your heart won't."

McIntosh smiled sheepishly. "I was hurryin'."

"Well, take it from me, you ain't no spring chicken."

"I know."

"Maybe we ought to start walking at lunch time, like the clerks do."

"I wouldn't mind that," said Seay.

"Aw Horace," rejoined McIntosh. "You just wanna watch Mary Thornton's boobs bounce." He scratched his head and grinned.

Roberts laughed lightly. "Shit fellas. Okay. Merv. Tell me what you left at the pool when you collected evidence."

Not much, except ordinary type things," answered McIntosh. "The pool supplies, vacuum, brooms, all that stuff. All the housekeeping stuff under the sink. There was a cabinet of glasses and such like, which didn't look used. Drinks in the back of the refrigerator. I tried to take anything that had been used, you know, touched, recently. I probably took too much, now that I see it all laid out in here."

"What about towels?'

McIntosh thought for a minute. "I wanna say I didn't see any, but the one. There was shelves in the shower room, but nothing on 'em. No. There won't towels down there."

"Those people must've air-dried," said Seay. "Maybe that's why the girl's top was off."

"Horace," said Roberts, "I think you need some time off."

* * *

Lewis Brown bought a Mountain Dew from a machine at the Citgo before reentering his Crown Victoria. He lit a cigarette, then used his cell phone to call dispatch.

"Yeah," Willie Painter answered the call.

"This is Brown. Anything for me?"

"Some fella called. Said you called him. Wouldn't leave a name, just a number."

The number was to a cellular telephone. "Thanks Willie."

"Yeah. And Okra was lookin' for you. Said you hadn't returned a call."

"I forgot."

"I can't keep on being no secretary for this bunch."

"Okay Willie," answered Brown. *I thought relaying messages was his job,* he complained to himself as he dialed the number.

"Hullo."

"This is Lieutenant Lewis Brown of the Lafayette County Sheriff's department. I was asked to call this number."

"Yeah. Why you callin' me?"

Brown knew the answer before he asked. "Is this Jeff Smith?"

"Yeah. Wha'ju want with me anyway?"

"I need to talk to you."

"Then talk."

"Is there some place I can meet you?"

"Man I ain't got time for no meetin'."

Brown wondered whether Smith would be as genial with Roberts, or Seay. "I can meet you at home, after work."

"You got trouble understandin' English?"

"Listen to me Smith. You're a material witness to a murder. If you won't see me, I'll get yuh ass picked up. We can lock up a material witness." The threat seemed to work on television.

There was a brief silence on Smith's end, then, "Maybe you better jus' lock me up. Give me one more reason to sue you."

Brown doubted that he had grounds to obtain an order directing that Smith be held; his bluff was being called. Nothing was more galling than being outflanked by Jeff Smith, once again. "That's your call. Make it easy or make it hard. Gonna happen sooner or later. And all for nothin'. All I want to do is talk to you. I know you gave her crack, you told me that. I'm not interested in crack. I'm workin' a murder."

"Yeah. From what I heard, y'all is interested in crack."

Brown had no authority to promise Smith anything concerning McIntosh's possible distribution changes, but he was confident that he had maneuver room for the night of August twenty-first. "I don't care what you traded, sold, swapped or what that night."

"Yeah. Well is that a promise?"

"Yes."

"Come to my grandmother's at seven tonight. Don't bring no army wif you."

* * *

Brown met Okra Alexander in the courthouse parking lot. The latter was washing his patrol car. "You needed me?" asked the lieutenant.

"Yeah. Might have a lead on one of those guns stolen in the Cove. I was working on a theft and went to Hermie's Pawn in Waynesboro. Happened on a pawn by Aaron Bota. Gun's been sold, but I got the buyer's address too if you wanted it."

"How'd you manage that?"

"Got lucky. I asked if Aaron Bota had pawned anything. Asked about several suspects while I was there."

"Damn," said Brown as he took the slip of paper from Okra. "Good work."

Okra touched the brim of his Stetson in an informal salute. "Hope it helps."

This was the break he needed, but Brown's mood wasn't ebullient. Roberts's first question would be why the lieutenant himself hadn't bothered to canvas pawn shops. The answer that Roberts would provide for him was that Brown hadn't thought of it. Brown, turning to walk to his basement office, saw the sheriff's car in its reserved parking place. *I don't need more of his crap,* thought Brown. He retraced his steps to his Crown Victoria.

Anita Smith lived on a winding secondary road that led from Morgan to Oak Grove. Her small Jim Walter house was one of several clustered together near Saint Samuel's Baptist Church. Three cars were parked in the dirt driveway that stopped at her front door steps, and in the back, sandwiched in among invading Paradise trees, were four decrepit automobiles long since discharged from their intended purpose. Like an entomologist's straight pin protruding from the thorax of a beetle, one sapling had pushed through the hoodless engine compartment of an old Mercury. A tiny boy was circling the house in an electric jeep when Brown made his first pass by the residence.

Brown was early, so he continued along the road until he passed Oak Grove Baptist Church. After passing the church he pulled into the narrow rutted lane leading to the Sand Lot and turned the Crown Victoria back in the direction of Anita Smith's. Night was quickly falling when Brown parked beside the other cars in Smith's front yard. After straightening his tie he walked to the front door and tapped several times on the storm door. For several minutes the only sound from within was that of a television program.

El Fago Henderson eventually answered Brown's knock. "Ut-oh. What I done now? I don't got to report to jail fo' another week." The odor of beer followed his words.

"You live here?"

"No. Jus' visitin'. They's my people. Anita's mama was married to my uncle."

Jeff Smith, a ball cap backward on his head, appeared at Fago's shoulder. "He not here to see you," he said to Fago.

"Oh," said Fago. "I figured that fat ass Debbie Washington was lyin' on me again," after which he promptly turned and disappeared.

Smith opened the door and joined Brown on the stoop. "Don't pull that gun on me Brown."

"Do I need to?" responded Brown. The words came out automatically and Brown cursed silently for letting Smith set the tone. "Where you wanna talk?" he asked quickly.

"Right here okay with me."

Brown remembered Roberts's preference for sitting during an interview, a predilection made more compelling by the turn of events when last Brown tried to talk to Smith. "Let's talk in my car. No use everybody hearing our business." Brown turned and started down the steps without awaiting a reply.

Smith grumbled something unintelligible and after a moment's delay began following the lieutenant.

Brown let himself into his cruiser and unlocked the passenger door. Smith slid into the other seat and peered straight ahead into the false blue light cast by the dusk-to-dawn lamp in the neighbor's yard. Brown was trying to decide how to begin his questioning when Smith spoke.

"Whatcha need from me?" asked Smith.

"Everything you can tell me about Miranda Noble."

"Yeah. Then what. Charge me? My lawyer say y'all got charges you holdin'. Why should I talk to you, then get screwed."

"If you tell the truth, it'll help with that other stuff."

"How you know if I be tellin' the truth? You wouldn't be here if you already knew it all. You know what I'm sayin'? You don't have no clue yet do you? Still don't know who done it."

"I wouldn't be here if I couldn't verify your information." Given the Negative Retinal Image ruse, a half lie wasn't going to hurt anything.

"Yeah. Okay. How about this help?"

"I'll work that out with the commonwealth's attorney," answered Brown. *Cross'll probably tell me to go to hell,* he warned himself. "He got you cut loose didn't he?"

"How long I set in that jail before y'all did that?"

"Look Jeff. You wouldn't talk to me. Remember. You coulda cleared yourself. You ran and then wouldn't talk. What was I supposed to think?"

Smith was silent a moment, then: "What you do? White people think a black man killed a freak—a rich white girl. What you do?"

"You got that wrong. Black cop thought you killed a crack head. So don't go there. Just tell me what was goin' on with her. When did you start sellin' her crack?"

"Okay man, lemme check my records," answered Smith. "They be at the main office."

"Why don't you just cut the bullshit."

"Now I really be scared."

Brown wiped his chin involuntarily. "Do it your way. Distribution carries five to forty."

"And I get what? Probation? Shit."

"Okay Smith. Thanks." Brown pushed the keys into the ignition. "Okay. We done. See ya when we serve the indictments."

Smith looked at Brown before responding, then: "Why you think I know so much? Bitch bought some a couple of times."

"At the Sand Lot?"

"Yeah. Drove in and bought. You know what I'm sayin'?"

"Anyone with her?"

"Like I gonna be noticin' that."

"Anybody with her you didn't know?"

"Do I be a fool? Hell no. Was anyone with her I didn't know, I'd remember that."

"How about at the Quik Mart?"

"Just saw her, maybe once, with some dude."

"How many times you deliver to her?"

"One time. And that's why I'm sittin' here. Called me at home and axed for me to bring it. Said we could party a little."

"Party?"

"Okay Brown. Ack like you never been around nobody black. Party. Fuck. You know what fuck means?"

"Okay Smith. You're real funny. Is that what she meant?"

"Yeah."

"So?"

"I went on over there. Figured she don't have cash. She offered me a drink and I said fine and I made me one, but I come to party. She knew right then what I meant and she didn't waste no time. I give her the rock, three rocks—was worth it."

"When did you leave?"

“Around five. I don’t know. Was early.”

“What were you driving?”

“My Volvo.”

“What about the Buick?”

“That was bein’ worked on.”

“And where’d you go?”

“To a party in Hogantown.”

Brown eyed Smith for a moment. “Party? So you mean a real party this time.”

Smith looked sullenly at the lieutenant. “Whatever.”

“When you were at Miranda’s, what did she say?”

“I ain’t go over there for no conversatin’.”

“You made that clear. Did she say anything about anybody?”

“I don’t know man. Just talk. She won’t acting like somebody was gonna show up and kill her, if that’s what you mean.”

“You said she called you.”

“Somebody give me the message, my grandmother I think, that she was at her daddy’s”

“Is that why you called at Senator Noble’s?”

“She didn’t leave no number. That was the only one I could get. Nobody answered.”

“I know.”

“She called back later and we hooked up. That’s it. That’s what I know.”

* * *

Gene Roberts waited until evening to call Clara Wood. The pool towels were striped, and she had washed all of them on Friday and left them stacked in the laundry room; the towels were always washed on Friday, whether clean or not, because Rita had a phobic fear of spiders. The beige monogrammed towel was from the bathroom on the first floor. Clara was certain of this because each bathroom’s linens were assigned a different color, and besides, on the following Monday she had found a bath towel missing from that bathroom.

Roberts was surprised that Clara could recall so clearly such an insignificant detail. “How is it you remember something like that?” he asked her.

There was a pause before she responded. “Mr. Roberts. If something isn’t where it’s supposed to be at, Miz Noble is gonna think I stole it. That’s the way she is. So I told her the minute I saw it missing. And she said ‘yes I know.’”

**CHAPTER 31**

Saturday, October 24th

"Should I wear these black pants or these silk ones?" she asked Ev.

Ev was standing by his dresser looking for blue socks. "Either one," he answered.

"Which one looks better on me?"

Ev turned with the intention of saying it made no difference. Across the room in a scanty black bra and panties stood Polly holding up the two pieces of clothing for him to examine. He did not look at the clothes and Polly quickly responded by putting the garments in front of her.

"I see The Look. Now tell me which pair."

"Wanna do it?" asked Ev. Nothing ventured, nothing gained.

"No Ev. We've got to get ready. Maybe later."

"It won't take that long."

"Ev. Which one?"

Ev took a few steps toward Polly and she responded by backing almost into the closet. "Evander Cross. Not now"

"Okay," sighed Ev.

"But I probably ought to. You're just going to be thinking about it and want to leave the party ten minutes after we get there."

"That's a good reason."

Polly made a sour face. "Too bad. I'm not in the mood. You've got to get the sitter." She laid the black pants aside and leaned forward to pull on the silk ones.

"Now you're torturing me," said Ev. "Don't women ever enjoy a little spontaneity?"

Polly ignored the question. She straightened and tossed her blonde hair out of her face. "These?" She turned around once, slipped the pants off, and repeated the exercise with the black variety. "Or these?"

"You'd look good in overalls Polly."

"You're not helping."

Ev turned again to the dresser. "Then put a shirt on. I might not be so distracted."

Polly snatched a white blouse from the pile of possibilities and pulled it on. "Okay. Look at these and then I'll change again."

The process continued, with additional alternatives, until Ev finally, and arbitrarily, choose the black pants. The format was repeated in the selection of the blouse and Ev again chose black.

The decision finally made Ev left to retrieve Gloria who was going to stay with the boys. Polly was in front of the bathroom mirror upon his return. She had changed from the clothes Ev had approved and was now wearing beige silk pants and a burgundy blouse.

"I'm glad you asked my opinion. Now hurry up."

"I changed my mind."

"The sooner we get there, the sooner we can leave."

"I changed my mind about the clothes, Ev. Now how do I look?" She turned to face him.

"Great."

"Only great?"

"What do you want me to say? I'm already having to walk around with my hands in my pockets."

"You're gross."

"I guess you're not wearing anything black are you?"

Polly smiled and flipped some of her locks over her left eye. "You'll just have to guess."

Ev and Polly were passing the barn on the long driveway leading to the Appersons. "Who's driving home?" asked Ev.

"You are. This has been an If day. So don't start asking me to leave as soon as you've thrown down your two drinks."

"An If day?"

"Yes. If I have to put up with your mother, I get to drink what I want."

Ev laughed before responding. "Evelyn will have champagne, won't she?"

"Two cases."

"Champagne always makes me patient."

"You don't drink…." Polly stopped speaking and hit Ev on the knee. "You're going to worry me to death. Why don't you just pull over behind the barn and let's get it over with."

"I would, but there's still enough light for someone to see the car before we get behind it. There is a road just past—"

"I'm teasing you, Ev," said Polly evenly.

"That's either a Freudian slip or a confession."

"Oh Ev." Polly was looking at the knots of guests scattered around the front of the house. "Rich and Carol Garrison are here," she observed. "Together."

Ev glanced across Polly at the couple as he pulled to the side of the drive to park. "Are you going to leave that button undone?" asked Ev, referring to her blouse. "You're showing."

"Now just stop it. Nothing is going to show."

"There's quite a bit to show."

"Stop it. Look at Carol. She's lost a ton of weight."

"Nothing like adultery, divorce, or widowhood for improving a woman's looks, well, some of her looks." Even if she had regained the figure of a Barbie doll, there was still the face of a Gargoyle.

Polly paused in her open door. "You are stuck in the gutter. Now go find Glenn. He might appreciate your humor."

The night air was pleasantly cool, a perfect Indian Summer evening. Guests were lingering out of doors under a bright waxing moon, and a sinking feeling was overtaking Ev. The Appersons had eased into a new circle—the Jet Set—the rich and not so famous who were new to Lafayette and who made their way turning old farms into ten acre farmettes, or from a trust fund or alimony, or both. With the Jet Set there was always a vague shroud of mystery about where they were reared, where they went to school, how they had come into money, and what had occupied them before they appeared in Lafayette. It was if they had been beamed into the county from another world. The Set spawned a subset: the second wives, whose poster child was Rita Noble, and Ev was here tonight only because the Nobles weren't.

The front door was standing open in the October air and Lydia McDonald, a champagne flute in hand, met the Crosses as they entered the center hall. She sported a spaghetti-strap top and a pair of jeans small enough for Sam Cross to wear, and her blonde hair was tightly pulled into a small knot at the back of her head.

"Polly, darling, and Ev. Isn't this simply wonderful?" She hugged Polly quickly and turned her cheek for Ev to kiss.

Ev delivered the expected peck to her scented cheek and wondered who was next on her list.

Polly looked over her shoulder as they continued down the hall, hoping to see whether Lydia was going to join the Garrisons, which she did, hot tub notwithstanding. Ev, noticing her effort, winked at her and Polly, seeing his reaction, quickly stuck her tongue out.

"You better watch yourself around Lydia," she whispered.

"Hey. When in Rome, do as the Romans," answered Ev.

Polly punched him with her elbow.

"What are you two doing?" laughed Evelyn Apperson as she handed Polly a flute of champagne.

"He's been an ass all afternoon," said Polly.

"What's new? That's a universal male trait, Polly," said Evelyn.

Ev poured Jack Daniels over ice and replied. "Whoever gets two down first doesn't have to drive."

"That's not the deal," said Polly. "It's an If day." She turned and before reaching the other side of the room was intercepted by the realtor Todd Kidd and his wife Tonya who promptly bored her with their trip to the Caymans and a new Volvo.

Glenn Apperson joined Ev at the bar. "Opportunity for a window of opportunity, Ev. We've got two cases of man's best friend."

Before Ev could respond, a slender young man, dressed in blue jeans, a plaid woolen shirt, and hiking boots, appeared beside Glenn who introduced him as Dick Van Eaton. "Dick is the general manager for Noble Development," said Glenn. "He bought the old Roosevelt Campbell farm a couple of years ago."

Crossing Ev's mind was the thought that he could not go anywhere without encountering some Noble tentacle, even a strange bird like this, who was either modeling for L.L. Bean or competing for the miniature lumberjack award.

"He's primarily involved with Clyde's Copperhill golf course and subdivision," continued Glenn.

"That's a big project," managed Ev.

"Damn right. Biggest project this county's ever seen," said Glenn as he took the opportunity of the introduction to walk away.

*Thanks for leaving me with this clown,* thought Ev.

Van Eaton poured a goblet of wine and looked back at Ev. "So what brought you to Lafayette County?" he asked as he raised the goblet to his lips.

"Well," replied Ev evenly, a stranger in his own land, "I'm from here." *And I have a full set of teeth to boot.*

"From here," repeated Van Eaton. "So what do you do?"

And so it went, as Ev ignored his two-drink rule, and waited for Polly.

* * *

Polly whispered that she was ready to leave without Ev having to plead, for she too grew tired of hearing about money and travel, their money and travel, and about their husband's mendacious former marital partners, usually from women who secretly considered themselves trophy wives, but who in Polly's estimation were, at best, consolation prizes. With her clutching his arm and talking, they walked to the station wagon. "Carol Garrison got our address, for her Christmas party."

"My reward for keeping secret her husband's public affair."

"Oh Ev. We have to do something occasionally." After a pause: "Our life is pretty boring, isn't it?"

"Not boring enough, sometimes."

"You know what I mean."

"Well, I'll admit, the prettiest girl at the party certainly deserves more excitement, but there's not much I can do about it." Ev opened the passenger door as he spoke.

Polly wrapped her arms around Ev's waist. "Yes you can," she said, and, "I love you."

"That's good to know, the way Rich Garrison followed you around."

"Yuck," said Polly as she leaned into the car. Ev could not see her unfastening another button on her blouse.

Ev let himself into the driver's side. "I'm surprised you wanted to leave so early."

Polly scooted across the seat and nestled against Ev. "I got tired of hearing about all the exciting things they do." She allowed Ev to turn the ignition before wiggling under his right arm.

Ev looked at the blonde head resting against him. "What's this? A window of opportunity?"

"Maybe."

Ev backed the car into the driveway. "Hold that thought," he said while resigning himself to the sandman beating him to the punch.

Polly pulled Ev's left hand over the open top of her blouse. "I'm showing now."

"I can tell."

"I think we should do something exciting." Ev was now putty in her hands and she knew it. She brushed his neck with her lips and breathed the sweet odor of champagne softly on his chin.

"I'm open to suggestions."

"I've been thinking about your idea since we got here."

"My idea?"

"Yes. Drive behind the barn."

"That was your idea."

"The What was your idea. The Where was mine."

"You're teasing me again aren't you?"

Polly pushed his hand inside her blouse. "Pull behind the barn."

"You're serious?"

"Pull behind the barn. I might say that naughty word, too."

# CHAPTER 32

Monday, November 2$^{nd}$

Three quick sentencings occupied Ev Cross in circuit court in the morning, and during the lull before a bond hearing he met with Brown, Roberts and Hawkes.

Brown presented the trio's findings. Roberts, as watchful as a chain gang guard, kept his eyes riveted on his protégé. Hawkes, hands clasped and his large frame leaning forward, stared at the floor. Cross smoked one of Brown's cigarettes when the lieutenant was finished.

"I guess it's fish or cut bait time isn't it," said Cross finally.

No one responded.

Cross rotated his swivel chair to the side and stared at the map of Lafayette County hanging on the wall. "Obviously, we go direct indictment. I'll need to tell Jim Crawford. He probably won't hear it…a sitting senator's wife. A retired judge will get the job, I guess." Ev spun his chair back and faced his three visitors. "I'm probably gonna get my ass whipped." He took off his glasses and studied the lenses.

"It won't be the first time," said Roberts.

"Thanks a million," replied Cross.

"You don't have any doubts, do you?" asked Roberts.

Ev shook his head slowly. "A murder at Onan, lots of spilt seed. I couldn't have picked three worse witnesses. I guess there isn't much more you can do is there?"

Brown answered. "I'm waiting for Pittsburg to call me back. A double check on whether Rita has any history there."

"That's it Ev," added Roberts. "We spent Friday studying the case. Something else might drop in our laps, but we can't think of anything else to pursue. But, you know me, there still a few imponderables."

"That's really encouraging," said Ev. "Like what?"

"Well, this passing out when she's on crack, shouldn't she be wired? And what was used to smother her? The towel doesn't make sense."

Brown rubbed his chin. "I don't know about the wired part, but there were plastic bags in the trash, just too wet and nasty to be tested."

Said Ev, "if you thought of it the defense will too."

Hawkes straightened in his chair. "Passed out or not, somebody smothered her."

"And two more things, and we've got a split opinion," continued Roberts.

"Rita and Clyde," answered Ev.

"Bingo," said Brown.

"I wonder what she's said to Clyde," said Ev. "I mean, she must be positioning herself, she's not stupid. I'm surprised Clyde hasn't called somebody raising hell."

Hawkes grunted. "My bet is she isn't breathing a word to him. She doesn't want to get him suspicious unnecessarily, you know, start him to thinking. I say let it hit the fan and then see what he does."

Roberts reached for his coat pocket as he spoke. "I say hot box 'em both. Tell 'em where we're going with this. That's been my view all along." He pulled his hand away with a murmured curse.

Ev looked at Brown. "Lieutenant?"

"I'm leaning toward R. C. We talked to Rita, and I think she's finished talking. We go see Clyde, with no charges, and he'll just blow up. After she's indicted, he'll know we aren't fishin'."

Cross slid his glasses back onto the bridge of his nose. "I'm with Gene. But we've got some time to decide. What about this will? Nobody's seen it."

"There might be no will," answered Roberts. "It might've been in the discussion stage. Anyway, will or no will, the possibility of one is all we need to prove."

"We can get it with a subpoena after we indict," said Ev. He stood and reached for his coat. "See you later gents. I've got a bond hearing." Ev waited for Brown and Hawkes to clear the room. "Gene," he said quietly. "What about the sheriff?"

Roberts paused in the threshold. "Sticky wicket."

"Can we get by with not telling him right away?"

"We can get by. Some of us might not stay employed. He is my boss."

"I thought you were retiring."

"Shit. Right," laughed Roberts. "I can't afford the health insurance."

"You'll have to be the judge then. But I really don't want him in the loop. He's gonna play it both ways at some point anyway."

"I'll do my best Ev. It shouldn't be a surprise. Lewis gave him a rundown last week."

* * *

Ev followed Jim Crawford into chambers following the bond hearing. Crawford settled into his chair and reached for his pipe. "What's going on with Alec?" referring to Alec Dickson, the defense attorney in the bond hearing.

"I don't know," said Ev.

"I got a pretty strong whiff when he spoke to me this morning."

"Me too."

Ev and Dickson had talked in the hallway before the hearing, the unmistakable odor of metabolizing alcohol following Dickson's words. So alerted Ev noticed that Dickson's face was not its normal color, but the shiny red of someone regularly drinking far too much. Dickson was no stranger to the bottle. He had been to the edge enough times that everyone in the courthouse was aware of his affinity, but Ev had never heard of him coming to court lubricated. Alec's father had been a chronic drunk as well as a capable lawyer, but not at the same time. The senior Dickson would periodically hole up in his home for several weeks—down with the summer flu as it was politely called—and send his housekeeper to the liquor store to replenish his stock. Yet no one had ever accused Alec's father of drinking seriously while trying to practice law.

"I hope he doesn't get himself into trouble," said Crawford. "I thought he was doing okay. What else is new?"

Ev pulled a chair away from the conference table and sat down. He managed a wry smile before responding. "We're ready to indict on the Noble murder. It's a case you won't have to hear."

Crawford knitted his brows and looked up from his pipe. "What's this?"

"Mrs. Senator Rita Noble."

"You're serious aren't you?"

"Serious as a heart attack."

"Yeah, you're probably right. I don't think I can hear that. How'd it boil down to her?"

Ev gave a brief synopsis of the evidence.

Crawford shook his head and released a plume of a smoke. "You sure drew the low hand on witnesses."

"And this isn't high-low poker. Anyway, she'll have a team of lawyers that'll put that football player's to shame. I doubt their coaching is going to be second rate. You know the big firm tricks. Hire jury consultants. Video practice cross-examinations with her. She'll be as drilled as a Florida State football team. If she makes a mistake, it'll be with her eye shadow or earrings or something like that."

Crawford shrugged and puffed again. "You stay in this business long enough, you get a nasty case."

"I guess. Sure would be a better existence riding a tractor every day. No phones. No people."

"That reminds me of your Uncle E's observation. I was just starting my practice and caught him one day when he was harried and he said, you know, if I could make a living farming, people would only see me at church and at the liquor store."

Ev laughed lightly. "That's E alright."

"How are you gonna handle her attorneys? Let them know before hand?"

"I guess I should call Oliver Farnsworth the day before the grand jury. Any more notice than that will just cause problems." Ev grunted. "Oliver claimed to be representing Jason, so he should figure out he has a conflict. I guess some Richmond firm will get retained."

Crawford put his pipe in his ashtray and checked his watch. "Well. Good luck. I've got to finish off a marriage at eleven-thirty. Sure you don't want to join me?"

"I think I'd rather deal with Rita Noble."

* * *

After matching the guns at the pawn shop to several that had been stolen from the Cove, Brown obtained a search warrant from the magistrate and at nine o'clock that night he and Horace Seay executed it at the home of Danny Bota. In a collapsing shed behind Bota's house they found three more of the missing weapons. Under Aaron's bed they found a coffee can containing cash and a plastic grocery bag stuffed with women's panties. Aaron Bota sat in the kitchen with his seething half-drunk father, and with tears running down his face, told the two officers that he and Ronnie Snidlett had committed every one of the eleven burglaries.

* * *

Ev Cross, oblivious to the cool twilight of the waning autumn, drove home absorbed with making and revisiting a mental list of things he must resolve before the trial of Rita Noble. The list's entries refused ordering; no sooner had he focused on one conundrum than another crowded into view. Should he put Rita's statements into evidence as part of his case-in-chief, or wait and use them in her cross-examination? But if she didn't testify her statements would never come in. She had to testify, but that assumed she would demand a jury. Should he request a jury if Rita didn't? Should Jeff Smith be saved for rebuttal? How could he make a jury believe Lester Snidlett? Why did he believe Snidlett? Of his lay witnesses, only Clara Wood would make a good impression on a jury. Would she stick to her story?

Juries. An old saw held that if you're guilty and didn't confess, you want a jury. The jury is an enigma in the system of criminal justice, a relic of the original precept of the Anglo-American notion of liberty. Appellate judges, educated and, sometimes, experienced with the battlefield of a trial, pour gallons of ink on thousands of pages of a stream of opinions, all dealing with the intricate procedures used to bring an accused to justice. These procedures are applied by trial judges, lawyers, and police, daily. But in the final analysis twelve people off the street, accustomed to justice occurring in a one hour television show, armed with stilted instructions of law and abruptly inundated with a mass of facts, lies, and innuendo,

272

closet themselves in a small windowless room and decide the ultimate issue. That juries were unpredictable was not simply an understatement, it was a cardinal rule.

Among the many vagaries of jurors was their reluctance to believe that the flesh and blood defendant, spruced and calm at the defense table, could actually do something as bad as the jury was being told. The defendant who had had the rare good sense not to admit his guilt to the police was perfectly positioned to exploit that reluctance. And Rita Noble had made no such admission.

A scattering of criminal practitioners—the ones who were paid to speak at seminars and who appeared as commentators on talk show news programs—claimed never to have lost in a murder case, or had been ten years without a defeat in a felony trial. Ev and anyone else who practiced law in the trenches knew why: these lawyers never took a close call to trial; these supermen either settled those charges with a plea bargain or gave the case to someone else in the office. Let some supernumerary take the courtroom whipping. Rita Noble was not going to plead to anything and Ev had no supernumerary to serve as the fall guy.

Another thing about jurors is that they have trouble believing unappealing people. Trials are full of unappealing people. As Ev had learned the hard way, juries will not convict if all the Commonwealth can offer is the testimony of a fellow bad actor. Ev's greatest concern was how to avoid disaster with the triumvirate of Smith, Thomasson, and Snidlett on his witness list.

Polly was sitting outside when Ev arrived home. At her feet were Jasper and Chief, and cradled in her hands was any empty wine goblet.

"Couldn't wait cocktail hour?" asked Ev as he approached her. Chief lazily arose and walked to meet Ev.

Polly briefly looking at Ev through narrow eyes, raised the empty glass. "Mother's little helper."

"That kind of day?" asked Ev.

"An If day," said Polly finally.

"Oh," responded Ev quietly. "I think I'll get a drink first." Polly waved her empty goblet for Ev to refill.

At his return, Ev seated himself beside Polly and handed her the replenished goblet. "My mother?" he asked.

"Who else?"

"I thought she was in South Carolina."

"She was. She's not now."

Ev didn't answer, for Polly was not going to need prompting.

"First she called to tell me about the houses she was looking at and the club she was going to join. Then she called to tell me about the trip to Sicily that Amanda and Richard had planned, and by then she was sniffling, talking about how *special* Sicily was to the family because your father had fought there. How *special* it was that he fought in two wars. We all should be excited that Amanda was taking this *special* trip. Why does she do this to me? Is this some weird first son thing? Is she jealous?"

*Maybe that's it,* she thought. Margaret was jealous, envious of Polly's standing—her standing before she married a Cross, her education, even her looks. Understanding the problem, though, did nothing to make it easier to bear.

"How poor was your mother when she was a child?" asked Polly.

Ev looked at Polly over his glasses. "They weren't poor, and they certainly weren't rich. I guess you could say they didn't have any extras."

"Your grandfather lost his farm?"

"Yes. Why?"

"I've just been trying to figure out why she treats me like shit."

"Well, now that we've got your favorite word on the table, tell me your theory."

Polly looked away before answering. "I don't see any humor in this."

"Why do you let her get to you?"

"You don't understand." Polly arose and walked to the edge of her withered garden.

"You've got two more months Polly," said Ev.

"Trust me. The only way this is going to end is if I outlive her."

Ev looked at Polly's back and then at his now empty tumbler. "We decided to indict Rita Noble."

Polly turned to face Ev. "Something new develop?"

"It's a combination of things. The bottom line is that she hated the girl and went there and she's lying to us about it. And then there's the bathroom towel. But it's going to be a tough case. And a lot of unhappy Democrats."

"Well, given what I learned, I'd say Rita could do it. Get twelve married women for jurors. They'll understand."

Ev paused as he added the advice to the growing mental list. Yet another rule was that women jurors seldom fail to see through the lies of a woman on the witness stand.

"So when's the trial?" asked Polly.

"We have to indict fist. Then we'll need a judge assigned. Then the case will be set. I don't know. March, June. It's up to the defense."

"A judge? Jim won't be the judge?"

"The General Assembly elects the judges. Clyde Noble is a senator. It's a conflict for Jim, or at least he sees it that way."

"So everybody gets to run for cover?"

"Something like that," said Ev as he swirled the ice in his empty glass. "I'm going in. It's getting dark."

Polly did not follow.

Ev walked to the counter and poured another drink. Sam appeared at his side.

"Daddy. What's a baster?"

"A baster. I don't know." Polly dealt with the children's education, and Ev was not in the frame of mind to walk through a tutorial on some vocabulary word Sam was mispronouncing.

"You don't know?"

"How was it used? Is this homework?"

"A boy on the bus said you was a baster."

Ev, regretting that he had let Sam begin riding the bus in the afternoons, looked at his son's quizzical face. "What boy?"

"A big boy."

"What's his name?"

"I don't know. He said you were a baster who put his daddy in jail."

Ev paused for a moment, wondering what to say. Finally, "The word is bastard, which is a bad word. So don't use it."

"Do you put people in jail?"

"Yes. Sometimes." There was no use trying to explain any neat distinctions.

"Wow," said Sam softly.

**CHAPTER 33**

Tuesday, December 1st

It was not yet eight o'clock when Ev arrived at his office and already the telephone was ringing. He let it ring.

The Noble trial scheduling hearing was set for two and Ev wanted once again to look over his list of imponderables before going to court. Rita's new lawyers had told him the week before that they wanted an early trial date. He hadn't any idea how early they intended, but their determination was made clear by the motions that flowed from the facsimile machine on Wednesday following term day. Some big firm underling had spent most of his Thanksgiving weekend researching and crafting the pleadings.

Ev heard the door open and the squeaky tread of Linda Masencup's rubber-soled shoes. "Linda," he called from the conference room, "hold my calls." He heard a ripple of quiet laughter.

"That kind of day already?" she answered.

The telephone rang again before Linda finished speaking. Linda answered, and Ev could hear her laughing. Laughter was always a good sign.

"Wil Bledsoe needs to talk to you about the hearing today," she called from her desk.

"Top of the mornin' Mr. Commonwealth," said Wil, "you go to the UVA-Tech game on Saturday?"

Ev wished that he could have been born with Bledsoe's nonchalance. "Missed it Wil. Watched it on TV."

"One of my Virginia Tech buddies has extra tickets and takes me every year. The fans led me to a realization on the aging process. With young people, men are always having to wait for women to get in and out of the bathroom. So coming out of the game, guess what? A crowd of women—all looking well over fifty—were standing around the men's room waiting for the men. I was on my way there myself. I bet I get up twice every night to go to the john. Hell to get old. Anyway, I called on your Noble case."

*Now what is this about?* wondered Ev.

"The big boys in Richmond decided they needed a local boy at the table, so they associated me as co-counsel. They drove up here yesterday to review the case with me. I figure they clipped Clyde for some three thousand for something we could have talked about on the phone."

"Ganging up on me," said Ev, not knowing how else to respond.

"Damn right."

"They're asking for trial right away. How soon is soon?"

"About two weeks."

"Bullshit."

"I'm serious Ev. Between you and me, what's going on is Clyde doesn't want this hanging over the campaign. He wants it over, at all costs, and that's a blank check to make the big firm heart—where the heart should be—patter. Plus he's told them acquittal is a certainty."

"Clyde Noble or not, two weeks is unheard of." Ev's mind was spinning as he spoke. Lawyers usually wanted forever to prepare a case for trial; the haste fairly shouted that Roberts and company had missed something big. Something that would nail the charge between the eyes.

"They told me Brockenbrough Taliferro was going to be the judge," said Bledsoe.

"I got Jim Crawford's letter yesterday. That's who it is."

"Have you ever had a case with him?"

"No."

"Well, I'll tell you. A defendant couldn't ask for a better judge. Two weeks won't bother him. I mean, the thing is, if you indict, then the Commonwealth's case is ready. His theory, anyway. So we'd like to see your file today, and Roberts's too."

"Linda will have mine here. You need to call Roberts for his."

"Thanks. I'll put on my war paint."

* * *

In the courtroom huddled at defense table were the Nobles and their lawyers. Eight people, murmuring among themselves, were sitting in the gallery. Angela Keating and Varney Mitchell were among them and Ev surmised the rest were reporters as well.

The youngest of the three lawyers, Ellen Mathieson, nodded toward Ev as she said something to Paul Avery, the other Richmond lawyer. Ev had met them briefly on term day when they appeared to request a scheduling hearing. Rita had appeared as well and surrendered herself to Okra Alexander as soon as the grand jury returned a true bill on her first degree murder indictment. The magistrate, with Clyde and Rita Noble staring him in the face, must have doubted the strength of the Commonwealth's case for he had set bail at twenty thousand dollars, a sum promptly secured by Clyde's extensive real estate holdings. Unlike any other murder defendant, Rita had seen neither handcuffs nor the inside of a cell; she was still being treated like a duchess.

Avery finished replying to Mathieson and started walking toward Ev. A small man with gray flecked black hair and gold rim glasses like Ev's, he looked as if he had been born in his gray suit and blue necktie. Bledsoe and Mathieson followed

277

him. Mathieson, who looked to be in her thirties, was wearing a dark blue pants suit and around her neck a colorful silk scarf. Graduates of Randolph Macon Woman's College, Polly's alma mater, had a penchant for scarves—in consequence Polly refused to even own a scarf—and Ev wondered whether Mathieson had done her undergraduate work at RMWC. Bledsoe, his double-breasted pinstriped suit and cowboy boots making him wholly out of place beside the Richmond lawyers, was not attempting to suppress a smirk.

"Good morning Ev," Avery greeted the commonwealth's attorney.

"Mr. Cross," added Mathieson.

Bledsoe smiled through his smirk and halted a step behind the Richmond duo.

"What are your thoughts on how long the trial should take? Three days at most?" asked Avery.

"That's what I figure," said Ev. He wondered how Avery could estimate the trial's length when the defense hadn't had time to digest the Commonwealth's evidence. "With a jury," he added.

"And we're asking for jury," replied Avery. "We were looking at December sixteenth through nineteenth."

"That probably isn't enough time to summons the witnesses," replied Ev. Another thought occurred to Ev. Juries were known to be generous just before Christmas, and generosity ran in the favor of the defendant. Ev had asked Gene Roberts to come to the hearing, and he had seen Brown walk in, but not Roberts. Ev motioned to Brown and introductions were made. "The suggestion," said Ev, "is to set this case for December sixteenth. What do you think?"

Brown looked at Ev with a puzzled expression. It sounded like a trick question he might hear as the accused in the dock. "Of next year?" he finally answered.

The lawyers laughed politely before Ev spoke. "I can't agree to such an early date. Too many things to coordinate in too little time. We can shoot for mid-January, and that's pushing it."

"We can't agree to that," said Avery.

Avery's stance was making Ev more nervous by the minute. He and Roberts had discussed the urgency being pressed by the defense and they had both reached the same conclusion: the defense had an ace in the hole that the investigation had somehow overlooked. The broad hint, like a slap in the face rather than a whisper, led Roberts to grouse that further interviews of the Nobles might have prevented the surprise that was surely coming.

Mathieson, meanwhile, addressed Brown. "Did you go to William and Mary Lieutenant Brown?"

"Yes I did," answered Brown, wondering how she knew. He had forgotten that he was wearing a green tie speckled with yellow WM monograms.

"Did you play football?"

"No," Brown answered curtly.

"Oh…I went to law school there, and I guess I saw you sometime. Going to class perhaps." Mathieson flushed slightly before smiling weakly and turning to join Bledsoe and Avery.

Brown followed Ev to the Commonwealth's table. "Okay Lewis," asked Ev, "why did you lie to her?"

"Pissed me off. Since I'm black she just assumed I played football."

"Well you did play football, Lewis."

"Beside the point."

Ev was still laughing quietly when Avery again approached him.

"Should we go to chambers and see the judge first? I haven't met him," said Avery.

"Me either," said Ev.

Brockenbrough Barton Taliferro, appointed to the bench before Ev was born, had been retired for more than a decade. Retirement was no impediment as he sat as a substitute judge as often as he had as an active circuit court judge. He was tall and snowy-headed with a ruddy complexion and a deep gravelly voice. He wouldn't wear glasses, whether he needed them or not. His home was in the Shenandoah Valley where his circuit for thirty-four years covered six rural counties. He moved a trial at a fast clip and brooked no posturing by attorneys. Everyone, including his wife, children, and friends, addressed him as Judge. This suited him as most people could not pronounce Brockenbrough, and he had never liked the diminutive Bart that, in his long-distant youth, had evolved from Barton.

His pet peeve, however, was the pronunciation of his surname. Taliferro, like Brockenbrough, was an old Virginia name, and the only people who knew how to pronounce it were superannuated Virginians. Given the modern tendency to pronounce every letter in a word, the unenlightened tortured his name into Tal-i-fair-ro. Properly said, Taliferro sounded exactly like Toliver. The Judge had long-since learned to instruct the bailiffs in the courts he visited to open the courtroom for B. B. Toliver.

The Judge had already given Okra Alexander his lesson for the morning. As he did with all visiting judges, Okra asked the clerk beforehand for the judge's name and wrote it on a small slip of paper in the event of a memory lapse at the critical moment. Okra was prone to memory lapses.

The four lawyers found the Judge reading the newspaper in chambers. Looking like a thespian Zeus, he arose immediately when they entered the room. "Good afternoon counsel. I'm B. B. Taliferro." He sounded like Zeus, too.

The four introduced themselves, Bledsoe last.

"I haven't been to Lafayette for—what is it Wil—three decades? I heard a case where one of your deputies beat his wife's boyfriend to death. All the circuit's judges recused themselves. Wil defended, and," he looked at Ev, "your uncle prosecuted. Jury let him off."

"I remember that well," said Bledsoe. "My first murder trial. The boy that was killed was the son of a doctor in Lynchburg. Boy, after that verdict, I started going to see Charlottesville doctors."

"Juries can be a fickle lot," said Taliferro. "What became of the deputy?"

"He became an electrical contractor. Did right well. I still represent him here and there," said Bledsoe.

"And his wife?" asked the Judge.

"They're just as happy as clams, Judge. Still married. I guess a good woman's hard to find."

Ev glanced at Ellen Mathieson, and although she was smiling at the remark, there was no mirth in her eyes.

The Judge too looked at Ellen before returning to his chair. "Okay. What do we have today? Only scheduling?"

"Yes sir," said Bledsoe.

"Any thoughts?" asked the Judge.

"Your honor," said Avery, "we would like to start the trial in two weeks."

Taliferro's left eyebrow raised slightly. "Mr. Cross?"

"I don't think that's in the realm of possibility," said Ev.

Taliferro pursed his lips a moment before responding. "I would think the Commonwealth's case is ready. You've been before the grand jury. And a legal proceeding isn't red wine, it doesn't get better with age."

Bledsoe darted a smug glance at Ev. Ev saw the look and ignored it.

"How long should it take?" asked Taliferro.

"We believe three days will be enough," said Avery.

"I'm glad to hear that," said the Judge. "I thought you might say three weeks. Murder trials are lasting that long in Northern Virginia now. I can't figure out what they do to stretch a murder trial into three weeks. Do you have a date to propose?"

"December sixteenth," said Avery.

"And you're opposed?" Taliferro asked Ev.

"Yes sir," responded Cross. "And if it does run over, we're pushing Christmas and the jury won't be pleased."

"Well, let's put it on the record," said Taliferro. "I'll decide from the bench. I'll be out in a few minutes."

The four lawyers excused themselves and left chambers. Wil smiled and said, "See what I mean Ev?"

Ev's thoughts were elsewhere, rapidly spinning possibilities that were limited only by his imagination. The defense team wanted to see his files and it occurred to him that, like Isaiah Christmas, the Richmond lawyers might assume they had no duty to reciprocate. Bledsoe knew the informal rules Ev followed, but Avery might not, and he, unquestionably, was calling the shots. Ev spoke before the foursome entered the courtroom. "I trust you'll provide the reciprocal discovery I would be entitled to."

Avery paused at the door. "Of course. Obviously there are no scientific tests. But we do have an alibi. Mrs. Noble left Richmond, intending to go home, but changed her mind. She was never there." Avery, when he finished speaking, opened the door and led Mathieson into the courtroom.

Bledsoe waited beside Ev until the other lawyers had crossed the room. "I don't envy you, Ev. A dork, a dirtball, and a drug dealer for witnesses."

"Thanks Wil," said Ev dryly.

* * *

B. B. Taliferro listened to Avery and then to Cross. When both were finished, the Judge set the trial for December sixteenth.

Ev gathered his files and motioned for Brown to follow him. "We've got a lot to do," he told the lieutenant.

Angela Keating was at Ev's side before Brown could respond. "Ev. Can we have a few minutes of your time?"

"Angela," began Ev.

"Now be fair to us. I know you tipped the local paper on the indictment," she interrupted.

Ev paused at the door to the hallway. From the corner of his eye he could see the other reporters hovering near defense table, waiting to follow the Nobles and their attorneys outside.

"Okay Angela, just a few questions." He had called Varney Mitchell before grand jury, as he had promised he would, and the weekly *Lafayette County Times* had been the medium to break the news of the indictment. Things could get ugly if he didn't accommodate Keating.

Ev, Keating, and Brown stepped into the hallway where four cameramen were waiting. Angela, blonde and wispy thin, waved to her cohort, a tall husky young black man who looked more like her bodyguard than a camera operator. He swung his camera to his shoulder and activated its stark bright light.

"Mr. Cross, will the judge's decision setting the trial in two weeks affect your case?"

Ev tried to avoid blinking under the harsh light. Still seething from the judge's ruling, he felt an urge to be both glib and sarcastic. He swallowed the urge. "Our investigation is complete, we'll be ready for trial."

"Were you surprised by the early court date?"

281

"I wasn't expecting it."

"Is trial so soon unusual?"

Ev knew better than to say anything impugning Taliferro. "No. Not unusual." Ev didn't need an insulted judge presiding over the trial.

"But doesn't it put you at a disadvantage, since you have no assistants?"

"I'm accustomed to that disadvantage, happens with all my trials."

"Are you going to request help in view of the seriousness of the charge?"

"No ma'am." Ev ignored the connotation that he couldn't handle a high profile murder.

"Does the fact that Rita Noble is a state senator's wife change any of your strategy?"

"It's a first degree murder charge regardless who did it."

"Well, hypothetically, if someone well-known is charged, don't they tend to be harder to convict?"

Lie again, or concede the point and lay the groundwork for an excuse if Rita were acquitted? He decided not to sandbag himself. "People in the public eye tend to draw more attention, I don't believe that changes the dynamics of their trials." Ev wondered if Angela would catch his careful correction of her politically correct but linguistically incorrect syntax.

She didn't, and wouldn't let go her line of questioning either. "So when someone is politically connected, you don't expect to find it harder to make your case against them?"

"The prosecution must prove the elements of the charge. So no, I don't think that makes a difference." Ev began turning in the hope that Keating would get the hint.

"One more question." Keating paused so that her editors would have no problem deleting the prefatory statement. "What problems do you foresee in the prosecution of Rita Noble?"

"I can't comment on the specifics of the case." Ev paused too, for the same reason as Keating. "I really must go Angela."

Keating pursed her lips and nodded toward her cameraman. The vicious light was extinguished. "Thank you Ev. Now please call us if something develops. Don't play favorites. And by the way, those little lies you gave me were pretty convincing."

Ev forced a smile for a response and quickly turned away. From the corner of his eye he could see another reporter gesturing in his direction, but the Nobles' exit from the courtroom diverted the reporter's attention. "Let's get the hell out of here," Ev muttered to Brown.

Once at his secretary's desk Ev informed Linda of the trial date. "Get our witness list to the clerk. Also, draft me a subpoena for Clyde Noble and Oliver

Farnsworth asking for wills, drafts of wills, notes, and so forth." Turning to Brown he continued, "What else needs quick attention?"

"I don't know Ev. I haven't sprinted in a long time."

"Not since the Quik Mart."

"Thanks Ev."

"Where's Roberts?"

"He went to the doctor."

"He didn't tell me he had an appointment."

"I think he's having some problems."

"Shit. That's just great. Bledsoe and Avery want to see your files, today. What else are you working on?"

"Well I still don't have an answer from Pittsburg on her criminal record."

"Call 'em again. Linda. Start scheduling the witnesses to come in to see me. Lewis, you or Gene will need to be here for that. Also, Linda, move all my cases from the week of trial. I can't be in three courts at once. Damn that old crusty bastard for doing this to me." Ev abruptly turned and left the anteroom.

"It's not going to be pleasant around here for the next two weeks," said Linda softly. "And I thought the last two were bad."

"That's puttin' it mildly," answered Brown as he opened the door to the hallway. Reverend John Henry Johnson Senior met him in the threshold.

"How y'all gettin' along?" Johnson greeted Linda and the lieutenant. Without waiting for a response, "Is the Commonwealth able to see me for just a minute?"

"He's tied up today, Reverend Johnson," answered Linda.

Ev, having heard Johnson's voice, called from his office. "I've got a few minutes."

Johnson asked Brown about his parents and Linda about her husband before going in to see Ev. "I won't hold you up, Mr. Commonwealth. I was up here paying my taxes and says to myself, I oughta drop in and see how my old friend be doin'.'"

"I'm here. That's about it," replied Ev. "Have a seat."

Johnson settled into a chair across from Ev's desk. "Sometimes somebody has to be your ears cause you can't hear what people don't say to you."

Ev leaned back in his chair and took off his glasses.

Johnson continued. "Lots of times I just listen, even though you knows I like to talk. And Sunday I was listenin' to the sheriff."

The mention of the sheriff made Ev's stomach start knotting. As planned, the indictment of Rita Noble was kept from Hank Burke; Roberts broke the news to his boss the day before term day. Burke was beside himself, first for being kept in the dark, then because Clyde Noble's wife was going to be the accused. When he finished reminding Roberts who did the hiring and firing in the sheriff's department, he marched up to Ev's office.

Ev knew what was coming when the red faced Burke appeared at his desk.

"Since nobody around here seems to remember, I'm Sheriff Henry R. Burke," he thundered. "I don't appreciate bein' the last one to know what y'all are doing."

Ev took a deep breath and folded his hands together tightly.

"Y'all are fixin' to indict Rita Noble, and just last week I called Senator Noble askin' for his endorsement. Now what kinda dumb ass does that make me? Y'all don't have the evidence to convict nobody, let alone her."

The mention of an endorsement was all Ev needed to hear. Burke wasn't interested in the crime, he was concerned about his political hide. "We discussed this Hank," answered Ev calmly even while his ears were pounding with surging blood. "You agreed we would work the case and then fill you in."

"It's a big difference between workin' cases on Jeff Smith and workin' cases on Rita Noble, and then wait to the last minute and set it off in my face like a hand grenade. Now I'm gettin' calls from Hampton Coleman and that Dillon Cobb fella asking what in the hell we're up to. Don't expect nothin' from me. You've dug your own grave and I'll be damned if I'm going to be buried in it with you."

"It's a tough case and I had to make the call," said Ev. He was relieved that Coleman and Klobb hadn't been pestering him as well, and felt a little smug that they hadn't dared.

"Well you remember that," said Burke. He twisted the gun belt on his hips and left the room as quickly as he entered.

Linda Masencup walked in seconds later. "What's his problem?"

"The problem is that the job of sheriff was created so that a little man would have a shot at being a demi-god for some short time in his life."

"Is he serious? Didn't he have a clue that Rita was a suspect?"

Ev mulled the question, and for a moment, wondered if Burke was being honest about his ignorance. "He knew enough," said Ev. "He's running for political cover."

Johnson leaned forward in his chair. "Now I know you got your job to do. And you the right man to do it. I know your uncle, knew your daddy and your granddaddy, and I know your people gonna do the right thing. Might not be plain at first. Now the sheriff, he sayin' you don't have much on Senator Noble's wife. He sayin' he feels right sorry for her. People listen to the sheriff. So they wonderin', what's goin' on?"

"Not much I can do about the sheriff, John."

Johnson chuckled before responding. "No. I reckon not. But I wish there was. Everybody seem to have forgot there's a girl dead."

"The people will understand when we put on our evidence." Ev wished he could feel as confident as he sounded.

"That's what I told 'em. But, you know, they figure the sheriff know what he's talkin' about. Leaves you standin' out there by yourself. They don't see me, or Joe Lewis Brown, or the others what have faith in you. So you just gotta do the Lord's work."

"Thank you John."

"Well. I tied you up long enough. Tell your mother I was thinkin' of her, what with her movin' and all. And soon you'll be in the old home house. That's the way it oughta be."

* * *

Half-filled boxes sat in every room of the house and Polly couldn't muster the steam to finish filling them. Boxes for Bounty towels and Clorox bleach, collected from the IGA, served to remind her that Ev was adamant that they couldn't afford professional movers, and Polly, despite her protests, silently agreed. Everything on a shoestring and there had been not one bite on the house they needed to sell—had to sell.

Evelyn Apperson had not called and hadn't returned Polly's calls since the news of the indictment broke the Wednesday before. Polly knew what was happening. Ev was now a pariah with the Nobles' circle and she, by association, along with him. She knew better than to expect the invitation for Carol Garrison's party; the Crosses, never full members on anybody's social list, were now blacklisted.

And now Polly was having difficulty resisting Ev's doom and gloom attitude. There were just so many ways she could tell him the world would not come to an end if he lost, especially when he might be right.

Upon his arrival Ev walked straight to the cabinet and retrieved the Jack Daniels. "My trial is in two weeks."

"I know." Linda Masencup had already tipped Polly to the day's events.

"The designated judge must have thought it was funny to do that to me. He's probably got hardening of the arteries."

"I hope you're sure about this."

"Me too."

"Your mother told me she overheard the sheriff telling someone that no jury would convict Rita."

"Sounds like he wanted that to get back to me."

"That's not fair, sandbagging you like that."

Ev shook his head. "I had a friend in law school, from Georgia. His observation on fair was this: When the doctor pulled you out into the world and smacked you on the hiney, he didn't say one word about life being fair. Anyway, I hope the boys can stand waiting a little longer for the Christmas tree."

* * *

Gene Roberts ignored his doctor and returned to the sheriff's office after his appointment. The three notebooks lay in front of him, taunting him, stirring a tense butterfly feeling in his stomach. *What am I missing?* He flipped open the first notebook and looked at the evidence log, the document which described each item of physical evidence together with its assigned number and the location where it was found.

Beer cans, cigarette butts, he had studied the list until he had memorized it. He turned the pages until he came upon the sketch of the crime scene. The number of each item was supposed to be marked on the sketch at the point where it had been retrieved. He started comparing the log to the sketch. Item forty-seven, a plastic Dr. Pepper bottle, was not on the sketch, yet the log recited that it had been recovered behind an azalea near the pool fence.

"Damn, McIntosh," mumbled Roberts as he flipped to the laboratory submissions. The bottle had been sent in, but there were no finger prints of value. Perhaps Pepe Lopez had pitched the bottle while he was mowing the yard—the grounds, Roberts corrected himself. Roberts pulled a dog-eared sheet from beneath his telephone and found Mervin McIntosh's number. He dialed it, left a message on the answering machine, and decided to call it quits for the day.

# CHAPTER 34

Sunday, December 13th

The only way for Ev to focus his full attention on the preparation for trial was to come to the office on a weekend. No telephone interruption, no walk-ins. He emptied the contents of the Noble files on the conference table. For each potential witness there was a manila folder filled with statement transcripts, investigation reports, and his own notes. A pile of photographs and documents awaited the designation of exhibit numbers. The master jury list was spread in front of him.

The jury was a crapshoot; they were a collective croupier. No one could predict how it would come out once the case was theirs. And choosing the jury was no better than five card draw. A pat hand was a rarity, so a few obviously must be discarded, some were keepers, others were a mystery, and twelve had to be empanelled on the basis of an attorney's instinct and crossed fingers. No experienced lawyer would claim to foretell what minutiae, what insignificant detail, what piece of evidence not before the jury, might be the determining factor. No one except the jurors knew, if they did, what was going through their minds.

Ev scanned the jury list; he had already circulated it among the various courthouse offices and Gene Roberts, asking for comments on the potential jurors—his informal jury screening process. Ev was certain that the defense team would have a high-dollar jury selection expert available to assist with the selection of the jurors and to whisper to Avery and company his reaction to each potential juror's eye movement, dress, and perfume odor.

Several of the names on the list were familiar. Elliot Masencup, his secretary's great uncle, was fine, and had little chance of being seated. Todd Carson, one of Wimpie Carson's innumerable relatives, was acceptable, but would probably be stricken since he was a kinsman of a deputy.

Mariah Reynolds, Ev's cousin, was also on the list. Ev was uncertain of the consanguinity, something on the order of second cousins thrice removed, but Mariah, who knew the Cross genealogy back to William the Conqueror, was not in doubt. Mariah was a dedicated spinster and a confirmed eccentric; she loved dogs and detested most Yankees, the only Democrats she had ever voted for were Ev and E, and George McGovern, and she made clear that those who drank blended scotch instead of single malt belonged to the lowest order of the rabble. She refused to respond to anyone who mispronounced her name as Ma-ree-ah and she smoked Lucky Strikes incessantly. She was also brilliant (B.A. Smith College; Masters, University of Virginia; Doctorate, North Carolina). As for men she considered few her equal, and those few were related to her, with the exception of one. She had been jilted at the altar, and being incurably and secretly a romantic, she never replaced him.

Mariah would make a good juror and Bledsoe knew her well enough to think otherwise. Linda Masencup had drawn a line through Oscar Hogg, and noted, simply, "crazy." Roberts had marked through two names with no reason given. Some of the potential jurors, a retired nurse, a bank teller, a farm manager, Ev recognized but didn't know.

Several others he knew and wanted to avoid at all costs. Andrew Reske and Emily Wilko were in the Dillon Klobb circle of from-somewhere-else former flower children, good Democrats all, and conflicted about authority. Who knew where black jurors stood, given the sheriff's perfidious whisperings. One-third of the jury pool was under thirty-five; Ev wanted as few young people on the jury as possible. Young people, familiar only with the fantasy world of television crime drama, got lost in their deliberations; they would want to know whether the pool water could be tested for DNA or if satellite images were available.

Some were people Ev had prosecuted for minor offenses: DUI, speeding and so forth; they might harbor a personal grudge against the prosecutor. The majority, however, were strangers; evidence of the influx of new people into Lafayette County.

Finished with his review, Ev was left with only a handful with whom he was comfortable, and the defendant would probably strike them. It would be a crapshoot.

Ev laid the list aside and pulled an empty yellow pad in front of him. He had to decide not only what witnesses to call, but in what order. The guts of the case were Rita Noble and Lester Snidlett. The jury had to believe one or the other, or they could throw up their hands, decide they couldn't decide whom to believe, and acquit. The evidence against Rita was circumstantial and the only reason to believe Snidlett was the circumstantial evidence against Rita. Ev could feel his head spinning. He reasoned that the same thing would happen to the jury. There must be something else.

Ev thumbed through the documents he would put into evidence and stopped at the draft will that had been produced in response to his subpoena to Clyde Noble. Noble's current worth was some six million dollars. Miranda was to get the lump sum of two hundred-fifty thousand dollars at Clyde's death, and one-third of a two million dollar trust when Rita died. Miranda was cut in for a little under a million, Rita and her two children would get over five. Money begets money, and any appreciation in Clyde's wealth before his death would also go to Rita. The average person, whose family lived on forty or fifty thousand a year, would think that Rita wouldn't concern herself with a million when she would control five; the average person was not intimately familiar with the Rita Noble.

Ev's concentration wandered again. Why wasn't the defense taking the position that Rita found the body, assumed Jason had committed the murder, and then lied to protect Jason? The defense chose alibi before knowing precisely what Jason had told the police, or much of anything else for that matter. Did Avery's team know something that Ev didn't, or maybe it was simple: no jury would believe Lester Snidlett over Rita Noble. Actually it was basic, not simple. Rita must be adamant that she never went home that night. Avery and Bledsoe were stuck with what she told them, and that left alibi, and the corollary defense, SODDI: Some Other Dude Did It. Still, discounting Snidlett, the defense team needed some explanation for the bathroom towel, a silver car, threats, and motive. Rita might prove her own worst enemy by arrogantly dictating a defense that didn't mesh with the evidence. Arrogance or survival? What would Clyde Noble do if Rita admitted she was there, saw his daughter at the bottom of the pool, and returned to Richmond with her lips firmly clamped? Kiss the five million goodbye.

Ev and Gene Roberts had met with Paula Noble the day before Rita was indicted. Dreading the meeting, Ev put it off until the last minute. But Paula's reaction was not what he expected; she heard his announcement without blinking, as if somehow she had suspected it all along, and finally, quietly, she asked, "How will you prove it?"

Ev, with no assistants, was unaccustomed to laying out his full trial strategy to another person, and in any event, was always guarded in what he revealed to victims and their families as non-lawyers had their own views about which facts were important and, ignorant of the rules of evidence, on what would be admissible. Ev put his characteristic caution aside and explained each facet of his case against Rita Noble. When he was finished, Paula, staring at her lap, sighed quietly and pushed at a tear in her eye. "How could she be so cold, so evil?" she asked, looking up.

"That's something I wish I could explain to the jury, but I don't have anything else," answered Ev. "I have to depend on her lies."

"Anybody who knew her would know she would lie about anything. So that doesn't help you."

"The jury won't know her, personally anyway."

"What about Clyde?"

"He's an unknown factor."

"How in God's name can he choose that woman over his flesh and blood?"

"He must believe her."

"Like a jury could," said Paula.

Ev had also expected an explosion from Clyde Noble, instead there was nothing. A confrontation might have been preferable just to get it behind him. But Clyde was obviously taking another tact, waiting until the trial was over before he undertook Ev's methodical political demolition. Ev based his conclusion on two facts. First was the inherent cutthroat nature of politics. Second was Clyde Noble's interview following the scheduling hearing. Surrounded by more cameras than his nascent candidacy had ever generated, Clyde had rattled his saber.

Lobbing him a slow pitch, Angela Keating asked: "Will Miz Noble prevail in the trial in two weeks?"

"Of course," replied Noble. "It's already obvious to me that someone connected with the investigation has experienced a monumental lapse in judgment."

"Any thoughts on who that would be?" came a voice from the huddle of reporters. Noble paused very briefly. "We think that problem is best addressed after our trial is behind us." Clyde, like every politician, loved the royal plural pronoun.

Ev received three telephone calls from reporters asking whether Noble was speaking of the prosecutor. He lied when he answered that he had no idea what the senator was suggesting.

*It's all about politics, baby,* Ev thought ruefully. He chased the rambling thoughts from his mind and once again forced his attention to the yellow tablet.

* * *

At home, Gene Roberts was restless. The plastic Dr. Pepper bottle was still annoying him.

Mervin McIntosh could not remember the exact location of the bottle, just generally that it was on the east side of the pool, behind the fence and some azaleas. Without prints the bottle was of little significance and it could have been where it was found for weeks before the murder. More than likely, one of the Noble children had pitched it over the fence. Still, if he couldn't tie the bottle to the crime, then perhaps he could exclude it.

Gene drove over Scott's Mountain, stopped at the Onan Trading Post, then back tracked a mile and pulled into the driveway of Hector Lopez. The Lopez home was a small frame farm house provided by Clyde Noble. Lopez opened the door before Roberts could knock.

"What I can do for you?" asked Lopez.

"Mr. Lopez, I'm Gene Roberts—"

"Yes. I know. You are the policeman."

"Can we sit down and talk for a few minutes?"

Lopez glanced over Roberts's shoulder as if expecting to see someone.

"I'm alone," said Roberts.

"Eez not that. Come in."

Lopez guided Roberts past the Lopez family gathered in front of the wood stove and television and led him into the kitchen.

290

"Are you expecting someone?" asked Roberts. "Is this a bad time?"

"Eez not that. My boss… I maybe not supposed to talk to you."

Gene pulled out a kitchen chair and settled himself at the table. "Whether you talk to me is up to you." Mexicans, given the reputation of the police in parts of Mexico, usually talked for fear they would be beaten or simply disappear.

Lopez chewed at his lower lip, then joined Roberts at the table. "What?"

"You told me you keep the yard at the Nobles."

"Yes. And Pepe. He cut the grass."

Gene pulled a plastic Dr. Pepper bottle from his coat pocket, one he had just purchased and drained in the parking lot at the Onan Trading Post, and set it on the table while still watching Lopez. "You told me Pepe cut the grass the Wednesday before Miranda was killed, right?"

Lopez eyed the bottle cautiously. "Yes. He cut the grass then. It was dry. He cut only once a week."

"You drink these?"

"Sometimes."

"Did you leave this by the pool?"

"I leave nothing. The Mrs. Noble, she would, you know, take my job if she see anything in the grass. Once, she have friends there, and she see a candy paper from one of the children, and she tell me no more, or I go back to Mexico." Lopez shook his head emphatically.

*Must have been off her meds,* thought Roberts. "What about Pepe? Does he drink these?"

"Yes, I think. Maybe."

"Could he come in here for a minute?"

Lopez yelled in Spanish for Pepe, who appeared at the door promptly. He was short and pudgy, and as serious as his father. Lopez spoke again in Spanish and Pepe joined the two men at the table.

"Pepe," began Roberts. "Do you drink these?"

Pepe glanced at his father before answering. "Yes. Sometimes." There was barely a trace of accent in his response.

"Did you leave one of these by the pool, in August, when Clyde Noble's daughter was killed?"

Pepe's eyes widened. He looked at his expressionless father for a moment, and receiving no instructions, looked back at Roberts. "I could have," he answered quietly.

"When?"

Pepe looked at the tabletop.

A staccato of Spanish burst from Lopez and Roberts suddenly regretted that he had not brought Brown with him. "What did your father tell you?" asked Roberts.

"To tell you the truth."

"Well then, tell me the truth."

Pepe released a deep sigh.

* * *

Ev finished the listing of his witnesses for his case-in-chief and laid his pencil aside.

> Bennie Thomas
> Horace Seay
> Jeanette DeWease
> Mervin McIntosh
> Jeff Junior Smith, III
> Jason Thomasson
> Lester Snidlett
> Manfred Fitzgerald
> Sunny Dawn Grogan
> Juanita Lopez
> Trooper J. M. Gregory
> Clara Wood
> Lewis Brown
> Gene Roberts

Ev had to explain to the jury the presence of three men's semen, yet there was no clean way to put in the evidence of the trio of degenerates—Smith, Thomasson and Snidlett—that would lessen their negative impact, so he decided to call them back to back and hope the last of his witnesses would overcome them. He added the car rental agent from the Richmond Mercedes dealership to prove the mileage put on the loaner. To deal with contingencies, and rebuttal, he had another list of witnesses. Poochie Essex and four crack customers could verify Smith's alibi. They were terrible witnesses, but they were all he had. Ev always called Roberts last, twenty plus years as a cop, a polished witness and error proof, Ev couldn't finish any stronger. He wondered how three days would be enough.

The telephone interrupted his thoughts, and Ev decided to answer it as only Polly knew he was at the office.

"Ev." It was Bledsoe's voice. "You're havin' to work like a real lawyer."

"I wouldn't have answered if I knew you were calling."

"Damn Ev. Anyway, I saw your Bronco in the sheriff's lot and decided to see if you're ready to throw in the towel."

"I'm certainly ready to get it over with."

292

"Off the record, what else you got on Rita?"

Ev laughed. "When is anything off the record with a defense lawyer? But you've got what I've got."

"I'll grant you she's a first rate bitch, but guilty? I don't think so. I told you awhile back that she reminded me of my first wife. That wasn't fair, even my first wife had a few good points. For one thing, she did have a set of knockers."

Ev decided to fish as well. "I bet you and Avery wish she had told you she did go home and then panicked because Jason had been there, right?"

"How'd you guess?"

"But you believe her?"

"If I wasted my time trying to figure out whether my clients were truthful, I'd end up drunk more often than Alec Dickson, probably more than Gooseneck. By the way, a client brought me some peach brandy; we oughta crack it after this trial."

"Wil. The phones are probably bugged."

"I didn't say it was illegal," laughed Bledsoe. "Listen Ev. Are you people sure Snidlett didn't kill that girl? I mean, that's where the evidence points. Frigged her, and then when the buggery didn't work, he got pissed and killed her. Even better, he probably raped her. He's a mean drunk."

"A mean drunk would choke her or beat her to death, not carefully smother her and drop her into the pool. Besides, you've got the polygraph."

"Yeah. Inconclusive on killing her."

"Almost truthful. The state police err on the side of caution. And almost truthful is one thing Rita Noble is not."

"Sneaky; ain't she? Make sure you get some nookie before trial. Keeps your mind from wandering."

Ev laid the receiver in its cradle and stared at the print of the Rotunda hanging on his conference room wall. *Bledsoe won't die of a heart attack.*

The telephone rang again. "Must be Polly this time," said Ev. The caller was Gene Roberts.

"You tracked me down, too," said Ev.

"You know I don't call you at home unless I need to. Polly said you were at your office. Thought you might want this. Another witness has surfaced."

Ev felt butterflies. "Another witness for Rita?"

"Nope. For us. I guess. Pepe Lopez. The thirteen year old. Ev. The boy was there."

"Try that again."

"Pepe. Hector's son. He cuts the Nobles' grass. He would sneak over to watch Miranda in her bikini. Hide behind the fence. One day he caught her doing it with Jason. The kid had a private hoochie-coochie act. So he was constantly sneaking over there, trying to catch some more. He slipped out of his room Friday night and walked over there, it's not a half mile, and got there in time to see her fun with Smith. He hung around, and before long, Thomasson shows up. He gets an eyeful of round one and sticks around for the fight. He leaves after Thomasson leaves. He thinks around eight-thirty."

"So he's not there for the finale."

"Afraid not."

"Damn."

"He might take some of the heat off of us on Smith and Thomasson. Anyway, he ran home and kept his mouth shut. Figured the family would be on their way to Mexico if he breathed a word."

Ev was silent.

"Are you there?" asked Roberts.

"I think so," said Ev. "How'd you get this?"

"Chasing rabbits. A Dr. Pepper bottle. Got lucky."

"I'd rather be lucky than good. Do you think the kid'll hold up? The Nobles know how to use pressure."

"I don't know Ev. He seems to be a good kid. But you know how things can change."

"Well type it up. I want to hand Wil the report. I sure wish he'd stuck around."

"Me too. I guess we're at the end of the tether. I'm going to watch a football game now."

Ev slowly re-laid the receiver. It was helpful stuff, but Pepe' wasn't going to resolve the SODDI question. The defense would probably say Pepe killed Miranda. He penciled Pepe's name in after Lewis Brown.

* * *

Polly sat at her computer staring at the screen. There was a story somewhere in Margaret's doings, but she wasn't sure whether to pen an anecdote, or a novel. *My mother-in-law,* thought Polly, *a good title. Or maybe, my mother-in-law, a witch revisited.* Witch needed to be worked in somehow. That aside, where to start? The hidden silver, Kitty Carson, the chandelier, vodka? The vodka drinking witch? Vodka and the Witch? Words were jumbled, like her thoughts, and nothing would flow from her imagination to her fingers at the keyboard. Then the telephone rang. It had been three days since the witch had called, so Polly knew she was due.

"Polly," said the voice. Margaret was sober. "I'm in South Carolina, at my sister's. I forgot to tell you I was coming down. Can you check the cats?"

"Yes ma'am," said Polly evenly.

"You're a keeper."

The last line was a dead give-away that Margaret's sister must be nearby, or else Margaret would never have bothered with a term of endearment.

"You'll never guess," continued Margaret. "I found a Tom who looks just like Kitty Carson. Now at least. He had one white spot on his chest, so I dyed that black. Isn't that wonderful, Kitty's back. But I thought I better change the name a bit. So it's Kitten Carson."

"How nice," said Polly. *Another story for the book.*

"You weren't at the Coleman's Christmas party Friday. I asked Mae but she just looked surprised and didn't answer."

*The pariah infection is spreading*, thought Polly. "We weren't invited."

"Are you sure?"

"I'm sure."

"That must have been an oversight."

"No it wasn't, Mrs. Cross. Ev is prosecuting the wife of a prominent Democrat."

"And you think Hampton Coleman would be that way because he's such a Democrat?" There was a pause. "I'm sorry Polly. That's not right. If I'd known that, I would have declined. I never liked Hampton Coleman anyway. Nobody does."

"Thank you Mrs. Cross," said Polly quietly.

"Is there anything I can do?"

"I'm afraid not," answered Polly, feeling sheepish about her earlier thoughts.

"I haven't even moved yet and already I miss you, Ev, and the boys. Well, thank you for looking after the cats. Give the boys my love. Better not run up the telephone bill. Goodbye."

Polly replaced the receiver and walked to the door of the closed-in porch. The boys were quietly watching *Aristocats*. Suddenly she was no longer interested in the computer.

# CHAPTER 35

Tuesday, December 15th

Ev was in the conference room, the door closed, revising the outline of his opening statement. He briefly considered a reference to the Biblical Onan, but then decided that might create error in some federal judge's eyes in a later habeas corpus proceeding, assuming he could convict Rita in a state court. All the seminar experts agreed that a lawyer should never read his argument to the jury, but that was fine for those who could shoot from the hip. Ev wasn't going to read his opening, but he needed a prop. Besides, as E had reminded him, even eloquent Winston Churchill carefully wrote all of his speeches after an extemporized one proved an abject failure. The self-appointed experts differed on the most important part of the lawyer's case. Some said it was the opening, some said it was closing, and some, the cross-examination. Ev, his own expert, now a fledgling Kshatriya, believed that exhaustive attention to detail was the key. After that, wits and luck took over.

He stopped his review and looked at the telephone, hoping Brown would call to tell him that the Pittsburg police had finally produced some dirt on Rita. It was getting late in the game to expect a bombshell.

Linda opened the door. "Mr. Avery just faxed a motion."

"At four o'clock? The day before trial? How does that give me time to react?" Another motion was not the bombshell Ev had in mind. His tone of voice led Linda to keep quiet. He snatched the paper from her hand and began reading. The document was a motion *in limine*, which meant that the defense wanted B. B. Taliferro to rule beforehand that some piece of evidence could not be presented to the jury. The second numbered paragraph stunned Ev:

> 2. Prohibit the Commonwealth from presenting any evidence concerning reports to, or the investigative results of, any Harrisburg, Pennsylvania law enforcement agency.

Ev read the paragraph and then re-read it. Carefully oblique, and poorly phrased, probably on purpose, the motion told him something bad was out there without giving him the details necessary to track it down. What was Avery doing?

Ev had already told Wil Bledsoe that the prosecution had nothing else, except Pepe's statement which was faxed to Avery and Bledsoe on Monday. Perhaps Bledsoe and Avery were not talking. Why would the defense educate the prosecution at this late hour? Filing the motion at the last minute meant that the defense knew something and had some reason to believe that Ev was on to it. The eleventh hour motion was insurance both that the bad stuff wouldn't pop out in front of the jury, and that Ev, ignorant of the mystery as he was, wouldn't have time to chase any rabbits. *Avery thinks I'm hiding the ball, he thinks I know something I'm not telling them. He's outsmarted himself.*

Ev dialed Brown's number and received no answer; he did the same with Roberts with the same results. He then called dispatch and Reggie Williams answered. "Where are Roberts and Brown?"

"Roberts went to the doctor. Brown's out on a child abuse case."

"Well leave a message for them to call, ASAP." Ev banged the receiver down. "Shit. Shit. Shit. Linda! Get the telephone numbers for the Harrisburg police, the prosecutor and whatever else they have up there."

"Yes sir."

Armed with several numbers, Ev first called the prosecutor's office: none of the multitude of lawyers was available, so he left a message for one to call him. He then called the police department. Not knowing what he was looking for, Ev was shunted from one extension to another until finally he was connected with the records division. He explained his position and his need for information on Rita Thomasson.

"I'm sorry sir," replied the by-the-books voice of a young woman. "We can release information only to one of our officers or the D. A. Have you contacted the investigating officer?"

"If I knew that, I wouldn't be talking to you," Ev replied sharply. Regretting his outburst, he continued in a softer voice. "I understand your policy. My problem is that I need this information for a murder trial starting tomorrow, and I don't have anything but this name."

Ev's indelicate response had done its damage. "Since you understand, do I need to tell you again?"

"Can you direct me to someone who can help me with determining who this officer is?" asked Ev, sounding as contrite as he could manage.

"Homicide, Auto? Sir, I need some information."

"Pick one," said Ev.

The transfer connected Ev with Sergeant Castellano in Homicide. Ev explained his dilemma.

"Don't ring a bell with me," said Castellano.

Ev had assumed that much.

"Tell you what," continued the sergeant, "I'll check the computer. See if I find anything. When did this happen?"

"I don't know," said Ev. "Maybe two decades ago."

"I'll try and see if I get anything. Have an investigator call you. Probably tomorrow."

*Too close to five o'clock,* thought Ev. He thanked the officer and put the receiver down. Avery had sent him on a scavenger hunt with one item on the list, only it was like going door-to-door looking for a Confederate C-Note in a Cleveland suburb.

Linda Masencup re-appeared at the door. "Five o'clock Ev. Do you need me to stay?"

"No. Thanks anyway. Back in the front lines tomorrow."

Ev answered the telephone when it rang.

"This is Daphne Kesserling, Dauphin County D. A.'s office."

Ev explained what he was trying to find, which took several minutes.

There was a pause before Kesserling responded. "Do you have any idea about a time frame?"

"My guess is early eighties or late seventies. And that is a guess."

"And you say the defense attorney brought this up?"

"Look. Beats me too. But it must be something or he wouldn't be filing a motion on the outside chance I was aware of it."

Kesserling laughed. "I'm glad criminal cases in other jurisdictions are weird. I thought we had them all. Look, I'll see what I can find. But, you know, her problem—whatever it is—is so old that it's probably not on a computer. Maybe somebody will remember the name, though I don't think anybody in this office was here in the seventies. No luck with the police?"

"I couldn't tell them where to start."

"I'll get our investigator to call them."

"You're lucky to have one."

"More than one. I'll call when I have something."

"Let my secretary know. I'll be in court."

Ev looked through his notes for the hundredth time, made a few entries on his opening statement, and thought again about Avery's motion. The Commonwealth could not present evidence of the defendant's bad character; her prior bad acts would be hidden from the jury unless something happened during trial that, in legal parlance, opened the door. Ev could ask Rita about felony convictions, or misdemeanor convictions for lying and stealing, but there was none, to his knowledge. So what was Avery doing seeking to limit evidence that the prosecution was prohibited from putting in and didn't know about anyway? Something wasn't making sense and he didn't even know what it was that he didn't understand.

Other than hope for a call from Pennsylvania, Ev was as ready as he was going to be. He pulled on his father's overcoat, descended the quiet stairs of the deserted courthouse and entered the biting air of the cold December night. Three patrol cars were parked in the sheriff's lot, all idling and all devoid of occupants. *Is this a rich country or what?* Ev asked himself.

# CHAPTER 36

Wednesday, December 16th

Ev arose early on the mornings of jury trials. Polly did too. She couldn't sleep with his bumbling around, and anyway, the tension in his mood was infectious. The wise course of action, she knew from experience, was to get him on his way. Ev appeared in the kitchen in his blue wool suit, his only winter suit.

"Good luck Ev."

"I'll need it."

Polly kissed him on the cheek as he opened the door. She needn't worry that touching him might elicit a proposition, even though she wished it would. As Evelyn had once observed, men are never too drunk, sick, tired, hungover, or old to want to do it, but preoccupied was another matter. Polly watched through the window as Ev scraped the heavy frost from the Bronco's windshield, and as he turned around and drove down the driveway.

The trial had Polly as tense as Ev, but she was keeping the emotion to herself. He at least could go to court and do battle; she was in the rear where she could do nothing but wait, like Ike sitting in England agonizing for word from Normandy. In the normal course Polly discounted Ev's grousing about work. He was the one who had chosen a small town practice with small town money and then added the unpleasant layer of politics, but this case presented an additional twist. She resented the cold shoulder their friends had turned. Ev was doing the peoples' dirty work, regardless of the personal consequences, not a knight-in-shining-armor routine, but old fashioned duty, and she was proud of him.

Sam could sleep another hour before it was time to awaken him. Polly walked to the living-den and turned on the computer. Quiet time was rare and maybe, provided the jitters in her stomach would subside, something worth typing would form during the interlude. Maybe she should write about a murder.

* * *

Ev sat at his conference table drinking coffee and scanning again each witness file. Additional review was unnecessary; Ev came in early for the last phase of mental preparation, immersing himself in the quiet before the storm. Nothing he had experienced was like jury trial queasiness, but the hour before kick off was close. Ev remembered clearly sitting in the high school locker room, a team of boys, prisoners of their own thoughts, waiting to be told to take the field for warm-ups. The butterflies disappeared when the referee signaled the start of the contest. Likewise, his focus would reach a fine edge as soon as he began questioning his first witness. With mixed dread and anticipation, he wanted that moment to arrive as quickly as possible while, at the same time, wishing the ordeal would go away.

Lewis Brown and Linda Masencup walked into the office together. Brown was as nervous, in his father's words, as a cat in a room full of rocking chairs. Ev waved the lieutenant into the conference room and, without preliminaries, explained Avery's recent motion.

Brown rubbed his upper lip before replying. "When you know it all, sometimes it's best to keep your mouth shut. You had any luck tracking it?"

"I've got calls into Harrisburg. Maybe they'll call today."

"Sorta late."

"We were looking in the wrong place. It wasn't Pittsburg. Why tip us?"

"Beats me Ev. I guess people think that because we're the police, the Force is with us. That we can dig up anything."

"I guess you didn't get my message yesterday?" There was an edge in Ev's question.

"I was working a really bad child molestation. Really bad. I got home at twelve. No use talking about it now. I should be working it this minute. There ain't but one of me."

"Nobody can help you?"

"Everybody's tied up with this trial. Unless you want me to get Wimpie Carson involved."

"Shit no," murmured Ev as he began stacking the folders. "Help me carry this stuff to the courtroom. Then check on our witnesses, make sure they're all here."

The two entered the anteroom and Ev explained to Linda the calls he was expecting. "When you get something, bring a note down and slip it to me."

In silence Brown and Cross walked downstairs and along the corridor to the circuit court. The benches outside of the courtroom door were full. Inside, the gallery was overflowing; those without seats were leaning against the wall. The crowd rumbled in low voices.

Rita's Richmond lawyers were standing at the defense table; Rita was seated. Avery and Mathieson were methodically sorting through files and notebooks while Bledsoe leaned against the chancel rail talking to Hank Burke and Clyde Noble. Wearing his cowboy boots and a gray double-breasted suit, and smiling amiably, Wil looked as if he were passing the time between Sunday School and worship service. It was not lost on Ev that the sheriff had positioned himself on the defendant's side of the room, not as a grim-faced guard, but as a chatty friend.

Bledsoe caught sight of Ev and waved genially. *Nerves of steel or he doesn't give a rat's ass,* thought Ev. The sheriff glanced at Ev and then turned toward Clyde Noble.

Mathieson looked up at the same time. Catching Ev's eye, she arose and started toward him. She wasn't wearing a scarf. "Good morning Ev. Lieutenant." Her voice was formal, just short of officious. "Lieutenant, I happened to be looking through my yearbook. It appears the annual staff were under the impression you were a starting cornerback. Were they as mistaken as I?"

An embarrassed smile appeared on Brown's face.

"I told you about lying," said Ev.

"Okay. You got me," said Brown.

Mathieson kept a straight face. "Why didn't you ask me whether I played field hockey?"

"I'm not that fast on my feet."

"Unless you're in pads?" Mathieson allowed a small smile. "You had me going there for a while, thought I'd offended you. And by the way, I did play field hockey."

The three laughed as inconspicuously as they could manage.

"See Lewis, never try to fool a defense lawyer," said Ev. His smile disappeared. "Good luck Ellen."

"Good luck Ev," said Mathieson as she walked away.

Ev was arranging his files when Roberts and R. C. Hawkes appeared at his side. "Glad you fellas could make it," said Ev.

Roberts didn't smile. "I talked to Linda, dispatch gave me your message to call about an hour ago. That damn Reggie Williams. Got your note on the Harrisburg thing. We were trying to speed up the process, with no luck."

Ev nodded toward the sheriff. "He's planted himself over there. I guess he wants the potential jurors slash voters to see him yukking it up with the enemy."

"I'll take care of that," said Roberts. "Anything you need?"

"No. Anyway. Too late now. I might spring you or R. C. from the witness room to work on the Harrisburg business if I get anything."

Hawkes took a seat along the wall behind the Commonwealth's table while Roberts went over to whisper something to Burke. Burke nodded and left the room through the door leading to the main corridor.

Roberts walked by Ev on his way to take a seat by Hawkes, winking at the prosecutor as he passed.

*Wonder what the hell he told him,* mused Ev.

Okra's booming voice interrupted the crowd's hum. "All rise and give the Court your attention." B. B. Taliferro entered through the door behind Ev as Okra spoke. Okra glanced at the slip of paper in his hand and continued. "The Honorable B. B. Tal-i-fair-o presiding."

Taliferro, his shoulders flinching at the mispronunciation, mounted the steps to the bench and seated himself.

"Take your seats," said Okra.

"Good morning. I'm B. B. Toliver," said the judge in stentorian baritone. He glared briefly at Okra. "Alright Mr. Cross, are we ready for the case of Commonwealth versus Rita Thomasson Noble?"

Ev arose before responding as the press of the crowd required that all formalities be observed. "Yes, your honor."

"Mr. Avery?" asked Taliferro.

"The defense is ready," responded Avery.

Taliferro flipped through several pages of the file in front of him, then, "We'll proceed with arraignment. Mrs. Noble, please stand." The judge read the indictment and Rita responded firmly, not guilty. Taliferro continued with routine questions asked of every defendant and when finished, looked toward Okra. "Bring in the jury."

Okra disappeared through the side door and in several minutes, reappeared leading a long line of potential jurors, forty-five of them. The first twelve were directed into the jury box, and the others into the chairs along the wall behind Ev, and then, after Okra had cleared the first two rows of the gallery, into those seats as well. The displaced spectators piled into the rear of the courtroom along the wall, blocking the front door, and looked at one another quizzically. During the reshuffling a nattily dressed graying man arose from the seats behind the defense table and slid into a chair by Avery. *The jury expert,* thought Ev.

The screening of the jurors began with questioning by Taliferro. The first question was not out of his mouth before crazy Oscar Hogg raised his hand. "Yes sir," said Taliferro.

"I'm hard of hearing," said Hogg.

"What's your name?"

"What's that?" called Hogg loudly, a smirk poorly concealed. There was a titter in the gallery.

"You'll be excused," replied Taliferro in a voice that could have been heard at the Quik Mart.

Question four asked whether the jurors had information of the case from the news media or other sources. More than thirty hands went up. Taliferro finished the question, "Will this information affect your impartiality in this case?"

Twenty-nine heads nodded no. Andrew Reske raised his hand.

"Your name?" asked the judge.

"Andy Reske."

"You don't believe you can set what you've heard aside and decide the case impartially?"

"It's difficult to say. I know Senator and Mrs. Noble personally. And of course, the news can't cover everything. At the beginning of the investigation, when another person was arrested—"

"Thank you Mr. Reske, you're excused," interrupted Taliferro.

Ev glanced at Avery. Whispers were being exchanged at defense table and Ev could guess their concern. They needed only one juror, one Andy Reske, to hang up the jury, or even better, to sway the other eleven. For an instant Ev thought Avery would object, but the moment passed, perhaps in part because Emily Wilko had not raised her hand.

"Is there anyone else who thinks he or she can't be impartial as the result of things you've heard or read?"

In light of Reske's being excused, two other jurors, but not Emily Wilko, expressed their doubts in light of the news coverage in a weakly disguised effort to avoid jury duty. Their efforts were not so successful. Ev put tic marks by their names anyway; he wasn't comfortable with either. Unwilling jurors were lousy jurors. Besides, both were in their twenties.

Ev peered at his jury list. The judge had asked about whether jurors were related by blood or marriage to Rita, and whether the media coverage had tainted their ability to serve impartially. Surely Reske was not the only one of the forty-five who had some connection to Clyde Noble. Noble was not only homegrown, but was the county's state senator. Wilko was obviously hiding the ball, but were others?

Ev wondered whether he was edging toward paranoia. He rationalized that Clyde Noble was far beyond casual contact with the masses and that Rita probably hated them altogether. If Ev were to ask outright whether any of the potential jurors knew the Nobles personally, he would also succeed in identifying the ones who claimed no such relationship, a backhanded way of suggesting to the defense whom to strike. Moreover, the judge would enter the fray, asking the particulars of the relationship, thus giving full vent to Noble's connections to the county, and with no guarantee that Taliferro would excuse every juror who had some connection. Ev decided he wouldn't ask, and the defense wouldn't either. Avery probably assumed that Rita was some sort of local royalty, like a Kennedy in Massachusetts, and the last thing he would want was to cleanse the jury of people who knew the Nobles. Avery needed only one juror, Ev needed twelve.

The opportunity for questioning fell next to the attorneys, the Commonwealth first. He asked whether any of the panel had been represented by the defense lawyers, and a few hands went up. He then asked the nature of the representation: a will, a speeding ticket, a divorce, all by Bledsoe. Ev put a tic mark by the speeder. He asked whether the jurors or members of their families had been prosecuted for a serious offense. Two hands went up. Ev looked at his list.

"Mrs. Snead I believe. What kind of offense?"

"Thelma Snead. My brother is in jail for habitually offending. Not for the first time either."

Ev, sensing a hint of bitterness in her statement, put a tic mark by her name. "And Mr. Thornton?" He was Robert Thornton, the father of Alphonso Thornton, whose murder had never been solved, the murder which in some fashion involved Jeff Junior Smith the third.

"My son was charged with dope," said Thornton.

Ev put a question mark next to his name. There were innumerable Thorntons in the county and this Thornton's significance had not occurred to him when first he reviewed the jury list. He wondered why Gene had not flagged him. Maybe Gene wasn't concerned.

Following two more questions intended to be innocuous, Ev was finished. A third hand went up before Ev could seat himself. "Yes sir?"

"A D.U.I. The way the police acted, I guess it's a serious offense. And my name is Aubrey Campbell, in case you don't remember me Mr. Cross."

"Can you render an impartial verdict in this case?" asked Taliferro.

"Yes sir," answered Campbell crisply.

There were also innumerable Campbells in Lafayette, and Ev did not remember either Aubrey or his case. But Campbell's tone of voice boded ill; Ev put a tic mark beside the name.

Avery then arose and began as Ev had, asking whether any of the jurors had been represented by Ev when he was in private practice. Two hands went up. Both explained that Ev had handled real estate closings for them years ago. Ev had forgotten that he had done so.

Avery asked whether any were related to law enforcement officers. Numerous hands were raised. Avery asked each one about the relationship, and whether he would believe a policeman over the other witnesses.

When Todd Carson was asked the question, he shook his head. "Knowin' my cousin Wimpie, it's probably just the opposite."

There was a murmur of laughter in the gallery.

Avery asked some general questions and then paused when the jury expert pushed a yellow tablet in front of him.

"Have any of you served on a criminal jury before?" Four hands were raised, including Mariah Reynolds's.

"Miz Reynolds?" asked Avery, looking at his list and then at Mariah.

"Yes, and it's Miss Reynolds. I take it you're asking whether I sat in a criminal trial, and not whether all the jurors were criminals."

There was general laughter. Bledsoe covered his mouth with his hand.

*Don't blow it Mariah,* thought Ev.

Avery smiled as best he could; lawyers loathe being corrected in the courtroom. "Yes ma'am."

"Once," said Mariah.

"Did your jury convict or acquit?"

Ev rose to interpose an objection, but Taliferro needed no prompting. "I think that's going a little too far."

Bledsoe leaned forward and whispered something to Avery. Avery pursed his lips, looked at the judge, and announced that he had no other questions.

The clerk reworked her jury list and handed it to Okra who delivered it to Ev. A line was drawn after the twentieth name. Both the defense and the Commonwealth had four peremptory strikes in the twenty and would take turns striking a name.

Ev scanned the twenty. Anna Wilko, Thelma Snead, Aubrey Campbell, Robert Thornton, the speeder, one of the two young people Ev had checked, and one that Roberts had blacklisted were in the twenty. Four strikes and seven questionable jurors. Todd Carson and two other of those related to cops also were in the twenty, along with Mariah, and the two people—middle aged women—that Ev had represented in real estate closings. Ev expected the defense to strike their four from this six. But the first strike was easy: Anna Wilko. He handed the list to Okra who delivered it to the defense table.

The list soon returned. The defense struck a former client. Ev struck Aubrey Campbell. The defense struck Ev's other former client. Ev: one of the young people he had marked. The defense: a well dressed older woman Ev didn't know. The defense was following the rule that women can see through another woman's lies.

Ev lingered on number four. Would Thornton distrust the sheriff's department's work; they certainly failed him with his son's murder. He wished now that he had quizzed Roberts on his objections to the two the investigator had marked. Would Thelma Snead hold it against the prosecutor that her brother was in jail? Ev surveyed the faces of the remaining possible jurors. Roberts's suspect was a young man with scraggly goatee-like-beard—a mangina. Ev struck him.

The defense lingered too over their last choice. When the list returned, stricken was an older woman whose nephew was an Alexandria policeman.

The croupiers were selected. Six women. Six men. Ten white. Two black. Three young, nine old enough.

Why did the defense leave Mariah Reynolds on the panel? Bledsoe, who undoubtedly was a key player in the winnowing process, must have a reason. Ev could ponder that later.

Taliferro swore in the jury and released those who had escaped service. He then called for the witnesses to be sworn. Following Ev's lengthy list, the defense identified Rita, her Methodist minister, a fire company captain, a public health nurse, and a retired school teacher. Rita would testify. Surely the defense would not have her sworn and then have her sit mute. The other four, assumed Ev, were character witnesses. Half the county served in a volunteer fire company and the other half had been taught by the teacher. But what drew Ev's attention was the absence of Clyde Noble. The senator was part of Rita's alibi; what were the defense lawyers thinking? Had Noble insisted on watching the proceeding, which witnesses could not do until released, or was it a tactic: have the county's state senator sitting behind his wife throughout the proceeding. Ev toyed with announcing that Clyde would be a Commonwealth witness, then let the moment pass. Something was afoot and he didn't have time to determine just what.

The witnesses were sworn, instructions given, a brief break taken and then opening statements.

Opening. Every lawyer needed a single simple theme and the theme came first in opening. Ev went first. "The Commonwealth will prove in this trial that Rita Noble murdered her stepdaughter. And for age-old reasons: greed and hate." As he spoke, he turned and gestured, but did not point, toward Rita even as he looked her in the eye, and the jurors' eyes followed his lead. He had read somewhere that the prosecutor in opening had to look the defendant in the eye. Rita didn't disappoint him. She stared back, cold and impersonally, like she was watching a snake she was about to kill.

In the sequence he hoped to follow with his witnesses, Ev told the story of Miranda's last evening, of her disputes with Rita, and of the will. The jurors watched him impassively. When Ev was finished, Avery arose.

"We do not quibble with much of what the commonwealth's attorney says," he began. "This family," he waved toward Rita and Clyde Noble, "has suffered a grievous loss. And at the end, we are confident you will conclude that Rita Noble did not commit this evil crime."

Ev glanced at Paula Noble who was sitting in the gallery. She was staring at the floor, unable to look at Rita's defender.

"This young woman's death came at the hands of someone else. Rita Noble was never at the Noble home that awful night."

As suspected, SODDI and alibi.

Avery continued, mentioning repeatedly the DNA proof of three men's semen. There seemed to be an edge in his remarks, as if the dead girl had asked for it, and Ev wondered whether Avery might be laying it on a little too thick.

Avery finished his remarks and took his seat.

Taliferro looked at Ev. "Call your first witness Mr. Cross."

Ev called the rescue squad chief, Bennie Thomas. He followed with Mervin McIntosh, whose principal job was identifying all of the physical evidence. Seay, next, identified the photographs. Saved for last was the picture of Rita with the folded bathroom towel in her hands. Avery put only a few questions. Even Jeanette

DeWease, the medical examiner, escaped hard questions from Avery. He was saving the big guns for the three degenerates.

Linda Masencup tiptoed to Ev's side during Avery's questioning of DeWease and slid a note in front of him. "Call Daphne Kesserling ASAP," it read. A telephone number followed.

Ev, his thoughts racing, had trouble concentrating on Avery's last questions. He was tense with anticipation when Taliferro dismissed the jury to lunch after the medical examiner's testimony was concluded.

Ev went immediately to his office and dialed Kesserling's numbers. She was at lunch. "Shit. Shit. Shit," said Ev loudly as he banged the receiver down. He was quickly eating a pack of nabs when he tried her number again fifteen minutes later.

Daphne Kesserling was at her desk when Ev made his second call. "What did you find out?" asked Ev.

"Oh, you'll love this," said Kesserling.

Ev had the tingling stomach of a six year old waiting for his parents before he could run to the Christmas tree on the magic morning.

Kesserling continued. "Rita Thomasson was investigated for embezzlement and blackmail. In 1979. She was stealing from a highway contractor whose wife happened to be in the state legislature. State money was involved, it got sticky, and no charges were ever placed."

"What about the blackmail?"

"Her boss, the contractor, failed to observe his marital vows. So when he discovered the embezzlement, Thomasson threatened to tell his wife about their affair, plus, she wanted more money."

"And it wasn't prosecuted."

"Can't tell you why. The district attorney declined to prosecute and the officer closed his file. You're lucky the officer is still a cop." Kesserling gave Ev the officer's name and telephone number. "Hope you can use it."

"You've gone above and beyond the call Miss Kesserling. Whether I get to use it is up to the defendant." Ev rang off and immediately dialed the officer's number, the response was an answering machine. Ev left a brief message and rehung the receiver. "Linda. An officer Kyle Derwinski will probably call. Tell him I must speak to him, so get his day and night numbers." Ev drained a Coke and pulled on his suit jacket. "When you go to lunch Linda, get me a pack of Camels."

Linda's mouth dropped open.

"I know, I know," said Ev. "Can't be helped."

Ev, altering his planned order of witnesses, decided to get through the afternoon without calling Lester Snidlett. Given Avery's tactics thus far, Snidlett would be pivotal, and Ev didn't want the jury to go home that night wondering, after a blistering cross-examination, whether Snidlett was the killer. Better to start

Thursday morning with Snidlett and end the second day with stronger witnesses. Primacy and recency. Follow the experts' rules.

If there were a wild card, it was Jason Thomasson. Jason had some damning things to say, if he didn't hedge. He also could be cast as a possible killer, in the unlikely event Rita would let Avery pursue that angle. But first there was Jeff Junior Smith the third.

Smith, dressed in baggy blue jeans and a loose white tee-shirt bearing a single large black X, front and back, walked to the witness stand as if he were expecting to be knighted. Seated, he glared at the jury, and several jurors, obviously uncomfortable, broke eye contact with him. Ev asked a few introductory questions and then turned Smith loose to tell his part. Smith was cautious, but smug, when he described the trade he made with Miranda. Ev finished with having Smith describe his whereabouts that night, and thinking of no reason to prolong the ordeal, asked no more questions.

Avery was out of the blocks quickly. "You were charged for this murder, weren't you?"

"Yeah."

"In fact, when Lieutenant Brown tried to question you, you took off into the woods, and he had to chase you down."

"Yeah."

"And then the charge was dropped."

"Yeah."

"You could be charged with distributing cocaine."

"Brown said they wouldn't. But, you know, I got to testify."

"So you were let off the murder charge and get a free pass on selling cocaine, if you testify?"

"Yeah."

"Who can say where you were Friday night, after you left Miranda?"

"Some of my associates. Lots of 'em."

"People who buy crack cocaine from you."

"I said my associates."

"Who buy cocaine from you?"

"What difference does that make?"

Taliferro spoke without moving. "Answer the question Mr. Smith."

"Sometimes," grunted Smith. "Whatever. But I didn't kill nobody."

"Sometimes," repeated Avery. "And this girl's murder is not the first one that's led to you as a suspect, is it?"

Ev arose from his chair. "Objection."

Smith ignored the interruption. "Is that a question? Whadya mean, suspeck?"

"Keep quiet Mr. Smith," said Taliferro. "Objection sustained."

Smith looked at the judge. "What's he sayin'?"

"I said keep quiet Mr. Smith," boomed Taliferro. "Ask your next question Mr. Avery."

The damage was done, objection or not. Robert Thornton would fill the jury in on the rest; he would have anyway. Avery seemed to gloat for a moment, then looked at the judge. "No more questions."

"Next witness Mr. Cross," said Taliferro.

"Jason Thomasson."

Thomasson, dressed in a blue blazer and tie, looked like a Woodberry Forest student as he took the stand. Avery was probably responsible for his improved appearance and Ev wondered whether his testimony had been groomed as well. Ev began with questions about Rita's dismay with Jason's interest in Miranda. Thomasson was forthcoming, but contrite, and at times barely audible. When Ev came to the telephone call at the pool, Jason paused.

"Mr. Thomasson," repeated Ev, his voice slightly elevated, "did Miranda receive a call at the pool?"

"I think so. I'm hazy on that."

*The little son of a bitch,* thought Ev. "You mean you can't remember?"

Jason jumped at the opportunity. "Not really."

Ev flipped through Jason's witness folder, pulled out a transcript of Brown's interview with him, and walked to the witness stand. "You remember talking to Lieutenant Brown on October fourteenth?"

"I think so."

"Will you please read this—"

"Objection," said Avery while still seated. "He can't read that to the jury."

"Mr. Cross?" asked Taliferro.

"Had Mr. Avery given me a chance, I was going to ask Mr. Thomasson to read his own statement to himself for the purpose of refreshing his recollection."

"Overruled."

Thomasson silently read the part of the transcript Ev provided him.

"Can you remember now?"

Jason's voice was so low as to be inaudible.

"Speak up," said Taliferro.

"I said not really," replied Thomasson.

*Screw you,* thought Ev. He arose and addressed the judge. "I ask leave of court to examine him as an adverse witness."

"Objection," spat Avery.

*Good. Good,* thought Ev. *Let Avery keep objecting.* The jury always wondered what a lawyer was hiding when there were objections.

"Mr. Cross?" asked Taliferro.

"He's the defendant's brother. On top of that, he's proved himself adverse."

"Overruled. Go ahead Mr. Cross. You may treat the witness as adverse."

With a whipped-dog glance at Rita, which Ev hoped the jury noticed, Jason caved. He meekly agreed that he had made each statement Ev read to him. Ev was careful to include every line using the word fuck that Jason had attributed to Rita. Fuck didn't go over well with juries, and certainly didn't fit the royalty image.

Ev ended his questioning and unconsciously took off his eyeglasses.

Avery arose, positioned himself at the chancel rail, and began asking about each of the police visits to Jason's apartment. Then: "You thought they were going to arrest you, right?"

Jason had no trouble with the volume of his response. "I sure did."

"Each time they came."

"Yeah."

Rita wasn't going to allow Avery to suggest that Jason killed Miranda, but he could continue to paint the investigation as inept and desperate. "You were scared weren't you?"

"I sure was."

"You were trying to convince them, the police, that you didn't do it."

"Of course. I mean, who wouldn't. I was innocent."

"Didn't you realize your statements were pointing the police to your sister?"

"I was scared man."

"Is that why you kept giving the police bits of story at a time?"

"Yeah. I thought it would get them off my back."

"Were you telling the truth?"

Jason looked at the floor. "Rita was just checking on me. She thought they were going to charge me. What I told the cops, I sorta added to it."

"What did you add?"

"Those parts about her saying I was messing everything up. Like I was scared. Rita was scared for me. That's all. This is all my fault." Jason pushed at one eye as if wiping a tear.

Avery seemed content to leave this vague damaging statement to linger in the jury's mind, and he probably had no idea what Jason might say if he pressed him. Avery turned, glanced at the jury, and sat down.

Ev arose with the interview transcript in his hand. "I'll ask again. You said, Rita Noble made this statement: I'm on my way there, and your ass and his ass better not be around when I get to that fucking pool."

"I said that."

"Under the penalty of perjury, Mr. Thomasson, is that what you heard her say?"

"Yes," answered Thomasson quietly.

"You left between eighty-thirty and nine."

"Yes."

"And when you got to your apartment you called Miranda, at the pool."

"Yes."

"When?"

"Nine-thirty. Maybe. Coulda been a little earlier or a little late than that."

"And Miranda was alive."

"Objection," said Avery in a bored monotone. "We've been over this once, on direct."

Ev raised the transcript to shoulder level and then slowly lowered it. "No more questions." He could feel his face flushing and decided it was time to stop. More questioning was not going to improve matters.

"It looks like we have time for one more witness," said Taliferro.

"I call Pepe Lopez," said Ev, wondering at the same time whether Avery and the Nobles had managed to poison his testimony as well.

Pepe stayed the course, however.

Avery asked two questions. "You weren't there after nine o'clock, were you?"

"No sir."

"You don't know what happened after nine do you?"

"No sir."

Ev went straight to his office following the dismissal of the jury. Linda Masencup was gone, but on his desk were Derwinski's telephone numbers and a pack of unfiltered Camels. Ev dialed the first number.

"Derwinski," a gruff voice finally answered.

Ev explained yet again the purpose for his call.

"I was brand new in the fraud unit," began Derwinski. "This guy, Michael O'Donnell, came in with the story that his bookkeeper was stealing from him. O'Donnell was a road contractor and it probably helped that his wife was in the legislature. Mrs. O'Donnell was with him when I interviewed him. Something was fishy from the get-go. Your girl, Rita Thomasson, denied everything. We put our auditors on it and figured she had taken about twenty-five Gs. O'Donnell fired her and she threatened to sue O'Donnell. That's when he 'fessed up to sleeping with her and gave me a tape of a telephone conversation that she wanted ten grand to keep her mouth shut about everything. We were ready to indict her, but the D. A. said no. Mrs. O'Donnell didn't want the publicity. For some reason the state debarred him from road contracts. O'Donnell went belly-up and then his wife divorced him. Just another slice of life."

"We get jaded don't we," said Ev as he lit one of the Camels.

"How can you help it?"

"What was fishy?"

"Just the way Representative O'Donnell was involved. I think she figured it out and pushed her husband into coming to the police. You know, like she knew there was more to it. My bet is the debarment was her handiwork, too. Basically hung him out to dry."

"A woman scorned."

"Yep."

"You still have the tape?"

"Sure do."

"Do you think you could be here on Friday to testify?"

"I'd love to. Thomasson drew the get-out-of-jail-free card here."

"How about O'Donnell?"

"I bet he would, too. If we can track him down. He wanted to prosecute, his wife nixed it. Politics. You know anything about that?"

"Unfortunately, yes."

"Look it. I'll try to find him. Call you tomorrow. Tonight if you're still at the office."

"I'll be here awhile. I can't thank you enough."

"I've been wanting to take a trip south. Good luck."

Ev heard the door closing as he put the receiver down. Gene Roberts appeared.

"Bad day?" asked Roberts.

"Smith was bad.  Jason, well, to use a time-honored phrase, Jason rat-fucked us."

"Okra told me about Jason."

"Yeah. The little snot."

"You weren't surprised were you?"

"I guess I didn't think he'd lie outright. Damn. I forgot to ask him about the time of the call to Tamara Harding."

"Does it matter?" asked Roberts.

"Who knows? I can call him later on if I need that little tidbit, and the phone bill. But let me fill you in on a new twist." Ev explained the story of Michael O'Donnell.

"That's promising. Anything I can do?"

"Not now. I'll keep you posted."

"What about the motion *in limine*?"

"Avery didn't raise it with the judge and there was no reason for me to. It will come up fast enough if this embezzlement stuff surfaces."

Roberts eyed the cigarettes and smiled wryly. "This law enforcement business needs a warning from the surgeon general. See you tomorrow."

# CHAPTER 37

Thursday, December 17th

Okra Alexander called court to order promptly at nine-thirty, and managed this time, under Taliferro's careful scrutiny, to announce the judge's name correctly.

There was still no word from Kyle Derwinski, but Ev could not now worry about that. He called Lester Hester Snidlett as his first witness.

Snidlett entered the courtroom half smiling, half sneering, as if he deserved the attention focused on him. He was dressed in what was probably his only decent shirt, a polyester button-down with too-short sleeves that revealed most of his substantial arm. Tight blue jeans and scuffed cowboy boots rounded out his court attire. Ev walked the witness through his testimony, and as with Jeff Smith, Snidlett seemed to relish telling the jury about sex with Miranda, which the jury couldn't miss, but he didn't stray from what he had told the investigators.

Ev ended his questions with the call Miranda received and turned the witness over to the defense. He had warned Snidlett the week before that the defense lawyers would try to rattle him, and to keep his cool, and he assumed his breath was wasted.

Ellen Mathieson rustled in her chair and then arose. She wore a scarf today.

*What the hell?* thought Ev. *Using the brief bag toter?* Then just as quickly he understood the defense strategy. Their game plan was clear in its simplicity: they would use the pretty young woman to bait Snidlett, to challenge his masculinity, which was his whole world, his only world. Ev leaned back, steepled his fingers beneath his chin, and waited.

"Mr. Snidlett," began Mathieson. "You lied to Investigator Roberts the first time he asked you about Friday night…didn't you?"

"Uh-huh."

"That's yes?"

"Yeah."

"You lied to them right up till they told you they had a match on your DNA, and Sunny quit covering for you."

"I figured they'd just say I did it."

"You were afraid you'd be charged."

"Wouldn't you be?"

"You're the witness Mr. Snidlett. You need to answer questions, not ask them. Now, again, you were scared you'd be charged, right?"

"I won't scared, ma'am. I just figured they'd lay the blame on me."

"You said lights came on at the Noble house, didn't you?"

"Uh-huh. And heard the door slam too."

"But you didn't tell the police that until after they had Sunny's new story and your DNA."

"Yeah. I came clean."

"You came clean when the police had enough to arrest you."

"Okay."

"You heard about the murder didn't you?"

"They said she drowneded at first."

"Later you heard it was murder."

"Later."

"But you didn't call the police. To tell them you were there, that Miranda was alive when you left, and that the lights came on."

"I didn't see nothin' would say who done it."

"You were scared out of your wits."

Snidlett stiffened in the witness chair. "I won't scared. I was nervous."

"Rape with murder carries the death penalty. Good reason to be…nervous."

"Now look. Won't no rape neither." Snidlett was beginning to flush.

"You injured her. You used force."

"Like I told him," Snidlett pointed to Ev with his thumb, "we was drunk and, you know, we won't…we should've been more careful. We tried and it just wouldn't…we couldn't do it."

"More careful? She was passed out."

"No she won't. Now she was drunk. She was drunk-drunk. On that crack and all. That's why I thought she'd drowneded. But she won't passed out when I left. I mean, we was together Wednesday night, and we did it then. So it's like this. What we done Friday was A-okay with her."

"Enough force to tear her flesh was okay with her?"

"You're so sure it was me. How about them other two there before me? One of them coulda done it."

"You didn't tell the police you had that kind of sex on Wednesday."

"Didn't no one ask me."

"You were an angry man when you left there weren't you."

"I won't in no good mood."

"Angry because you couldn't finish the kind of sex you wanted?"

"No. No. Angry cause I had to leave. Not at her. That light and door and all. Angry cause I was goin' home."

"Angry because she'd been seeing a black man, Jeff Smith."

"I didn't know about no Jeff Smith."

"So angry you went home and started tearing up your trailer."

"Sunny jumped in on me, and I was drunk as a fart, and I did lose it. Yes ma'am I did. Ain't no happy place there with that woman when she breaks western.

Anyway what's that got to do with it?" Snidlett was leaning forward, his chin jutting menacingly.

"You've beaten Sunny haven't you?"

Ev started to his feet, his mind racing whether to object.

"I didn't touch her that night." Snidlett's eyes were riveted to Mathieson.

Ev was still rising when he changed his mind. Taliferro would probably allow the line of questioning, and even if his objection were sustained, the jury would likely get lost in speculations about just what badness Snidlett had done to Sunny. Ev lowered himself into his chair.

"You've beaten Sunny other times, haven't you?" continued Mathieson.

"We've got into it before. She gives as good as she gets."

"You beat her October fourth, and that's when she changed her story on your whereabouts for the Friday night of the murder."

"We got into it that night. She was mad 'cause she figured I was with the girl—"

"The girl? Miranda Noble?"

"Miranda Noble. So we got into it."

"And you were charged with assaulting her."

"Yeah."

"For the second time."

"Okay."

"And this second charge is still pending?"

"I reckon so."

"The Commonwealth offer you a deal to testify here?"

"No. I sat in jail awhile."

The question was a cheap shot. The defense team knew that Ev had offered Snidlett nothing on his pending charge.

"And that's when, in your words, you came clean. When nobody was left to cover for you, right?"

"That's right. That's right." So tight was Snidlett's grip on the arm of the witness chair that his fists were bone-white. Snidlett continued, his voice loud. "Nothing left to do but tell 'em what happened. And then some fancy lawyer tries to make it out I killed her. Well no damn way." He was leaning forward rigidly as he finished speaking.

Mathieson walked briskly to within an arm's length of Snidlett. "Were you angry then, when you couldn't force yourself on her, like you are now?"

His eyes bulging, Snidlett's lips quivered as he tried to answer.

Taliferro's voice interrupted like rolling thunder. "Please stand back and give the witness room Miss Mathieson."

"I won't angry about her Miss—whatever your name is."

"Mathieson," she responded as she stepped back. "Do you have trouble remembering women's names?"

Ev arose quickly. "Objection."

"Sustained," said Taliferro.

Mathieson walked to the defense table and positioned herself behind her empty chair. Avery handed her a sheet of paper, and after she had scanned it, she looked back at Snidlett. "Do you remember talking to Sergeant Seay and Lieutenant Brown on October fifth?"

"No. Talked to 'em so much I don't know a date."

"But you talked to them?"

"Guess so."

"Let me show you this." Mathieson handed him the transcript of Brown's and Seay's interview with Snidlett while he was in jail. "You can read can't you?"

"I can read," answered Snidlett sullenly as he took the papers.

When he was finished Mathieson started again. "Brown asked, did you do any other things, sexually, with Miranda. And you said no, she passed out. Did you say that?"

"I mighta."

"Five minutes ago you said she wasn't passed out."

Snidlett twisted in his chair. "She won't. I told 'em that."

"The next day, your story changed, when Lieutenant Brown asked you about anal intercourse, and you said she was passed out. And you got tired of waiting. So you were pissed off and tried it. Would have done it but for hearing the door slam. Your words, right?"

Snidlett breathed deeply and looked at Mathieson. "Look. She was so drunk she was like being passed out. And we done that thing the night before, so I just tried and it didn't work."

"Well what's the truth Mr. Snidlett? What you said on October fifth or October sixth, or when Roberts first interviewed you, or what you're telling the jury today?"

"I was drunk. She was drunk. I ain't got no crystal clear memory of anything."

"Do you remember how she was smothered?"

"That's another fancy question—"

"Mr. Snidlett," began Taliferro, booming, "Just answer the question."

"She was laying there drunk as a coot and alive when I left. Read that from those papers. 'Cause that's what I told 'em. Read that."

"Brown asked you, you were forcing yourself on her while she was passed out. And you said yes, she wouldn't have known."

"If that's what I said, but she won't passed out. She was drunk-drunk."

"I don't have any more questions, your honor," said Mathieson. She sat down and glanced sideways at Avery's pleased smirk.

"Mr. Cross?" came Taliferro's quick response.

The lecture circuit experts would say that Ev needed to ask more questions to take the sting out of Mathieson's cross-examination. Rehabilitate the witness. As far as Ev was concerned, he stood a better chance of walking onto the Tennessee football team than he did of rehabilitating Lester Snidlett.

"Mr. Cross," repeated Taliferro.

*Oh hell. Here goes.* Ev leaned forward. "Mr. Snidlett. Did you rape Miranda Noble?"

"No suh."

"Did you kill Miranda Noble?"

"No suh."

"Has my office cut you any deals on this charge Miss Mathieson mentioned?"

"If you did, nobody told me."

"Did Miranda receive a call while you were there?"

"From that other guy."

"Are you telling the truth?"

"Yes suh. Now that lie-detector—"

"Objection," shouted Mathieson and Avery simultaneously.

Snidlett glared at the defense table. "They callin' me a liar and—"

"Keep quiet," said Taliferro in a menacing growl. "Ladies and gentlemen of the jury, no testimony regarding a lie-detector—polygraph—is admissible, one way or the other. You must disregard any reference to one." He looked at Avery before continuing. "Do you need a moment?"

Ev knew what the judge's question was about. He was giving the defense team an opportunity to request a mistrial: stop this one and start over with a new jury. There was no analogy to the misfortune of a mistrial although Bledsoe had come close by comparing it to *coitus interruptus*.

Avery huddled with Mathieson and the Nobles. When his whispered explanation was finished, Clyde Noble shook his head promptly and emphatically. Clyde was as anxious as Ev to bring the ordeal to a final conclusion.

Avery pursed his lips and paused. Then, moving slowly, he arose. "We're ready to continue your honor."

Ev wondered if the jury could hear his sigh of relief.

"Mr. Cross," said Taliferro.

Ev thought as quickly as his jumbled thoughts would allow. The jury might just think that Snidlett had passed a lie-detector test. It was senseless to try to improve on that possibility. "No more questions."

"Mr. Snidlett, you're excused to the witness room," said Taliferro.

The jurors, their chins tucked against their chests, watched Snidlett from the top of their eyes as he walked heavily away from the witness stand to return to the witness room. The Commonwealth's case was at its nadir, and everyone in the courtroom knew it. Ev concluded that his guess about the polygraph slip was sadly misplaced.

Taliferro broke the auspicious silence left when Snidlett passed through the side door. "We'll recess for ten minutes."

The jury arose and began filing out of the courtroom through the same door. Ev, the defense attorneys, and the Rita Noble stood as the jurors departed. Standing for the jury was a tradition, whose origins were lost, which recognized that the jurors once sworn were the judges of the facts and entitled to the same deference as the robed figure behind the bench.

Ev walked quickly out of the courtroom in route to his office. He was at his desk lighting a cigarette and looking through his pink message slips when Paula Noble walked in.

"Ev," she said quietly.

"Yes." Ev looked up.

"It's not going well is it?"

"No. It's not." His voice was flat. Discouraging observations from the gallery were certainly not going to be of any help.

"Is there anything I can do?"

Ev shook his head. "I wish there were. You heard Snidlett. Do you believe him?"

Paula looked at the floor. "Just listening, I find it hard. But if that big logger got angry, and was raping her too, he'd leave some bruises.  And DeWease said there was none."

"That's my view, too," said Ev. "I hope the jury is thinking along those lines."

"I hope I didn't bother you. Keep up the fight." Paula left as quickly as she had appeared.

Ev walked into the anteroom. "Linda, any call from Pennsylvania?"

"Nothing."

* * *

Taliferro's lips were bowed impatiently as Ev quickly entered the courtroom. "Okay sheriff, *now* you can bring in the jury."

The courtroom waited in silence for the jury. Several minutes elapsed without their appearance. Some juror had probably settled in on the toilet.

Taliferro was slowly rocking in his chair when the jury finally filed in. "The jury are present," he announced. "Call your next witness Mr. Cross."

"Manfred Fitzgerald."

Fitzgerald entered the room dressed in a flannel shirt as orange-red as his hair. He smiled at the judge and jury as he took his seat. "Whew, hot in that waitin' room," he said to no one in particular.

Ev needed Fitzgerald for two simple points: that Snidlett had been in his store the night of the murder and to identify the cash register slip which listed the time of the purchases as nine-fifty-six. Given these simple facts and with the crush of the abrupt trial date, Ev had not interviewed Fitzgerald.

Fitzgerald was a harmless witness and Ev doubted that the defense would have any questions. He was wrong.

Mathieson, fresh from drawing Snidlett's blood, arose from defense table. She began with general questions about Fitzgerald's store hours and whether the cash register accurately recorded time. She smiled and Fitzgerald smiled back. No harm was done. Then she paused, and while looking at the jury, asked, "Wouldn't you say he was a little too intoxicated to be buying beer?"

Fitzgerald turned a little redder than his normal crimson. Selling alcohol to a drunk customer was a violation of his ABC license, although routinely done, and it was clear to Ev that Manfred erroneously feared that his testimony could get him into trouble. Mathieson was setting him up to prevaricate.

"I wouldn't say so. I mean, he didn't look that way to me. Now he'd had something to drink, but I, you know, couldn't tell how much. You know, some people are different. Alcohol does 'em differently." Fitzgerald had tried to ramble his way out of the question and Ev doubted that the jury was fooled.

"But you wouldn't sell to him drunk would you?"

"Oh no ma'am. Lose my license."

*Well done,* thought Ev. *She's set him up for something. The jury knows Snidlett was drunk.*

"Did you two chat for a few minutes?"

"I'm not…I don't know. Probably. He's a regular."

"I don't want you to speculate."

"I'm sure we talked."

"Anything in particular?"

"He was his regular self. Jokin' and callin' me Red Man. That's an old nickname that just won't go away." Fitzgerald smiled nervously.

Ev scanned Brown's notes in Fitzgerald's witness file. There was nothing about any conversation. *Damn Brown,* thought Ev. *Where's this going?*

"So he was his regular self?" repeated Mathieson, a hint of disbelief in her voice.

"Yep. Said he needed beer cause he was going home to his old lady and you had to be drunk to put up with her."

"So he wasn't drunk…yet?"

"Not that I could tell."

"And he was joking and his regular self."

"Sure was."

"And you two are pretty good friends."

"Well, I've been knowin' him since grade school."

"And you're good friends."

"I guess you could say that."

"And you found this cash register slip on October twenty-first…two months later."

"Sounds right." Fitzgerald's eyes suddenly widened as if he were just realizing what Mathieson was doing to him. "I got a right sloppy accounting system. Oughta check it more often."

"Nothing further," said Mathieson crisply.

Ev stared at Fitzgerald's blood red profile. Mathieson had taken a neutral innocuous witness and nailed him to the wall. There was nothing to do but push the envelope. "Mr. Fitzgerald, there's been prior testimony that Lester Snidlett was drunk and angry just before he—"

"Objection," interrupted Mathieson brusquely. "He can't start characterizing—"

"Miss Mathieson," interrupted Taliferro, drowning her voice. "I don't need a speaking objection. What are the grounds?"

"Characterizing prior testimony, your honor," said Mathieson.

"Mr. Cross?"

"Let me rephrase your honor. Mr. Fitzgerald, Snidlett didn't tell you where he had been?"

"No sir."

"And, at the time, you knew nothing about Miranda Noble and him?"

"Still don't know much."

"So you don't know what he was up to, or how he was acting, before he got to the store?"

"No way I could know."

"Was he in the store long?"

"No sir. Walked in. Got beer. Sorta chit-chat while he's doing that. Don't have his money. Signs the printout. And leaves. I was ready to close up, so, you know. It wasn't long."

"How'd you find the receipt?"

"About once a month I go through the box—it's a cigar box—and see who needs prodding. He came in and I said to him, what about this beer receipt. And he lit up like a Christmas tree and said the sheriff's department needed it. So he paid it and took it."

"Did he say why the sheriff's department needed it?"

"Just said they needed it. And I'm thinking why in the world do they want a beer receipt?"

"When did you find out the receipt was involved with this murder case?"

"When Joe Lewis Brown came to talk to me a couple days later, after I gave it to Lester Hester. I mean, he didn't say exactly what it was about, but I gotta general idea."

"You knew Miranda Noble."

"Yes sir."

"Just before she was killed, did she try to make purchases with checks?"

"Yes sir."

"Would you take them?"

"I did. But they started bouncing. And the Nobles would cover 'em. Then Mrs. Noble—"

"Objection," said Mathieson quickly. "I'd like to be heard outside of the jury's presence."

Taliferro pursed his lips and looked at Mathieson a moment before responding. With the jury positioned in front of the bench, there was no place for the lawyers and the judge to whisper—a sidebar conference. Taliferro arose and pointed to the side door. Mathieson, Avery, and Cross followed.

In the hall outside the door, Taliferro spoke. "Okay. Where's this going Mr. Cross?"

"Mr. Fitzgerald will say that Mrs. Noble told him that the Nobles wouldn't be covering anymore of the victim's checks. Goes to the defendant's state of mind and attitude about her stepdaughter, motive."

"Miss Mathieson?" asked Taliferro.

"It's irrelevant. Also, he's introducing new material on redirect," answered Mathieson.

"Objection sustained," said Taliferro. "Now let's go in and move this along."

Ev reentered the courtroom with is teeth tightly clenched. Maybe he should have asked the question during direct examination. Maybe Bledsoe's prediction about Taliferro was again proving itself. In any event, he couldn't end his questioning on an objection.

"How far is your store from the Nobles?"

"About two miles."

"Do you know where Hester Lopez lives?"

"Yes sir. He's about a mile from the Nobles."

"No more questions." Ev jotted a note to himself to ask Rita about the checks assuming she testified. He glanced at his witness list. Sunny Grogan was next, yet Ev was having second thoughts. The jury had heard a steady stream of battered witnesses, Ev needed to turn the tide before they gave up on his efforts. "Call Juanita Lopez," said Ev.

Juanita required an interpreter which made questioning miserable. Ev kept it simple, eliciting that she had seen a silver sedan turn into the Noble driveway. She volunteered that it was shortly after nine, and Avery, fumbling back and forth through the interpreter, could not shake her.

Next was the dealership rental manager who explained that the Nobles were lent a silver LeSabre, and in two days put two hundred sixty-one miles on the odometer. Avery asked no questions, and from the corner of his eye, Ev saw Mariah Reynolds and Robert Thornton leaning forward, their interest piqued, and both undoubtedly performing mental mileage calculations: Richmond to Onan was almost exactly one hundred miles.

Trooper J. M. Gregory was next. Three more jurors perked up when he testified that only miles from the exit to Onan, traveling toward Richmond, he had given Rita a speeding ticket at ten-twenty-one. Avery, again, asked no questions. Ev studied the poker face of the defense team. They couldn't deny that Rita was on the road from Onan; they were conserving their ammunition for a different front.

Clara Wood followed Gregory. Ev had her explain how Miranda had reentered her father's world and then began guiding her through her observations of Rita Noble's reactions. The old woman spoke quietly, toying with a handkerchief, and though she occasionally glanced at Ev, most of the time she stared at the floor in front of the jury. Ev then asked about the will.

"Will?" she repeated.

"Did Mrs. Noble mention a will?"

"She done more'n that. She fussed after Mr…Senator Noble a lot. Girl already got too much of his money. He needed to be doin' for his own chil'ren, which was her two."

"What did Mr. Noble say?" asked Ev, refusing to refer to him as Senator.

"Objection," called Mathieson. "Hearsay."

"Let me try it another way," said Ev. "When was the last time you heard the Nobles argue about the will?"

"Objection," said Mathieson again, "there's no evidence of arguing."

"Mr. Cross?" said Taliferro.

"I'll lay a foundation, your honor. Did the Nobles argue about the will?"

"Objection," said Avery yet again. "Leading."

Taliferro spun a pencil in his fingers. "Overruled."

"Did they argue about the will?" repeated Ev.

"Oh yes sir. More'n too many times."

"When was the last time they argued?"

"Thursday. That's when Miz Noble changed the burglar 'larm numbers."

"Who had the new numbers?"

"Mr. Clyde, Miz Noble, and the two little chil'ren, but they can't remember it."

"Did Miranda have the new combination?"

"Objection."

"Miss Mathieson," said Taliferro impatiently, "she can testify to what she knows. And you may cross-examine."

Clara looked at Rita Noble before continuing. "She couldn't. She didn't come there after it was changed. Except Friday, when nobody was there."

"The lights on the terrace. Where are the switches?"

"In the dining room and kitchen."

"If you're standing at those doors, can you see the pool?"

"Plain as day."

"Did you find a towel missing from a bathroom, after Miranda…was killed?"

"Yes sir. The downstairs one. When I come Sunday evening."

Ev walked to a table positioned under the window behind him and retrieved the towel. "Was it one like this?"

"Yes sir. That's a downstairs towel. Each bathroom's got its own color towels. And that's downstairs."

"Wouldn't be at the pool?"

"No sir. Miz Noble won't allow it."

Ev paused for a moment. "Were there any towels at the pool on Friday? This one or any other?"

"No sir. I collected the pool towels to wash and was going to put 'em back down there later. Miz Noble wants 'em washed every Friday even if nobody don't use 'em."

*Here goes,* thought Ev. *I hope she'll say the hard part.* He looked at Clara steadily as he spoke. "Why would you check the downstairs bathroom for towels?"

"I'm always checking everywhere 'cause Miz Noble would blame—"

"Objection," called Avery, rising to his feet.

Taliferro leaned forward in his chair. "Mr. Avery. She is going to testify. Go ahead Mrs. Wood." The Judge liked the old woman.

"Miz Noble would blame me for stealin'. Anything gets misplaced, I'm the first one she blames. And I never took anything from anybody."

Ev glanced at Robert Thornton from the corner of his eye. Thornton's jaw was set, and when Clara finished speaking, he cast a cold glance at Rita Noble.

Ev paused a moment to let her answer have its full effect. Then, "Mrs. Wood. Tell us about Wednesday."

"That last Wednesday. Mister Clyde was gone. And Miranda was asleep. And Miz Noble just went up and bust in the room. I was in the chil'ren's bathroom. And she called her terrible things."

"What did Mrs. Noble say? Use the words. We've heard them."

"I prob'bly shouldn't say 'em in here."

Taliferro spoke quickly from the bench. "It's alright Mrs. Wood. Tell us what was said."

Clara drew a long breath. "She said, get up you…f-ing whore. Go somewhere else to steal money to buy drugs. Go whore for it. Things like that. Her last thing, made me almost cry, was, I never wont to see you here again." Clara wiped the corners of her eyes with her handkerchief. "And she didn't, not after that awful Friday."

Ev looked at Clara steadily in the silence that followed. He knew, and she knew, that her employment was finished. Rita plowed through people's lives as if they were dirt, getting the chaff, stubble and everything else under and out of her way. The courtroom was no place for a lawyer to succumb to emotions, but Ev was having difficulty suppressing the anger rising within him.

"Those are my questions," said Ev softly.

Avery arose and buttoned his coat in one polished movement.

"You were quite fond of Miranda, weren't you?" he asked.

"Yes."

"You were hurt that Mrs. Rita Noble didn't share your affection for her."

"I didn't understand it."

"Miranda didn't like her stepmother did she?"

"I don't think she did."

"That day they argued, Miranda cursed her stepmother back didn't she?"

"Yes," said Clara quietly. "It was awful."

"You'll have to admit that Mrs. Noble had been putting up with some bad behavior wouldn't you."

"Sometimes."

"But Miranda was still welcome there anytime wasn't she?"

"Until that Wednesday. Seemed like Miz Noble took the last straw that day."

"You didn't happen to leave that towel at the pool did you?"

Ev looked at Avery while awaiting Clara's answer; another trap was unfolding.

"No sir."

"Didn't you expect Miranda to sneak over with the Nobles away?"

"I didn't study on that."

"But it was possible."

"Yes."

"One more thing. Have you ever been convicted of lying, or cheating, or stealing?"

Ev's eyes jerked away from his notepad. What was this? Why ask the question and get a resounding no unless they knew something Ev didn't?

Clara looked at her lap. "I been convicted of something. A bad check. Two of 'em."

Ev had not checked Clara's criminal history; he had no reason to suspect that she had ever been in a criminal court. Ev looked at Bledsoe who was studying the floor at this feet. *The sorry bastard. He probably represented her; that's how they knew.*

"Two bad check convictions," repeated Avery as he seated himself.

Ev didn't wait for Taliferro to turn the witness back to the Commonwealth. "How long ago was that Mrs. Wood?"

"Twelve years. Happened when my husband was dying of cancer. I just got down and didn't know how to get up." A tear rolled down her check after she answered. "I paid 'em though."

Ev glanced at the jury. The other black juror, Edna Wilson, pushed a tear from the corner of her eye. Avery had made a monumental error; instead of rendering Clara's testimony unworthy of belief because she had criminal convictions, he had needlessly humiliated a gentle old woman and earned himself at least one enemy on the jury.

"Twelve years ago," repeated Ev. "Nothing else."

"You're excused Mrs. Wood," said Taliferro softly before looking at the wall clock over the side door. "This is a good time to break for lunch."

* * *

Ev hurried to his office, as anxious to dodge the lurking press corps as he was to check his telephone messages.

"You have calls," Linda answered his query, "but not the two you wanted."

Ev ignored the pink message slips, lit a Camel and opened a pack of nabs. His thoughts turned to Roberts and Brown, who, in the foregoing order, would be his last witnesses. At this point his preference for calling Roberts last didn't jibe with the evidentiary sequence. Their job was to paint Rita as a liar. If their efforts failed to sway the jury, then the rest of the trial would be a massacre.

* * *

"Call Investigator Roberts," announced Ev once court was re-assembled.

After Roberts identified himself, Ev asked his favorite question. "How long have you been in the business of law enforcement?"

"Twenty-nine years, this month."

* * *

It was almost four o'clock when Roberts was called to testify. Ev had changed his order of witnesses and Brown was all but certain that he would be the prosecution's last witness, the end-on-a-high note witness. He knew the principal goal of Roberts's and his testimony: discredit Rita by laying out her evolving story. Though it seemed much longer to Brown, Roberts was on the stand no more than thirty minutes.

"You're up, Lewis," said Roberts when he reentered the witness room.

Brown looked at Roberts quizzically, expecting some bit of advice, or forewarning, but Roberts said nothing as he re-took his seat and picked up the novel he had been reading. Brown straightened his tie for the hundredth time and chastised himself for the apprehension enveloping him like pre-game jitters, yet the tension tenaciously resisted. His stomach was aflutter when he took the witness stand.

"Tell the jury your name and position, please," said Ev.

His official title still being somewhat fluid, Brown paused before answering, and was certain he must look like he was floundering with the simplest question he would hear. Then, "Lewis Brown, Lieutenant, Lafayette County Sheriff's Department."

After the introduction Ev guided Brown sequentially through the lieutenant's investigation. The interviews, the video tapes, the hotel bill with the telephone call, and lastly, the final confrontation with Rita Noble. *Smooth as silk,* thought Brown, pleased with his efforts.

Mathieson arose when Ev stopped questioning.

"Lieutenant Brown," began Mathieson. "You arrested Jeff Smith for this murder didn't you?"

Ev, stating the obvious, had told Brown to be prepared for this question, and Roberts had admonished Brown to admit no error when giving his response. The wrong man was arrested and jailed; Brown hadn't quite decided how to finesse that one.

"I arrested Jeff Smith," answered Brown.

"The arrest, of course, was an error."

"At the time there was no error. Later, we learned that Mister Smith could not have committed the crime," Brown thought he had handled that question faultlessly.

326

"At the time, there was no error. Later you discovered he was not the murderer."

"Later we discovered evidence that exonerated Mr. Smith." As an afterthought Brown added, "We discovered he was a witness."

"So as I understand it, evidence before you can lead you to, let's say, the wrong conclusion."

Brown was not going to dance around the bitter pill any longer, Roberts be damned. "The evidence I had then led me that way, and it turned out to be wrong. The main thing was that Smith took off when I tried to talk to him about Miranda. Of course later I learned he had cocaine in his pocket, which is probably the reason he ran."

"It took you several weeks to realize the error."

"That sounds right."

"He was arrested September seventeenth."

"I think so."

"And the charges dropped September twenty-eighth?"

"That sounds correct."

"Rita Noble was indicted on November twenty-fourth."

"Yes."

"You were the lead investigator after Gene Roberts's heart attack on September twenty-sixth."

"With Special Agent Hawkes, yes."

Mathieson walked to her seat at counsel table and whispered something to Avery. Brown sat rock still. He hadn't missed the analogies she was drawing. The questions about the time needed to discover and rectify the mistake were expected; but he hadn't prepared himself for the possibility that Mathieson would make it personal, tying his mishandling of Smith with the potential for his mishandling of Rita Noble.

Finished with her whispering, Mathieson looked back toward Brown. "Three men told you they were at the Nobles' pool the evening Miranda died."

"Yes."

"The semen from each man was determined to be present in Miranda."

"Yes."

"Each man denies killing her."

"That's correct; and our evidence—"

"Just answer the question lieutenant," interrupted Mathieson. "Mrs. Noble never admitted to being at the pool."

"She—"

"Yes or no."

"No. She did not."

"And you don't have one witness who saw her there?"

"Not alive," said Brown, regretting the quip but not being able to restrain himself.

Mathieson maintained an innocent calm during the pause that followed. "How long have you been in law enforcement, lieutenant?"

"Three years."

"Three years...that's all I have, your honor." Mathieson spun smoothly toward the jury, glanced at them, and took her seat.

Brown was seething that Mathieson had attacked him professionally. Local lawyers never called a cop's abilities into question, at least not while he was on the stand; lawyers had to live with the police just like they had to live with the judges and the other lawyers. Mathieson would be back in Richmond Friday night, and as likely to see Halley's Comet twice in her lifetime as she was of seeing Brown on the stand again. He bit his lower lip and looked at Ev, wondering what would follow on redirect.

"Mr. Cross," said Judge Taliferro as he glared at the clock on the wall.

"One moment, your honor," answered Ev, scrambling to devise a few questions to soften Mathieson's parting shots.

"It's late Mr. Cross. We need to move along."

"Where'd you go to college, lieutenant?" asked Ev.

"William and Mary."

"And your major?"

"Psychology."

Ev arose and walked toward the witness stand. "Did you interview Juanita Lopez the first time?"

"No sir. Investigator Roberts did."

"He doesn't speak Spanish."

"No sir."

"Do you?"

"Yes sir."

"Is that when you learned of the silver car going into the Nobles?"

"Yes sir."

Ev hoped that Brown knew where this was going. "Was that a turning point in your investigation?"

"Very much so."

Brown, Ev sighed to himself, had not missed the opening.

"Did something about hillbillies come up during your investigation?"

Mathieson and Avery both looked at Ev quizzically. Bledsoe hid a smirk with his hand.

A thin smile appeared on Brown's taut face. "Mrs. Noble told Jason that we hillbillies would give up on the case sooner or later."

Mathieson and Avery both jumped to their feet, but before they could object, Ev announced firmly, "the Commonwealth rests."

Mathieson's effort at "objection" was drowned by Taliferro's voice. "The Commonwealth has rested. The jury is excused until tomorrow at nine-thirty."

* * *

Ev made straight for his office to escape the reporters who wanted a couple of sound bites for the late news. Among the pink message slips, most of which listed a reporter, Ev found Michael O'Donnell's name and number. Ev lit a cigarette with one hand as he dialed with the other.

"This is O'Donnell," answered a reedy voice.

"Mr. O'Donnell, this is Evander Cross, prosecutor in Lafayette County, Virginia...."

"Yeah. Mr. Cross. Kyle Derwinski told me what you wanted. I'm going to be up front. I'm not getting involved again with that bitch, now or ever."

Disappointment froze Ev's tongue.

"I'm sorry Mr. Cross. But she wrecked my life and my business. And my ex wouldn't let her be charged. You know about the ex-Mrs. O'Donnell? She's still trying to be Congresswoman O'Donnell."

"I can't say as I blame you," managed Ev in resignation.

Roberts and Brown appeared at the door and Ev waved them in.

O'Donnell continued, "Can you get by with Derwinski as a witness? He knows it all."

"I'd need you both," answered Ev. "Can you give me the details?"

"Sure. She was stealing. And while she was stealing, we were having an affair. I began to expect an embezzler, but not that she was doing it, so I got the police involved. Their investigation led straight to her. That's when she decided to try to blackmail me. Well, as luck would have it, she was taking money from a little fund that I used to grease some skids. You had to with state contracts. So I was jammed up and my ex put two and two together. Her career was more important than mine. So I got screwed. A little tail cost me, probably, ten million dollars. I mean, you can tell. All this in court won't help, and Rita'll probably figure some way to stick it to me again. I'll look like the crook. I sub with a trucking business now, hauling gravel. My dear wife finished me with state contracts. I can't get wiped out again."

"I understand Mr. O'Donnell. I'll manage without you. Thanks for the call."

"No problem. I hope you convict the little bitch."

Ev rang off and looked glumly at Brown and Roberts. "I won't get anywhere with the Harrisburg stuff. It was a long shot anyway."

"Any better today?" asked Roberts.

"We looked a lot better in the stretch," answered Ev. "You two and Clara Wood were welcome relief after dealing with those three shits."

"You ought to be in the witness room with them," said Brown. "Smith and Snidlett both think they know it all and that damn Poochie Essex wouldn't shut up."

Roberts grunted and nodded his head.

"By the way," continued Brown. "Thanks for giving me a shot after Mathieson's questions. Damn, she was heartless."

"That'll teach you about pretty smiling lawyers," said Roberts. "She buttered you up with that football stuff and was plotting the whole time how to bust your ass wide open."

"You told Gene?" asked Ev.

"Oh yeah," answered Brown.

"You'll be happy to know Lewis, that Mathieson barely questioned Gene. That twenty-nine years of police experience kept her in line."

"So the trick is, I gotta live long enough to look like I know what I'm doing," said Brown.

Roberts stood and spun the diminished pack of Camel's lying on Ev's desk. "Anything we can do?"

Ev shook his head. "Nothing more I can do about our evidence now. Just try to figure out what Rita will say, if she says anything. That, and sketch my closing argument."

"Good luck," said Brown as he left the room.

Gene nodded his farewell and followed the Lieutenant.

Ev picked up the telephone and called Derwinski's number. There was no reason for the police officer to come to Virginia if O'Donnell wasn't going to testify.

* * *

Polly was half asleep when Ev came to bed. She felt a pat on her lower back. "Goodnight," she murmured.

"Goodnight," he replied quietly.

330

# CHAPTER 38

Friday, December 18th, a.m.

Cross looked at the poker faces of two of the opposing Richmond counsel while the courtroom awaited Taliferro's appearance. Bledsoe was leaning over the gallery rail, whispering and smiling with Angela Keating. Serenely self-confident in a dark blue wool suit, Rita sat motionless at counsel table. Several seats away in the row behind counsel table was Clyde Noble. Would she testify, Ev asked himself for the hundredth time. The Commonwealth's case was rattled, but Rita's lies to the police were unexplained and damaging. Avery might well take the easy route and deny the jury an opportunity to hear her and Ev the opportunity to cross-examine on her conflicting stories. After all, the duchess did not have to prove her innocence, Ev had to prove her guilt. And regardless, with Michael O'Donnell's decision, there was no hope now that Ev could put the Harrisburg shenanigans before the jurors. Rita would be polished, perfect, pristine—the consummate practiced bitch.

Taliferro appeared and took his seat without glancing at Okra who had now mastered the judge's name. With the jury seated all eyes turned to the defense table. Ev expected the defense to begin by calling the character witnesses.

"Call your witness," grumbled Taliferro.

"We call Rita Noble," answered Avery.

*I'll be damned,* thought Ev. Feeling Bledsoe's gaze, Ev involuntarily looked at the cowboy-booted lawyer at the end of the defense table. Bledsoe cocked the corner of his mouth in a half smile and then raised his eyebrows.

*What does he know?* thought Ev.

Rita walked to the stand, was sworn, and seated herself erectly behind the witness podium.

Avery asked no preliminary questions, such as her name. Instead, "did you kill Miranda, Rita?"

*Cute,* groused Ev. *Everything cozy and personal.*

"Absolutely not," answered Rita quietly, slowly and with the intonation that she was holding back a tear just for being questioned on such a ludicrous proposition.

"What did happen that night?"

Rita waded in, moving straight to the telephone call.

"Why did you call Miranda, Rita?"

"A premonition, a feeling. Call it what you will. Something wasn't right."

"Did you say the things your brother testified to?"

Rita sighed and carefully paused before answering. "I spoke to Jason, not Miranda. I was angry with him. I told him he'd better not be there." Rita looked at each juror in turn as she answered. "Clyde and I were very upset that the young people would use our home when we were away. I was furious he thought so little of me that he'd ignore what we'd asked. So I, without stopping to think about it, went straight to the car and started for Lafayette County. It was my home—my home."

*You can't hide all of it can you Rita?* thought Ev.

"And then what did you do?" asked Avery.

"I drove to my home in Onan."

A pin dropping would have sounded like cymbals.

Avery turned and looked in the direction of the window behind defense counsel's table.

Ev could feel his eyes bulging. Surprises in the courtroom were as commonplace as flatulence on a boys' camping trip; this went beyond surprise. There was little wonder that Avery had averted his face from Ev, the jury, and the judge. Given Avery's opening statement, Ev harbored no doubt but that Rita had sprung this newest story on Avery at the last minute, probably this morning, giving him no time to develop a strategy. Then Clyde Noble caught Ev's eye. The senator's mouth was ajar, his flesh ashen: she was telling him for the first time.

Avery kept his gaze on the window. "What did you find?"

"I saw Jason's car in the driveway, and Miranda's, too."

"And then?" asked Avery.

"So I parked and walked to the pool. Miranda was lying on a beach lounge, with a towel on her face. Jason was sitting at the pool edge. Oh my God I… I must have yelled, and he looked up, like he was waking up. And he said she's dead. His speech was slurred so I knew he was drunk. And then he said—I couldn't say a word—then he said she'll never cheat on anybody again. Then he got up and half-staggered past me and I tried to grab him and he pushed past and ran to his car and left." Rita dabbed at her left eye with a Kleenex she had conveniently produced from somewhere.

Rita continued. "I ran to the lounge and pulled the towel off and shook her. I felt for a pulse, but I knew there was nothing I could do. And then I panicked. I was there with my dead stepdaughter that my brother had just killed." And on she went. Panic, fear, anxious to cover for her brother. Agonizing over her dishonesty with the senator. Lying to the police. Until today, when the evidence forced her to tell the truth, else face the prospect of being in prison, away from her children for a crime she did not commit.

"How did Miranda end up in the pool?" asked Avery.

Rita managed a quick sob, one Ev hoped seemed as orchestrated to the jury as it was to him. "I…I was trying to protect Jason. I hoped, I thought it would look like she drowned. He's my brother." She covered her mouth with the tissue for a moment before erupting into a flood of tears.

Ev cast a glance at the jury. They were watching her carefully, their faces a cipher. Were they buying the lie? Why was Rita fingering her brother, why not Snidlett? The only explanation Ev thought plausible was that blaming Jason gave her an excuse for her string of canards, and an explanation for not reporting Miranda's death immediately; she could exonerate herself and still have an angle to play with Clyde Noble: cover all the bases, except Jason's.

Avery looked at Taliferro. "May we have a moment, your honor?"

The judge nodded his head, his face, too, expressionless.

Ev looked past Rita, over Avery's shoulder, at the wall behind defense table. Colonel-judge-delegate Alexander Spotswood Dickson, one of Alec Dickson's ancestors, sternly peered back at him from his portrait on the wall. To the left of Colonel Dickson was a window, then the likeness of Ev's great-great-grandfather, William Cross. Something beyond the window was amiss. From his vantage point, this window framed the flag pole at the edge of the courtyard. The American flag didn't look right—the stars were in perfect vertical alignment. A gust of wind rippled the flag open.

*No way,* thought Ev. *I'm in a time-warp. How the hell did a forty-eight star flag get there?*

The diversion was brief. Rita took a deep breath, dabbed her eyes, and looked up. "Thank you Mr. Avery."

Avery managed to focus his attention directly on his witness. "Did you call Jason when you and the senator returned?"

"I did. I finally got my wits together and wanted an explanation. He was crying and pleading for me to protect him. And I said I would if he told me the truth. He said he had been to my house to see Miranda. They fought at the pool, over her drug problem, and he left. He got to his apartment and turned around to come back, to make up."

*She's too clever by half,* thought Ev.

Rita was picking up steam. "He arrived and walked around and up on the terrace and saw that awful Snidlett person on top of her, just as he said. Snidlett got up suddenly, like he'd seen Jason, pulled up her bathing suit bottom, and left in a hurry. Miranda moaned, like she was calling a name."

*She's about to slip into the first person,* mused Ev.

Avery seemingly reached the same conclusion. "And what next did Jason tell you?"

"He said he was frozen, then he just went mad. He ran down yelling at her, but she just moaned something he couldn't understand. Then he heard her say something about Lester. He grabbed the towel and…and, that was the end."

"Was the towel from a bathroom?"

"Yes."

"How did it come to be at the pool?"

"I have no idea. I suspect Clara left it there for her."

"You didn't go inside the house?"

"No."

"Were the lights on, on the terrace?"

"They could have been. I…my attention was elsewhere."

"Have you told your husband all this?"

Ev watched as the jurors looked toward Clyde Noble who was seated in the row behind defense table. His hands hung loosely between his legs and his eyes were fixed on the floor.

"I couldn't. I've hurt him and I'm sorry."

Ev rolled his eyes toward the ceiling.

"I have no further questions," said Avery.

Barely twenty minutes of testimony from the defendant and now it was Ev's turn, with his meager cross-examination plans in shambles. The obvious former plan of attack was to ask Rita about each variation and contradiction of her stories to Roberts and Brown. He had expected the Avery team to blunt, pre-emptorally, the edges on many of them; but Rita's tearful confession today had swept that table: everything was a lie to protect Jason and she was more than happy to keep repeating the excuse.

"Mr. Cross," said Taliferro.

"May I have a few minutes," said Cross, trying to buy time while he struggled to devise something to ask. Scanning his notes, it struck him that Rita had testified to no times. Avery had avoided the topic too, and for the obvious reason that Rita's new story didn't mesh. Cross wasn't the only lawyer who had made a time line. He could only imagine Avery's consternation upon being informed by Rita—mid-trial—of an entirely new story.

"Mr. Cross," snapped Taliferro.

"Yes your honor, I'm ready. Mrs. Noble. You agree you left Richmond at seven-thirty-eight."

"I wasn't aware of the time," answered Rita coldly.

"You have no reason to dispute the videotapes."

"I have no reason."

"You arrived at your home after nine."

"Mr. Cross, I wouldn't know."

"Mrs. Lopez saw your silver Buick turn in at that time, correct?"

"She said that, yes."

"You were stopped for speeding at ten-twenty-one."

“Yes.”

“You would agree you left your house ten to fifteen minutes before the police stopped you?”

“Probably.”

“And you got to the hotel at eleven fifty-one.”

“Yes.”

“So you were there, at your house, about one hour.”

“I wasn’t there that long.”

“Forty-five minutes.”

“Probably.”

“Where else did you go?”

Rita eyed Ev coldly. “I didn’t go anywhere else.”

“So you’re there from about nine-fifteen until ten, ten-o-five.”

“I suppose so. Yes.”

“You didn’t see Lester Snidlett.”

“Most certainly not.”

Ev glanced at the jury. Mariah was pushed back in her chair as if trying to put as much space between Rita and herself as she could manage. Thelma Snead and Edna Wilson, seated beside one another, were unflinching in their attentiveness.

“Jason was staggering drunk.”

“He had too much.”

“And you saw him leave, say, nine-twenty?”

“Once again, I have no idea.”

“So he was there, what, five minutes, with you.”

“If that.”

“Jason leaves at nine-twenty.”

“He must have,” answered Rita irritably.

Ev glanced at his time line. Jason made his call to Tamara Harding at nine-forty-one, information Ev had forgotten to put into evidence when Jason testified. How could Rita be ignorant of this? Surely Avery had gone over the evidence with her before trial. Was Mrs. Rita Noble so arrogant as to think the call unimportant, or had she forgotten about it when Ev neglected to have Jason tell about it? Maybe Ev was lucky, and lucky was better than good.

“You’ve been to Jason’s apartment?”

“Of course.”

“At least a forty minutes, probably forty-five minute drive?”

“I think so,” answered Rita. “But I have no idea how fast he was driving.”

“Let me get this straight. Jason told you he left, went to his apartment, came back, found Snidlett there, killed Miranda, then left again?”

“That’s what he said Mr. Cross.” Her words were cold and clipped.

"He left at nine-twenty."

"Asked and answered," objected Avery.

"Move along Mr. Cross," said Taliferro.

"And got home in time to call Tamara Harding at nine-forty-one," continued Cross.

Rita's face darkened, her eyes blinked, and then: "I couldn't tell you. I don't know who called who at nine-forty-one."

"Jason testified he left between eight and eight-thirty."

"He wasn't being truthful."

"Pepe said Jason left at eight-thirty, is he lying?"

"You're putting words in my mouth. Jason left and came back."

"You heard Lester Snidlett say he was there an hour or more, until almost ten?"

"Mr. Cross. He's a drunken liar."

"Mr. Snidlett lied about being there?"

"He obviously doesn't remember when he was there, so he's making the times up."

"If Jason left at eight-thirty, he would get home at nine-fifteen, correct?"

Rita did not answer.

"If he turned around immediately and came back, he would get to your house around ten."

"I don't know," answered Rita in a low voice

"Well, if you left there at ten or ten-o-five, and you were there forty-five minutes, then you arrived at nine-fifteen."

"I couldn't tell you."

"And Jason could not have been there."

"Jason lied to you and to me. All I know is that he was there when I got there. Maybe he didn't go to his apartment."

"Was Manfred Fitzgerald lying about Lester Snidlett being at his store just before ten?"

"I wouldn't know."

"Was Clara Wood lying when she quoted you as calling Miranda a fucking whore?"

Rita turned a steely gaze on Ev before answering. "I didn't say that."

"That Clara was lying?"

"I didn't call Miranda those words."

"Was Clara lying when she said you said you never wanted to see Miranda again?"

"I never said that...to Miranda."

*Keep going Rita,* Ev cheered himself. "Was Clara lying when she testified that you argued with your husband about the will?"

"We didn't argue. I questioned whether Miranda would be responsible with so much money."

Ev retrieved the will from the table behind him. "Never argued. Is this the will?" He held it up for Rita to see.

"I wouldn't know."

Ev walked toward the witness. "Please look at it then."

"I think I've seen this but I certainly haven't read it," answered Rita, after flipping quickly through the document.

Ev paused momentarily as he took the will from Rita's hand. "Well here, on page three—"

"Objection," interposed Avery. "She just said she's never read it."

"Mr. Cross?" asked Taliferro.

"I withdraw the question. Mrs. Noble, did you know that Mr. Noble intended to leave two-hundred fifty thousand outright—"

"Your honor," interrupted Avery.

"This is cross-examination Mr. Avery," replied Taliferro. "Go ahead Mr. Cross."

"Mr. Noble intended to leave her outright a quarter million…" Ev liked the twist of using million instead of thousands, "as well as a one third interest in a two million dollar trust?"

Rita glanced at her husband, who by now was watching her with lifeless eyes. "That sounds familiar," she answered quietly.

"And that left you with only a little more than five million? In today's money."

"I'm not sure."

"And you weren't happy, were you?"

"I was afraid she'd misuse it, hurt herself."

"With drugs."

"I had every reason to think that."

"Mrs. Wood said you wanted it all for your children."

"Mrs. Wood, as you can gather, doesn't like me. I never said that."

Clyde Noble's jaw trembled, the only sign that he was alive.

Ev glanced at the jury. Mariah Reynolds was now watching Clyde Noble with equal intensity.

"And Jason was lying when he said he went home while Miranda was still alive."

"Yes Mr. Cross. He was lying. I can't blame him. Of course he would—"

"Your honor," spoke Ev firmly, "please instruct the witness to limit her response to my questions."

"Just answer the question," replied Taliferro, weariness creeping into his voice.

"Yes," said Rita.

"Jason, Pepe, Snidlett, Fitzgerald and Mrs. Wood, either lying…or mistaken?"

"I can only tell you what I experienced Mr. Cross. I simply don't know why the others have said what they said."

"Except Jason."

"Except Jason."

"Because you caught him red-handed."

"Yes," said Rita.

"And until today—this morning—you were covering for him?"

"Yes. A decision I regret." Rita looked toward Clyde as she spoke.

The salient question returned: why sacrifice Jason when, with a few twists to her tale, Rita could have pointed the finger at Snidlett? Was there something else, something Rita wasn't saying or that Ev was missing? With Rita's fertile imagination he could not violate lawyer rule number one: don't ask the question unless you know the answer. Then again, maybe this story was the essence of Rita Noble. She could kill her stepdaughter and then offer up Jason for the noose, and not miss one night's sleep, but that was closing argument material.

"And Mrs. Noble." Said Ev. "You lied every time you spoke to the police and to your husband."

"I explained, already—"

"You lied."

"I was trying to protect Jason."

"You lied."

"Objection," came Avery's voice. "Asked and answered."

"Overruled. She hasn't answered," said Taliferro.

"You lied," repeated Cross.

"I had to," answered Rita menacingly.

Ev couldn't resist the next question. "To save Rita Noble and her fortune." Their eyes locked.

Rita faced Ev squarely, "How dare you say that, you…you insignificant…." Her mouth remained open for a moment, then snapped shut.

Ev didn't blink, allowing the silence to accentuate her response—and resisting the urge to bait her further.

The quiet seemed to agitate Rita. She looked back at the jury. "I didn't know what else to do. What would you do? What would anyone do?" She sobbed softly.

"And today, you're the only person telling the truth."

Her sobs replaced by a venomous curl to her lips, Rita faced Ev. "I'm telling the truth."

Ev paused for a moment. He couldn't think of anything more to do with the change of story, yet he sensed that he had not inflicted the necessary damage. He had never been able to dunk a basketball, and just now, Ev wondered if he would ever be able to grab the jugular in cross-examination. He was out of safe questions and concluded he'd better observe lawyer rule number one. "I have no other questions your honor."

Avery arose, buttoning his coat.

Ev wondered what the other man could ask; Avery was equally ignorant of how Rita might answer a question, so redirect damage control was risky business. Lawyer rule number one was hobbling the other team too.

Finally. "Mrs. Noble," Avery, probably unconsciously, had abandoned the informality of addressing her as Rita, "Mr. Cross has suggested all these times to you. Were you checking your watch?"

Rita shook her head slowly, "Of course not. It's all a blur."

"Do you know, from your knowledge, what time you found Jason at the pool?"

"No Mr. Avery."

Avery sat down and glanced at the yellow pad in front of him. "I have no other questions."

"Mr. Cross?" asked Taliferro.

"No questions," answered Cross.

In quick succession Avery called the minister, the retired teacher, the nurse and the volunteer fire company chief to answer mechanical questions about Rita's reputation for truthfulness and nonviolence in the community. Ev had no way to attack their testimony, so he asked nothing. Instead, he used the time to think through how he would question Jason Thomasson when he called him as a rebuttal witness. Rebuttal evidence could be counterproductive. For one thing, the jury had heard both sides' evidence and didn't need to be bored with anything repetitive. For another, rebuttal often called for questioning on matters Ev had not covered with the witness, thus trenching on lawyer rule number one. And most importantly, Jason was a pissant; he might be incapable of the indignation necessary to satisfy the jury of his innocence.

Avery rested after the fire chief's glowing endorsement of Rita Noble. Apparently the only thing she hadn't done was rescue a blind child from a burning house.

"This is a good time to break for lunch," said Taliferro.

Ev gathered some of his notes and promptly left the courtroom. In his office, with a cigarette and a Coca-Cola, he mentally sketched his questions for Jason—Jason would be his only rebuttal witness. Avery would probably have a field day revisiting Jason's evolving story to the police, but there was no choice.

# CHAPTER 39

Friday, December 18th, p.m.

"Call Jason Thomasson," announced Ev once court had reconvened.

Jason entered the courtroom cautiously, looking pale and for all the world like he was the guilty one, and Ev felt a cold foreboding as he watched him. Once on the stand Jason glanced first at Rita, then toward the prosecutor. Ev began by carefully retracing Jason's timing of events: the easy part. Then, after a pause, Ev redirected his efforts.

"Did you see your sister that night?"

Jason looked up at Ev questioningly. "No."

"Did you return to the Noble home after leaving at around eight-thirty?"

"No."

"Your sister said you killed Miranda. Did you?"

Ev had his eyes riveted on Jason. He wanted to watch the jurors' reaction too, but couldn't do both. The silence in the courtroom told him that every ear was carefully tuned.

Jason jerked his head to face Ev. "Say what?" Just as quickly, he then turned his head the other way to look at Rita. She met his confused eyes with a cold, determined stare. The head pivoted back to Ev. "No way Mr. Cross."

"She said you left, came back at nine-fifteen—"

"Objection," interrupted Avery.

"Overruled," answered Taliferro quickly.

"—when she got there, you were there and told her Miranda was dead, and the next day you told her you killed her." Jason had turned gray. *Damn him,* thought Ev, *he looks like he did it.*

Jason snapped his head in the direction of Rita. "Did you tell them that?"

Rita's shark eyes did not blink.

"Answer Mr. Cross, Mr. Thomasson," boomed Taliferro.

When Jason's head pivoted back to Ev, the gray was replaced with a deep flush. "That's totally bull shit. She's set me up. She's knows I didn't kill her. I wasn't there. She wanted me to help cover it up, now I know why. That's why she told me it was my fault. That's why she told me to keep quiet. To set me up." Jason was breathing deeply when he sputtered to a halt.

"Who is Tamara Harding?" asked Ev.

"A girl I used to date."

"Did you call her that Friday night?"

"Yes."

"Long distance."

"Yes."

Ev arose and handed the telephone bill to Jason. "Is the call on this bill?"

"Yes."

Ev handed Jason a pencil. "Circle the call. What time did you make it?"

"Says right here. Nine-forty-one."

"How long does it take you to drive from the Noble home to your apartment?"

"Forty-five minutes or more." Jason then glanced back at his sister, shook his head, and returned his attention to Ev.

"Did you leave your apartment after that call, and go back to your sister's?"

Jason's jaw was set. Ev had not thought him capable of such determination.

"Absolutely not. I mean, if…I don't know what all she's said, but it's totally wrong. I thought I was helping cover for her. She was the one acting so weird. That's what I told Brown. I mean at first, I don't know, but later I got suspicious. But she's my sister…was my sister. Now I'm totally convinced."

"Objection your honor," said Avery.

Taliferro answered in a low voice. "Don't give opinions Mr. Thomasson. The jury will ignore the opinion of the witness."

"The statement you gave Brown about Rita Noble's calls to you were truthful?"

"Yeah. Absolutely. I know I didn't tell everything at first. I mean, Rita had me scared. Like I was going to be charged. But you had so much. Finally I just told what I knew. That's why she told me to keep my mouth shut. That I'd fuck up everything. Her words, not mine."

"Two days ago, under oath, you had trouble remembering these statements to the police?"

"I know. I didn't have trouble, I remembered it all. But I thought I was helping Rita. So this is my reward. Those big dollar lawyers and her set me up and screwed me, just like she screwed that contractor up in—"

Avery and Mathieson lurched to their feet, "Objection!" erupting from both of them.

"Remember that Rita?" asked Jason facing his sister.

"'Mr. Thomasson," said Taliferro.

"Broke it off in him too," continued Jason.

Taliferro picked up the gavel, for the first time, and banged it as if driving a nail. The jury and everyone else in the courtroom jumped at the explosion. Okra's right hand reflexively went to his holstered pistol. The clerk was almost beneath her desk when she realized the noise came from a gavel and not a gun.

"Mr. Thomasson. One more unnecessary word and you will be held in summary contempt and jailed. Is that clear? Is that clear Mr. Thomasson?" Taliferro's voice could probably be heard in Hogantown.

"Yes sir," answered Jason firmly.

"Your honor," said Avery in a plaintive voice.

"Do you want to be heard on this?" asked Taliferro, looking at the defense table.

Ev doubted that Avery wanted to say much, further comment would emphasize the outburst, and the most that he could expect from Taliferro was another cautionary instruction to the jury.

"No judge," responded Avery after a moment's hesitation.

Taliferro then addressed the backs of the twelve heads sitting in front of him. "The jury will disregard the witness's statement about other events at other times. It is not evidence and may not be considered by you. Proceed Mr. Cross."

"You weren't there at nine-fifteen?" asked Ev.

"I was probably almost home. You said this little Mexican boy saw me leave."

"Did you call Miranda?"

"Yeah. Shortly after I got home. She really blasted me. So I called Tamara. Got blasted by her too."

"And you didn't kill Miranda."

"No. That's a lie. Her lie." He looked back at Rita as he finished his answer.

Ev looked toward Taliferro. "Nothing else."

Mathieson took the floor for the defendant. With painful accuracy she retraced every variation Jason had given the police. "Even two days ago," she continued, "in front of this jury, you changed your story."

"I shoulda said I remembered everything."

"Didn't you change your story just a few minutes ago?"

"I told the truth."

"On Wednesday, you told the jury that this was all your fault didn't you."

"Alright, I said that. But I… it wasn't. I was trying to help Rita on Wednesday. I didn't know whether she did it or not. And maybe it is my fault, if I hadn't come to the—"

Mathieson cut him off. "The bottom line is that you say whatever you need to when you need to."

"Her saying I did it is what I get for trying to help her, and do what she says."

"You caught Miranda with Lester Snidlett didn't you?"

"I don't even have a clue who he is. Not until this trial."

"Miranda said some awful things to you that night."

"Okay."

"And it made you angry."

"I know that. Like. I called her some things too and left. Then I called to apologize."

"That's what you say, you have no witnesses."

"Ask Mr. Cross. That Snidlett or whoever he is was there when I called her."

Mathieson paused. The changing story was good stuff, but she was making little headway with Rita's new theory, and Ev sensed that she wanted to find a graceful way to end the questioning. For that matter, like Ev, both Mathieson and Avery seemed anxious to bring the matter to an end. Bledsoe was nonchalant, there was nothing he could do and he knew it.

"You didn't tell the police and Mr. Cross about that call until months later, when you were suspected."

"I know. That was dumb."

"Just another little curve ball."

Jason shrugged his shoulders.

"I have nothing else," said Mathieson.

Ev had no questions and with Jason's reinforcement of Snidlett's earlier testimony about the call, no more witnesses. It was over. Once again Taliferro sent the jury to their holding pen while he took up the matter of instructions with the lawyers. Most of the gallery occupants filed into the hallway, a few went outside to smoke cigarettes in the cold December afternoon.

"Are we ready for closing arguments?" asked Taliferro once the instructions to the jury were completed.

The closing argument Ev had written the night before was useless now in light of Rita's changed story. He would have to shoot from the hip, and his accuracy was pretty poor from that angle.

Taliferro answered his own question. "It's late, so I'll give you ten minutes."

Most legal pundits and all of Hollywood—with the exception of Perry Mason—seemed to think that closing argument was a trial's pinnacle. Ev didn't buy the theory. Jurors were human and had heard three days of testimony; he could not accept that each juror's mind was a slate full of dots awaiting a crafty lawyer's words of wisdom to make the connections. Nevertheless, it was foolhardy to assume anything.

The ten minutes seemed like ten seconds. Taliferro reentered, took his seat and called for the jury. When the latter had settled Taliferro looked at the commonwealth's attorney. "You may argue the case Mr. Cross."

Ev positioned himself in front of the witness stand, several feet from the rail separating the jury. His only prop was his time line, annotated with Rita's version of the facts.

"Thank you ladies and gentlemen. It's been a long three days. You're tired, I'm tired and they're tired." Ev gestured toward the defense table. "My remarks won't take long." The latter statement might not be accurate, but it gave the jury hope. "This case, like so many, boils down to one issue: credibility. Who's telling the truth? Do you believe Rita Noble? If you do, you must believe all the other witnesses are lying. I want to compare what they've had to say." Ev then began to trace the events as presented by his witnesses, carefully listing the time each had given. A poster size rendition of his time line would have been helpful, but he had decided not to prepare one since the shifting sands of trial might render it useless. He now regretted the decision.

He then turned to Rita's timing of events. After listing them, he paused for effect; then, "Mrs. Noble's story leaves no time for Lester Snidlett to be at the pool. Jason left around eight-thirty, unless both Pepe and Jason are lying, and, according to Mrs. Noble, he was there again shortly after nine. Even if you accept, as her story would have you, that Snidlett rode around for an hour after leaving the pool and before going to Manfred Fitzgerald's store, when could he have been at the pool? Is Snidlett lying or is Rita Noble? And how could Jason have left after nine-fifteen and been at his apartment at nine-forty-one to make a telephone call. And is it reasonable to believe that Jason Thomasson, just finished with killing one girlfriend, would speed to his apartment—fly is more like it—to make a telephone call to a former girlfriend? To give himself an alibi? Mrs. Noble said he was staggering drunk. A staggering drunk devising such an alibi? Is Jason lying or is Rita Noble? And what of the towel? No one could get in the house but Mr. Noble, Mrs. Noble, and Clara Wood. Is Mrs. Wood lying about the towel, or is Rita Noble?"

Ev was trying to move his concentration from juror to juror, their attention was thoughtful, but not rapt. He lingered with Edna Wilson as he spoke of Clara Wood, and received from her a barely perceptible nod. *I've got one,* he rallied himself.

"So why would Rita Noble lie? Because she was finished competing with her stepdaughter. Miranda was sharing her home—remember the defendant's words, it is my home—and someday she would be sharing part of Clyde Noble's millions, a small part. She made it clear to Miranda, as Clara Wood said, that she didn't want to see her again. She made it clear that Miranda shouldn't receive one dime. She was consumed with greed and it turned into hatred.

"Then on the last day of trial, Mrs. Noble changes her story. You remember Mr. Avery's opening remarks, that the defendant was never there. Not only does she change her story at the last minute, but she lays the crime on her own flesh and blood. What could be more telling? What could be more revealing of her venal, corrupt absorption with herself? What could better explain the remorseless heart and mind that compelled her to kill her husband's daughter? Kill Miranda and let Jason hang for it.

"That's the essence of it. The Commonwealth's witnesses corroborate one another—like pieces of a puzzle fitting together. A few pieces are missing, but you know what the picture is. Rita Noble's pieces don't fit, they can't. So is Rita Noble lying, with every reason to, or is everyone else? I ask that you return a verdict of guilty."

Ev knew he had concluded abruptly, but the words ran out and it was better to stop than to fumble around trying to talk for the sake of talking. No sooner was he seated than a tumble of things he should have mentioned rolled through his thoughts.

Taliferro wasted no time. "Mr. Avery."

"Yes your Honor, Miz Mathieson will address the jury," answered Avery.

*One last stab at peeling away the women,* thought Ev.

Ellen Mathieson, in a dark gray skirt and jacket, projected a Puritan austerity. She arose with a determined air and took the center before the jury. Speaking without either notes or pause she attacked the recollection of each Commonwealth witness, saving her harshest words for Lester Snidlett and Jason Thomasson.

Then she shifted focus. "Mr. Cross asked the question, why would Rita Noble lie? The question is, why did she lie to the investigators? The answer is human nature. Fundamental human nature. Her brother had murdered her husband's daughter. Rita put it best—what else could she do. Torn between her husband and her own brother, she tried to protect both. Was that a mistake? Yes. In hindsight, most assuredly, yes. But she acted from the heart. She could not bring back Miranda, but possibly she could save Jason from prison. Her conscience, either way, would be her tormentor."

The corner of Ev's eye caught Mariah turning her head to look at Clyde Noble. He was not watching Mathieson; his eyes seemed to be trained at his feet. The mention of his status as husband elicited one twitch of the jaw, and nothing else.

Mathieson continued in this vein for several minutes. Then, for the first time, she paused, walked in front of the jury box and stopped so that she was positioned between Rita Noble and the jurors. "The sheriff's department went through three suspects before settling on Rita." She pointed toward her client with an open, supplicating hand. "Those three changed their stories and are not charged. Rita, foolishly protecting her brother, stuck by him. Would we be here today if she too had changed her story, and provided the police with the truth about Jason? We would not. Ladies and gentlemen. Someone murdered Miranda Noble. It wasn't Rita."

Mathieson had not reached her chair when Taliferro spoke. "Rebuttal argument Mr. Cross?"

Ev toyed with using this last chance to revisit the things he had forgotten to address initially. He glanced at the jury. Most of the jurors were looking at their feet or studying their watches. They had heard enough. Few lawyers still breathing would miss the opportunity to have the last word, but today Ev elected to be one of the few. "No further argument your honor."

* * *

It was four-fifty-two when the jury filed out of the courtroom on their task of deciding Rita Noble's fate.

Ev remained standing after the jury departed, stress and tension draining from him like water through a sieve. There was no more he could do. Suspense was the only emotion remaining. Roberts and Brown joined Ev at the table as Taliferro declared court in recess.

The investigator and lieutenant, having first heard of Rita's changed story during closing arguments, looked at Ev expectantly.

Ev read their minds. "Yeah. She put it on Jason. Even Clyde Noble, I'm sure, didn't know she was going to spring that one."

"I think you got her on the times," said Brown, his youthful confidence genuine.

Roberts grimaced. "We started out with a tough circumstantial evidence case and it's still circumstantial. The jury could go in there and say, we can't be certain."

Ev took off his glasses and rubbed his eyes. "No eyewitness and no confession. It's no great leap for them to decide no one will ever know for sure what happened, and when they do that, it's over. They don't even need to believe Rita to acquit."

"They need to believe she's a liar," said Roberts.

"Anybody taking any bets?" asked Brown.

Ev smiled. "It's over." He turned to Roberts. "I've been meaning to ask you Gene, how'd you get the sheriff out of here Wednesday morning?"

Roberts replied. "A call came to dispatch before I left for court. A tree fell on Conway Lawson."

Ev's eyes widened in surprise.

"You didn't know?" asked Roberts.

"I haven't been keeping up with current events this week. Is he okay?"

"Well, he died yesterday."

"Damn. Poor bastard. The occupational hazard of cutting wood."

"Anyway," continued Roberts, "when you pointed out Hank's little lovefest with Clyde Noble, I decided to tell him about it and suggested he make an appearance at the hospital to show his sympathy, and pretend there was nothing blatantly political about it. Poor old Conway, he couldn't even fell trees in the right direction. The sheriff ordered the courthouse flag delivered to the family for the casket. Hank lost interest in this trial as soon as his opposition disappeared."

Ev motioned to the window framing the flag pole. "Check out the replacement."

Brown and Roberts looked without recognition.

"Forty-eight stars," said Ev. "Who's responsible for that?"

Roberts laughed. "The janitor, he handles most of the executive decisions around this place. Only in Lafayette County."

"Man," said Brown. "This is like one of those old *Twilight Zone* shows."

"Listening to Rita was *Twilight Zone* material, too," said Ev. "I'm going to my office."

* * *

Polly regretted buying the boys Pokémon cards. Will was too young to grasp the nuances of the game and, in consequence, lost to Sam in every bout. Unbeknownst to Polly, until this afternoon, the stakes in each game was one of the loser's cards. The fight erupted when Sam snatched a Squirtle which Will was unwilling to part with regardless of the bet. Will, leaning forward over the space between the two boys, was using both hands to grapple with Sam's card-filled left fist.

"Moron!"

"Cheater!"

Polly was one step away when Sam's right hand darted toward Will's head, and in the coordinated twinkling of a Three Stooges' act, slammed his brother's forehead into the floor. Will's head ricocheted off the floor like a basketball; dazed from the blow, his mouth fell silently open. Sam was a breath away from re-administering the punishment when Polly caught his arm and yanked him to his feet. "Go to your room."

Sam backed carefully away, his left fist still clutching his Pokemon cards. "I told him," he said quietly.

Will's shriek deteriorated into long sobs as he rocked back and forth, his hands clutching his head. Polly pulled him to his feet and guided him to a chair. "Sit down," she said. "Let me look at you." A goose egg was forming on his forehead. "You probably have a concussion. Just sit here."

Polly filled a plastic bag with ice and gave it to the moaning child to hold to his head. She was walking toward the telephone, intending to call the pediatrician's office, when the machine rang. Ev's office number was on the caller ID.

"Yes," she answered.

"The jury just went out," said Ev.

The crisis of her moment prevented Polly from questioning Ev as she would have. "Then it's almost over. If we're not home when you get here, it's because I've taken Will to the doctor. Sam slammed his head onto the floor."

"Stitches?" asked Ev.

Ev's diffidence was irritating. "No Ev. Maybe a concussion."

348

"I don't know how long they'll be out."

"I'll handle Will, Ev. So don't worry. Good luck."

Polly rang off and then dialed the pediatrician's office.

* * *

Ev lit a cigarette, annoyed that there was a budding crisis at home and there was nothing he could do to help. At this point there was nothing he could do about anything. He paced the office until the cigarette was a nub. He was at his desk when Paula Noble entered the office.

"You did everything you could, Ev," she began. "What do you think they'll do?"

Ev arose as she spoke. "Sit down Paula. And thank you. As for the jury, I don't have a clue. I never do."

"For what it's worth, I thought it sounded like the giant lie it was, especially after what her lawyer said in the beginning."

"I guess that's what we're pinning our hopes on."

There was a brief silence before Paula spoke. "There is just you here, I mean, you and your secretary."

"We are it."

"I don't know how you do it. There were three lawyers on the other side."

"But only one can talk at a time."

A smile brightened Paula's wan face. "Well, I guess that's so." Arising from the chair, she continued. "What do you do while you wait?"

"Wait," replied Ev. He tried to return her smile.

"Thank you again Ev. You did a good job, whatever happens."

Ev nodded in response as Paula left his office. Doing a good job, even a great job, was absolutely meaningless if the result were defeat. He lit another cigarette to ease the butterflies, but it didn't help. When the cigarette was spent he ambled down to the hallway outside of the courtroom. Bledsoe was holding forth from one of the benches with Okra Alexander. Bledsoe waved Ev over.

"I was just telling Okra about the time poor old Conway Lawson fell asleep in a jury trial and started snoring. He always served as bailiff in a jury trial so he could be seen by all the voters, bless his heart."

"That's bad about Conway," said Ev.

"Let's go see Taliferro," said Bledsoe.

Swapping stories with the judge and other lawyers while awaiting the jury was a time-honored occurrence in small courthouses. The tradition was the last of the front porch rocking chair conviviality that existed before judges closeted

349

themselves in the locked and guarded chambers afforded by the new courthouses in sprawling impersonal suburban counties.

Taliferro was drinking a Coca-Cola when the two entered chambers.

"Think we'll finish tonight, judge?" asked Bledsoe.

"Unless someone has a mighty good reason, we are going to finish tonight," answered Taliferro. "The jurors no more want to come back tomorrow than I do."

"I wanted to turkey hunt in the morning," said Bledsoe.

"Don't let us stand in the way," answered Taliferro. "That was awful news about Conway Lawson."

"It was," agreed Ev.

Taliferro pushed back in his chair and smiled—for the first time thought Ev—before speaking. "Conway, just elected sheriff, was a character witness for your deputy in that murder trial Wil. And you asked whether he was aware of the deputy's reputation as a peaceable, law abiding citizen. And Conway looked at the jury and said 'the onliest time I ever saw the defendant really angry was when his wife was with someone else.' Jury still acquitted."

And so the conversation went until Ev realized that he was hungry and excused himself to buy a Coca-Cola to wash down a pack of Nabs.

At eight-thirty the judge ordered supper for the jury from the General Lafayette Inn. Ev walked over to the sheriff's department and listened to Brown and Roberts complain about Wimpie Carson. Roberts borrowed one of Cross's cigarettes and promised that he wasn't going to ask for another one. Ev and Roberts debated whether long deliberations suggested a conviction; they agreed that a quick verdict almost always meant acquittal. Matters were well beyond the quick verdict stage, but the passage of time didn't encourage them: the jury could be in the process of hanging.

Ev returned to his office and looked through his pink telephone message slips. One was from Glenn Apperson and contained Linda's note that Glenn wanted Ev to call after the trial dust settled. He was at his desk at eleven-forty reading three days' mail when Okra Alexander stuck his head in the door. "They've got a verdict."

Ev drew a deep breath. This was it: the scorecard on three days of work, winner takes all. Pulling on his blazer he eyed the pack of cigarettes. There wasn't time for one. There was something about a verdict that isolated Ev, leaving him with the sense that he was the only person in the world. He felt utterly and singularly alone; he couldn't imagine what the defendant must be feeling, and didn't care.

He walked briskly to the courtroom. Even at this late hour—eleven-forty-nine—there were still people moving to the gallery: most of the reporters, Paula Noble and her sister and mother, Clyde Noble's mother, Rita's minister. Rita Noble and her entourage filed in after Ev. Roberts was placing deputies around the room for security. Except for the minister and police, not one witness, not even Jason, had stayed to hear the outcome. Other than Roberts's almost inaudible instructions to the deputies; there was no talking.

Okra waited for the rustling to subside before leaving the room to escort Taliferro to the bench. The bailiff reappeared leading the judge. "All rise," he called.

Taliferro mounted the steps and took his seat. "Alright. Bring in the jury."

Everyone in the courtroom, except Taliferro, arose when Okra reappeared. The gallery had quickly conformed to the rule of standing when the jury entered and exited.

Ev turned to look at the jurors as they filed into the jury box. Yet another rule was that convicting jurors would not look at the defendant. Conversely, acquitting jurors often glanced at the defendant, some would even smile at the accused they were setting free. Mariah Reynolds and Robert Thornton glanced toward the defense table and Ev felt a hollowness in the pit of his stomach.

There was more rustling as the onlookers and jurors settled into their seats. Only the deputies posted about the room remained standing. There was dead silence.

"Ladies and gentlemen," rumbled Taliferro, "who was elected foreman?" Taliferro had not adopted the use of the anatomical sounding 'foreperson.'

Mariah Reynolds raised her hand.

"Have you reached a verdict?"

"We have."

"Please hand it to the sheriff."

Okra walked to the jury box, retrieved the typed verdict form, and handed it to Taliferro.

Taliferro opened the document then returned it to Okra who in turn walked to the clerk and handed it to her.

"Is this verdict of each of you?" asked Taliferro.

Twelve heads nodded in the affirmative.

"Alright Mrs. Noble. Please stand."

The formalities seemed to be in slow motion, like the movement of cold molasses.

Rita and her three lawyers came to their feet. The lawyers each faced the clerk. Rita stared at the wall behind Ev. Clyde Noble leaned forward in his seat as if he, too, would stand, then, as if thinking better of it, slid back.

"Madame Clerk," said Taliferro, "please read the verdict."

Ev looked at the jurors. All of them save Mariah were occupied with the floor at their feet. Mariah, her jaw set, was focused on the wall behind the gallery. They were motionless. He heard the clerk's voice, it sounded oddly distant.

"On the indictment of murder in the first degree, we the jury find...."

Several of the spectators in the gallery leaned forward expectantly.

"...the accused...."

Ev was conscious of the fact that he was not thinking; he was observing but nothing was registering. His mind was in a bizarre warp, suspended animation: the dice were about to hit the table.

# CHAPTER 40

Saturday, December 19th

"Guilty," finished the clerk.

A muffled sob and a sigh drifted from the gallery, otherwise the room was silent—an eerie quiet. Rita looked toward the judge, her face a ghostly white and her lips quivering as if she would speak.

"Please be seated," said Taliferro. "Is there a motion to poll the jury?"

"Yes your honor," replied Avery in a raspy voice.

The clerk addressed each juror, beginning with Robert Thornton. "Robert Thornton, is this your verdict?"

"Yes," he answered in a firm voice.

The last juror called was Thelma Snead. She hesitated, dabbing her eyes with a handkerchief. Edna Wilson, still seated beside her, patted Thelma's other hand. Then, "yes."

There was a rustling in the gallery and a sprinkling of whispers.

"The court still has business," said Taliferro, instantly quieting the spectators. "Are counsel ready to proceed to the sentencing phase?"

Avery and Mathieson leaned toward the defendant, and after a moment's quiet exchange, Avery announced that the defense was ready.

Ev concurred. For evidence at this stage, the Commonwealth could present only prior criminal convictions. Since Rita had none, Ev stood, advised the court he had no evidence, and rested.

What would the defense do? Put Rita on the stand to…to say what? Screw you jurors for convicting me? He sensed that Rita, at this moment, was a loose cannon. Maybe Clyde Noble. But Ev doubted that the senator was in any condition to testify. Moreover, Ev could not read the other man's emotions; and he doubted whether Avery was having any more success.

Mathieson and Avery again huddled with Rita Noble. Meanwhile, Wil Bledsoe studied his fingers. "We have no evidence." said Avery finally.

The judge read the brief instructions necessary for the jury to reach a sentence. Their options ranged from twenty years to life.

The lawyers again were allowed to address the jury. One o'clock was fast approaching and Ev could see the weariness in the jurors' faces. His stock sentencing speech was short, and he made it shorter this morning.

"Ladies and Gentlemen. You are the representatives of the people of Lafayette County. You, tonight, are the conscience of the whole. I make no recommendations as to the sentence you should impose. Instead, I ask that you set the sentence you believe appropriate for this awful thing. Thank you."

Avery was slow in rising. Ev couldn't blame him. There was little the defense counsel could do but plead for leniency, a painful about-face after having assured the jury from beginning to end that his client was innocent.

Avery walked slowly to the front of the witness stand and began speaking in a quiet, solicitous voice. He mentioned Rita's young children, her church, the evil of narcotics and the stress of life. He managed to consume ten minutes without saying anything, then sat down.

The jury was again led to their deliberating confines. The judge disappeared to chambers.

The hall door was not yet closed when every voice in the gallery began speaking. Paula Noble walked immediately to Ev's table, tears running down her face, and shook his hand. She repeated "Thank you" several times before her sister joined her, putting her arm around Paula and grasping Ev's forearm. Several reporters dashed to the door in the vain hope that they might beat a deadline.

Lewis Brown felt one emotion: vindication. The second guessing ended the moment the word guilty fell off the clerk's lips; the insult of Mathieson's cross-examination was suddenly a distant memory, like a first quarter missed tackle in a game his team had won by a half dozen touchdowns. Rising from his seat against the wall, Brown clapped Roberts on the shoulder, who responded with a surly glare, then walked to Ev's side. As soon as Paula and her sister had turned to walk away, he extended his hand toward the prosecutor. "Good job Ev." Brown was beaming.

Ev shook the proffered hand. "Lieutenant. As much as I'd like to think that my great lawyering carried the day, the simple fact is Rita Noble decided this case for the jury. And that happened because good police work backed her into a corner."

"Don't be too modest," answered Brown, Ev's compliment warming him like a Christmas Eve fireside.

"Anyway, you and Roberts earned the day off."

"It's already Saturday, boss," laughed Brown.

"Take it anyway."

Brown was still lingering at defense table when Avery walked over to extend his hand to Ev—a hale fellows well met end to their contest. Across the room Mathieson stood with her arms crossed as she talked to Bledsoe. A vindictive urge told the Lieutenant to walk to the two. After a moment's hesitation he resisted the thought.

* * *

The jury needed twenty minutes to decide a sentence: twenty-five years in the penitentiary. This time Rita Noble was led away in handcuffs. Clyde Noble wasn't present. He had disappeared following the jury's exit to consider sentencing.

* * *

Stale cigarette smoke in the investigator's office prompted Gene Roberts to wonder what attracted him to the habit. The confounding thing was that he still wanted to light a cigarette and settle in behind his desk. There was no better way to unwind. Cigarette or not, he needed a few minutes of quiet. Lewis Brown, Horace Seay, Mervin McIntosh and R.C. Hawkes were ebullient after the trial, and while he shared their pleasure with success, his strongest emotion was one of relief. With the other officers gone he could share a post mortem with himself in the quiet.

The investigation had not been conducted to his standards—and as investigator, the fault was his; the missteps and oversights had nearly cost them the case, and but for Rita Noble's fortuitous blunder, he wondered whether the prosecution would have succeeded. He chastised himself that any number of things could have been handled differently, then countered that Monday morning quarterbacking was the avocation of nonparticipants. Matters always looked clearer in retrospect. Investigation and trial were strictly human endeavors, and with humans involved, the chaos theory was at the helm.

"Damn I must be tired," grumbled Roberts, chasing the esoteric thoughts, temporarily, from his head. Brown wanted help with the child rapist he was targeting and the next morning was already upon him.

* * *

Polly was dozing in front of the television with Wil asleep on the sofa when Ev came to the door. There was a gleam in his eye and spring to his step that answered her question before she asked it. "Did you win?"

"Yep," answered Ev, shedding his father's overcoat. "Twenty-five years."

Polly arose and hugged him. "I'm happy, for you."

Ev shrugged. "I hope there's a bottle here." He entered the kitchen, found the Jack Daniels, and poured a tumbler almost full. After adding ice he sat down at the kitchen table and drained half the glass.

"Tell me about it," said Polly.

"I don't know where to start. It was wild. Rita changed her story. This morning she took the stand and said Jason killed Miranda. How's Will?"

"He's okay. I made him sit up for a long time. What did she say?"

"That she went to the pool and Jason was there and then later told her he killed her. You didn't need to go to the doctor?"

"No. So the jury didn't buy that?"

"I guess not. Damn. What a win. Is Sam okay?"

"Oh yes. His guilt kept him quiet, for about thirty minutes. Why do you think they didn't believe her?"

Ev drained the glass and poured another. "Her story didn't fit. Man. If she hadn't changed her story, I might have lost. But I'd rather be lucky than good."

"I wonder if Evelyn will speak to me now."

"Glenn called and left me a message. Evelyn won't be far behind."

"Maybe we still have two friends."

"The hell with the rest of them."

That was easy for Ev to say. Polly had been isolated since the day the indictment was returned.

Ev continued. "Look. With the Jet Set, this will pass. A week or two and it will be as if the waters opened and simply swallowed Rita up. Out of sight, out of mind."

"I hope so," said Polly, unconvinced.

Ev finished the drink. Adrenalin and alcohol were animating him. "The hell with all of them, and with the Hampton Colemans too. I think I'm finished with my party. They abandoned me before I lost, everybody but John Henry Johnson."

"In your job, what difference does party make?"

"None. Maybe I should run as an independent."

"That's a problem for another day."

"You would not have believed how awful, simply awful, Lester Snidlett was. Is. Did you know an Ellen Mathieson at Randolph-Macon?"

"The name's familiar. A few years behind me I think. Why?"

"She was a defense attorney. With a scarf. I thought so." Ev polished off the drink and poured another.

"You didn't tell me about her."

"I don't know what I've told anybody. You've been in bed every night when I got home."

"You weren't the kind of company during the trial I wanted to keep."

Ev smiled over the tumbler at his lips. "Anything different tonight?"

"Ev."

"Damn. It's like I've been on another planet."

Polly wasn't sure how Ev meant that, but it wasn't far from her own feeling of disengagement from the world. Without Evelyn and an occasional brush with the Jet Set, she, too, might as well have been on another planet—stuck there with Margaret Cross. "Your mother has called here twice a day wanting to know what's happening."

Ev shook his head in disinterest. "Those fools left Mariah Reynolds on the jury."

"Your eccentric cousin?"

"Damn Hampton Coleman. Fat air bag. Not inviting us to his Christmas party."

"I didn't know you noticed."

"I noticed."

"I guess our Christmas can start now."

"I doubt the boys have been waiting."

It was after three when Polly convinced Ev it was time for bed. He didn't argue, the bottle was empty, and, disproving Evelyn's theory, he was too drunk to pester Polly.

**CHAPTER 41**

Wednesday, December 23<sup>rd</sup>

Rhonda Gooden met Ev at the top of steps just down the hall from the general district courtroom. "Mr. Cross," she said in, for her, an unusually quiet voice, "Kin I talk to you for a minute?" Her blue jeans and tank top were so tight that she could have won a wet tee-shirt contest without a drop of water. The winter weather appeared to be of little consequence to her, other than the effect it had on two portions of her anatomy.

Ev struggled to keep his eyes level with her flashing green ones. He looked down the hall, and seeing only an old man on one of the benches, motioned toward the opposite end.

"Well, it's sorta personal," said Rhonda.

The old man looked up at this, surveyed Rhonda from head to toe, and smiled crookedly at Ev.

Sorta personal was not a combination of words Ev liked hearing and during the pause while he tried to devise an alternative, Rhonda spoke again.

"We kin go in that little room the lawyers use." Rhonda had been to court enough to know where conferences were held.

Ev shrugged his shoulders and followed her to the coffee-copier room. Rhonda walked in ahead of him and Ev, following, left the door slightly ajar.

"Mr. Cross. No reason to get ol' Romey in any trouble. I done took care of it. I mean Skeeter got cut out, which was the whole problem. So I fixed that. Rhonda leaned against the counter as if posing for a tabloid cover, perhaps biker girl of the month.

Ev wanted to smile but decided to suppress it.

"I mean he done got his fair share now. The deal was to drop the charges on Romey. You know what I mean?"

"I believe so," answered Ev.

"Well Wil Bledsoe told me to tell you so you'd drop the charges."

"Oh he did, did he?"

"Yeah. He called it something. A court and satisfaction. Well, I done the satisfaction part. I reckon the court part's yours." Rhonda had a twinkle in her eye, which led Ev to believe she was enjoying the locker room semantics. "You wont me to s'plain it to the judge?"

Ev shook his head and laughed quietly in spite of himself. "That won't be necessary. Just come up to the front when the case is called." No sense in depriving Abner Lincoln of a viewing.

358

"Thanks a million Mr. Cross. I owe you one," said Rhonda as she left the tiny room.

*No thanks*, thought Ev. He waited until Rhonda was in the courtroom, then made his way to the file room. Bledsoe was sitting on a table.

"Mr. Commonwealth," said Bledsoe, "fresh from kickin' my ass in court. Did you speak to Miss Gooden?"

"Oh yeah Wil. I got the message."

Bledsoe erupted in a cackling laugh. "Puts new meaning in accord and satisfaction don't it."

"Best resolution of a case I've ever seen. Did you tell her how to dress?"

"Something about that might have come up. Was a real sight wasn't it? She was something else in her day."

"I guess you have firsthand knowledge."

"Missed that one. I'm a lot older than I look. Abner's almost done with the unrepresented docket. We can get Romey outa the way. You got much?"

"No. Christmas Eve eve. Your case is it."

Bledsoe rubbed his knees thoughtfully. "I guess you figured that Rita will appeal, after sentencing."

"I figured. But so what? There's no error."

"She gotta little too cute. Changing her story on us in midstream."

"She was doing that from day one. I saw the look on your faces. Was pretty clear she decided to say she was there at the last minute."

"I don't know why someone'll spend fifty thousand dollars for lawyers and then not tell them what they're gonna say. The little bitch hung herself."

"Well. Bless her heart. I wasn't very confident when I rested. She, or you all, must have had a different reaction."

"Clara Wood, and Roberts and Brown," answered Bledsoe. "They had Rita rattled."

"My guess was that she was trying to beat me and save face with Clyde, and sacrificing Jason was the only way."

"I told Avery and Ellen you weren't going to make any mistakes. You did a good job."

The compliment embarrassed Ev. "Thanks Wil. But I'm not so sure it was anything other than Rita and the jury."

Bledsoe arose from the table. "In a case like that, you never really know what happened. Never will. Anyway, someday, maybe when Rita's out of prison, I've got a few tidbits for you."

"A confession?"

Bledsoe laughed. "No. I'd know what happened if she'd confessed."

"Well, I still say she convicted herself."

"Yes. But that doesn't mean she's guilty."

"Oh. You know something."

"I'm simply saying her screwin' up the case doesn't prove she's guilty. It proves she pissed off the jury. Anyway, at least you're not eaten up with hubris. That's the media's favorite word now isn't it? Hubris. By the way, do you think your Democratic buddies will get over this?"

"It's not my party."

Bledsoe smiled. "What's this?"

"My party turned on me like I was a leper. No thanks. I might run as an independent."

"Hell, you might run as a Republican. Hampton Coleman will shit all over hisself." Bledsoe laughed. "Ev Cross. Republican. I like that."

"I'm not sure I'm ready for that, Wil. Here's a question you might be free to answer. Why'd you keep Mariah Reynolds on the jury?"

"The jury expert. I told 'em to strike her."

"What did he use? A Ouija board?"

"Tarot cards. I said get rid of the older women, especially Mariah. I knew you wanted to keep them. But the expert said something about Mariah being sympathetic because she was in the same social stratum. I liked that. Social stratum."

"Mariah and Rita in the same social stratum?" Ev laughed. "What world was he in?"

"Look, I got one-seventy an hour to sit around and look dumb. Good work if you can get it. Especially for a hillbilly."

"I thought you'd like that part."

"I should tell Rita I prefer to be called an Appalachian-American. That's the politically correct approach. On another subject, your secretary said you're getting your mother's house."

"We are, but getting might not be the right word."

"That means moving. I hate that."

"Not anytime soon. Polly says it has to be painted inside before we move or it will never get done."

Bledsoe laughed. "I guess that means you. Come on, let's go in and see if Abner's ready for the Rhonda Gooden show."

The two walked through the side door into the courtroom. Lincoln concluded the last of the traffic cases and called Romey Bryant's name. Bryant, Hawkins and Gooden filed to the front and stood before the bench. Ev watched as Lincoln cast a brief glance at Gooden's tank top before raising the warrant, as if to block the view, and began reading the charge aloud.

Ev interrupted. "We have an agreement your honor."

"Okay," said Lincoln, laying the paper down and giving himself another opportunity to dart a glance at Rhonda's equipage.

"Reduced to misdemeanor assault and battery, and dismissed on accord and satisfaction after payment of costs," continued Ev.

"Mr. Bledsoe?"

"That's right, judge. You agree, Skeeter?" asked Bledsoe.

"Oh yeah. I'm satisfied."

Rhonda giggled.

"Okay Mr. Bryant," said Lincoln, "see the clerk and you're free to go."

The departing trio left the courtroom devoid of litigants.

"What didja think of that judge?" asked Bledsoe.

Lincoln smiled. "Setting me up, were you?"

"I was hoping Ev would get her to tell you the satisfaction part."

"So," said Lincoln, "as hard as it is to believe, there's more to it than meets the eye?"

Bledsoe explained the circumstances leading to the charge and its resolution. Okra Alexander, sitting in his corner, laughed aloud.

Lincoln sputtered with laughter himself, and after Bledsoe was finished, he looked at Ev. "Now I've heard of some deals in court before, but I've got to hand it to you, this one's the best. All round. Your idea?"

"Hell no," said Bledsoe. "Mine. I got Romey and Rhonda in my office and told Rhonda to screw Skeeter's brains out and the whole thing would go away."

Okra slapped his knee before arising. "I'd like to stay to hear the rest of this, but we got one more, judge. Gooseneck." Okra left the room to call the jail.

"Well shit," said Bledsoe. "Might as well stick around. Christmas with Gooseneck. This stuff is better than sex and almost as good as whiskey." He dropped into the witness chair facing the bench.

Lincoln leaned forward. "Did you really tell her that?"

"Damn right, Abner. She laughed at first, then got thoughtful, and said okay. Romey didn't give a tinker's dam. It's all in a day's work. The majesty of the law."

"Maybe she thought better of that *ménage a trois* business coming out in court," said Lincoln.

"Naw," replied Bledsoe. "Wouldn't faze her. It was just her sense of fair play. Justice for all."

"I bet it was," said Lincoln. The judge looked at Ev. "Has Wil got over the pasting you gave him last week?"

Ev colored at the question.

Bledsoe spoke before Ev could answer. "I was third string Abner."

"Not your fault, huh?" said Lincoln.

"Six women on the jury, Richmond lawyers, and Rita Noble on the stand. Clarence Darrow would've had trouble."

Lincoln shook his head. "Poor Clyde Noble."

The door to the courtroom opened and in shuffled Gooseneck Smoot with Wimpie Carson at his side. The prisoner was dressed in the re-invigorated black and white striped jail garb, his long neck thrust forward like the bowsprit of a schooner.

"Elwood Smoot," said Lincoln.

"Abner. Merry Christmas." Gooseneck halted at the bench and leaned forward on his elbows. "Gonna let me out fer Santa, judge?"

"Elwood, you're charged with drunk in public and possession of alcohol after interdiction. What's the plea?"

"Oh. I guess guilty. I been in three weeks. That's long enough."

"If I let you out, you'll freeze to death."

"If I freeze to death, it's my fault, not yours."

Lincoln leaned back in his chair. "I don't want to read on Christmas morning that you froze on Christmas Eve."

"Y'all worry about me more than I worry about myself."

"Social Services got you a place to live in Charlottesville. Why didn't you stay?"

"I'm a rolling stone," smiled Gooseneck. "Look. You put me in jail for my safety and I thank you. But I hate it. If I liked it so much I'd just turn myself in."

"Well I've got to put you in. To keep you warm."

"Let me out the twentieth of March, like last year?"

"Six months, you pull three."

Gooseneck nodded slowly. "I can live with that. How about four months?"

"Six months. You know the alcohol's going to kill you."

"I hate alcohol. But I love it more'n I hate it. So I'm gonna make a resolution. Get myself organized for a change." Wimpie tugged at Gooseneck's arm. "Well okay. Have a good Christmas. Think about me sittin' in jail while y'all are at home in front of a fire."

Wimpie Carson guided Gooseneck to the door of the courtroom. "Wimpie, gotta cigarette?" asked the prisoner as they passed through the door.

Bledsoe arose from the witness chair. "There you go. Our job: managing the masses. We're the three wise men. Put Gooseneck in jail for Christmas for his own good, that was our gift. The little match girl wouldn't have frozen to death if we'd been around. Someone would've arrested her for vagrancy or panhandling and locked her up in detention. Merry Christmas judge."

## THE END